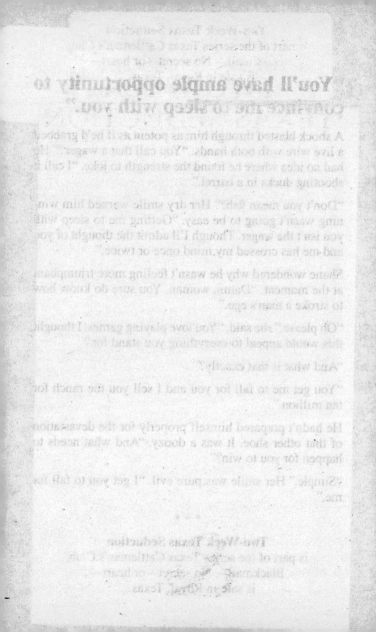

TWO-WEEK TEXAS SEDUCTION

BY
CAT SCHIELD

First Published in Great Britain 2017
By Mills & Boon, an imprint of HarperCollins*Publishers*
1 London Bridge Street, London, SE1 9GF

Special thanks and acknowledgement are given to Cat Schield for her contribution to the Texas Cattleman's Club: Blackmail series.

ISBN: 978-0-263-92807-5

51-0217

Our policy is to use papers that are natural, renewable and recyclable products and made from wood grown in sustainable forests. The logging and manufacturing processes conform to the legal environmental regulations of the country of origin.

Printed and bound in Spain
by CPI, Barcelona

Cat Schield has been reading and writing romance since high school. Although she graduated from college with a BA in Business, her idea of a perfect career was writing books for Mills & Boon. And now, after winning the Romance Writers of America 2010 Golden Heart® Award for Best Contemporary Series Romance, that dream has come true. Cat lives in Minnesota with her daughter, Emily, and their Burmese cat. When she's not writing sexy, romantic stories for Mills & Boon Desire, she can be found sailing with friends on the St. Croix River, or in more exotic locales, like the Caribbean and Europe. She loves to hear from readers. Find her at www.catschield.com and follow her on Twitter, @catschield.

For everyone trying to make ends
meet while keeping your dreams alive.
Never give up, never surrender.

One

Before she'd moved to Royal, Texas, few people had ever done Brandee Lawless any favors. If this had left her with an attitude of "you're damned right I can," she wasn't going to apologize. She spoke her mind and sometimes that ruffled feathers. Lately those feathers belonged to a trio of women new to the Texas Cattleman's Club. Cecelia Morgan, Simone Parker and Naomi Price had begun making waves as soon as they'd been accepted as members and Brandee had opposed them at every turn.

Her long legs made short work of the clubhouse foyer and the hallway leading to the high-ceilinged dining room where she and her best friend, Chelsea Hunt, were having lunch. At five feet five inches, she wasn't exactly an imposing figure, but she knew how to make an entrance.

Instead of her usual denim, boots, work shirt and cowboy hat, Brandee wore a gray fit-and-flare sweater dress with lace inset cuffs over a layered tulle slip, also in gray.

She'd braided sections of her long blond hair and fastened them with rhinestone-encrusted bobby pins. She noted three pair of eyes watching her progress across the room and imagined the women assessing her outfit. To let them know she wasn't the least bit bothered, Brandee made sure she took her time winding through the diners on her way to the table by the window.

Chelsea looked up from the menu as she neared. Her green eyes widened. "Wow, you look great."

Delighted by her friend's approval, Brandee smiled. "Part of the new collection." In addition to running one of the most profitable ranches in Royal, Texas, Brandee still designed a few pieces of clothing and accessories for the fashion company she'd started twelve years earlier. "What do you think of the boots?"

"I'm sick with jealousy." Chelsea eyed the bright purple Tres Outlaws and grinned. "You are going to let me borrow them, I hope."

"Of course."

Brandee sat down, basking in feminine satisfaction. With all the hours she put in working her ranch, most saw her as a tomboy. Despite a closet full of frivolous, girlie clothes, getting dressed up for the sole purpose of coming into town for a leisurely lunch was a rare occurrence. But this was a celebration. Her first monthlong teenage outreach session was booked solid. This summer Hope Springs Camp was going to make a difference in those kids' lives.

"You made quite an impression on the terrible trio." Chelsea tipped her head to indicate the three newly minted members of the Texas Cattleman's Club. "They're staring at us and whispering."

"No doubt hating on what I'm wearing. I don't know why they think I care what they say about me."

It was a bit like being in high school, where the pretty, popular girls ganged up on anyone they viewed as easy prey. Not that Brandee was weak. In fact, her standing in the club and in the community was strong.

"It's pack mentality," Brandee continued. "On their own they feel powerless, but put them in a group and they'll tear you apart."

"I suppose it doesn't help that you're more successful than they are."

"Or that I've been blocking their attempts to run this club like their personal playground. All this politicking is such a distraction. I'd much rather spend my time holed up at Hope Springs, working the ranch."

"I'm sure they'd prefer that, as well. Especially when you show up looking like this." Chelsea gestured to Brandee's outfit. "You look like a million bucks. They must hate it."

"Except I'm wearing a very affordable line of clothing. I started the company with the idea that I wanted the price points to be within reach of teenagers and women who couldn't afford to pay the designer prices."

"I think it's more the way you wear your success. You are confident without ever having to build yourself up or tear someone else down."

"It comes from accepting my flaws."

"You have flaws?"

Brandee felt a rush of affection for her best friend. An ex-hacker and present CTO of the Hunt & Co. chain of steak houses, Chelsea was the complete package of brains and beauty. From the moment they'd met, Brandee had loved her friend's kick-ass attitude.

"Everyone has things about themselves they don't like," Brandee said. "My lips are too thin and my ears stick out. My dad used to say they were good for keeping my hat from going too low and covering my eyes."

As always, bringing up her father gave Brandee a bittersweet pang. Until she'd lost him to a freak accident when she was twelve, he'd been her world. From him she'd learned how to run a ranch, and the joys of hard work and a job well done. Without his voice in her head, she never would've had the courage to run from the bad situation with her mother at seventeen and to become a successful rancher.

"But you modeled your own designs for your online store," Chelsea exclaimed. "How did you do that if you were so uncomfortable about how you looked?"

"I think what makes us stand out is what makes us interesting. And memorable. Think of all those gorgeous beauty queens competing in pageants. The ones you remember are those who do something wrong and get called out or who overcome disabilities to compete."

"So the three over there are forgettable?" With a minute twitch of her head, Chelsea indicated the trio of mean girls.

"As far as I'm concerned." Brandee smiled. "And I think they know it. Which is why they work so hard to be noticed."

She'd barely finished speaking when a stir in the air raised her hackles. A second later a tall, athletically built man appeared beside their table, blocking their view of the three women. Shane Delgado. Brandee had detected his ruggedly masculine aftershave a second before she saw him.

"Hey, Shane." Chelsea's earlier tension melted away beneath the mega wattage of Shane's charismatic white grin. Brandee resisted the urge to roll her eyes. Shane would love seeing proof that he'd gotten to her.

"Good to see you, Chelsea." His smooth Texas drawl had a trace of New England in it. "Hello, Brandee."

She greeted him without looking in his direction. "Delgado." She kept her tone neutral and disinterested, masking the way her body went on full alert in his presence.

"You're looking particularly gorgeous today."

Across from her, Chelsea glanced with eyebrows raised from Shane to Brandee and back.

"You're not so bad yourself." She didn't need to check out his long legs in immaculate denim jeans or the crisp tan shirt that emphasized his broad shoulders to know the man looked like a million bucks. "Something I can do for you, Delgado?" She hated that she was playing into his hands by asking, but he wouldn't move on until he'd had his say.

"Do?" He caressed the word with his silver tongue and almost made Brandee shiver.

She recognized her mistake, but the damage was done. Her tone grew impatient as she clarified, "Did you just stop by to say hello or is there something else on your mind?"

"You know what's on my mind." With another man this might have been a horrible pickup line, but Shane had elevated flirting to an art form.

Brandee glanced up and rammed her gaze into his. "My ranch?" For years he'd been pestering her to sell her land so he could ruin the gorgeous vistas with a bunch of luxury homes.

To his credit, the look in his hazel eyes remained friendly and compelling despite her antagonism. "Among other things."

"You're wasting your time," she told him yet again. "I'm not selling."

"I never consider the time I spend with you as wasted." Honey dripped from every vowel as he flashed his perfect white teeth in a sexy grin.

Brandee's nerve endings sizzled in response. Several times in the last few years she'd considered hooking up with the cocky charmer. He possessed a body to die for and offered the perfect balance of risk and fun. Sex with him would be explosive and memorable. Too memorable. No doubt she'd spend the rest of her days wanting more. Except as far as she could tell, Shane wasn't the type to stick around for long. Not that she was looking for anything long-term, but a girl could get addicted to things that weren't necessarily good for her.

"In fact," he continued, sex appeal rolling off him in waves, "I enjoy our little chats."

"Our chats end up with me turning you down." She gave him her best smirk. "Are you saying you enjoy that?"

"Honey, you know I never back down from a challenge."

At long last he broke eye contact and let his gaze roam over her mouth and breasts. His open appreciation electrified Brandee, leaving her tongue-tied and breathless.

"Good seeing you both." With a nod at Chelsea, Shane ambled away.

"Damn," Chelsea muttered, her tone reverent.

"What?" The question came out a little sharper than Brandee intended. She noticed her hands were clenched and relaxed her fingers. It did no good. Her blood continued to boil, but whether with lust or outrage Brandee couldn't determine.

"You two have some serious chemistry going on. How did I not know this?"

"It's not chemistry," Brandee corrected. "It's antagonism."

"Po-tay-to. Po-tah-to. It's hot." Either Chelsea missed Brandee's warning scowl or she chose to ignore it as she continued, "How come you've never taken him for a test drive?"

"Are you crazy? Did you miss the part where he's been trying to buy Hope Springs Ranch for the last three years?"

"Maybe it's because it gives him an excuse to stop by

and see you? Remember how he came by the day after the tornado and stayed to help?" Two and a half years earlier an F4 tornado had swept through Royal. The biggest to hit in almost eighty years, it had taken out a chunk of the west side of town including the town hall and a wing of Royal Memorial Hospital before raging on to cause various degrees of damage to several surrounding ranches.

"He wasn't being altruistic. He was sniffing around, checking to see if because of the hit the ranch took whether I was in a position where I had to sell."

"That's not why he spent the next few days cleaning up the storm damage."

Brandee shook her head. Chelsea didn't understand how well Shane hid his true motives for being nice to her. He lived by the motto "You catch more flies with honey than vinegar." The smooth-talking son of a bitch wanted Hope Springs Ranch. If Brandee agreed to sell, she'd never hear from Shane again.

"Where Shane Delgado is concerned, let's agree to disagree," Brandee suggested, not wanting to spoil her lunch with further talk of Shane.

"Okay." Chelsea clasped her hands together on the table and leaned forward. "So, tell me your good news. What's going on?"

"I found out this morning that Hope Springs' first summer session is completely booked."

"Brandee, that's fantastic."

Since purchasing the land that had become Hope Springs Ranch, Brandee had been working to create programs for at-risk teens that helped address destructive behaviors and promote self-esteem. Inspired by her own difficult teen years after losing her dad, Brandee wanted to provide a structured, supportive environment for young adults to learn goal-setting, communication and productive life skills.

"I can't believe how well everything is coming together. And how much work I have to do before the bunkhouses and camp facilities are going to be ready."

"You'll get it all done. You're one of the most driven, organized people I know."

"Thanks for the vote of confidence."

It had taken years of hard work and relentless optimism, but she'd done her dad proud with the success she'd made of Hope Springs Ranch. And now she stood on the threshold of realizing her dream of the camp. Her life was perfect and Brandee couldn't imagine anything better than how she felt at this moment.

Shane strode away from his latest encounter with Brandee feeling like he'd been zapped with a cattle prod. Over the years, he'd engaged in many sizzling exchanges with the spitfire rancher. After each one, he'd conned himself into believing he'd emerged unscathed, while in reality he rarely escaped without several holes poked in his ego.

She was never happy to see him. It didn't seem fair when everything about her brightened his day. Usually he stopped by her ranch and caught her laboring beside her ranch hands, moving cattle, tending to the horses or helping to build the structures for her camp. Clad in worn jeans, faded plaid work shirts and dusty boots, her gray-blue eyes blazing in a face streaked with sweat and dirt, she smelled like horses, hay and hard work. All tomboy. All woman. And he lusted after every lean inch of her.

She, however, was completely immune to him. Given her impenetrable defenses, he should have moved on. There were too many receptive women who appreciated that he was easy and fun, while in Brandee's cool gaze, he glimpsed an ocean of distrust.

But it was the challenge of bringing her around. Of knowing that once he drew her beneath his spell, he would satisfy himself with her complete surrender and emerge triumphant. This didn't mean he was a bad guy. He just wasn't built to be tied down. And from what he'd noticed of Brandee's social life, she wasn't much into long-term relationships, either.

And so he kept going back for more despite knowing each time they tangled she would introduce him to some fresh hell. Today it had been the scent of her perfume. A light floral scent that made him long to gather handfuls of her hair and bury his face in the lustrous gold waves.

"Shane."

His mental meanderings came to a screeching halt. He nodded in acknowledgment toward a trio of women, unsure which one had hailed him. These three were trouble. Cecelia, Simone and Naomi. A blonde, brunette and a redhead. All three women were gorgeous, entitled and dangerous if crossed.

They'd recently been admitted to the Texas Cattleman's Club and were making waves with their demands that the clubhouse needed a feminine face-lift. They wanted to get rid of the old boys' club style and weren't being subtle about manipulating votes in their favor.

Brandee had been one of their most obstinate adversaries, working tirelessly to gather the votes needed to defeat them. She'd infiltrated the ranks of the oldest and most established members in order to preach against every suggestion these three women made. The whole thing was amusing to watch.

Shane responded to Naomi's wave by strolling to their table. "Ladies."

"Join us," Cecelia insisted. She was a striking platinum blonde with an ice queen's sharp eyes. As president of To The Moon, a company specializing in high-end children's furniture, Cecelia was obviously accustomed to being obeyed.

Putting on his best easy grin, Shane shook his head. "Now, you know I'd love nothing more, but I'm sorry to say I'm already running late." He glanced to where his best friend, Gabriel Walsh, sat talking on his cell phone, a half-empty tumbler of scotch on the table before him. "Is there something I can do for you ladies?"

"We noticed you were talking with Brandee Lawless," Simone said, leaning forward in a way that offered a sensational glimpse of her ample cleavage. With lush curves, arresting blue eyes and long black hair, she, too, was a striking blend of beauty and brains. "And we wanted to give you some friendly advice about her."

Had the women picked up on his attraction to Brandee? If so, Shane was losing his touch. He set his hands on the back of the empty fourth chair and leaned in with a conspiratorial wink.

"I'm always happy to listen to advice from beautiful women."

Cecelia nodded as if approving his wisdom. "She's only acting interested in you because she wants you to vote against the clubhouse redesign."

Shane blinked. Brandee was acting interested in him? What had these three women seen that he'd missed?

"Once the vote is done," Simone continued, "she will dismiss you like that." She snapped her fingers and settled her full lips into a determined pout.

"Brandee has been acting as if she's interested in me?" Shane put on a show of surprise and hoped this would entice the women to expound on their theories. "I thought she was just being nice."

The women exchanged glances and silently selected Naomi to speak next. "She's not nice. She's manipulating you. Haven't you noticed the way she flirts with you? She knows how well liked you are and plans to use your popularity to manipulate the vote."

Shane considered this. Was Brandee flirting with him? For a second he let himself bask in the pleasure of that idea. Did she fight the same intoxicating attraction that gripped him every time they met? Then he rejected the notion. No. The way she communicated with him was more like a series of verbal jousts all determined to knock him off his white charger and land him ass-first in the dirt.

"Thank you for the warning, ladies." Unnecessary as it had been. "I'll make sure I keep my wits about me where Brandee is concerned."

"Anytime," Naomi murmured. Her brown eyes, framed by long, lush lashes, had a sharp look of satisfaction.

"We will always have your back," Cecelia added, and glanced at the other two, garnering agreeing head bobs.

"I'll remember that." With a friendly smile and a nod, Shane left the trio and headed to where Gabe waited.

The former Texas Ranger watched him approach, a smirk kicking up one corner of his lips. "What the hell was that about? Were you feeding them canaries?"

"Canaries?" Shane dropped into his seat and gestured to a nearby waiter. He needed a stiff drink after negotiating the gauntlet of strong-willed women.

"That was a trio of very satisfied pussycats."

Shane resisted the urge to rub at the spot between his shoulder blades that burned from several sets of female eyes boring into him. "I gave them what they wanted."

"Don't you always?"

"It's what I do."

Shane flashed a cocky grin, but he didn't feel any satisfaction.

"So what did they want?" Gabe asked.

"To warn me about Brandee Lawless."

Gabe's gaze flickered past Shane. Whatever he saw made his eyes narrow. "Do you need to be warned?"

"Oh hell no." The waiter set a scotch before him and Shane swallowed a healthy dose of the fiery liquid before continuing. "You know how she and I are. If we were kids she'd knock me down and sit on me."

"And you'd let her because then she'd be close enough to tickle."

"Tickle?" Shane stared at his best friend in mock outrage. "Do you not know me at all?"

"We're talking about you and Brandee as little kids. It was the least offensive thing I could think of that you'd do to her."

Shane snorted in amusement. "You could have said *spank*."

Gabe closed his eyes as if in pain. "Can we get back to Cecelia, Simone and Naomi?"

"They're just frustrated that Brandee has sided against them and has more influence at the club than they do. They want to rule the world. Or at least our little corner of it."

On the table, Gabe's phone chimed, signaling a text. "Damn," he murmured after reading the screen.

"Bad news?"

"My uncle's tumor isn't operable."

Several weeks ago Gabe's uncle Dusty had been diagnosed with stage-four brain cancer.

"Aw, Gabe, I'm sorry. That really sucks."

Dale "Dusty" Walsh was a dynamic bear of a man. Like

Gabe he was a few inches over six feet and built to intimidate. Founder of Royal's most private security firm, The Walsh Group, he'd brought Gabe into the fold after he'd left the Texas Rangers.

"Yeah, my dad's pretty shook up. That was him sending the text."

Gabe's close relationship with his father was something Shane had always envied. His dad had died when Shane was in his early twenties, but even before the heart attack took him, there hadn't been much good about their connection.

"Hopefully, the doctors have a good alternative program to get Dusty through this."

"Let's hope."

The two men shifted gears and talked about the progress on Shane's latest project, a luxury resort development in the vein of George Vanderbilt's iconic French Renaissance château in North Carolina, but brimming with cutting-edge technology. As he was expounding on the challenges of introducing the concept of small plates to a state whose motto was "everything's bigger in Texas," a hand settled on Shane's shoulder. The all-too-familiar zap of awareness told him who stood beside him before she spoke.

"Hello, Gabe. How are things at The Walsh Group?"

"Fine." Gabe's hazel eyes took on a devilish gleam as he noticed Shane's gritted teeth. "And how are you doing at Hope Springs?"

"Busy. We've got ninety-two calves on the ground and another hundred and ninety-seven to go before April." Brandee's hand didn't move from Shane's shoulder as she spoke. "Thanks for helping out with the background checks for the latest group of volunteers."

"Anytime."

Shane drank in the soft lilt in Brandee's voice as he

endured the warm press of her hand. He shouldn't be so aware of her, but the rustle of her tulle skirt and the shapely bare legs below the modest hem had his senses all revved up with nowhere to go.

"See you later, boys." Brandee gave Shane's shoulder a little squeeze before letting go.

"Bye, Brandee," Gabe replied, shifting his gaze to Shane as she headed off.

All too aware of Gabe's smirk, Shane summoned his willpower to not turn around and watch her go, but he couldn't resist a quick peek over his shoulder. He immediately wished he'd fought harder. Brandee floated past the tables like a delicate gray cloud. A cloud with badass boots the color of Texas bluebonnets on her feet. He felt the kick to his gut and almost groaned.

"You know she only did that to piss off those three," Gabe said when Shane had turned back around. "They think she's plotting against them, so she added fuel to the fire."

"I know." He couldn't help but admire her clever machinations even though it had come with a hit to his libido. "She's a woman after my own heart."

Gabe laughed. "Good thing you don't have one to give her."

Shane lifted his drink and saluted his friend. "You've got that right."

Two

Afternoon sunlight lanced through the mini blinds covering the broad west-facing window in Brandee's home office, striping the computer keyboard and her fingers as they flew across the keys. She'd been working on the budget for her summer camp, trying to determine where she could siphon off a few extra dollars to buy three more well-trained, kid-friendly horses.

She'd already invested far more in the buildings and infrastructure than she'd initially intended. And because she needed to get the first of three projected bunkhouses built in time for her summer session, she'd been forced to rely on outside labor to get the job done.

Brandee spun her chair and stared out the window that overlooked the large covered patio, with its outdoor kitchen and fieldstone fireplace. She loved spending time outside, even in the winter, and had created a cozy outdoor living room.

Buying this five-thousand-acre parcel outside Royal four years ago had been Brandee's chance to fulfill her father's dream. She hadn't minded having to build a ranch from the ground up after the tornado had nearly wiped her out. In fact, she'd appreciated the clean slate and relished the idea of putting her stamp on the land. She'd set the L-shaped one-story ranch house half a mile off the highway and a quarter mile from the buildings that housed her ranch hands and the outbuildings central to her cow-calving operation.

The original house, built by the previous owner, had been much bigger than this one and poorly designed. Beaux Cook had been a Hollywood actor with grand ideas of becoming a real cowboy. The man had preferred flash over substance, and never bothered to learn anything about the ranching. Within eighteen months, he'd failed so completely as a rancher that Brandee had bought the property for several million less than it was worth.

Brandee was the third owner of the land since it had been lifted from unclaimed status ten years earlier. Emmitt Shaw had been the one who'd secured the parcel adjacent to his ranch by filing a claim and paying the back taxes for the five thousand acres of abandoned land after a trust put into place a century earlier to pay the taxes had run out of money. Health issues had later compelled him to sell off the land to Beaux to pay his medical bills and keep his original ranch running.

However, in the days following the massive storm, while Brandee was preoccupied with her own devastated property, Shane Delgado had taken advantage of the old rancher's bad health and losses from the tornado to gobble up his ranch to develop luxury homes. If she'd known how bad Beaux's situation had become, she would've offered to buy his land for a fair price.

Instead, she was stuck sharing her property line with his housing development. Brandee liked the raw, untamed beauty of the Texas countryside, and resented Delgado's determination to civilize the landscape with his luxury homes and fancy resort development. Her father had been an old-school cowboy, fond of endless vistas of Texas landscape populated by cattle, rabbits, birds and the occasional mountain lion. He wouldn't be a fan of Shane Delgado's vision for his daughter's property.

Her smartphone chimed, indicating she'd received a text message. There was a phone number, but no name. She read the text and her heart received a potent shock.

Hope Springs Ranch rightfully belongs to Shane Delgado.
–Maverick

Too outraged to consider the wisdom of engaging with the mysterious sender, she picked up the phone and texted back.

Who is this and what are you talking about?

Her computer immediately pinged, indicating she'd received an email. She clicked to open the message. It was from Maverick.

Give up your Texas Cattleman's Club membership and wire fifty thousand dollars to the account below or I'll be forced to share this proof of ownership with Delgado. You have two weeks to comply.

Ignoring the bank routing information, Brandee double-clicked on the attachment. It was a scan of a faded, handwritten document, a letter dated March 21, 1899, written by someone named Jasper Crowley. He offered a five-thousand-acre parcel as a dowry to the man who married his daughter, Amelia. From the description of the land, it was the five thousand acres Hope Springs Ranch occupied.

Brandee's outrage dissipated, but uneasiness remained.

This had to be a joke. Nothing about the documentation pointed to Shane. She was ready to dismiss the whole thing when the name Maverick tickled her awareness. Where had she heard it mentioned before? Cecelia Morgan had spoken the name before one of the contentious meetings at the TCC clubhouse. Was Cecelia behind this? Given the demands, it made sense.

Brandee had been doing her best to thwart every power play Cecelia, Simone and Naomi had attempted. There was no way she was going to let the terrible trio bully their way into leadership positions with the Texas Cattleman's Club. Was this their way of getting her to shut up?

She responded to the email.

This doesn't prove anything.

This isn't an empty threat, was the immediate response. Shaw didn't search for Crowley's descendants. I did.

That seemed to indicate that Maverick had proof that Crowley and Shane were related. Okay, so maybe she shouldn't ignore this. Brandee set her hands on the edge of the desk and shoved backward, muttering curses. The office wasn't big enough for her to escape the vile words glowing on the screen, so she got up and left the room to clear her head.

How dare they? She stalked down the hall to the living area, taking in the perfection of her home along the way.

Everything she had was tied up in Hope Springs Ranch. If she wasn't legally entitled to the land, she'd be ruined.

Selling the cattle wouldn't provide enough capital for her to start again. And what would become of her camp?

Sweat broke out on Brandee's forehead. Throwing open her front door, she lifted her face to the cool breeze and stepped onto the porch, which ran the full length of her home. Despite the chilly February weather, she settled in a rocker and drew her knees to her chest. Usually contemplating the vista brought her peace. Not today.

What if that document was real and it could be connected to Shane? She dropped her forehead to her knees and groaned. This was a nightmare. Or maybe it was just a cruel trick. The ranch could not belong to Shane Delgado. Whoever Maverick was, and she suspected it was the unholy trio of Cecelia, Simone and Naomi, there was no way this person could be right.

The land had been abandoned. The taxes had ceased being paid. Didn't that mean the acres reverted back to the government? There had to be a process that went into securing unclaimed land. Something that went beyond simply paying the back taxes. Surely Emmitt had followed every rule and procedure. But what if he hadn't? What was she going to do? She couldn't lose Hope Springs Ranch. And especially not to the likes of Shane Delgado.

It took a long time for Brandee's panic to recede. Half-frozen, she retreated inside and began to plan. First on the agenda was to determine if the document was legitimate. Second, she needed to trace Shane back to Jasper Crowley. Third, she needed to do some research on the process for purchasing land that had returned to the government because of unpaid back taxes.

The blackmailer had given her two weeks. It wasn't a lot of time, but she was motivated. And if she proved Shane was the owner of her land? She could comply with Maverick's demands. Fifty thousand wasn't peanuts, but she had way more than that sitting in her contingency fund. She'd pay three times that to keep Shane Delgado from getting his greedy hands on her land.

And if she absolutely had to, she could resign from the Texas Cattleman's Club. She'd earned her membership the same way club members of old had: by making Hope Springs a successful ranch and proving herself a true cattleman. It would eat at her to let Cecelia, Simone and Naomi bully her into giving up the club she deserved to be a part of, but she could yield the high ground if it meant her programs for at-risk teenagers would be able to continue.

Bile rose as she imagined herself facing the trio's triumphant smirks. How many times in school had she stood against the mean girls and kept her pride intact? They'd ridiculed her bohemian style and tormented anyone brave enough to be friends with her. In turn, she'd manipulated their boyfriends into dumping them and exposed their villainous backstabbing to the whole school.

It wasn't something Brandee was proud of, but to be fair, she'd been dealing with some pretty major ugliness at home and hadn't been in the best frame of mind to take the high road.

When it came to taking care of herself, Brandee had learned how to fight dirty from her father's ranch hands. They'd treated her like a little sister and given her tips on how to get the upper hand in any situation. Brandee had found their advice useful after she'd moved in with her mother and had to cope with whatever flavor of the month she'd shacked up with.

Not all her mother's boyfriends had been creeps, but enough of them had turned their greedy gaze Brandee's way to give her a crash course in manipulation as a method of self-preservation.

And now those skills were going to pay off in spades.

Because she intended to do whatever it took to save her ranch, and heaven help anyone who got in her way.

Standing in what would eventually become the grotto at Pure, the spa in his luxury resort project, The Bellamy, Shane was in an unhappy frame of mind. He surveyed the half-finished stacked stone pillars and the coffered ceiling above the narrow hot tub. In several months, Pure would be the most amazing spa Royal had ever seen, offering a modern take on a traditional Roman bath with a series of soothing, luxurious chambers in which guests could relax and revive.

Right now, the place was a disaster.

"I'm offering people the experience of recharging in an expensive, perfectly designed space," Shane reminded his project manager. "What about this particular stone says expensive or perfect?" He held up a sample of the stacked stone. "This is not what I ordered."

"Let me check on it."

"And then there's that." Shane pointed to the coffered ceiling above the hot tub. "That is not the design I approved."

"Let me check on that, as well."

Shane's phone buzzed, reminding him of his next appointment.

"We'll have to pick this up first thing tomorrow." Even though he was reluctant to stop when he had about fifty more details that needed to be discussed, Shane only had fifteen minutes until he was supposed to be at his mother's home for their weekly dinner, and it was a twenty-minute drive to her house.

Shane wound his way through The Bellamy's construction site, seeing something that needed his attention at every turn. He'd teamed with hotelier Deacon Chase to create the architectural masterpiece, and the scope of the project—and the investment—was enormous.

Sitting on fifty-plus acres of lavish gardens, the resort consisted of two hundred and fifty luxury suites, tricked out with cutting-edge technology. The complex also contained fine farm-to-table dining and other amenities. Every single detail had to be perfect.

He texted his mother before he started his truck, letting her know he was going to be delayed, and her snarky response made him smile. Born Elyse Flynn, Shane's mother had left her hometown of Boston at twenty-two with a degree in geoscience, contracted to do a field study of the area near Royal. There, she'd met Shane's father, Landon, and after a whirlwind six-month romance, married him and settled in at Bullseye, the Delgado family ranch.

After Landon died and Shane took over the ranch, Elyse had moved to a home in Pine Valley, the upscale gated community with a clubhouse, pool and eighteen-hole golf course. Although she seemed content in her six-thousand-square-foot house, when Shane began his housing development near Royal, she'd purchased one of the five-acre lots and begun the process of planning her dream home.

Each week when he visited, she had another architectural design for him to look over. In the last year she'd met with no fewer than a dozen designers. Her wish list grew with each new innovation she saw. There were days when Shane wondered if she'd ever settle on a plan. And part of him dreaded that day because he had a feeling she would then become his worst client ever.

When he entered the house, she was standing in the doorway leading to the library, a glass of red wine in her hand.

"There you are at last," she said, waving him over for

a kiss. “Come see how brilliant Thomas is. His latest plan is fantastic.”

Thomas Kitt was the architect Elyse was currently leaning toward. She hadn’t quite committed to his design, but she’d been speaking of him in glowing terms for the last month.

“He’s bumped out the kitchen wall six inches and that gives me the extra room I need so I can go for the thirty-inch built-in wine storage. Now I just need to decide if I want to do the one with the drawers so I can store cheese and other snacks or go with the full storage unit.”

She handed Shane the glass of wine she’d readied for him and gestured to the plate of appetizers that sat on samples of granite and quartz piled on the coffee table.

Shane crossed to where she’d pinned the latest drawings to a magnetic whiteboard. “I’d go with the full storage. That’ll give you room for an extra sixty bottles.”

“You’re right.” Elyse grinned at her son. “Sounds like a trip to Napa is in my future.”

“Why don’t you wait until we break ground?” At the rate his mother was changing her mind, he couldn’t imagine the project getting started before fall.

“Your father was always the practical one in our family.” Elyse’s smile faded at the memory of her deceased husband. “But you’ve really taken over that role. He’d be very proud of you.”

Landon Delgado had never been proud of his son.

You’ve got nothing going for you but a slick tongue and a cocky attitude, his father had always said.

Elyse didn’t seem to notice the dip in her son’s mood as she continued, “Is it crazy that I like the industrial feel to this unit?” She indicated the brochure on high-end appliances.

Shane appreciated how much fun his mother was having with the project. He wrapped his arm around her and dropped a kiss on her head. "Whatever you decide is going to be a showstopper."

"I hope so. Suzanne has been going on and on about the new house she's building in your development to the point where I want to throw her and that pretentious designer she hired right through a plate-glass window."

Growing up with four older brothers gave Elyse a competitive spirit in constant need of a creative outlet. Her husband hadn't shared her interests. Landon Delgado had liked ranching and believed in hard work over fancy innovation. He'd often spent long hours in the saddle moving cattle or checking fences. His days began before sunup and rarely ended until long after dinner. When he wasn't out and about on the ranch, he could be found in his office tending to the business side.

To Landon's dismay, Shane hadn't inherited his father's love of all things ranching. Maybe that was because as soon as Shane could sit up by himself, his father had put him on a horse, expecting Shane to embrace the ranching life. But he'd come to hate the way his every spare moment was taken up by ranch duties assigned to him by his father.

You aren't going to amount to anything if you can't handle a little hard work.

About the time he'd hit puberty, Shane's behavior around the ranch had bloomed into full-on rebellion, and when Shane turned fifteen, the real battles began. He started hanging out with older friends who had their own cars. Most days he didn't come home right after school and dodged all his chores. His buddies liked to party. He'd been forced to toil alongside his father since he was three years old. Didn't he deserve to have a little fun?

According to his father, the answer was no.

You're wrong if you think that grin of yours is all you need to make it in this world.

"So what have you cooked up for us tonight?" Shane asked as he escorted his mother to the enormous kitchen at the back of the house.

"Apricot-and-Dijon-glazed salmon." Although Elyse employed a full-time housekeeper, she enjoyed spending time whipping up gourmet masterpieces. "I got the recipe from the man who catered Janice Hunt's dinner party. I think I'm going to hire him to cater the Bullseye's centennial party," Elyse continued, arching an eyebrow at her son's blank expression.

Shane's thoughts were so consumed with The Bellamy project these days, he'd forgotten all about the event. "The centennial party. When is that again?"

"March twenty-first. I've arranged a tasting with Vincent on the twenty-fourth of this month so we can decide what we're going to have."

"We?" He barely restrained a groan. "Don't you have one of your friends who could help with this?"

"I do, but this is *your* ranch we're celebrating and *your* legacy."

"Sure. Of course." Shane had no interest in throwing a big party for the ranch, but gave his mother his best smile. "A hundred years is a huge milestone and we will celebrate big."

This seemed to satisfy his mother. Elyse was very social. She loved to plan parties and when Shane was growing up there had often been dinners with friends and barbecues out by the pool. Often Shane had wondered how a vibrant, beautiful urbanite like his mother had found happiness with an overly serious, rough-around-the-edges Texas rancher. But there was no question that in spite of their differences, his parents had adored each other, and the way Landon had doted on his wife was the one area where Shane had seen eye to eye with his father.

At that moment Brandee Lawless popped into his mind. There was a woman he wanted to sweep into his arms and never let go. He imagined sending her hat spinning away and tunneling his fingers through her long golden hair as he pulled her toward him for a hot, sexy kiss.

But he'd noticed her regarding him with the same skepticism he used to glimpse in his father's eyes. She always seemed to be peering beyond his charm and wit to see what he was made of. He'd never been able to fool her with the mask he showed to the world. It was unsettling. When she looked at him, she seemed to expect…more.

Someday people are going to figure out that you're all show and no substance.

So far he'd been lucky and that hadn't happened. But where Brandee was concerned, it sure seemed like his luck was running out.

Three

After snatching too few hours of sleep, Brandee rushed through her morning chores and headed to Royal's history museum. She hadn't taken time for breakfast and now the coffee she'd consumed on the drive into town was eating away at her stomach lining. Bile rose in her throat as she parked in the museum lot and contemplated her upside-down world.

It seemed impossible that her life could implode so easily. That the discovery of a single piece of paper meant she could lose everything. In the wee hours of the morning as she stared at the ceiling, she'd almost convinced herself to pay Maverick the money and resign from the TCC. Saving her ranch was more important than besting the terrible trio. But she'd never been a quitter and backing down when bullied had never been her style. Besides, as authentic as the document had looked, there was no reason to believe it was real or that it was in the museum where anyone could stumble on it.

Thirty minutes later, she sat at a table in the small reference room and had her worst fears realized. Before her, encased in clear plastic, was the document she'd been sent a photo of. She tore her gaze from the damning slip of paper and looked up at the very helpful curator. From Rueben Walker's surprise when she'd been waiting on the doorstep for the museum to open, Brandee gathered he wasn't used to having company first thing in the morning.

"You say this is part of a collection donated to the museum after Jasper Crowley's death?" Brandee wondered what other bombshells were to be found in the archives.

"Yes, Jasper Crowley was one of the founding members of the Texas Cattleman's Club. Unfortunately he didn't live to see the grand opening of the clubhouse in 1910."

"What other sorts of things are in the collection?"

"The usual. His marriage license to Sarah McKellan. The birth certificate for their daughter, Amelia. Sarah's death certificate. She predeceased Jasper by almost thirty years and he never remarried. Let's see, there were bills of sale for various things. Letters between Sarah and her sister, Lucy, who lived in Austin."

Brandee was most interested in Jasper's daughter. The land had been her dowry. Why hadn't she claimed it?

"Is there anything about what happened to Amelia? Did she ever get married?"

Walker regarded Brandee, his rheumy blue eyes going suddenly keen. "I don't recall there being anything about a wedding. You could go through the newspaper archives. With someone of Jasper's importance, his daughter's wedding would have been prominently featured."

Brandee had neither the time nor the patience for a random search through what could potentially be years' worth of newspapers. "I don't suppose you know of anyone who would be interested in helping me with the research? I'd be happy to compensate them."

"I have a part-time assistant that comes in a few times a week. He might be able to assist you as soon as he gets back from helping his sister move to Utah."

"When will that be?"

"Middle of next week, I think."

Unfortunately, Maverick had only given her two weeks to meet the demands, and if the claims were true, she needed to find out as soon as possible. Brandee ground her teeth and weighed her options.

"Are the newspaper archives here?"

The curator shook his head. "They're over at the library on microfiche."

"Thanks for your help." Brandee gave Reuben a quick nod before exiting the building and crossing the street.

The library was a couple blocks down and it didn't make sense for her to move her truck. She neared Royal Diner and her stomach growled, reminding her she hadn't eaten breakfast. As impatient as she was to get to the bottom of Maverick's claim, she would function better without hunger pangs.

Stepping into Royal Diner was like journeying back in time to the 1950s. Booths lined one wall, their red faux leather standing out against the black-and-white-checkerboard tile floor. On the opposite side of the long aisle stretched the counter with seats that matched the booths.

Not unexpectedly, the place was packed. Brandee spotted local rancher and town pariah, Adam Haskell, leaving the counter toward the back and headed that way, intending to grab his seat. As she drew closer, Brandee noticed a faint scent of stale alcohol surrounded Haskell. She offered him the briefest of nods, which he didn't see because his blue bug-eyes dropped to her chest as they passed each other in the narrow space.

Once clear of Haskell, Brandee saw that the spot she'd been aiming for was sandwiched between an unfamiliar fortysomething cowboy and Shane Delgado. Of all the bad luck. Brandee almost turned tail and ran, but knew she'd look silly doing so after coming all this way. Bracing herself, she slid onto the seat.

Shane glanced up from his smartphone and grinned as he spotted her. "Well, hello. Look who showed up to make my morning."

His deep voice made her nerve endings shiver, and when she bumped her shoulder against his while sliding her purse onto the conveniently placed hook beneath the counter, the hairs on her arms stood up. Hating how her body reacted to him, Brandee shot Shane a sharp glance.

"I'm not in the mood to argue with you." She spoke with a little more bluntness than usual and his eyes widened slightly. "Can we just have a casual conversation about the weather or the price of oil?"

"I heard it's going to be in the midfifties all week," he said, with one of his knockout grins that indicated he liked that he got under her skin. "With a thirty percent chance of rain."

"We could use some rain."

Heidi dropped off Shane's breakfast and took Brandee's order of scrambled eggs, country potatoes and bacon. A second later the waitress popped back with a cup of coffee.

"Everything tasting okay?" Heidi asked Shane, her eyes bright and flirty.

"Perfect as always."

"That's what I like to hear."

When she walked off, Brandee commented, "You haven't taken a single bite. How do you know it's perfect?"

“Because I eat breakfast here twice a week and it’s always the same great food.” Shane slid his fork into his sunny-side up eggs and the bright yellow yolk ran all over the hash on his plate.

Brandee sipped her coffee and shuddered.

“What’s the matter?” Shane’s even white teeth bit into a piece of toast. He hadn’t looked at her, yet he seemed to know she was bothered.

“Nothing.” Brandee tried to keep her voice neutral. “Why?”

“You are looking more disgusted with me than usual.” His crooked smile made her pulse hiccup.

“It’s the eggs. I can’t stand them runny like that.” The same flaw in human nature that made people gawk at car accidents was drawing Brandee’s gaze back to Shane’s plate. She shuddered again.

“Really?” He pushed the yolk around as if to torment her with the sight. “But this is the only way to eat them with corn-beef hash.”

“Why corn-beef hash and not biscuits and gravy?”

“It’s a nod to my Irish roots.”

“You’re Irish?”

“On my mother’s side. She’s from Boston.”

“Oh.” She drew out her reply as understanding dawned.

“Oh, what?”

“I always wondered about your accent.”

“You thought about me?” He looked delighted.

Brandee hid her irritation. Give the man any toehold and he would storm her battlements in a single bound.

“I thought about your accent,” she corrected him. “It has a trace of East Coast in it.”

Shane nodded. “It’s my mom’s fault. Even after living in Texas for nearly forty years, she still drops her *r*’s most of the time.”

"How'd your mom come to live in Texas?"

Even as Brandee asked the question, it occurred to her that this was the most normal conversation she and Shane had ever had. Usually they engaged in some sort of verbal sparring or just outright arguing and rarely traded any useful information.

"She came here after college to study oil reserves and met my dad. They were married within six months and she's been here ever since." Shane used his toast to clean up the last of the egg. "She went back to Boston after my dad died and stayed for almost a year, but found she missed Royal."

"I'm sure it was you that she missed."

Shane nodded. "I am the apple of her eye."

"Of course." Brandee thanked Heidi as the waitress set a plate down on the counter. With the arrival of her breakfast, Brandee had intended to let her side of the conversation lapse, but something prompted her to ask, "She didn't remarry?"

Never in a million years would Brandee admit it, but Shane's story about his mother was interesting. Shane's father had died over a decade earlier, but Elyse Delgado had accompanied her son to several events at the TCC clubhouse since Brandee had bought Hope Springs Ranch. Her contentious relationship with Shane caused Brandee to avoid him in social situations and she'd never actually spoken to his mother except to say hello in passing. Yet, Brandee knew Elyse Delgado by reputation and thought she would've enjoyed getting to know the woman better if not for her son.

"There've been a couple men she's dated, but nothing serious has come out of it. Although she was completely devoted to my father, I think she's enjoyed her independence."

"I get that," Brandee murmured. "I like the freedom to run my ranch the way I want and not having to worry about taking anyone's opinions into account."

"You make it sound as if you never plan to get married." Shane sounded surprised and looked a little dismayed. "That would certainly be a shame."

Brandee's hackles rose. He probably hadn't intended to strike a nerve, but in the male-dominated world of Texas cattle ranching, she'd faced down a lot of chauvinism.

"I don't need a man to help me or complete me."

At her hot tone, Shane threw up his hands. "That's not what I meant."

"No?" She snorted. "Tell me you don't look at me and wonder how I handle Hope Springs Ranch without a man around." She saw confirmation in his body language before he opened his mouth to argue. "Thanks to my dad, I know more about what it takes to run a successful ranch than half the men around here."

"I don't doubt that."

"But you still think I need someone."

"Yes." Shane's lips curved in a sexy grin. "If only to kiss you senseless and take the edge off that temper of yours."

The second Brandee's eyes cooled, Shane knew he should've kept his opinion to himself. They'd been having a perfectly nice conversation and he'd had to go and ruin it. But all her talk of not needing a man around had gotten under his skin. He wasn't sure why.

"I have neither a temper nor an edge." Brandee's conversational tone wasn't fooling Shane. "Ask anyone in town and they'll tell you I'm determined, but polite."

"Except when I'm around."

Her expression relaxed. "You do bring out the worst in me."

And for some reason she brought out the worst in him. "I'd like to change that." But first he had to learn to hold his tongue around her.

"Why?"

"Because you interest me."

"As someone who sees through your glib ways?"

"I'll admit you've presented a challenge." Too many things in his life came easily. He didn't have to exert himself chasing the unachievable. But in Brandee's case, he thought the prize might be worth the extra effort.

"I've begun to wonder if convincing me to sell Hope Springs had become a game to you."

"I can't deny that I'd like your land to expand my development, but that's not the only reason I'm interested in you."

"Is it because I won't sleep with you?"

He pretended to be surprised. "That never even occurred to me. I'm still in the early stages of wooing you."

"Wooing?" Her lips twitched as if she were fighting a smile. "You do have a way with words, Shane Delgado."

"Several times you've accused me of having a silver tongue. I might have a knack for smooth talking, but that doesn't mean I'm insincere."

Brandee pushed her unfinished breakfast away and gave him her full attention. "Let me get this straight. You want us to date?" She laughed before he could answer.

He'd thought about it many times, but never with serious intent. Their chemistry was a little too combustible, more like a flash bang than a slow burn, and he'd reached a point in his life where he liked to take his time with a woman.

"Whoa," he said, combating her skepticism with lighthearted banter. "Let's not get crazy. How about we try a one-week cease-fire and see how things go?"

Her features relaxed into a genuine smile and Shane

realized she was relieved. His ego took a hit. Had she been dismayed that he'd viewed her in a romantic light? Most women would be thrilled. Once again he reminded himself that she was unique and he couldn't approach her the same way he did every other female on the planet.

"Does that mean you're not going to try to buy Hope Springs for a week?" Despite her smile, her eyes were somber as she waited for his answer.

"Sure."

"Let's make it two weeks, then."

To his surprise, she held out her hand like it was some sort of legal agreement. Shane realized that for all their interaction, they'd never actually touched skin to skin. The contact didn't disappoint.

Pleasure zipped up his arm and lanced straight through his chest. If he hadn't been braced against the shock, he might have let slip a grunt of surprise. Her grip was strong. Her slender fingers bit into his hand without much effort on her part. He felt the work-roughened calluses on her palm and the silky-smooth skin on the back of her hand. It was a study in contrasts, like everything else about her.

Desire ignited even as she let go and snatched up her bill. With an agile shift of her slim body, she was sliding into the narrow space between his chair and hers. Her chest brushed his upper arm and he felt the curve of her breasts even through the layers of her sweater and his jacket.

"See you, Delgado."

Before he got his tongue working again, she'd scooped her coat and purse off the back of the chair and was headed for the front cash register. Helpless with fascination, he watched her go, enjoying the unconscious sashay of her firm, round butt encased in worn denim. The woman knew how to make an exit.

"Damn," he murmured, signaling to the waitress that

he wanted his coffee topped off. He had a meeting in half an hour, but needed to calm down before he headed out.

A cup of coffee later, he'd recovered enough to leave. As he looked for his bill, he realized it was missing. He'd distinctly recalled Heidi sliding it onto the counter, but now it was gone. He caught her eye and she came over with the coffeepot.

"More coffee, Shane?"

"No, I've got to get going, but I don't see my bill and wondered if it ended up on the floor over there." He indicated her side of the counter.

"All taken care of."

"I don't understand."

"Brandee got it."

Had that been the reason for her brush by? In the moment, he'd been so preoccupied by her proximity that he hadn't been aware of anything else. And he understood why she'd paid for his meal. She was announcing that she was independent and his equal. It also gave her a one-up on him.

"Thanks, Heidi." In a pointless assertion of his masculinity, he slid a ten-dollar tip under the sugar dispenser before heading out the door.

As he headed to his SUV, he considered his action. Would he have been compelled to leave a large tip if Gabe or Deacon had picked up his tab? Probably not. Obviously it bothered him to have a woman pay for his meal. Or maybe it wasn't just any woman, but a particular woman who slipped beneath his skin at every turn.

Why had he rejected the idea of dating her so fast? In all likelihood they'd drive each other crazy in bed. And when it was over, things between them would be no worse. Seemed he had nothing to lose and a couple months of great sex to gain.

As he headed to The Bellamy site to see how the project was going, Shane pondered how best to approach Brandee. She wasn't the sort to be wowed with the things he normally tried and she'd already declared herself disinterested in romantic entanglements. Or had she?

Shane found himself back at square one, and realized just how difficult the task before him was. Yet he didn't shy from the challenge. In fact, the more he thought about dating Brandee, the more determined he became to convince her to give them a shot.

But how did a man declare his intentions when the woman was skeptical of every overture?

The answer appeared like the sun breaking through the clouds. It involved the project nearest and dearest to her heart: Hope Springs Camp for at-risk and troubled teenagers. He would somehow figure out what she needed most and make sure she got it. By the time he was done, she would be eating out of his hands.

Brandee left the Royal Diner after paying for Shane's breakfast, amusing herself by pondering how much it would annoy him when he found out what she'd done. She nodded a greeting to several people as she headed to the library. Once there, however, all her good humor fled as she focused on finding out whether there was any truth to Maverick's assertion that Shane was a direct descendant of Amelia Crowley.

It took her almost five hours and she came close to giving up three separate times, but at long last she traced his family back to Jasper Crowley. Starting with newspapers from the day Jasper had penned the dowry document, she'd scrolled through a mile of microfiche until she'd found a brief mention of Amelia, stating that she'd run off with a man named Tobias Stone.

Using the Stone family name, Brandee then tracked down a birth certificate for their daughter Beverly. The Stones hadn't settled near Royal but had ended up two counties over. But the state of Texas had a good database of births and deaths, and the town where they'd ended up had all their newspapers' back issues online.

Jumping forward seventeen years, she began reading newspapers again for some notice of Beverly Stone's marriage. She'd been debating giving up on the newspapers and driving to the courthouse when her gaze fell on the marriage announcement. Beverly had married Charles Delgado and after that Brandee's search became a whole lot easier.

At last she was done. Spread across the table, in unforgiving black and white, was the undeniable proof that Shane Delgado was legally entitled to the land where Hope Springs Ranch stood. A lesser woman would have thrown herself a fine pity party. Brandee sat dry-eyed and stared at Shane's birth certificate. It was the last piece of the puzzle.

In a far more solemn mood than when she'd arrived, Brandee exited the library. The setting sun cast a golden glow over the street. Her research had eaten up the entire day, and she felt more exhausted than if she'd rounded up and tagged a hundred cattle all on her own. She needed a hot bath to ease the tension in her shoulders and a large glass of wine to numb her emotions.

But most of all she wanted to stop thinking about Shane Delgado and his claim to her land for a short time. Unfortunately, once she'd settled into her bath, and as the wine started a warm buzz through her veins, that proved impossible. Dwelling on the man while lying naked in a tub full of bubbles was counterproductive. So was mulling over their breakfast conversation at the Royal Diner, but she couldn't seem to shake the look in his eye as he'd talked about kissing her senseless.

She snorted. As if her current problems could be forgotten beneath the man's chiseled lips and strong hands. She closed her eyes and relived the handshake. The contact had left her palm tingling for nearly a minute. As delightful as the sensation had been, what had disturbed her was how much she'd liked touching him. How she wouldn't mind letting her hands wander all over his broad shoulders and tight abs.

With a groan Brandee opened her eyes and shook off her sensual daydreams. Even if Shane wasn't at the center of her biggest nightmare, she couldn't imagine either one of them letting go and connecting in any meaningful way.

But maybe she didn't need meaningful. Maybe what she needed was to get swept up in desire and revel in being female. She'd deny it until she was hoarse, but it might be nice to let someone be in charge for a little while. And if that someone was Shane Delgado? At least she'd be in for an exhilarating ride.

The bathwater had cooled considerably while Brandee's mind had wandered all over Shane's impressive body. She came out of her musings to discover she'd lost an hour and emerged from her soaking tub with pruney fingers and toes.

While she was toweling off, her office phone began to ring. It was unusual to have anyone calling the ranch in the evening, but not unheard-of. After she'd dressed in an eyelet-trimmed camisole and shorts sleepwear set she'd designed, Brandee padded down the hall to her office, curled up in her desk chair and dialed into voice mail.

"I heard you're looking for a couple horses for your summer camp." The voice coming from the phone's speaker belonged to Shane Delgado. "I found one that might work for you. Liam Wade has a champion reining horse that he had to retire from showing because of his bad hocks. He wants the horse to go to a good home and is interested in donating him to your cause."

Brandee had a tight budget to complete all her projects and was doing a pretty good job sticking to it. When she'd first decided to start a camp, she'd done a few mini-events to see how things went. That was how she'd funded the meeting hall where she served meals and held classes during the day and where the kids could socialize in the evenings. Thanks to her successes, she'd forged ahead with her summer-camp idea. But that required building a bunkhouse that could sleep twelve.

With several minor issues leading to overages she'd hadn't planned for, getting a high-quality, well-trained horse for free from Liam Wade would be awesome. She already had three other horses slated for the camp and hoped to have six altogether to start.

Brandee picked up the phone and dialed Shane back. Knees drawn up to her chest, she waited for him to answer and wondered what he'd expect in return for this favor.

After three rings Shane picked up. "I take it you're interested in the horse."

"Very." Her toes curled over the edge of the leather cushion of her desk chair as his deep, rich voice filled her ear. "Thank you for putting this together."

"My pleasure."

"It was really nice of you." Remembering that he had the power to destroy all she'd built didn't stop her from feeling grateful. "I guess I owe you…" She grasped at the least problematic way she could pay him back.

"You don't owe me a thing."

Immediately Brandee went on alert. He hadn't demanded dinner or sexual favors in exchange for his help.

What was this new game he was playing? Her thoughts turned to the blackmailer Maverick. Once again she wondered whether Shane was involved, but quickly rejected the idea. If he had any clue she was squatting on land that belonged to his family, he would be up front about his intentions.

"Well, then," she muttered awkwardly. "Thank you."

"Happy to help."

After hanging up, she spent a good ten minutes staring at the phone. Happy to help? That rang as false as his "you don't owe me a thing." What was he up to? With no answers appearing on the horizon, Brandee returned to her bedroom and settled in to watch some TV, but nothing held her attention.

She headed into the kitchen for a cup of Sleepytime herbal tea, but after consuming it, she was more wide-awake than ever. So she started a load of laundry and killed another hour with some light housekeeping. As the sole occupant of the ranch house, Brandee only had her cook and cleaning woman, May, come in a couple times a week.

Standing in the middle of her living room, Brandee surveyed her home with a sense of near despair and cursed Maverick. If she found out who was behind the blackmail, she'd make sure they paid. In the meantime, she had to decide what to do. She sank down onto her couch and pulled a cotton throw around her shoulders.

Her choice was clear. She had to pay the fifty thousand dollars and resign from the Texas Cattleman's Club. As much as it galled her to give in, she couldn't risk losing her home. She pictured the smug satisfaction on the faces of the terrible trio and ground her teeth together.

And if Maverick wasn't one or all of them?

What if she'd read the situation wrong and someone else was behind the extortion? She had no guarantee that if she met the demands that Maverick wouldn't return to the well over and over. The idea of spending the rest of her life looking over her shoulder or paying one blackmail demand after another appalled Brandee. But what could she do?

Her thoughts turned to Shane once more. What if she could get him to give up his claim to the land? She considered what her father would think of the idea and shied away from the guilt that aroused. Buck Lawless had never cheated or scammed anyone and would be ashamed of his daughter for even considering it.

But then, Buck had never had to endure the sort of environment Brandee had been thrust into after his death. In her mother's house, Brandee had received a quick and unpleasant education in self-preservation. Her father's position as ranch foreman had meant that Brandee could live and work among the ranch hands and never worry that they'd harm her. That hadn't been the case with her mother's various boyfriends.

She wasn't proud that she'd learned how to manipulate others' emotions and desires, but she was happy to have survived that dark time and become the successful rancher her father had always hoped she'd be. As for what she was going to do about Shane? What he didn't know about his claim on Hope Springs Ranch wouldn't hurt him. She just needed to make sure he stayed in the dark until she could figure out a way to keep her land free and clear.

Four

At Bullseye Ranch's main house, Shane sat on the leather sofa in the den, boots propped on the reclaimed wood coffee table, an untouched tumbler of scotch dangling from the fingers of his left hand. Almost twenty-four hours had gone by since Brandee had called to thank him for finding her a horse and he'd been thinking about her almost nonstop. She'd sounded wary on the phone, as if expecting him to demand something in return for his help. It wasn't the response he'd been hoping for, but it was pure Brandee.

What the hell was wrong with the woman that she couldn't accept a kind gesture? Well, to be fair, he hadn't acted with pure altruism. He did want something from her, but it wasn't what she feared. His motive was personal not business. Would she ever believe that?

His doorbell rang. Shane set aside his drink and went to answer the door. He wasn't expecting visitors.

It was Brandee standing on his front porch. The petite blonde was wearing her customary denim and carrying a bottle wrapped in festive tissue. She smiled at his shocked look, obviously pleased to have seized the upper hand for the moment.

"Brought you a little thank-you gift," she explained, extending the bottle. "I know you like scotch and thought you might appreciate this."

"Thanks." He gestured her inside and was more than a little bewildered when she strolled past him.

"Nice place you have here." Brandee shoved her hands into the back pockets of her jeans as she made her way into the middle of the living room.

"I can't take the credit. My mom did all the remodeling and design."

"She should have been an interior designer."

"I've told her that several times." Shane peeled the paper off the bottle and whistled when he saw the label. "This is a great bottle of scotch."

"Glad you like it. I asked the bartender at the TCC clubhouse what he'd recommend and this is what he suggested."

"Great choice." The brand was far more expensive than anything Shane had in his house and he was dying to try it. "Will you join me in a drink?"

"Just a short one. I have to drive home."

Shane crossed to the cabinet where he kept his liquor and barware. He poured shots into two tulip-shaped glasses with short, stout bases and handed her one.

Brandee considered it with interest. "I thought you drank scotch from tumblers."

"Usually, but you brought me a special scotch," he said, lifting his glass to the light and assessing the color. "And it deserves a whiskey glass."

"What should we drink to?" she asked, snagging his gaze with hers.

Mesmerized by the shifting light in her blue-gray eyes, he said the first bit of nonsense that popped into his head. “World peace?”

“To world peace.” With a nod she tapped her glass lightly against his.

Before Shane drank, he gave the scotch a good swirl to awaken the flavors. He then lifted the glass to his nose and sniffed. A quality scotch like this was worth taking the time to appreciate. He took a healthy sip and rolled it around his tongue. At last he swallowed it, breathed deeply and waited. At around the six-second mark, the richness of the scotch rose up and blessed him with all its amazing flavors—citrus, pears, apples and plums from the sherry barrels it was aged in, along with an undertone of chocolate and a hint of licorice at the very end.

“Fantastic,” he breathed.

Brandee watched him with open curiosity, then held up her glass. “I’ve never been much of a scotch drinker, but watching you just now makes me think I’ve been missing out. Teach me to enjoy it.”

She couldn’t have said anything that pleased him more.

“I’d be happy to. First of all you want to swirl the scotch in the glass and then sniff it. Unlike wine, what you smell is what you’ll taste.”

She did as he instructed, taking her time about it. “Now what?”

“Now you’re going to take a big mouthful.” He paused while she did as instructed. “That’s it. Get it onto the middle of your tongue. You’ll begin to tease out the spice and the richness.” He let her experience the scotch for a few more seconds and then said, “Take a big breath, swallow and open your mouth. Now wait for it.”

She hadn’t blinked, which was good. If she had, it would mean the scotch flavor was too strong. Her expression grew thoughtful and then her eyes flared with understanding.

"I get it. Tangerine and plum."

"The second sip is even better."

Together they took their second taste. The pleasure Shane received was doubled because he was able to share the experience with Brandee. She didn't roll her eyes or make faces like many women of his acquaintance would have. Instead, she let him lead her through an exploration of all the wonderful subtleties of the scotch.

Fifteen minutes later, they had reached a level of connection unprecedented in their prior four years of knowing each other. He was seeing a new side of Brandee. A delightful, sociable side that had him patting himself on the back for putting her in touch with Liam. Convincing her they should give dating a try was going to be way easier than he'd originally thought.

Brandee finished her last sip of scotch and set the glass aside. "I had another reason for dropping by tonight other than to say thank-you."

Shane waited in silence for her to continue, wondering if the other shoe was about to drop.

"I thought about what you said in the diner yesterday." She spoke slowly as if she'd put a lot of thought into what she was saying.

Shane decided to help her along. "About you needing to be kissed senseless?" He grinned when he saw the gap between her eyebrows narrow.

"About us calling a truce for two weeks," she countered, her tone repressive. "I know how you are and I realized that after those two weeks, you'd be back to pestering me to sell the ranch."

Right now, he didn't really give a damn about buying her ranch, but he sensed if he stopped pestering her about it she would forget all about him. "You have a solution for that?"

"I do. I was thinking about a wager."

Now she was speaking his language. "What sort of wager?"

"If I win you agree to give up all current and future attempts to claim Hope Springs Ranch and its land."

"And if I win?"

"I'll sell you my ranch."

A silence settled between them so loud Shane could no longer hear the television in the den. Unless she was convinced she had this wager all sewn up, this was a preposterous offer for her to make. What was she up to?

"Let me get this straight," he began, wanting to make sure he'd heard her clearly. "After years of refusing to sell me your land, you're suddenly ready to put it on the table and risk losing it?" He shook his head. "I don't believe it. You love that ranch too much to part with it so easily."

"First of all, what makes you think you're going to win? You haven't even heard the terms."

He arched one eyebrow. "And the second thing?"

"I said I'd sell the land. I didn't say how much I wanted for it."

He'd known all along that she was clever and relished the challenge of pitting his wits against hers. "Ten million. That's more than fair market value."

Her blue-gray eyes narrowed. She'd never get that much from anyone else and they both knew it.

"Fine. Ten million."

The speed with which she agreed made Shane wonder what he'd gotten himself into. "And the terms of our wager?"

"Simple." A sly smile bloomed. "For two weeks you move in and help me out at the ranch. Between calving time and the construction project going on at my camp, I'm stretched thin."

Shane almost laughed in relief. This was not at all what he'd thought she'd propose. Did she think he'd shy away from a couple weeks of manual labor? Granted, he rarely came home with dirt beneath his fingernails, but that didn't mean he was lazy or incompetent. He knew which end of the hammer to use.

"You need someone who knows his way around a power tool." He shot her a lecherous grin. "I'm your man."

"And I need you to help with the minicamp I have going next weekend."

Now he grasped her logic. She intended to appeal to his altruistic side. She probably figured if he got a close look at her troubled-teen program that he would give up trying to buy the land. This was a bet she was going to lose. He didn't give a damn about a camp for a bunch of screwed-up kids who probably didn't need anything more than parents who knew how to set boundaries.

"That's it?" He was missing something, but he wasn't sure what. "I move in and help you out?" Living with Brandee was like a dream come true. He could survive a few backbreaking days of hard work if it meant plenty of time to convince her they could be good together for a while.

"I can see where your mind has gone and yes..." She paused for effect. "You'll have ample opportunity to convince me to sleep with you."

A shock as potent as if he'd grabbed a live wire with both hands blasted through him. His nerve endings tingled in the aftermath. He struggled to keep his breathing even as he considered the enormity of what she'd just offered.

"You call that a wager?" He had no idea where he found the strength to joke. "I call it shooting ducks in a barrel."

"Don't you mean fish?" Her dry smile warned him winning wasn't going to be easy. "Getting me to sleep with you isn't the wager. You were right when you said I was lacking male companionship."

Well, smack my ass and call me a newborn. The phrase, often repeated by Shane's grandma Bee, popped into his head unbidden. He coughed to clear his throat.

"I said you needed to be kissed senseless."

She rolled her eyes at him. "Yes. Yes. It's been a while since I dated anyone. And I'll admit the thought of you and I has crossed my mind once or twice."

"Damn, woman. You sure do know how to stroke a man's ego."

"Oh please," she said. "You love playing games. I thought this would appeal to everything you stand for."

"And what is that exactly?"

"You get me to say I love you and I sell you the ranch for ten million."

He hadn't prepared himself properly for the devastation of that other shoe. It was a doozy. "And what needs to happen for you to win?"

"Simple." Her smile was pure evil. "I get you to say 'I love you' to me."

Brandee stood on her front porch, heart beating double-time, and watched Shane pull a duffel out of his SUV. In his other hand he held a laptop case. It was late afternoon the day after Brandee had pitched her ridiculous wager to Shane and he was moving in.

This was without a doubt the stupidest idea she'd ever had. Paying Maverick the blackmail money and quitting the TCC was looking better and better. But how would she explain her abrupt change of heart to Shane? No doubt he would consider her backpedaling proof that she was afraid of losing her heart to him.

At least she didn't have to worry about that happening. There was only room in her life for her ranch and her camp. Maybe in a couple years when things settled down she could start socializing. She'd discovered that as soon as she'd started thinking about seducing Shane, a floodgate to something uncomfortably close to loneliness had opened wide.

"Hey, roomie," he called, taking her porch steps in one easy bound.

Involuntarily she stepped back as he came within a foot of her. His wolfish grin was an acknowledgment of her flinch.

"Welcome to Hope Springs Ranch."

"Glad to be here."

"Let me show you to your room. Dinner's at seven. Breakfast is at six. I don't know what you're used to, but we get up early around here."

"Early to bed. Early to rise. I can get on board with the first part. The second may take some getting used to."

Brandee let out a quiet sigh. Shane's not-so-subtle sexual innuendo was going to get old really fast. It might be worth sleeping with him right away to get that to stop.

"I'm sure you'll manage." She led the way into the ranch house and played tour guide. "Kitchen. Dining room. Living room."

"Nice." Shane took his time gazing around the uncluttered open-plan space.

"Your room is this way." She led him into a hallway and indicated a door on the left. "Guest bedrooms one and two share that bathroom. I put you in the guest suite. It has its own bathroom and opens to the patio."

Shane entered the room she indicated and set his duffel on the king-size bed. "Nice."

The suite was decorated in the same neutral tones found

throughout the rest of the house. It was smaller than her master bedroom, but she'd lavished the same high-end materials on it.

"You'll be comfortable, then?" She imagined his master suite at Bullseye was pretty spectacular given what she'd seen of his living room.

"Very comfortable." He circled the bed and stared out the French doors. "So where do you sleep?"

He asked the question with no particular inflection, but her body reacted as if he'd swept her into his arms. She shoved her hands into her back pockets to conceal their trembling and put on her game face. She'd get nowhere with him if he noticed how easily he could provoke her.

"I'll show you."

Cringing at the thought of inviting him into her personal space, Brandee nevertheless led the way back down the hall and past the kitchen. When she'd worked with the architect, she insisted the master suite be isolated from the guest rooms. Passing her home office, Brandee gestured at it as she went by and then strode into her private sanctuary. It wasn't until Shane stood in the middle of her space, keen eyes taking in every detail, that she realized the magnitude of her mistake.

It wasn't that giving him a glimpse of her bedroom might clue him in to what made her tick. Or even that she'd imagined him making love to her here. It was far worse than that. She discovered that she liked having him in her space. She wanted to urge him into one of the chairs that faced her cozy fireplace and stretch out in its twin with her bare feet on his lap, letting him massage the aches from her soles with his strong fingers.

"Nice."

Apparently this was his go-to word for all things related to decorating. She chuckled, amusement helping to ease her anxiety.

Shane shot her a questioning look. “Did I miss something?”

“You must drive your mother crazy.”

“How so?”

“She loves to decorate. I imagine she’s asked your opinion a time or two. Tonight, your reaction to every room we’ve been in has been—” she summoned up her best Shane imitation “—nice.” Her laughter swelled. “I’m imagining you doing that to your mother. It’s funny.”

“Obviously.” He stared at her as if he didn’t recognize her. But after a moment, his lips relaxed into a smile. “I’ll make an effort to be more specific from now on.”

“I’m sure your mother will appreciate that.”

Deciding they’d spent more than enough time in her bedroom, Brandee headed toward the door. As she passed Shane, he surprised her by catching her arm and using her momentum to swing her up against his body.

“Hey!” she protested even as her traitorous spine softened beneath his palm and her hips relaxed into his.

“Hey, what?” He lowered his lips to her temple and murmured, “I’ve been waiting too many years to kiss you. Don’t you think it’s time you put me out of my misery?”

She should’ve expected he’d make his move as soon as possible, and should’ve been prepared to deflect his attempt to seduce her. Instead, here she was, up on her toes, flattening her breasts against the hard planes of his chest and aching for that kiss he so obviously intended to take.

“I’m going to need a couple glasses of wine to get me in the mood,” she told him, stroking her fingers over his beefy shoulders and into the soft brown waves that spilled over his collar.

“You don’t need wine. You have me.” His fingers

skimmed the sensitive line where her back met her butt, sending lightning skittering along her nerve endings.

She trembled with the effort of keeping still. Seizing her lower lip between her teeth, she contained a groan, but the urge to rub herself all over him was gaining momentum. She needed to decide the smart move here, but couldn't think straight.

Summoning all her willpower, she set her hands on his chest and pushed herself away. "It's not going to happen, Delgado."

Shane raked both hands through his hair, but his grin was unabashed and cocky. "Tonight or ever?"

"Tonight." Lying to him served no purpose.

Given the seesaw of antagonism and attraction, she couldn't imagine them lasting two weeks without tearing each other's clothes off, but she refused to tumble into bed with him right off the bat.

"Fair enough."

Brandee led the way back into the main part of the house and toward the kitchen. When she'd made this wager, she hadn't thought through what sharing her home with Shane would entail. She hadn't lived with anyone since she'd run away from her mother's house twelve years earlier. Realizing she would have to interact with him in such close quarters threw her confidence a curve ball.

"I'm going to open a bottle of wine. Do you want to join me or can I get you something else?" She opened the refrigerator. "I have beer. Or there's whiskey."

"I'll have wine. It wasn't an I-could-use-a-beer sort of day."

Brandee popped the cork on her favorite Shiraz and poured out two glasses. "What sort of day is that?"

"One where I spend it in the saddle or out surveying the pastures." His usually expressive features lost all emotion.

And then he gave her a meaningless smile. "You know, ranch work."

"You don't sound as if you're all that keen on ranching."

Because he seemed so much more focused on his real-estate developments, she'd never considered him to be much of a rancher. He gave every appearance of avoiding hard work, so she assumed that he was lazy or entitled.

"Some aspects of it are more interesting than others."

With an hour and a half to kill before dinner, she decided to build a fire in the big stone fireplace out on her covered patio. The cooler weather gave her a great excuse to bundle up and enjoy the outdoor space. She carried the bottle of wine and her glass through the French doors off the dining room.

The days were getting longer, so she didn't have to turn on the overhead lights to find the lighter. The logs were already stacked and waiting for the touch of flame. In a short time a yellow glow spilled over the hearth and illuminated the seating area.

Choosing a seat opposite Shane, Brandee tucked her feet beneath her and sipped her wine. "You do mostly backgrounding at Bullseye, right?"

Backgrounding was the growing of heifers and steers from weanlings to a size where they could enter feedlots for finishing. With nearly fourteen thousand acres, Shane had the space to graze cattle and the skills to buy and sell at the opportune times. He had a far more flexible cattle business than Brandee's, which involved keeping a permanent stock of cows to produce calves that she later sold either to someone like Shane or to other ranches as breeding stock.

"I like the flexibility that approach offers me."

"I can see that."

She'd suffered massive losses after the tornado swept through her property and demolished her operations. She hadn't lost much of her herd, but the damage to her infrastructure had set her way back. And loss of time as she rebuilt wasn't the sort of thing covered by insurance.

Shane continued, "I don't want to give everything to the ranch like my father did and end up in an early grave." Once again, Shane's easy charm vanished beneath a stony expression. But in the instant before that happened, something like resentment sparked in his eyes.

This glimpse behind Shane's mask gave Brandee a flash of insight. For the first time she realized there might be more to the arrogant Shane Delgado than he wanted the world to see. And that intrigued her more than she wanted it to.

She couldn't actually fall for Shane. Her ranch was at stake. But what if he fell in love with her? Until that second, Brandee hadn't actually considered the consequences if she won this desperate wager. And then she shook her head. The thought of Shane falling for her in two weeks was crazy and irrational. But wasn't that the way love made a person feel?

Brandee shook her head. She wasn't in danger of losing her heart to Shane Delgado, only her ranch.

Five

Tossing and turning, his thoughts filled with a woman, wasn't Shane's style, but taking Brandee in his arms for the first time had electrified him. After a nearly sleepless night, he rolled out of bed at five o'clock, heeding her warning that breakfast was at six. The smell of coffee and bacon drew him from the guest suite after a quick shower.

He'd dressed in worn jeans, a long-sleeved shirt and his favorite boots. He intended to show Brandee that while he preferred to run his ranch from his office, he was perfectly capable of putting in a hard day's work.

Shane emerged from the hallway and into the living room. Brandee was working in the kitchen, her blond hair haloed by overhead recessed lighting. With a spatula in one hand and a cup of coffee in the other, she danced and sang to the country song playing softly from her smartphone.

If seeing Brandee relaxed and having fun while she flipped pancakes wasn't enough to short-circuit his equilibrium, the fact that she was wearing a revealing white cotton nightgown beneath a short royal blue silk kimono hit him like a two-by-four to the gut.

Since she hadn't yet noticed him, he had plenty of freedom to gawk at her. Either she'd forgotten he was staying in her guest room or she'd assumed he wasn't going to get up in time for breakfast. Because there was no way she'd let loose like this if she thought he'd catch her.

The soft sway of her breasts beneath the thin cotton mesmerized him, as did the realization that she was a lot more fun than he gave her credit for being. Man, he was in big trouble. If this was a true glimpse of what she could be like off-hours, there was a damn good chance that he'd do exactly what he swore he wouldn't and fall hard. He had to reclaim the upper hand. But at the moment he had no idea how to go about doing that.

"You're into Florida Georgia Line," he said as he approached the large kitchen island and slid onto a barstool. "I would've pegged you as a Faith Hill or Miranda Lambert fan."

"Why, because I'm blond or because I'm a woman?"

He had no good answer. "I guess."

She cocked her head and regarded him with a pitying expression. "The way you think, I'm not surprised you have trouble keeping a woman."

He shrugged. "You got any coffee?"

"Sure." She reached into her cupboard and fetched a mug.

The action caused her nightgown to ride up. Presented with another three inches of smooth skin covering muscular thigh, Shane was having trouble keeping track of the conversation.

"What makes you think I want to keep a woman?"

"Don't you get tired of playing the field?"

"The right woman hasn't come along to make me want to stop."

Brandee bent forward and slid his mug across the concrete counter toward him, offering a scenic view of the sweet curves of her cleavage. In his day he'd seen bigger and better. So why was he dry-mouthed and tongue-tied watching Brandee fixing breakfast?

"What's your definition of the right woman?" She slid the plate of pancakes into the oven to keep them warm.

"She can cook." He really didn't care if she did or not; he just wanted to see Brandee's eyes flash with temper.

She fetched a carton of eggs out of the fridge and held them out to him. "I don't know how to make those disgusting things you eat. So either you eat your eggs scrambled or you make them yourself."

This felt like a challenge. His housekeeper didn't work seven days a week and he knew how to fix eggs. "And she's gotta be great in bed."

"Naturally."

He came around the island as she settled another pan on her six-burner stove and got a flame started under it.

"So as long as she satisfies what lies below your belt, you're happy?" She cracked two eggs into a bowl and beat them with a whisk.

"Pretty much." Too late Shane remembered that their wager involved her falling in love with him. "And she needs to have a big heart, want kids. She'll be beautiful in a wholesome way, passionate about what she does and, of course, she's gotta be a spitfire."

"That's a big list."

"I guess." And it described Brandee to a tee, except for the part about the kids. He had no idea whether or not she wanted to have children.

"You want kids?"

"Sure." He'd never really thought much about it. "I was an only child. It would've been nice to have a bunch of brothers to get into trouble with."

Her silk kimono dipped off her shoulder as she worked, baring her delicate skin. With her dressed like this and her fine, gold hair tucked behind her ears to reveal tiny silver earrings shaped like flowers, he was having a hard time keeping his mind on the eggs he was supposed to be cracking. His lips would fit perfectly into the hollow of her collarbone. Would she quiver as she'd done the evening before?

Silence reigned in the kitchen until Shane broke it.

"Do you do this every day?" He dropped a bit of butter into his skillet.

"I do this most mornings. Breakfast is the most important meal of the day and trust me, you'll burn this off way before lunch."

Based on the mischief glinting in her eyes, Shane didn't doubt that. What sort of plan had she devised to torment him today? It was probably a morning spent in the saddle cutting out heavies, the cows closest to their due date, and bringing them into the pasture closest to the calving building.

It turned out he was right. Brandee put him up on a stocky buckskin with lightning reflexes. He hadn't cut cows in years and worried that he wouldn't be up to the task, but old skills came back to him readily and he found himself grinning as he worked each calf-heavy cow toward the opening into the next pasture.

"You're not too bad," Brandee said, closing the gate behind the pregnant cow he'd just corralled.

She sat her lean chestnut as if she'd been born in the saddle. Her straw cowboy hat had seen better days. So had her brown chaps and boots. The day had warmed from the lower forties to the midsixties and Brandee had peeled off a flannel-lined denim jacket to reveal a pale blue button-down shirt.

"Thanks." He pulled off his hat and wiped sweat from his brow. "I forgot how much fun that can be."

"A good horse makes all the difference," she said. "Buzz there has been working cows for three years. He likes it. Not all the ones we start take to cutting as well as he has."

Shane patted the buckskin's neck and resettled his hat. "How many more do you have for today?" They'd worked their way through the herd of fifty cows and moved ten of them closer to the calving building.

"I think that's going to be it for now." Brandee guided her horse alongside Shane's.

"How many more are set to go soon?"

"About thirty head in the next week to ten days, I think. Probably another fifteen that are two weeks out."

"And it's not yet peak birthing season. What kind of numbers are you looking at in March?"

With her nearly five thousand acres, Shane guessed she was running around seven hundred cows. That translated to seven hundred births a year. A lot could go wrong.

"It's not as bad as it seems. We split the herd into spring and fall calving. So we're only dropping three to four hundred calves at any one time. This cuts down on the number of short-term ranch hands I need to hire during calving and keeps me from losing a year if a breeding doesn't take."

"It's still a lot of work."

Brandee shrugged. "We do like to keep a pretty close eye on them because if anything can go wrong, chances are it will."

"What are your survival rates?"

"Maybe a little better than average. In the last three years I've only lost four percent of our calves." She looked pretty pleased by that number. "And last fall we only had two that were born dead and only one lost through complications." Her eyes blazed with triumph.

"I imagine it can be hard to lose even one."

"We spend so much time taking care of them every day between feeding, doctoring and pulling calves. It breaks my heart every time something goes wrong. Especially when it's because we didn't get to a cow in time. Or if it's a heifer who doesn't realize she's given birth and doesn't clean up the calf or, worse, wanders off while her wet baby goes hypothermic."

Over the years he'd become so acclimated to Brandee's coolness that he barely recognized the vibrant, intense woman beside him. He was sucker punched by her emotional attachment to the hundreds of babies that got born on her ranch every year.

This really was her passion. And every time he approached her about selling, he'd threatened not just her livelihood but her joy.

"My dad used to go ballistic if that happened," she continued. "I pitied the hand that nodded off during watch and let something go wrong."

"Where's your dad now?"

Her hat dipped, hiding her expression. "He died when I was twelve."

Finding that they had this in common was a surprise. "We both lost our dads too early." Although Shane suspected from Brandee's somber tone that her loss was far keener than his had been. "So, your dad was a rancher, too?"

She shook her head. "A foreman at the Lazy J. But it was his dream to own his own ranch." Her gaze fixed on the horizon. "And for us to run it together."

Shane heard the conviction in her voice and wondered

if he should just give up and concede the wager right now. She wasn't going to sell her ranch to him or anyone else. Then he remembered that even if he was faced with a fight he could never win, there was still a good chance she'd sleep with him before the two weeks were up. And wasn't that why he'd accepted the wager in the first place?

At around two o'clock in the afternoon, Brandee knocked off work so she could grab a nap. It made the long hours to come a little easier if she wasn't dead tired before she got on the horse. Normally during the ninety-day calving season Brandee took one overnight watch per week. She saw no reason to change this routine with Shane staying at her house.

Brandee let herself in the back door and kicked off her boots in the mudroom. Barefoot, she headed into the kitchen for a cheese stick and an apple. Munching contentedly, she savored the house's tranquillity. Sharing her space with Shane was less troublesome than she'd expected, but she'd lived alone a long time and relished the quiet. Shane had a knack for making the air around him crackle with energy.

It didn't help that he smelled like sin and had an adorable yawn, something she'd seen a great deal of him doing these last three days because she'd worked him so hard. In the evenings he had a hard time focusing on his laptop as he answered emails and followed up with issues on The Bellamy job site.

Today, she'd given him the day off to head to the construction site so he could handle whatever problems required him to be there in person. She didn't expect him back until after dinner and decided to indulge in a hot bath before hitting her mattress for a couple hours of shut-eye. It always felt decadent to nap in the afternoon, but she functioned better when rested and reminded herself that she'd hired experienced hands so she didn't have to do everything herself.

Since receiving Maverick's blackmail notice, she hadn't slept well, and though her body was tired, her mind buzzed with frenetic energy. Disrupting her routine further was the amount of time she was spending with Shane. Despite questioning the wisdom of their wager, she realized that having him in her house was a nice change.

Four hours later, Brandee was fixing a quiet dinner for herself of baked chicken and Caesar salad. Shane had a late business meeting and was planning on having dinner in town. He'd only been helping her for three days, but already she could see the impact he was having on her building project at the camp.

He'd gone down to the site and assessed the situation. Last night he'd studied her plans and budget, promising to get her back on track. As much as she hated to admit it, it was good to have someone to partner with. Even if that someone was Shane Delgado and he was only doing it to make her fall in love with him.

There'd been no repeat of him making a play for her despite the way she fixed breakfast every morning in her nightgown. Standing beside him in the kitchen and suffering the bite of sexual attraction, she'd expected something to happen. When nothing had, she'd felt wrung out and cranky. Not that she let him see that. It wouldn't do to let him know that she'd crossed the bridge from it's never going to happen to if it didn't happen soon she'd go mad.

Shane returned to the ranch house as Brandee was getting ready to leave. Her shift wouldn't begin for an hour, but she wanted to get a report on what had happened during the afternoon. As he came in the back door and met up with her in the mudroom, he looked surprised to see her dressed in her work clothes and a warm jacket.

His movements lacked their usual energy as he set his briefcase on the bench. "Are you just getting in?"

"Nope, heading out." She snagged her hat from one of the hooks and set it on her head. "It's my night to watch the cows that are close to calving."

"You're going out by yourself?"

She started to bristle at his question, then decided he wasn't being patronizing, just voicing concern. "I've been doing it for three years by myself. I'll be fine."

"Give me a second to change and I'll come with you."

His offer stunned her. "You must be exhausted." The words slipped out before she considered them.

He turned in the doorway that led to the kitchen and glared at her. "So?"

"I just mean it's a long shift. I spend between four to six hours in the saddle depending on how things go."

"You don't think I'm capable of doing that?"

"I didn't say that." Dealing with his ego was like getting into a ring with a peevish bull. "But you have worked all day and I didn't figure you'd be up for pulling an all-nighter."

"You think I'm soft."

"Not at all." She knew he could handle the work, but was a little surprised he wanted to.

"Then what is it?"

"I just reasoned that you don't…that maybe you aren't as used to the actual work that goes into ranching."

"That's the same thing."

Brandee regretted stirring the pot. She should have just invited him along and laughed when he fell off his horse at 2:00 a.m. because he couldn't keep his eyes open any longer.

"I don't want to make a big deal about this," she said. "I just thought you might want to get a good night's sleep and start fresh in the morning."

"While you spend the night checking on your herd."

"I took a three-hour nap." His outrage was starting to amuse her. "Okay. You can come with me. I won't say another word."

He growled at her in frustration before striding off. Brandee grabbed a second thermos from her cabinet. Coffee would help keep them warm and awake. To her surprise, Brandee caught herself smiling at the thought of Shane's company tonight. Working together had proven more enjoyable than she'd imagined. She didn't have to keep things professional with Shane the way she did when working with her ranch hands. She'd enjoyed talking strategy and ranch economics with him.

As if he feared she'd head out without him, Shane returned in record time. She handed him a scarf and watched in silence as he stepped into his work boots.

"Ready?" she prompted as he stood.

"Yes."

"Do you want to take separate vehicles? That way if you get…" She trailed off as his scowl returned. "Fine."

Irritation radiated from him the whole drive down to the ranch buildings. In the barn, she chatted with her foreman, Jimmy, to see how the afternoon had gone. H545 had dropped her calf without any problems.

"A steer," he said, sipping at the coffee Brandee had just made.

"That makes it fifty-five steers and fifty-two heifers." While the ratio of boys to girls was usually fifty-fifty, it was always nice when more steers were born because they grew faster and weighed more than the girls. "Anyone we need to keep an eye on tonight?"

"H729 was moving around like her labor was starting. She's a week late and if you remember she had some problems last year, so you might want to make sure things are going smoothly with her."

"Will do. Thanks, Jimmy."

The moon was up, casting silvery light across the grass when Shane and Brandee rode into the pasture. The pregnant cows stood or lay in clusters. A couple moved about in a lazy manner. H729 was easy to spot. She was huge and had isolated herself. Brandee pointed her out.

"She's doing some tail wringing, which means she's feeling contractions. I don't think she'll go tonight, but you can never tell."

"How often do they surprise you?"

"More often than I'd like to admit. And that drives me crazy because there's nothing wrong with nearly eighty percent of the calves we lose at birth. Most of the time they suffocate because they're breeched or because it's a first-calf heifer and she gets too tired to finish pushing out the calf."

"How often do you have to assist?"

"On nights like this it's pretty rare." The temperature was hovering in the low forties; compared to a couple weeks earlier, it almost felt balmy. "It's when we get storms and freezing rain that we have our hands full with the newborns."

Shane yawned and rubbed his eyes. Brandee glanced his way to assess his fatigue and lingered to admire his great bone structure and sexy mouth. It was an interesting face, one she never grew tired of staring at. Not a perfect face—she wasn't into that, too boring—but one with character.

"What?" he snapped, never taking his focus off the cows. Despite the shadow cast by the brim of his hat, Brandee could see that Shane's jaw was set.

"I was just thinking it was nice to have your company tonight."

For the briefest of moments his lips relaxed. "I'm glad to be here."

She knew that showing she felt sorry for him would only heighten his annoyance. Big strong men like Shane did not admit to weakness of any kind. And she rather liked him the better for gritting his teeth and sticking with it.

"That being said, you can take my truck and head back if you want. I don't think much of anything is going to happen tonight."

"I don't like the idea of you being alone out here."

"I've been doing this since I was ten years old."

"Not alone."

"No. With my dad. On the weekends, he used to let me ride the late-night watch with him."

"What did your mom say about that?"

"Nothing. She didn't live with us."

Shane took a second to digest that. "They divorced?"

"Never married."

"How come you lived with your dad and not your mom?"

Insulated by her father's unconditional love, Brandee had never noticed her mother's absence. "She didn't want me."

It wasn't a plea for sympathy, but a statement of fact. Most people would have said her mother was a bad parent or uttered some banality about how they were sure that wasn't true.

Shane shrugged. "You are kind of a pain."

He would never know how much she appreciated this tactic. Shane might come off as a glib charmer, but the way he watched her now showed he had a keen instinct for people.

"Yes," Brandee drawled. "She mentioned that often after my dad died and I had to go live with her."

Judging from his narrowed eyes, he wasn't buying her casual posture and nonchalant manner. "Obviously she wasn't interested in being a parent," he said.

Brandee loosed a huge sigh and an even bigger confession. "I was the biggest mistake she ever made."

Six

Shane's exhaustion dwindled as Brandee spoke of her mother. Although he'd grown up with both parents, his father's endless disappointment made Shane sympathetic of Brandee for the resentment her mother had displayed.

"Why do you say that?"

"She gave birth to me and handed me over to my dad, then walked out of the hospital and never looked back. After my dad died and the social worker contacted my mom, I was really surprised when she took me in. I think she wanted to get her hands on the money that my dad left me. He'd saved about fifty thousand toward the down payment on his own ranch. She went through it in six months."

"And you got nothing?"

"Not a penny."

"So your father died when you were twelve and your mother spent your inheritance."

"That about sums it up." Brandee spoke matter-of-factly,

but Shane couldn't imagine her taking it all in stride. No child grew up thinking it was okay when a parent abandoned them. This must have been what led to Brandee erecting her impenetrable walls. And now Shane was faced with an impossible task. The terms of her wager made much more sense. There was no way he was going to get her to fall for him.

After a slow circle of the pasture, Brandee declared it was quiet enough that they could return to the barn. Leaving the horses saddled and tied up, they grabbed some coffee and settled in the ranch office. While Brandee looked over her herd data, updated her birth statistics and considered her spring-breeding program, Shane used the time to research her.

"You started a fashion line?" He turned his phone so the screen faced her.

She regarded the image of herself modeling a crocheted halter, lace-edged scarf and headband. "A girl's got to pay the bills."

"When you were eighteen?"

"Actually, I was seventeen. I fudged my age. You have to be eighteen to open a business account at the bank and sell online."

"From these news articles, it looks like you did extremely well."

"Who knew there was such a huge hole in the market for bohemian-style fashion and accessories." Her wry smile hid a wealth of pride in her accomplishment.

"You built up the business and sold it for a huge profit."

"So that I could buy Hope Springs Ranch."

He regarded her with interest. "Obviously the fashion line was a moneymaker. Why not do both?"

"Because my dream was this ranch. And the company was more than a full-time job. I couldn't possibly keep up with both." She picked up her hat and stood. "We should do another sweep."

Back in the saddle, facing an icy wind blowing across the flat pasture, Shane considered the woman riding beside him. The photos of her modeling her clothing line had shown someone much more carefree and happy than she'd ever appeared to him. Why, if there'd been such good money to be made running a fashion company, had she chosen the backbreaking work of running a ranch?

Was it because she'd been trying to continue her father's legacy, molded by him to wake up early, put in a long day and take satisfaction in each calf that survived? From the way she talked about her dad, Shane bet there'd been laughter at the end of each day and a love as wide as the Texas sky.

He envied her.

"Is that the cow you were watching earlier?" He pointed out an animal in the distance that had just lain down.

"Maybe. Let's double-check."

When they arrived, they left their horses and approached the cow on foot. Judging from the way her sides were straining, she was deep in labor.

It struck Shane that despite spending his entire life on a ranch, he'd only witnessed a few births, and those had been horses not cows. He took his cue from Brandee. She stood with her weight evenly placed, her gloved hands bracketing her hips. Although her eyes were intent, her manner displayed no concern.

"Look," she said as they circled around to the cow's rear end. "You can see the water sack."

Sure enough, with the moon high in the sky there was enough light for Shane to pick out the opaque sack that contained the calf. He hadn't come out tonight expecting excitement of this sort.

"What did you expect?" It was as if she'd read his mind.

"Frankly I was thinking we'd be riding around out here while you kept me at arm's length with tales of your brokenhearted ex-lovers."

With her arms crossed over her chest, she pivoted around to face him, laboring cow forgotten.

"My brokenhearted what?"

"I don't know," he replied somewhat shortly. "I'm tired and just saying whatever pops into my mind."

"Why would you be thinking about my brokenhearted ex-lovers?"

"Are you sure she's doing okay?" He indicated the straining cow, hoping to distract Brandee with something important.

Unfortunately it seemed as if both females were happy letting nature take its course. Brandee continued to regard him like a detective interviewing a prime suspect she knew was lying.

"What makes you think that any of my lovers are brokenhearted?"

"I don't. Not really." In truth he hadn't given much thought to her dating anyone.

Well, that wasn't exactly true. To the best of his knowledge she hadn't dated anyone since moving to Royal. And despite the womanly curves that filled out her snug denim, she always struck him as a tomboy. Somehow he'd gotten it into his head that he was the only one who might've been attracted to her.

"So which is it?"

"Is that a hoof?"

His attempt to distract her lasted as long as it took for her to glance over at the cow and notice that a pair of hooves had emerged.

"Yes." And just like that she was back staring at him

again. "Do I strike you as the sort of woman who uses men and casts them aside?"

"No."

"So why would you think I would end my relationships in such a way that I would hurt someone?"

Shane recognized that he'd tapped into something complicated with his offhand remark and sought to defuse her irritation with a charming smile. "You should be flattered that I thought you would be so desirable that no one would ever want to break up with you."

"So you think I'm susceptible to flattery?"

He was in so deep he would need a hundred feet of rope to climb out of the hole he'd dug. What had happened to the silver-tongued glibness she liked to accuse him of having?

"Is she supposed to stand up like that?"

"Sometimes they need to walk around a bit." This time Brandee didn't spare the cow even a fraction of her attention. "She may be up and down several times."

"I think our arguing is upsetting her," he said, hoping concern for the cow would convince Brandee to give up the conversation.

"We're not arguing," she corrected him, her voice light and unconcerned. "We're discussing your opinion of me. And you're explaining why you assume I'd be the one to end a relationship. Instead of the other way around."

At first he grappled with why he'd said what he had. But beneath her steady gaze, he found his answer. "I think you have a hard time finding anyone who can match up to your father."

She obviously hadn't expected him to deliver such a blunt, to-the-point answer. Her eyes fell away and she stared at the ground. In the silence that followed, Shane worried that he'd struck too close to home.

Brandee turned so she was once again facing the cow.

The brim of her hat cast a shadow over her features, making her expression unreadable. Despite her silence, Shane didn't sense she was angry. Her mood was more contemplative than irritated.

"I never set out to hurt anyone," she said, her voice so soft he almost missed the words. "I'm just not good girlfriend material."

Was that her way of warning him off? If so, she'd have to work a lot harder. "That's something else we have in common. I've been told I'm not good boyfriend material, either."

Now both of them were staring at the cow. She took several steps before coming to a halt as another spasm swept over her. It seemed as if this would expel the calf, but no more of the baby appeared.

"Is this normal?" Shane asked. "It seems like she can't get it out."

"We should see good progress in the next thirty minutes or so. If we don't see the nose and face by then, there might be something wrong."

Shane was surprised at the way his stomach knotted with anxiety. Only by glancing at Brandee's calm posture did he keep from voicing his concern again.

"How do you do this?"

"I have around seven hundred cows being bred over two seasons. While I never take anything for granted, watching that many births gives you a pretty good feel for how things are going."

"Your business is a lot more complicated than mine." And offered a lot more potential for heartbreak.

He certainly wasn't standing in his field at three o'clock in the morning waiting for new calves to be brought into the world. He bought eight-month-old, newly weaned steers and heifers and sent them out into his pastures to grow up. Unless he was judging the market for the best time to sell, he rarely thought about his livestock.

"Not necessarily more complicated," Brandee said. "You have to consider the market when you buy and sell and the best way to manage your pastures to optimize grazing. There are so many variables that depend on how much rain we get and the price of feed if the pastures aren't flourishing."

"But you have all that to worry about and you have to manage when you're breeding and optimize your crosses to get the strongest calves possible. And then there's the problem of losing livestock to accidents and predators."

While he'd been speaking, the cow had once again lain down. The calf's nose appeared, followed by a face. Shane stared as she began to push in earnest.

"She's really straining," he said. "This is all still normal?"

"She needs to push out the shoulders and this is really hard. But she's doing fine."

Shane had the urge to lean his body into Brandee's and absorb some of her tranquillity. Something about the quiet night and the miracle playing out before them made him want to connect with her. But he kept his distance, not wanting to disturb the fragile camaraderie between them.

Just when Shane thought the whole thing was over, the cow got to her feet again and he groaned. Brandee shot him an amused grin.

"It's okay. Sometimes they like finishing the birthing process standing up."

He watched as the cow got to her feet, her baby dangling halfway out of her. This time Shane didn't resist the urge for contact. He reached out and grabbed Brandee's hand. He'd left his gloves behind on this second sweep and wished Brandee had done the same. But despite the worn leather barrier between them, he reveled in the way her fingers curved against his.

After a few deep, fortifying breaths, the cow gave one last mighty push and the calf fell to the grass with a thud. Shane winced and Brandee laughed.

"See, I told you it was going to be okay," Brandee said as the cow turned around and began nudging the calf while making soft, encouraging grunts.

A moment later she swept her long tongue over her sodden baby, clearing fluid from the calf's coat. The calf began to breathe and the cow kept up her zealous cleaning. Brandee leaned a little of her weight against Shane's arm.

That was when Shane realized they were still holding hands. "Damn," he muttered, unsure which had a bigger impact, the calf being born or the simple pleasure of Brandee's hand in his.

He hadn't answered the question before she lifted up on tiptoes and kissed him.

Being bathed in moonlight and surrounded by the sleepy cows seemed like an ideal moment to surrender to the emotions running deep and untamed through Brandee's body. At first Shane's lips were stiff with surprise and Brandee cursed. What had she been thinking? There was no romance to be found in a cold, windswept pasture. But as she began her retreat, Shane threw an arm around her waist and yanked her hard against his body. His lips softened and coaxed a sigh of relief from her lungs.

She wrapped her arms around his neck and let him sweep her into a rushing stream of longing. The mouth that devoured her with such abandon lacked the persuasive touch she'd expected a charmer like Shane to wield. It almost seemed as if he was as surprised as she.

Of course, there was no way that could be the case.

His reasons for being at her ranch were as self-serving as hers had been for inviting him. Each of them wanted to win their wager. She'd intended to do whatever it took to get Shane to fall in love with her. Her dire situation made that a necessity. But he'd been pestering her for years to sell and she was sure he'd pull out every weapon in his arsenal to get her to fall for him.

This last thought dumped cold water on her libido. She broke off the kiss and through the blood roaring in her ears heard the measured impact of approaching hooves all around them. It wasn't unusual for the most dominant cows in the herd to visit the newborn. Half a dozen cows had approached.

"He's looking around," she said, indicating the new calf. "Soon he'll be trying to get up."

Usually a calf was on its feet and nursing within the first hour of being born. Brandee would have to make sure her ranch hands kept an eye on him for the next twelve hours to make sure he got a good suckle. And they would need to get him ear-tagged and weighed first thing. The calves were docile and trusting the first day. After that they grew much more difficult to catch.

Brandee stepped away from Shane and immediately missed their combined body heat. "I think it's okay to head back."

"I'm glad I came out tonight," Shane said as they rode back toward the horse barn. A quick sweep of the pasture had shown nothing else of interest.

"You're welcome to participate in night duty anytime."

"How often do you pull a shift?"

"Once a week."

"You don't have to."

"No." But how did she explain that sitting on a horse in the middle of the night, surrounded by her pregnant cows, she felt as if everything was perfect in her world? "But when I'm out here I think about my dad smiling down and I know he'd be happy with me."

She didn't talk about her dad all that much to anyone. But because of Shane's awestruck reaction to tonight's calving, she was feeling sentimental.

"Happy because you're doing what he wanted?"

"Yes."

"How about what you want?"

"It's the same thing." Brandee's buoyant mood suddenly drooped like a thirsty flower. "Being a rancher is all I ever wanted to do."

"And yet you started a fashion business instead of coming back to find work as a ranch hand. You couldn't know that what you were doing with your clothing line would make you rich."

"No." She'd never really thought about why she'd chosen waitressing and creating clothing and accessories after running away from her mother's house over getting work on a ranch. "I guess I wasn't sure anyone would take me serious as a ranch hand." And it was a job dominated by men.

"You might be right."

When they arrived at the barn, this time Brandee insisted Shane take her truck back to the ranch house. She wasn't going to finish up work until much later. He seemed reluctant, but in the end he agreed.

The instant the truck's taillights disappeared down the driveway, Brandee was struck by a ridiculous feeling of loneliness. She turned on the computer and recorded the ranch's newest addition. Then, hiding a yawn behind her hand, she made her way to the barn where they housed cows and calves that needed more attention.

Cayenne was a week old. A couple days ago a ranch hand had noticed her hanging out on her own by the hay, abandoned by her mother. At this age it didn't take long for a calf to slide downhill, so it paid to be vigilant. Jimmy had brought her in and the guys had tended to a cut on her hind left hoof.

They'd given her a bottle with some electrolytes and a painkiller and the calf had turned around in two days. She was a feisty thing and it made Brandee glad to see the way she charged toward the half wall as if she intended to smash through it. At the very last second she wheeled away, bucking and kicking her way around the edge of the enclosure.

Brandee leaned her arms on the wood and spent a few minutes watching the calf, wondering if the mother would take back her daughter when they were reunited. Sometimes a cow just wasn't much of a mother and when that happened they'd load her up and take her to the sales barn. No reason to feed an unproductive cow.

Talking about being abandoned by her own mother wasn't something Brandee normally did, but it had proven easy to tell Shane. So easy that she'd also divulged the theft of her inheritance, something she'd only ever told to one other person, her best friend, Chelsea.

In the aftermath of the conversation, she'd felt exposed and edgy. It was partially why she'd picked a fight with him about his "brokenhearted ex-lovers" comment. She'd wanted to bring antagonism back into their interaction. Fighting with him put her back on solid ground, kept her from worrying that he'd see her as weak and her past hurts as exploitable.

At the same time his offhand comment had unknowingly touched a nerve. She'd asked if he saw her as the sort of woman who'd use a man and cast him aside. Yet she'd done it before and had barely hesitated before deciding to do so with Shane. She was going to make him fall for her and trick him into giving up his legal claim to Hope Springs Ranch. What sort of a terrible person did that make her?

Reminding herself that he intended to take the ranch didn't make her feel better about what she was doing. He had no clue about the enormity of their wager. Keeping him in the dark wasn't fair or right. Yet, if he discovered the truth, she stood to lose everything.

As during her teen years living with her mother, she was in pure survival mode. It was the only thing that kept her conscience from hamstringing her. She didn't enjoy what she was doing. It was necessary to protect what belonged to her and keep herself safe. Like a cat cornered by a big dog, she would play as dirty as it took to win free and clear.

Several hours later, after one final sweep of the pasture, she turned the watch over to her ranch hands and had one of them drop her off at home. She probably could've walked the quarter-mile-long driveway to her house, but the emotional night had taken a toll on her body as well as her spirit.

The smell of bacon hit her as she entered the back door and her stomach groaned in delight. With loud country music spilling from the recessed speakers above her kitchen and living room, she was able to drop her boots in the mudroom and hang up her coat and hat, then sneak through the doorway to catch a glimpse of Shane without him being aware.

Her heart did a strange sort of hiccup in her chest at the sight of him clad in baggy pajama bottoms, a pale blue T-shirt riding his chest and abs like a second skin. She gulped at the thought of running her hands beneath the cotton and finding the silky, warm texture beneath. While the man might be a piece of work, his body was a work of art.

"Hey." She spoke the word softly, but he heard.

His gaze shifted toward her and the slow smile that curved his lips gave her nerve endings a delicious jolt. She had to hold on to the door frame while her knees returned to a solid state capable of supporting her. He was definitely working the sexy-roommate angle for all it was worth. She'd better up her game.

"I'm making breakfast just the way you like it." He held up the skillet and showed her the eggs he'd scrambled. "And there's French toast, bacon and coffee."

Damn. And he could cook, too. Conscious of her disheveled hair and the distinctive fragrance of horse and barn that clung to her clothes, Brandee debated slinking off to grab a quick shower or just owning these badges of hard work.

"It all sounds great." Her stomach growled loudly enough to be heard and Shane's eyebrows went up.

"Let me make you a plate," he said, laughter dancing at the edges of his voice. "Here's a cup of coffee. Go sit down before you fall over."

That he'd misinterpreted why she was leaning against the doorway was just fine with Brandee. She accepted the coffee and made her way toward the bar stools that lined her kitchen island. Unconcerned about whether the caffeine zap would keep her awake, she gladly sipped the dark, rich brew.

"It's decaf," he remarked, sliding a plate toward her and then turning back to the stove to fill one for himself. "I figured you'd grab a couple hours before heading out again."

"Thanks," she mumbled around a mouthful of French toast. "And thanks for breakfast. You didn't have to."

His broad shoulders lifted in a lazy shrug. "I slept a few hours and thought you'd be hungry. How's the new calf?"

"On my last circuit he was enjoying his first meal."

"Great to hear." Shane slid into the seat beside her and

set his plate down. His bare feet found the rungs of her chair, casually invading her space. "Thanks for letting me tag along last night." He peered at her for a long moment before picking up his fork and turning his attention to breakfast.

"Sure."

As they ate in companionable silence, Brandee found her concern growing by the minute. The night's shared experience and his thoughtfulness in having breakfast ready for her were causing a shift in her impression of him. For years she'd thought of Shane as an egomaniac focused solely on making money. Tonight she'd seen his softer side, and the hint of vulnerability made him attractive to her in a different way.

A more dangerous way.

She had to stay focused on her objective and not give in to the emotions tugging at her. Letting him capture her heart was a mistake. One that meant she would lose everything. Her home. Her livelihood. And worst of all, her self-respect. Because falling for a man who wouldn't return her love was really stupid and she'd been many things, but never that.

Seven

It was almost six o'clock in the evening when Shane returned from checking on the building site at Brandee's teen camp. As he entered the house through the back door, the most delicious scents stopped him dead in his tracks. He breathed in the rich scent of beef and red wine as he stripped off his coat and muddy boots. In stockinged feet, he entered the kitchen, where Brandee's housekeeper stood at the stove, stirring something in a saucepan.

"What smells so amazing?"

"Dinner," May responded with a cheeky grin and a twinkle in her bright blue eyes.

The fiftysomething woman had rosy cheeks even when she wasn't standing over the stove. She fussed over Brandee like a fond aunt rather than a housekeeper and treated Shane as if he was the best thing that had ever happened to her employer.

"What are we having?"

"Beef Wellington with red potatoes and asparagus."

Shane's mouth began to water. "What's the occasion?"

"Valentine's Day." May pointed toward the dining table, where china and silverware had been laid. There were white tapers in crystal holders and faceted goblets awaiting wine. "You forgot?"

Eyeing the romantic scene, Shane's heart thumped erratically. What special hell was he in for tonight?

"I've been a little preoccupied," he muttered.

Between helping out at Hope Springs, keeping an eye on the construction at The Bellamy and popping in at Bullseye to make sure all was running smoothly, he hadn't had five minutes to spare. Now he was kicking himself for missing this opportunity to capitalize on the most romantic day of the year to sweep Brandee off her feet.

Obviously she hadn't made the same mistake.

May shook her head as if Shane had just proven what was wrong with the entire male sex. "Well, it's too late to do anything about it now. Dinner's in half an hour." She arched her eyebrows at his mud-splattered jeans.

Catching her meaning, Shane headed for his shower. Fifteen minutes later, he'd washed off the day's exertions and dressed in clean clothes. He emerged from his bedroom, tugging up the sleeves of his gray sweater. Black jeans and a pair of flip-flops completed his casual look.

Brandee was peering into her wine fridge as he approached. She turned at his greeting and smiled in genuine pleasure. "How was your day?"

"Good. Productive." It was a casual exchange, lacking the push and pull of sexual attraction that typified their usual interaction. Time to step up his game. "Did May head home?"

"Yes. She and Tim were going out for a romantic dinner."

"Because it's Valentine's Day. I forgot all about it."

"So did I." Brandee selected a bottle and set it on the counter. With her long golden hair cascading over the shoulders of her filmy top, she looked like a cross between a sexy angel and the girl next door. White cotton shorts edged in peekaboo lace rode low on her hips and bared her sensational, well-toned thighs. "Can you open this while I fetch the glasses? The corkscrew is in the drawer to your right."

"I guess neither one of us buys into all the romantic mumbo jumbo," he muttered.

He should've been relieved that the fancy dinner and beautifully set dining table hadn't been Brandee's idea. It meant that she hadn't set out to prey on his libido. But that didn't mean the danger had passed.

"Or we're just cynical about love." She gazed at him from beneath her long eyelashes.

Shane finished opening the bottle and set it aside to breathe. He worked the cork off the corkscrew, letting the task absorb his full attention. "Do you ever wonder if you're built for a long-term relationship?" He recognized it was a strange question to ask a woman, but he suspected Brandee wouldn't be insulted.

"All the time." She moved past him as the timer on the stove sounded. Apparently this was her signal to remove the beef Wellington from the oven. "I don't make my personal life a priority. Chelsea's on me all the time about it."

"My mom gives me the same sort of lectures. I think she wants grandchildren." And he was getting to an age where he needed to decide kids or no kids. At thirty-five he wasn't over the hill by any means, but he didn't want to be in his forties and starting a family.

"I imagine she's feeling pretty hopeless about the possibility."

"Because I haven't met anyone that makes me want to settle down?"

Brandee shook her head. "I can't imagine any woman being more important to you than your freedom."

And she was right. His bachelor status suited him. Having fun. Keeping things casual. Bolting at the first sign of commitment. He liked keeping his options open. And what was wrong with that?

"And what about you, Miss Independent? Are you trying to tell me you're any more eager to share your life with someone? You use your commitment to this ranch and your teen camp to keep everyone at bay. What are you afraid of?"

"Who says I'm afraid?"

Bold words, but he'd seen the shadows that lingered in her eyes when she talked about her mother's abandonment. She might deny it, but there was no question in Shane's mind that Brandee's psyche had taken a hit.

"It's none of my business. Forget I said anything." Shane sensed that if he pursued the issue he would only end up annoying her and that was not how he wanted the evening to go.

"Why don't you pour the wine while I get food on the plates." From her tone, she was obviously content to drop the topic.

Ten minutes later they sat down to the meal May had prepared. Shane kept the conversation fixed on the progress she was making at her teen camp. It was a subject near and dear to her heart, and helping her with the project was sure to endear him to her. Was it manipulative? Sure. But he wanted to buy her property. That's why he'd accepted the bet and moved in.

Shane ignored a tug at his conscience and reminded himself that Brandee was working just as hard as he was to make him fall for her. He grinned. She just didn't realize that she'd lost before she even started.

"This weekend I'm hosting a teen experience with some of the high school kids," Brandee said. "Megan Maguire from Royal Safe Haven is bringing several of her rescue dogs to the ranch for the teens to work with. Chelsea is coming to help out. I could use a couple more adult volunteers." She regarded him pointedly.

The last thing he wanted to do was spend a day chaperoning a bunch of hormonally charged kids, but he had a wager to win and since he'd dropped the ball for Valentine's Day, he could probably pick up some bonus points by helping her out with this.

"Sure, why not." It wasn't the most enthusiastic response, but he hoped she'd be pleased he'd agreed so readily.

"And maybe you could see if Gabe is interested, as well?"

If it made Brandee go all lovey-dovey for him, Shane would do as much arm-twisting as it took to get his best friend on board. "I'll check with him. I'm sure it won't be a problem."

After putting away the leftovers and settling the dirty dishes in the dishwasher, Brandee suggested they move out to the patio to enjoy an after-dinner scotch. This time, instead of taking the sofa opposite him, she settled onto the cushion right beside him and tucked her feet beneath her.

While the fire crackled and flickered, Shane sipped his drink and, warmed by alcohol, flame and desire, listened while Brandee told him about the struggling calf they'd saved and reunited with her mother today. He told himself that when Brandee leaned into him as she shared her tale she was only acting. Still, it was all Shane could do to keep from pulling her onto his lap and stealing a kiss or two.

"You know, it is Valentine's Day," she murmured, tilting her head to an adorable angle and regarding him from beneath her long lashes.

With her gaze fixed on his lips, Shane quelled the impulses turning his insides into raw need. She was playing him. He knew it and she knew he knew it. For the moment he was willing to concede she had the upper hand. What man presented with an enticing package of sweet and spicy femininity would be capable of resisting?

"Yes, it is," he replied, not daring to sip from the tumbler of scotch lest she see the slight tremble in his hand.

"A day devoted to lovers."

Shane decided to follow her lead and see where it took him. "And romance."

"I think both of us know what's inevitable."

"That you and I get together?" To his credit he didn't sound as hopeful as he felt.

"Exactly." She leaned forward to kiss him. Her lips, whether by design or intent, grazed his cheek instead. Her breath smelled of chocolate and scotch, sending blood scorching through his veins. "I've been thinking about you a lot."

Her husky murmur made his nerve endings shiver. He gripped the glass tumbler hard enough to shatter it. "Me, too. I lay in bed at night and imagine you're with me. Your long hair splayed on my pillow." Thighs parted in welcome. Skin flushed with desire. "You're smiling up at me. Excited by all the incredible things I'm doing to you."

From deep in her throat came a sexy hum. "Funny." Her fingertips traced circles on the back of his neck before soothing their way into his hair. "I always picture myself on top. Your hands on my breasts as I ride you."

Shane winced as his erection suddenly pressed hard against his zipper. "You drive me crazy," he murmured. "You know that, right?"

He set down his drink with a deliberate movement before cupping her head. She didn't resist as he pulled her close enough to kiss. Her lashes fluttered downward, lips arching into a dreamy smile.

Their breath mingled. Shane drew out the moment. Her soft breasts settled against his chest and he half closed his eyes to better savor the sensation. This wouldn't be their first kiss, but that didn't make it any less momentous. Tonight they weren't in the middle of a pasture surrounded by cows. This time, the only thing standing in the way of seeing this kiss through to the end was if she actually felt something for him.

Was that what made him hesitate? Worry over her emotional state? Or was he more concerned about his own?

"Let's go inside," she suggested, shifting her legs off the couch and taking his hand. Her expression was unreadable as she got to her feet and tugged at him. "I have a wonderful idea about how we can spend the rest of the evening."

The instant they stepped away from the raging fire, Brandee shivered as the cool February air struck her bare skin. She'd dressed to show off a ridiculous amount of flesh in an effort to throw Shane off his game. Naturally her ploy had worked, but as they crossed the brick patio, she wished she hadn't left the throw behind. Despite how readily Shane had taken her up on her offer, she was feeling incredibly uncertain and exposed.

In slow stages during their romantic dinner, her plan to methodically seduce him had gone awry. She blamed it on the man's irresistible charm and the way he'd listened to her talk about the calf and her camp. He hadn't waited in polite silence for her to conclude her explanation about the program she and Megan Maguire had devised to teach the teenagers about patience and responsibility. No, he'd asked great questions and seemed genuinely impressed by the scope of her project.

But the pivotal moment had come when she saw a flash of sympathy in his eyes. She'd been talking about one particular boy whose dad had bullied him into joining the football team when all the kid wanted to do was play guitar and write music. Something about the story had struck home with Shane and for several seconds he'd withdrawn like a hermit crab confronted by something unpleasant. She realized they were alike in so many ways, each burying past hurts beneath a veneer of confidence, keeping the world at bay to keep their sadness hidden.

As they neared the house, a brief skirmish ensued. Shane seemed to expect that Brandee would want their first encounter to be in her bedroom. That was not going to happen. She'd invited him into the space once and it had been a huge mistake. Her bedroom was her sanctuary, the place she could be herself and drop her guard. She didn't want to be vulnerable in front of Shane. Seeing her true self would give him an edge that she couldn't afford.

"Let's try out the shower in your suite," she suggested, taking his hand in both of hers and drawing him toward the sliding glass door that led to his bedroom. "I had such fun designing the space and haven't ever tried it out."

"The rain shower system is pretty fantastic."

The four recessed showerheads in the ceiling and integrated chromotherapy with mood-enhancing colored lighting sequences were ridiculous indulgences, but Brandee had thought her grandmother would get a kick out of it and had been right.

Shane guided her through the bedroom. His hand on the

small of her back was hot through the semisheer material of her blouse and Brandee burned. How was it possible that the man who stood poised to take everything from her could be the one who whipped her passions into such a frenzy? They hadn't even kissed and her loins ached for his possession. She shuddered at the image of what was to come, a little frightened by how badly she wanted it.

While Shane used the keypad to start the shower, Brandee gulped in a huge breath and fought panic. How was she supposed to pretend like this was just a simple sexual encounter when each heartbeat made her chest hurt? Every inch of her body hummed with longing. She was so wound up that she was ready to go off the instant he put his hands on her.

Shane picked that second to turn around. Whatever he saw in her expression caused his nostrils to flare and his eyes to narrow. Her nerve collapsed. Brandee backed up a step, moving fully clothed into the shower spray. She blinked in surprise as the warm water raced down her face. Shane didn't hesitate before joining her.

As he circled her waist, drawing her against his hard planes, Brandee slammed the door on her emotions and surrendered to the pleasure of Shane's touch. She quested her fingers beneath his sweater, stripping the sodden cotton over his head. The skin she revealed stretched over taut muscle and sculpted bone, making her groan in appreciation.

Almost tentatively she reached out to run her palm across one broad shoulder. His biceps flexed as he slid his hands over her rib cage, thumbs whisking along the outer curves of her breasts. She shuddered at the glancing contact and trembled as he licked water from her throat. Hunger built inside her while her breath came in ragged pants.

The water rendered her clothes nearly transparent, but

Shane's gaze remained locked on her face. He appeared more interested in discovering her by touch. His fingertips skimmed her arms, shoulders and back with tantalizing curiosity. If she could catch her breath, she might have protested that she needed his hands on her bare skin. An insistent pressure bloomed between her thighs. She felt Shane's own arousal pressing hard against her belly. Why was he making her wait?

In the end she took matters into her own hands and stripped off her blouse. It clung to her skin, resisting all effort to bare herself to his touch. Above the sound of the rain shower, she heard a seam give, but she didn't care. She flung the garment aside. It landed in the corner with a plop. At last she stood before him, clad only in her white lace shorts and bra. And waited.

Shane's breath was as unsteady as hers as he slipped his fingers beneath her narrow bra straps and eased them off her shoulders. Holding her gaze with his, he trailed the tips of his fingers along the lace edge where it met her skin. Brandee's trembling grew worse. She reached behind her and unfastened the hooks. The bra slid to the floor and she seized Shane's hands, moving his palms over her breasts.

Together they shifted until Brandee felt smooth tile against her back. Trapped between the wall and Shane's strong body, hunger exploded in her loins. She wrapped one leg around Shane's hip and draped her arms over his shoulders. At long last he took the kiss she so desperately wanted to give and his tongue plunged into her mouth in feverish demand.

Brandee thrilled to his passion and gave back in equal measures. The kiss seemed to go on forever while water poured over his shoulders and ran between their bodies. Shane's hands were everywhere, cupping her breasts, roaming over her butt, slipping over her abdomen to the waistband of her shorts.

Unlike his jeans with their button and zipper, her lacy cotton shorts were held in place by a satin ribbon. He had the bow loosened and the material riding down her legs in seconds. A murmur of pleasure slipped from his lips when he discovered her satin thong, but it was soon following her shorts to the shower floor.

Naked before him, Brandee quaked. In the early years of her fashion line, she'd modeled all the clothes up for sale at her online store, even the lingerie. She'd lost all modesty about her body. Or so she'd thought.

Shane stepped back and took his time staring at her. She pressed her palms against the tile wall to keep from covering herself, but it wasn't her lack of clothing that left her feeling exposed. Rather, it was the need for him to find her desirable.

"You are so damned beautiful," he said, sweeping water from his face and hair. His lips moved into a predatory smile. "And all mine."

She hadn't expected such a provocative claim and hid her delight behind flirtation. Setting her hands on her hips, she shot him a saucy grin. "Why don't you slip out of those wet jeans and come get me?"

Without releasing her from the grip of his intense gaze, he popped the button on his jeans and unzipped the zipper. He peeled off black denim and underwear. Brandee's breath lodged in her throat at what was revealed.

The man was more gorgeous than she'd imagined. Broad shoulders tapered into washboard abs. His thighs were corded with muscle. The jut of his erection made her glad she still had the wall at her back because her muscles weakened at the sight of so much raw masculinity.

"Come here." She had no idea how her voice could

sound so sexy and calm when her entire being was crazy out of control.

He returned to her without hesitation and captured both her hands, pinning them against the wall on either side of her head. His erection pressing against her belly, he lowered his head and kissed her, deep and demanding. Brandee yielded her mouth and surrendered all control.

This was what she needed. A chance to let go and trust. He was in charge, and in this moment, she was okay with that.

When he freed her hands, she put her arms around his neck, needing the support as he stepped between her feet, widening her stance. His teeth grazed her throat while his hand slid between their bodies and found her more than ready for his possession.

She moaned feverishly as he slid a finger inside her, the heel of his palm grazing the over-stimulated knot of nerves. Gasping, she writhed against his hand while hunger built. She needed him inside her, pumping hard, driving her relentlessly into a massive orgasm.

It was hard to concentrate as he masterfully drove her forward into her climax, but Brandee retained enough of her faculties to offer him a small taste of the torment he was inflicting upon her. She cupped her palm over the head of his erection and felt him shudder.

“Jeez” was all he could manage between clenched teeth.

“We need a condom.” She rode his length up and down with her hand, learning the texture and shape of him. “Now.”

“Yes.”

“Where?”

“Jeans.”

“You’re prepared.” A bubble of amusement gave her enough breathing room to stave off the encroaching orgasm.

"Since I arrived."

She bit her lip as his hand fell away from her body, but kept the dissatisfied groan from escaping while he took a few seconds to reach into his jeans pocket and pull out a foil-wrapped pack.

"Let me." She plucked it from his fingers and deftly ripped it open.

He winced as she rolled the condom down his length. Another time, she might have made more of a production of it to torment him, but her body needed to join with his, so she skipped the foreplay.

Almost as soon as she was done, he was lifting her off the floor and settling her back against the wall once more. Brandee stared out the shower door at the mirror that hung over the double vanity. She could just make out the back of Shane's head and her fingers laced in his hair. Every muscle in her body was tensed. Waiting.

"Look at me."

She resisted his demand. She needed him inside her, but she couldn't let him see what it would do to her. This wasn't just sex. Something was happening to her. In the same way she'd liked having him in her bedroom and found comfort riding beside him out in the pasture, she craved intimacy that went beyond the merely physical.

"Look at me." His rough voice shredded her willpower. "You're going to watch what you do to me."

That did it. She could no longer resist him. Her eyes locked with his. A second later he began to slide inside her, and Brandee began to shatter.

Eight

Shane wasn't sure what he'd said to make Brandee meet his gaze, but from the way her big blue-gray eyes locked on him, he was certain he'd regret it later. The ache she'd aroused needed release, but he took his time sliding into Brandee this first time. He wanted to remember every second, memorize every ragged inhalation of her breath and quiver of her body.

The first flutters of her internal muscles began before he'd settled his hips fully against hers. Her eyes widened to a nearly impossible size and she clutched his shoulders, her fingernails biting into him. As the first shudder wracked her, it was all he could do to keep from driving into her hard and fast and taking his own pleasure. Instead, he withdrew smoothly and pressed forward again. He watched in utter fascination as a massive orgasm swept over her, nearly taking him with it.

"Damn, woman." He thought he'd known lust and desire before, but something about what had just happened with Brandee told him he was diving straight off a cliff with nothing at the bottom to keep him from crashing and burning. "That was fast."

She gave him a dreamy smile as her head dropped back against the wall. Her lashes appeared too heavy to lift. "It's been a while," she said weakly. At long last her gaze found his and a mischievous glint lurked in the depths of her eyes. "And you're pretty good at this."

"You haven't seen anything."

She slid her fingers up his shoulders and into his hair, pressing the back of his head to urge his mouth toward hers. "Then let's get this party started."

"I thought we already had."

Before she could come up with another sassy retort, he claimed her mouth. Apparently the orgasm hadn't dampened her fire because Brandee kissed him back with ardent intensity.

Shane began to move inside her once more, determined to take his time and make her climax again. Had he ever been with a woman as wildly sensitive and willing to give herself wholeheartedly to pleasure as Brandee? Her whispered words of encouragement accompanied his every thrust and drove his willpower beyond its limits. But he held on until he felt the tension build in her body again. At last he let himself go in a rush of pleasure as her body bucked and she began to climax again. Sparks exploded behind Shane's eyes as they went over together.

In the aftermath, there was only the hiss of water pouring from the showerheads and ragged gasps as they strained to recover. But these were distant noises, barely discernible over the stunned, jubilant voice in Shane's head. He'd known making love to Brandee would be a singularly amazing experience, but he'd underestimated the power claiming her would have on his psyche.

"You should put me down," she said, her low, neutral tone giving nothing away. "Before something happens."

Something had already happened. Something immense and unforgettable. Powerful and scary. He was both eager and terrified to repeat the experience. But not yet. First he needed a few seconds to recover. And not just physically.

As soon as she was standing on her own, he reached to turn off the water, and the instant he took his eyes off her, she scooted out of the shower. He started to follow, but was slowed when a towel shot toward his face. The emotions that had been gathering in him, unsettling yet undeniable, retreated as he snatched the thick terry from the air.

Brandee had used his momentary distraction to slip a robe off the back of the door and wrap it around herself. Water dripped from the ends of her blond hair as she whirled to confront him, chuckling as she caught up another towel and knotted it around her head. Cocooned in plush white cotton, she watched him wrap the towel around his waist.

"Wow," she said with a bright laugh. "I knew that was going to be fantastic, but you exceeded my expectations."

Her delight found no matching gladness inside him. From her nonchalant cheerfulness, the experience hadn't been as transformative for her as it had been for him.

"That's me," he said, straining for a light tone. "Satisfaction guaranteed."

"I'll make sure I rate you five stars online." She yawned. "Well, it's been quite a day. And I still need to get a little work done. See you tomorrow, Delgado."

Shane had assumed there'd be a round two and now watched in stunned silence as Brandee blew him a kiss and disappeared out the bathroom door. Shane retreated to his room, shadowed by an uneasiness he couldn't shake. Chasing after her would only give her the upper hand in this wager.

Few knew his inner landscape didn't match the witty, life-of-the-party exterior people gravitated to. If he went after Brandee right now, he honestly didn't think he could pull off the cocky, charming version of himself that was his trademark.

She'd blown his mind and then walked away, leaving him hungry for more. But it wasn't so much his body that was in turmoil, but his emotions. And not because he was worried she might not be as into him as he'd thought.

He'd intended to make love to her again and then spend the night snuggling with her.

Snuggling.

With a groan, Shane flipped open his laptop and stared at the screen, unable to comprehend anything on it. Brandee had definitely won this round. Now it was up to him to make sure that didn't happen again.

The following day, Shane agreed to meet Gabe for a drink at the TCC clubhouse bar before dinner. While he waited on his friend, he followed up on a text he'd received a few minutes earlier. The call wasn't going well.

"I thought I told you last week that I needed that changed," Shane snarled into his cell phone. "Get it done."

"Sheesh," Gabe commented as he slid into the empty seat beside Shane. "Did you wake up on the wrong side of the bed, or what?"

The question hit a little too close to home. In fact, he hadn't woken up at all. He'd never fallen asleep. After Brandee's abrupt departure the night before, he'd busied himself until two o'clock and then laid awake thinking about her and replaying what had happened between them in the shower. And afterward.

Never before had a woman bolted so soon after making love. If anyone put on their clothes and got out, it was him.

"Sorry," Shane muttered. "Things are way behind at The Bellamy and we're due to open in a couple months."

"Things are always running behind. You usually don't take it out on your contractors."

Shane wasn't about to get into why he was so cranky. Not even with his best friend. So he shrugged his shoulders, releasing a little of the tension, and sipped his scotch.

"I'm feeling stretched a bit thin at the moment," he said. "I told you that I'm helping Brandee with her ranch. It's made me lose sight of some of the details at The Bellamy and I'm annoyed at myself."

"Oh."

Just that. Nothing more.

"Oh, what?" Shane demanded, not sure he wanted to hear what his friend had to say.

"It's just this wager of yours…" Gabe looked deep into the tumbler before him as if he could find the answer to life's mysteries at the bottom.

"Yes?" Shane knew he should just let it drop, but whatever was or wasn't happening between him and Brandee was like an itch he couldn't quite reach. And if Gabe had some insight, Shane wanted to hear it.

"It's just that I know you, Shane. I've seen you around a lot of women. You like this one. I mean really like her."

His first impulse was to deny it, but instead, he said, "Your point?"

"Let's say you somehow win the bet and she falls madly in love with you. Then what?"

"I guess we keep dating."

"You guess?" Gabe shook his head. "Do you really think she's gonna want to have anything to do with the guy who made her fall in love with him so he could take away the ranch she loves?"

"I don't have to buy the ranch." In fact, after spending time on it, he didn't really want the ranch to become home to hundreds of luxury estates. "I could just tell her I changed my mind."

"Have you?"

"Maybe."

"Does anyone ever get a straight answer out of you?"

"It depends."

"And what happens if Brandee wins?"

"That's not going to happen. I might really like this woman, but that's as far as it goes. She and I are too much alike. Neither one of us is interested in a relationship. We talked about it and we agree. Sex is great. Romance is..."

He'd been about to say *tiresome*, but he had to admit that over the course of several dinners and long talks by the fireplace on the patio, he was enjoying himself a great deal.

"Romance is...?" Gabe prodded.

"Too complicated, and you know I like things casual and easy."

With a nod, Gabe finished the last of his drink. "As long as you realize what you're doing can have repercussions and you're okay with whatever happens, my job as your conscience is done."

"I absolve you of all responsibility for any missteps I make with Brandee."

Gabe didn't look relieved as he nodded.

"One last thing before we get off the topic of Brandee," Shane said, remembering his promise to her the night before. "She asked me if you'd be willing to help tomorrow with her teen group. Apparently Megan Maguire from Safe Haven is bringing by some of her rescue dogs for the kids to work with."

"Sure. Let me know what time I need to be there."

Brandee surveyed the camp meeting hall for any details left undone. It was nearly ten o'clock in the morning and she was expecting a busload of teenagers to arrive at any moment. Megan had brought fifteen dogs, one for each teenager. Currently the rescues were running around in the paddock, burning off energy.

"Thank you for helping me out today," Brandee said to Gabe.

"My pleasure."

He and Chelsea had moved tables and organized the kitchen, while Brandee had helped Megan with the dogs and set up the obstacle course they would use later in the afternoon.

The plan for the day was for Megan to talk about the benefits of dog training for both the owner and pet and demonstrate her preferred method of clicker training. Then they would turn the kids loose in the paddock with the dogs so everyone could get to know each other.

After lunch, the teenagers would be issued clickers and dog treats. Megan was in charge of pairing up child with dog. Some of the kids had been through this before, so they would be given less experienced dogs. And the dogs that were familiar with clicker training would be matched with newcomers.

"Have you heard from Shane?" Gabe asked. "I thought he was going to be here today."

"He promised he would be, but he had something to check on at his hotel project."

"Well, hopefully that won't take him all day."

Brandee heard something in Gabe's tone, but before she could ask him about it, the camp bus appeared around a curve in the driveway. She pushed all thought of Shane's absence to the back of her mind. They'd completed the preliminary work without him, and there wouldn't be much to do while Megan spoke. Hopefully, Shane would arrive in time to help with lunch.

"Here we go." Megan Maguire came to stand beside Brandee. The redhead's green eyes reflected optimism. With her kind heart and patient manner, Megan was one of the most likable people Brandee had ever met. "I hope this group is as good as the last one."

"Me, too. We had such a great time."

"Of the ten dogs I brought that day, three of them were adopted almost immediately. The little bit of training they get here really helps."

"I know most of the kids enjoy it. Some act as if they are just too good for this. But it's funny, a couple of those girls that gave us such a hard time last month are back to do it again."

Brandee wasn't sure if it was because their parents were forcing them or if deep down inside they'd actually had fun. And what wasn't fun about hanging out with dogs all day?

The bus came to a halt and the door opened. The first teenager who emerged was Nikki Strait. She was one of the girls who'd been so bored and put out the prior month. She looked no better today. Neither did her best friend, Samantha, who followed her down the bus steps. Brandee sighed. Perhaps she'd been a little too optimistic about those two.

"Welcome to Hope Springs Camp," she said as soon as all the teenagers were off the bus and gathered in an ungainly clump. "On behalf of Megan Maguire of Royal Safe Haven and myself, we appreciate you giving up your Saturday to help with the dogs."

There were a couple smiles. A lot of looking around. Some jostling between the boys. All normal teenage behavior.

"We'll start our day in the camp meeting hall, where Megan will demonstrate what you'll be doing today. If you'll follow me, we can get started."

The teenagers settled into the folding chairs Chelsea had set up and more or less gave Megan their attention as she began speaking about Royal Safe Haven and the number of dogs that people abandoned each year in Royal.

"Dogs are pack animals," Megan explained. "They need a pack leader. Today it will be your job to assert yourself and take on that role. This doesn't mean you will mistreat the dogs or get angry with them. Most dogs perform better with positive reinforcement. That's why we use this clicker and these treats to get them to perform basic tasks such as recognizing their name, and commands such as *sit* and *down*. We'll also work with them on recalls and a simple but potentially life-saving maneuver I like to call 'what's this.'"

Megan set about demonstrating with her dog how effective the method was. She then switched to a nine-month-old Lab mix that had come to the shelter only the day before and was full-on crazy rambunctious.

Brandee surveyed the teens, noting which ones seemed engaged in the process and which couldn't be bothered. To her surprise Nikki was one of the former. The same could be said for Samantha.

Next, Megan brought the kids to the paddock so they could meet the dogs. Brandee turned her attention to lunch preparations. May had helped with the food. She'd fixed her famous lasagna and they would be serving it with salad, warm garlic bread and brownies for dessert. Last month they'd done chili and corn bread. As for next month…who knew if she'd even be around. With Maverick causing trouble, and Shane acting distant one minute and amorous the next, there were too many variables to predict.

A much more animated group of teenagers returned to the meeting hall. Playing with a group of dogs would do that.

Shane still hadn't arrived by the time the tables were cleared and the teenagers got down to the serious business of clicker training. Brandee shooed Gabe and Chelsea out of the kitchen with plates filled with lasagna and began the tedious job of cleaning up. She wrapped up what was left of the main meal and put the pans into the sink to soak while she nibbled at some leftover salad and scarfed down two pieces of May's delicious garlic bread.

It was almost one o'clock when Shane strolled into the meeting hall. Brandee had finished washing the plates and the silverware. All that was left was to scrub the pans.

"How's it going?" he asked, snagging a brownie. Leaning his hip against the counter, he peered at her over the dessert before taking a bite. "This is delicious."

"It's going fine," Brandee said, more than a little perturbed that after promising to help, he hadn't. "I didn't realize your business was going to take you all morning. You missed lunch."

"That's okay, I grabbed something in town."

"I thought you had a meeting at The Bellamy."

"I did, then David and I needed to chat, so we headed over to Royal Diner." He was gazing out the pass-through toward the gathered teenagers. "I'm here now. What can I do?"

She was tempted to tell him everything was done, but then she remembered the lasagna pans and grinned. "You can finish the dishes." She flung a drying towel over his shoulder and pointed at the sink. "I always leave the worst for last and now they're all yours."

As she went to join the others, her last glimpse of Shane was of him rolling up his sleeves and approaching the sink as if it contained a live cobra. She doubted the man had ever done a dish in his life and reminded herself to double-check the pans later to make sure they were clean to her standards.

Banishing Shane from her thoughts, Brandee circled the room to check on everyone's progress. To her surprise, Megan had paired Nikki with the hyper Lab mix. Nikki had seemed so disinterested the previous month, but with the puppy, she was completely focused and engaged. Already the teenager had the puppy sitting and lying down on command.

Brandee sidled up to Megan. "After how she was last month, what made you think to put Nikki and the Lab mix together?"

Megan grinned. "She and her mom have come by the shelter a couple times to help with the dogs and she has a real knack with them. I think last month she was bored with Mellie. This puppy is smart, but challenging. You can see how well it's going."

Next, Brandee turned her attention toward Justin Barnes. He'd isolated himself in a corner and was spending more time petting the dog than training her. It had been like this last month, too. The high school sophomore was disengaged from what was going on around him. She glanced in Gabe's direction, thinking he might be able to engage Justin, but Gabe was helping Jenny Prichard work with an adorable but very confused shih tzu/poodle mix.

Shane's voice came from right behind her. "Who's the kid over there?"

"Justin. He's the one I told you about whose dad wants him to play football rather than the guitar."

"Sounds like he and I might have a few things in common."

Brandee wasn't sure what Shane could say that might help Justin, but she'd asked for Shane to come today. It seemed wrong not to give him a chance to pitch in. "Maybe you could talk to him about it?"

"It's been a long time since I was a teenager, but I can give it a try."

"Thanks." Any animosity Brandee might have felt for his tardiness vanished. "I'll finish up the pans."

"No need. They're done."

"Already?"

"Just needed a little elbow grease." He arched an eyebrow at her. "It's not good for my ego that you look so surprised."

"I'm sure your ego is just fine." It was familiar banter between them, yet for one disconcerting moment, Brandee craved a more substantive connection. She dismissed the feeling immediately. What was she thinking? That she was interested in a *relationship* with Shane Delgado? Her stomach twisted at the thought, but the sensation wasn't unpleasant. Just troubling.

"You're right." He smirked at her. "It's great being me."

She watched him walk away and laughed at her foolishness. Even if she'd never made the bet with Shane, falling in love with him would be a disaster. They were too much alike in all the bad ways and complete opposites in the good ones. Nope, better to just keep things casual and breezy between them. Fabulous, flirty, sexy fun. That was all either of them wanted and all she could handle.

As he ambled toward Justin, Shane passed Gabe and raised his hand in greeting. Gabe acknowledged him with a broad grin and Shane wondered if he saw a touch of relief in his friend's eyes. No doubt Gabe appreciated that he was no longer the only guy.

Snagging a spare chair, Shane carried it to Justin's corner and set it down beside the kid, facing the dog.

"Hey," he said as he dropped a hand on the dog's caramel-colored head. "How's it going?"

"Fine." Justin mumbled the word and punched down on the clicker. The dog's ears lifted and he focused his full attention on the treat in Justin's hand.

"What's his name?" Shane indicated the dog.

"*Her* name is Ruby."

"Hey, Ruby." He fussed over the dog for a bit and then slouched back in his chair. "I'm Shane."

"Justin."

With niceties exchanged, the two guys settled down to stare at the dog, who looked from one to the other as if wondering where her next treat was coming from.

After a bit, Shane ventured into the silence. "What are you supposed to be doing?"

"Clicker training."

"How does that work?"

"Ruby."

The dog met Justin's glance. He clicked and gave her a treat.

"That's great."

Justin nodded.

So, obviously this whole connecting-with-kids thing wasn't easy. Shane's respect for Brandee's dedication grew. He shifted forward in the chair, propped his forearms on his thighs and mashed his palms together.

"She made me do dishes," he murmured. "Can you believe that?"

"Who did?"

"Brandee. She's always making me do stuff I don't want to."

"That sucks." Justin cast a sidelong glance his way. "Why do you do it?"

"Because she's pretty and I really like her. I'm not sure

she likes me, though. Sometimes I feel like no matter what I do, it's not good enough, ya know?"

"Yeah." More silence, and then, "It's like that with my dad. He makes me play football, but I hate it."

"My dad was the same way." After all these years, Shane couldn't believe he still resented his father, but the emotion churned in him. And really, it was all about not being good enough in Landon Delgado's eyes. "He expected me to follow in his footsteps and take over the family ranch, but I hated it." And in a community dominated by ranching, it felt like treason to criticize your bread and butter.

"What did you want to do instead?" Justin was showing more interest than he had a few seconds ago.

"I dunno. Anything but ranching." Shane thought back to when he'd been Justin's age. There wasn't much he'd been interested in besides hooking up with the prettiest girls in school and hanging out with his friends. He could see where his dad might've found that frustrating.

"So what do you do now?"

"Still have the ranch. And I develop properties. Heritage Estates is mine. And right now I'm working on a luxury hotel outside town called The Bellamy."

Justin's eyes had dimmed when Shane admitted he still had the ranch. "So you did what your father wanted you to do after all."

"The ranch has been in my family for almost a hundred years," Shane explained, deciding he better make his point awfully fast or he'd lose Justin altogether. "It wasn't as if I could walk away or sell it after my dad died. But I found a way to make it work so that I can do what I want and also respect my father's wishes."

"It isn't that easy for me."

"What do you want to do instead of playing football?" Shane asked, even though he already knew the answer."

"Play guitar and write music."

"Sounds pretty cool. How long have you been into that?"

"My dad gave me the guitar for my birthday a couple years ago."

"If your dad didn't want you to play the guitar, why did he buy you one?"

"He'd rather I play football," Justin said, his tone defensive and stubborn.

"Do you know why?"

"Because he did in high school and he got a scholarship to go to college." Justin gave a big sigh. "But I'm not that good. No college is going to want to put me on their team."

"Maybe your dad is worried about paying for your college?"

"I guess." Justin shrugged. "But I'm not really sure I want to go to college. I want to write songs and have a music career."

"You're way ahead of where I was at your age in terms of knowing what you want. That's pretty great." Shane had used money he'd inherited from his grandmother to start his real-estate development company shortly after graduating from college. When his dad found out what he'd done, he hadn't talked to him for a month. "I didn't know what I was going to do when I graduated high school, so I got a degree in business."

"College is expensive and I don't know if it would help me get what I want."

Shane wanted to argue that Justin would have something to fall back on if the music didn't work out, but he could see from the determined set of the boy's features that he would have a career in music or nothing else. Shane hoped the kid had some talent to back up his ambition.

"I'm sure this thing with your dad and football is because he's worried about your future. Maybe you could agree to try football in exchange for him agreeing to helping you with your music."

"Is that what you did with your dad?"

Not even close. "Absolutely. We came to an understanding and I figured out a way to keep ranching and at the same time pursue my interest in real estate."

"Was he proud of you?"

The question tore into Shane's gut like a chain saw. "My dad died before my business really got going, but I think he saw the potential in what I was doing and was impressed."

Shane didn't feel one bit bad about lying to the boy. Just because Shane hadn't been able to communicate with his father didn't mean Justin would have the same problem. And maybe if someone had offered him the advice he'd just given to the teenager, things with his dad might've gone better.

"I'll give it a try," Justin said.

"And if you want to talk or if you want me to have a heart-to-heart with your dad, here's my card. Call me anytime."

"Thanks." Justin slid the business card into his back pocket and seemed a little less glum. Or at least he showed more interest in the dog training.

Shane stuck around to watch him for a little while longer and then excused himself to go help a girl who seemed to be struggling with a brown-and-white mop of a dog.

Over the next thirty minutes, he worked his way around the room chatting with each kid in turn. By the time Megan called for everyone to take the dogs outside to the obstacle course, Shane had gotten everyone's story.

"How do you do that?" Brandee joined him near the back of the crowd. "Everyone you talk to was smiling by the time you walked away. Even Justin."

"How do you not realize what a great guy I am?" He grinned broadly and bumped his shoulder into hers. "I would think after living with me this past week you'd have caught the fever."

"The fever?" she repeated in a dubious tone.

"The Shane fever." He snared her gaze and gave her his best smoldering look. "Guaranteed to make your heart race, give you sweaty palms and a craving for hot, passionate kisses."

Her lips twitched. "I'm pretty sure I'm immune." But she didn't sound as confident as she once had.

"That sounds like a challenge."

"It's a statement of fact."

"It's your opinion. And if I'm good at anything, I'm good at getting people to see my point of view. And from my point of view, you're already symptomatic."

"How do you figure?"

With everyone's attention fixed on Megan, Shane was able to lean down and graze his lips across Brandee's ear. He'd noticed she was particularly sensitive there. At the same time, he'd cupped his hand over her hip and pulled her up against his side. The two-pronged attack wrenched a soft exclamation from her lips.

A second later he let her go and greeted her glare with a smirk. "Tell me your heart isn't racing."

"You aren't as charming as you think you are," she said, turning her attention to what was going on among the poles, small jumps and traffic cones set up near the meeting hall.

He let her get the last word in because he'd already annoyed her once that day and that wasn't the way to this woman's heart.

"Do you think there's something going on between Gabe and Chelsea?" Brandee asked after a couple more kids had taken their dogs through the obstacle course.

Shane followed the direction of her gaze and noticed the couple standing together on the outskirts of the crowd. "Going on how?"

"Like maybe they could be interested in each other?"

"Maybe." Shane paid better attention to the body language between the two and decided there might be an attraction, but he was pretty sure neither one had noticed it yet.

For a second Shane envied the easy camaraderie between Gabe and Chelsea. With the bet hanging over their heads, he and Brandee couldn't afford to let down their guards. And maybe that was okay. Sparring with Brandee was exciting. So was making love to her. He liked the way she challenged him, and figuring out how to best her kept him on his toes.

Besides, he wasn't in this for the long haul. This was his chance to have some fun and try to win a bet. Eventually he would move out of Brandee's house and life would return to normal. But what if it didn't? What if he wanted to keep seeing Brandee? He snuck a peek at her profile. Would she be open to continuing to see where things went? Or was this just about the wager for her?

Shane didn't like where his thoughts had taken him. He liked even less the ache in his chest. Gabe's words from several days earlier came back to haunt him.

As long as you realize what you're doing can have repercussions and you're okay with whatever happens...

It was looking more and more like he had no idea what he was doing and the repercussions were going to be a lot more complicated than he'd counted on.

Nine

To thank Chelsea, Gabe and Shane for their help at Hope Springs Camp's mini-event, Brandee treated them to dinner at the Texas Cattleman's Club. Their efforts were the reason the day had gone so smoothly and Brandee was able to relax at the end of the successful event.

As soon as they finished dinner and returned to the ranch house, she and Shane headed out to the patio to sit by the fire.

Brandee tucked her bare feet beneath her and sipped at her mug of hot, honey-laced herbal tea. "Despite your very late start," she said to Shane, keeping her tone light, "you were a huge help today. I think it was good to have both you and Gabe there. Usually we have trouble keeping the boys on task."

"A couple of them were a little rowdy while they were waiting for their turn at the obstacle course, but once they got working with the dogs it was better."

"The clicker training keeps both handler and dog engaged. Megan was very satisfied how the day went."

"She said she might even get some adoptions out of it."

"I wish Seth Houser could be one of them. He's been working with Sunny for almost three months. And making great strides." The Wheaton terrier was a great dog, but way too hyper. He'd been adopted twice and returned both times. A talented escape artist with abandonment issues, he needed to go to someone as active as he was.

"I was really amazed by how well Seth handled him." Shane puffed out a laugh. "I think Tinkerbell and Jenny were my favorite pair."

The adorable shih tzu/poodle mix with the bad underbite had been recently turned in by a woman who had to go into a nursing home. Jenny was a goth girl of fifteen who'd shuffled through the day with stooped shoulders and downcast eyes. But she'd bonded with her short-legged black-and-white dog and together they'd won the obstacle course.

"Megan has a knack for matching the right dog to the perfect handler."

They lapsed into silence for a time while the fire popped and crackled. The longer they went without speaking, the more Brandee could feel the tension building between them. The last time they'd sat together out here, she'd ended up dragging Shane into the shower.

The day after, she'd been busy with her cattle herd and hadn't gotten home until late every night. Part of her wondered if she'd been avoiding Shane. The way she'd felt as he'd slid inside her for the first time had shocked her. She'd expected to enjoy making love with Shane, but couldn't have predicted to what extent. It was like all the best sex she'd ever had rolled into one perfect act of passion.

And ever since, all she wanted to do was climb into the

memory and relive it over and over. But not the aftermath when she'd bolted for the safety of her room before Shane could notice that her defenses were down. Standing naked in the bathroom, she'd been terrified that, with his appetite satisfied, he wouldn't want her to stick around. So, she'd fled.

Now, however, after a couple days to regain her confidence, she was ready to try again. Anticipation formed a ball of need below her belly button. The slow burn made her smile. She was opening her mouth to suggest they retire to his bedroom when he spoke.

"I see why you find it so rewarding."

Brandee sat in confused silence for several seconds. "What exactly?"

"Working with teenagers."

With a resigned sigh, Brandee turned down the volume on her libido. "I wish I could say it was all success and no failure, but these kids don't have nearly the sorts of issues of some I've worked with."

"You do a good job relating to them."

He hadn't done so bad himself. Watching him with Justin, Brandee had been impressed with the way he'd gotten the kid to stop looking so morose.

"I remember all too well what it was like to have troubles at home," she said.

"Your mom?" Shane asked gently.

For a second Brandee was tempted to give a short answer and turn the topic aside, but part of her wanted to share what her childhood had been like after losing her dad. "It wasn't easy living with someone who only wants you around so she can steal your money."

"I can't imagine." Shane shifted his upper body in her direction until his shoulder came into companionable contact with hers.

Brandee welcomed the connection that made her feel

both safe and supported. "It didn't make me the ideal daughter."

"You fought?"

"Not exactly." Brandee let her head fall back. Her eyes closed and images of the cramped, cluttered house filled her mind. A trace of anxiety welled as memories of those five suffocating years rushed at her. "She yelled at me, while I said nothing because I'd tried arguing with her and she'd just freak out. So I learned to keep quiet and let her have her say. And then I'd rebel."

"By doing what?"

"The usual. Partying with my friends. Drinking. Drugs. For a while my grades slipped, then I realized she didn't give a damn about any of it and I was only hurting myself."

"So, what happened?"

"I cleaned up my act. Not that she noticed anything going on with me." Or cared. "But I continued to avoid the house as much as possible."

"That sounds a lot like how I spent my teen years. I made sure I was gone as much as possible. That way I wasn't around when it came time to help out on the ranch. It drove my dad crazy." Shane fixed his gaze on the hypnotic dance of the flames, but didn't seem to be seeing the fire. "He was a firm believer in hard work, a lot like your dad. He was fond of telling me I wasn't going to make anything of myself if I wasn't willing to work for it. I didn't believe him. I was pretty happy with what I had going. I had a lot of friends and decent grades. I was having a good time. And all he cared about was that I wasn't in love with ranching like he was."

Brandee didn't know how to react to the bitter edge in Shane's voice. She loved her ranch and couldn't imagine giving it up. That ranching was something Shane only did out of obligation was a disconnect between them that reinforced why she shouldn't let herself get too emotionally attached.

"What was it about the ranching you didn't like?" she asked, shifting to face him and putting a little distance between them.

"I don't honestly know. One thing for sure, I didn't see the point in working as hard as my dad did when there were more efficient ways to do things. But he wouldn't listen to anything I had to say. He expected me to follow exactly in his footsteps. I wasn't going to do that."

"What did you want to do?"

"Justin asked me that today, too. I guess I just wanted to have fun." He grinned, but the smile lacked his typical cocky self-assurance. "Still do."

She let that go without comment even as she was mentally shaking her head at him. "So, how'd you get into real-estate developing?"

"A buddy of mine in college got me into flipping houses. I liked the challenge." Satisfaction reverberated in Shane's voice. He obviously took great pride in his past accomplishments. And present ones, too. From everything she'd heard, The Bellamy was going to be quite a resort.

"I got my first job when I turned sixteen," Brandee said. "Stocking shelves at a grocery store after school and on weekends. It gave me enough money to buy a used junker with no AC and busted shocks. I didn't care. It was freedom. I used to park it around the corner from the house because I didn't want my mom knowing about it."

"What would've happened if she'd known about it?"

"She would've given it to Turtlehead or Squash Brain." Those days were blurry in her memory. "Mom always had some loser boyfriend hanging around."

"She lived with them?"

Brandee heard the concern in his voice and appreciated

it more than she should. "They lived with her. She rented a crummy two-bedroom house right on the edge of a decent neighborhood because she thought it was great to be so close to people with money. I don't know what she was like when my dad met her, but by the time I went to live with her, she wasn't what anyone would call a class act."

"What did she do?"

"She actually had a halfway-decent job. She cut hair at one of those chain salons. I think if she had better taste in boyfriends she might have been more successful. But all she attracted were harmless jerks." She thought back to one in particular. "And then Nazi boy showed up."

"Nazi boy?"

"A skinhead with the Nazi tattoos on his arms and all over his chest. For a while I just hung in there figuring he'd soon be gone like all the rest."

"But he wasn't?"

"No. This one had money. Not because he worked. I think he and his white-supremacist buddies jacked cars or ran drugs or something. He always had money for blow and booze." She grimaced. "My mom took a bad path with that one."

"How old were you?"

"I'd just turned seventeen."

"Did he bother you?"

"Not at first. He was more into my mom than a dopey-looking kid with bad hair and ill-fitting clothes. But his friends were something else. I think initially they started to bug me out of sheer boredom. I was used to having my ass grabbed or being shoved around by some of the other guys my mom hooked up with. Nazi boy's friends were different, though."

As she described her encounters, Shane's muscles tensed. "Did they hurt you?"

She knew what he was asking. "If you're trying to be delicate and ask if I got raped, the answer is no."

Shane relaxed a little. "So what happened?"

"For a while it was okay. I was hiding behind bad hygiene and a dim-witted personality. Then one day I was taking a shower and thought I was alone in the house."

"You weren't?"

"Nazi boy had taken off with his buddies to go do something and I wasn't expecting them back. I never showered when he was home. Most days I either took clothes to school and cleaned up there or did the same thing at a friend's house."

"That's pretty extreme."

The unfinished mug of tea had gone cold in Brandee's hands, so she set it on the coffee table. "I'd seen how he could be around my mom and it made me feel way too vulnerable to be naked in the house."

"So he came home unexpectedly and caught you in the shower?"

Those days with her mom weren't something she liked talking about and part of her couldn't believe she was sharing this story with Shane. The only other person she'd told was Chelsea.

"I was coming out of the bathroom wearing nothing but a towel. The second I saw him, I jumped back into the bathroom and locked the door. He banged on the door, badgering me to open it for twenty minutes until my mom came home."

"Did you tell her what happened?"

"No. Why bother? She'd just accuse me of enticing him. Either she was scared of him or she liked the partying too much. This one wasn't going away anytime soon."

"Did he come after you again?"

"For a while I tried to stay away as much as possible,

but sometimes I had to go home. When I did, I was careful to do so when my mom was home. He left me alone while she was around."

"I don't suppose you had a teacher or adult that could help you out."

"That might have been smart. But I felt like all the adults I'd reached out to had failed me. Instead, I found the biggest, meanest football player in our school and made him the most devoted boyfriend ever." She batted her eyelashes and simpered. "Oh, Cal, you're just so big and strong." Her voice dripped with honey. "Do you think you could get that terrible man who lives with my mother to stop trying to put his hands all over me?"

"Did that work?"

"Like a charm. Nazi boy was all talk and glass jaw. He knew it and I knew it. At five-ten and 170, he might have scared me, but he was no match for a six-five, 280-pound linebacker."

Shane regarded her with admiration and respect. "So your linebacker kept you safe until you finished high school?"

Brandee shifted her gaze out toward the darkness beyond the patio and debated lying to him. "I didn't actually finish high school."

"How come?"

"Because two months before graduation my mom finally figured out that her boyfriend was coming on to me and rather than kicking him to the curb, she blamed me. That's when I ran away for good."

Shane's first instinct was to curse out her mother, but the way Brandee was braced for his reaction, he knew he had to take a gentler approach or risk her fleeing back behind her defenses.

"Wow, that sucks."

This part of her story was different than the last. As she'd spoken of her difficulties with Nazi boy, she'd sounded strong and resilient. Now, however, she was once again that abandoned child, learning that she was the biggest mistake her mother had ever made. Her loneliness was palpable and Shane simply couldn't stand to be physically separated from her. He reached for her hand and laced their fingers together, offering her this little comfort.

"What did you do?" he asked.

"I should've gone to live with my grandmother in Montana."

"Why didn't you?"

Her fingers flexed against his as she tightened her grip on him. A second later she relaxed. "Because I was angry with her for not taking me in after my dad died."

"So what did you do instead?"

"I stayed with my best friend for a couple days until I found a room and a waitressing job that paid better."

"When did you start your business?"

"I'd learned how to crochet and knit from one of my friends' moms and had been making headbands and adding lace embellishments to stuff I found at the thrift store. I bought a used sewing machine and started doing even more stuff. It was amazing how well things sold online. All I did was waitress, sew and market my stuff."

"The rest is history?"

"Not quite. Nazi boy and his friends tracked me down. Fortunately I wasn't home. But the homeowner was. They shoved her around and scared her pretty good. After that they went into my room and took everything, including the five hundred dollars I'd saved."

"What happened then?"

"The homeowner pressed charges and they all got

picked up by the cops. But she kicked me out. Once again I had nowhere to go and nothing to show for all my hard work."

"Did you stay in Houston?"

"Nope. I moved to Waco and lived out of my car for two weeks."

"At seventeen?"

"Haven't you figured out I'm tougher than I look?" She gave a rueful laugh. "And I'd turned eighteen by then. In fact, I'd been out celebrating my birthday with friends when Nazi boy robbed me."

"What happened after that?"

"That's when things get boring. I found another waitressing job and another place to live. Took a second job at a tailoring shop. The owner let me use the machines after hours so I could create my designs. In four months I was making enough by selling my clothes and accessories online to quit my waitressing job. In a year I moved into a studio apartment and was bringing in nearly ten thousand a month."

Shane had a hard time believing her numbers could be real. "That's a lot for a solo operation."

"I didn't sleep, was barely eating and the only time I left my apartment was to get supplies or ship product."

"How long before it got too big for you to handle?"

"By the time I turned twenty, I had four seamstresses working for me and I was in over my head. I was paying everyone in cash and eventually that was going to catch up to me. So I talked to a woman at the bank I really liked and Pamela hooked me up with a website designer, lawyer and an accountant. But between the designing and running things, there was still too much for me to do, so I hired Pamela to manage the business side. And then things really took off."

"And now here you are running a ranch." He smiled ruefully. "It's not an ordinary sort of career move."

"Probably not, but it's a lot better for me. While I loved designing and promoting my fashion lines, I'm not cut out to sit in an office all day looking at reports and handling the myriad of practical decisions a multimillion-dollar business requires."

"You'd rather ride around in a pasture all night, keeping an eye on your pregnant cows."

She nodded. "Exactly."

"So, you sold the business."

"A woman in California bought it and has plans to take it global." Brandee shook her head. "It's still a little surreal how much the company has grown from those first few crocheted headbands."

"I can't help but think it was a lot to give up."

"It wasn't my dream. Hope Springs Ranch is. And I still design a few pieces each year. So, I get to be creative. It's enough. And now I expect to be busier than ever with Hope Springs Camp starting to ramp up."

His gaze fastened on her softly parted lips and a moment later, he'd slid his hand beneath the weight of her long hair and pulled her toward him. After the first glancing slide of his mouth over hers, they came together in a hungry crush.

Tongues danced and breath mingled. Shane lifted her onto his lap, the better to feel her soft breasts press against him through her cotton shirt. With her fingers raking through his hair, Shane groaned her name against the silky skin of her long neck. Despite the longing clawing at him these past few days, he'd underestimated his need for her.

"I can't wait to be inside you again," he muttered, sliding his tongue into the hollow of her throat while his fingers worked her shirt buttons free. "You are like no woman I've known."

Brandee stripped off her shirt and cast it aside. "You're pretty awesome yourself, Delgado." Her fingers framed his face, holding him still while she captured his gaze. "You've made me feel things I've never known before."

Her mouth found his in a sweet, sexy kiss that stole his breath. He fanned his fingers over her back, reveling in her satiny warmth, the delicate bumps of her spine and the sexy dimples just above her perfect ass. This time around, Shane was determined to take his time learning everything about what turned her on.

He shifted so that her back was against his chest and his erection nestled between her firm butt cheeks. This gave him full access to her breasts, stomach and thighs, while she could rock her hips and drive him to new levels of arousal. As trade-offs went, it wasn't a bad one.

Shane unfastened her bra and set it aside. As the cool night air hit her nipples, they hardened. He teased his fingertips across their sensitive surface and Brandee jerked in reaction. Her head fell back against his shoulder as a soft *yes* hissed past her teeth.

"Do that again," she murmured, her eyelids half-lowered, a lazy smile on her lips. "I love the feel of your hands on me."

"My pleasure."

He cupped her breasts and kneaded gently, discovering exactly what she liked. Each breathy moan urged his passion higher. His fingers trembled as they trailed over her soft, fragrant skin. Her flat stomach bucked beneath his palm as he slipped his fingers beneath the waistband of her leggings and grazed the edge of her panties.

"Let's get these off." His voice was whisky-rough and unsteady.

"Sure."

She helped him shimmy the clingy black cotton material over her hips and down her legs. He enjoyed sliding his hands back up over her calves and knees, thumbs trailing along the sensitive inner thigh. Catching sight of her lacy white bikini panties, Shane forgot his early determination to make her wait.

He dipped his fingertips beneath the elastic and over her sex. She spread her legs wider. Her breath was coming in jagged gasps and her body was frozen with anticipation as he delved into her welcoming warmth.

They sighed together as he circled her clit twice before gliding lower. He found a rhythm she liked, taking his cues from the way her hips rocked and the trembling increased in her thighs. She gave herself over to him. She was half-naked on his lap, thighs splayed, her head resting on his shoulder, eyes half-closed. She sighed in approval as he slid first one, then two fingers inside her.

The tension in her muscles increased as he slowly thrust in and out of her. He noted how her eyebrows came together in increased concentration, saw the slow build of heat flush her skin until all too soon, her lips parted on a wordless cry. And then her back arched. She clamped her hand over his and aided his movements as her climax washed over her in a slow, unrelenting wave. He cupped her, keeping up a firm, steady pressure, and watched the last of her release die away.

"We need to take this indoors," he murmured against her cheek, shuddering as she shifted on his lap, increasing the pressure of her backside against his erection. The sensation made him groan.

"Give me a second," she replied. "I'm pretty sure I can't walk at the moment."

Wait? Like hell.

"Let me help you with that." He lifted her into his arms and stood.

"Your room," she exclaimed before he'd taken more than two steps. "Please. I've been imagining you all alone in that big bed and thinking about all the things I'd like to do to you in it."

He liked the way her mind worked. "I've been picturing you there, as well." He slipped through the French doors and approached his bed. "We'll take turns telling each other all about it and then acting every scenario out."

"Sounds like we're going to have a busy night."

"I'm counting on it."

Tonight, he'd make sure she didn't have the strength to leave until he was good and ready to let her go.

Ten

The Royal Diner was packed at nine o'clock on Sunday morning, but Brandee had gotten there at eight and grabbed a table up front. As Chelsea slid into the red vinyl booth across from her, Brandee set aside the newspaper she'd been reading.

"Thanks for meeting me," Brandee said. "I needed to get out of the house. This thing with Shane is not going as I'd hoped."

"I told you it was a bad idea."

Brandee winced. "Let's put it down to me being in a desperate situation and not thinking straight."

"So, have you finally given in to that wild animal magnetism of his?"

"I haven't *given in* to anything," Brandee retorted. "However, we have been having fun." A lot of fun.

"You are such a fake." Chelsea laughed. "You act all cool chick about him, but I watched you yesterday. When he was talking to the kids, you were all moony. You've got it bad."

Brandee wasn't ready to admit this in the relative safety of her mind much less out loud to her best friend in a public restaurant. "It's just sex. I've been out of circulation for a long time and he's very capable."

Chelsea shook her head in disgust and picked up her menu. "Is that why you look so tired out this morning?"

"No. I actually got a good night's sleep."

That was true. After they'd worn each other out, Brandee had fallen into the deepest slumber she'd had since Maverick had sent that vile demand. Snuggling in Shane's arms, his breath soft and warm against her brow as she'd drifted off, she'd gained a new perspective on the amount of time she spent alone. Where she'd thought she was being smart to direct her energy and focus toward the ranch, what she'd actually done was maintain a frantic pace in order to avoid acknowledging how lonely she was.

"Thanks again for your help yesterday," Brandee said once they'd put in their breakfast orders and the waitress had walked away. "I couldn't have managed without you and Gabe and, once he showed up, Shane. I hope this wasn't my last mini-event."

"Anything new from Maverick?"

"No, but my resignation from the TCC and the money are due in two days. And I don't know if Shane's going to sign away his claim to Hope Springs Ranch before the deadline."

"You don't think Shane is falling in love with you?"

Brandee's heart compressed almost painfully at Chelsea's question. "I don't know. Do you think he is? Even a little?" She sounded very insecure as she asked the question.

"It's hard to tell with Shane. He hides how he feels nearly as well as you do." Chelsea eyed her friend over the rim of her coffee cup. "But given the way he looked at you during dinner last night, I'd say that he's more than a little interested."

Brandee still felt an uncomfortable pang of uncertainty. "That's something, I guess."

"Which makes the whole wager thing a bummer because it's going to get in the way of you guys being real with each other."

Thinking over the prior evening's conversation and the lovemaking that followed, Brandee wasn't completely sure she agreed. She'd felt a connection with Shane unlike anything she'd ever known before. Maybe sharing their struggles with their parents had opened a gap in both their defenses.

"I'd like to call off my wager with Shane," Brandee admitted. "What started out as a good idea has gotten really complicated."

"So do it."

"How am I supposed to explain my change of heart to Shane?"

"You could tell him that you really like him and want to start with a clean slate."

Brandee threw up her hands, her entire body lighting up with alarm. "No. I can't do that. He'll think he's won and I'll have to sell him Hope Springs."

Besides, leaving herself open to be taken advantage of—or worse, rejected—went against all the instincts that had helped her to survive since she was twelve years old. She didn't want to be that girl anymore, but she was terrified to take a leap of faith.

Chelsea blew out her breath in frustration. "This is what I'm talking about. You have to stop working the angles and just trust that he feels the same way."

"But what if he doesn't?" Already Brandee had talked

herself out of canceling the wager. "What if it's just that he's done a better job of playing the game than me?"

"And what if he's really fallen for you and is afraid to show it because that means you'll win the wager? Shane loves a challenge. You two have squared off against each other almost from the day you met. Frankly, I'm a little glad this Maverick thing came along to bring you two together."

Chelsea's frustrated outburst left Brandee regarding her friend in stunned silence. She'd never considered that being blackmailed could have an upside. Yet she couldn't deny that her life was a little bit better for having gotten to spend time with Shane.

The sound of angry voices came from a table twenty feet away.

Chelsea, whose back was to the drama, leaned forward. "Who is it?"

"Looks like Adam Haskell and Dusty Walsh are at it again." The two men hated each other and tempers often raged when they occupied the same space. "I can't quite tell what it's about."

"You're nothing but an ignorant drunk." Walsh's raised voice had the effect of silencing all conversation around him. "You have no idea what you're talking about."

"Well, he's not wrong," Chelsea muttered, not bothering to glance over her shoulder.

Brandee's gaze flickered back to her best friend. "He needs to learn to mind his own damn business." She remembered how when she first bought Hope Springs Ranch, Adam had stopped by to inform her that ranching wasn't women's work.

"You're gonna get what's coming to you." Haskell's threat rang in the awkward silence that had fallen.

"You two take it outside." Amanda Battle stepped from

behind the counter and waded into the confrontation. "I'll not have either of you making a ruckus in my diner."

Most people probably wouldn't have tangled with either Haskell or Walsh on a normal day, much less when they were going at each other, but Amanda was married to Sheriff Nathan Battle and no one was crazy enough to mess with her.

"He started it," Walsh grumbled, sounding more like a petulant five-year-old than a man in his sixties. It was hard to believe that someone like Dusty could be related to Gabe. "And I'm not done with my breakfast."

"Looks like you're done, Adam." Amanda glanced pointedly at the check in his hand. "Why don't you head on over to the register and let Karen get your bill settled."

And just like that it was over. Brandee and Chelsea's waitress appeared with plates of eggs, biscuits and gravy, and a waffle for them to share. She returned a second later to top off their coffee and the two women dug in.

After a while Brandee returned to their earlier conversation. "I've been thinking more and more about what Maverick brought to light."

"That it's not really fair to keep Shane from knowing that his family is the rightful owners of the land Hope Springs sits on?"

"Yes. I can't exactly afford to walk away from ten million dollars, but I can make sure that after I'm gone the land will revert back to his family."

Chelsea was silent for a long time. "This really sucks."

"Yes, it does." Brandee was starting to think that no matter what she did, her time with Shane was drawing to a close. "Whoever Maverick is, the person has a twisted, cruel personality."

"Still think it's one or all of the terrible trio?"

"I can't imagine who else." Brandee hadn't given up on her suspicions about Cecelia, Simone and Naomi. "Although it seems a little extreme even for them."

"But you've really been a burr in their blankets and I could see them siding with Shane."

"And considering what Maverick wants..."

"Money?"

"Fifty grand isn't all that much. I think Maverick asked for money more to disguise the real purpose of the blackmail, which was getting me out of the Texas Cattleman's Club." Something she could see the terrible trio plotting to do. "Regardless of what I do or don't know, the fact is that I can't afford for Shane to find out the truth."

"But if you don't win the wager, what are you going to do?"

"As much as I hate the idea, I think I'm going to do as Maverick demands."

"So, what does that mean for you and Shane?"

"I think from the beginning we were both pretty sure this thing was going to end up in a stalemate."

"So neither of you is going to admit that you've fallen for the other."

"Nope."

"And yet I'm pretty sure you've fallen for him."

"I can't let myself go there, Chels." Brandee rubbed her burning eyes and let her pent-up breath go in a ragged exhale. "There's too much at stake."

"And if the fate of your ranch didn't hinge on you admitting that you had it bad for him?"

"The problem is that it does." As much as Brandee wished she was brave enough to risk her heart, she could point to too many times when trusting in things beyond her control hadn't worked in her favor. "So, I guess that's something we'll never know."

* * *

The rain began shortly after three o'clock that afternoon. Brandee fell asleep listening to it tap on the French doors in the guest suite, a rapid counterpoint to the steady beat of Shane's heart beneath her ear. It was still coming down when she woke several hours later.

They hadn't moved during their nap and his strong arms around her roused a contentment she couldn't ignore. For as long as she could remember, she'd bubbled with energy, always in motion, often doing several things at once and adding dozens of tasks to the bottom of her to-do list as she knocked off the ones at the top.

Around Shane she stepped back from the frenetic need for activity. He had a way of keeping her in the moment. Whether it was a deep, drugging kiss or the glide of his hands over her skin, when she was with him the rest of the world and all its problems slipped away.

"Ten more minutes," he murmured, his arms around her tensing.

"I'm not going anywhere."

His breath puffed against her skin as his lips moved across her cheek and down her neck. "I can feel you starting to think about everything that needs to get done in the next twelve hours."

"I'm only thinking about the next twelve minutes." She arched her back as his tongue circled her nipple. A long sigh escaped her as he settled his mouth over her breast and sucked.

In the end it was twenty minutes before she escaped his clever hands and imaginative mouth and made her way on shaking legs to her shower. As tempted as she'd been by his invitation to stay and let him wash her back, they'd already lingered too long.

They grabbed a quick dinner of May's chili to fortify

them for the long, cold night, before heading out. With the number of cows showing signs of delivering over the next twenty-four hours, it was all hands on deck.

Icy rain pelted Shane and Brandee as they maneuvered the cows. By three o'clock in the morning, Hope Springs Ranch had seen the addition of two heifers and three steers. On a normal night, emotions would be running high at all the successful births, but a sharp wind blew rain into every gap in their rain gear, leaving the group soaked, freezing and exhausted.

Brandee cast a glance around. Although most of the newborns were up on their feet and doing well, a couple still were being tended to by their moms. That left only one cow left to go. The one Brandee was most worried about: a first-time heifer who looked like she was going to be trouble.

"We might want to take this one back to the shed," Brandee shouted above the rain, moving her horse forward to turn the heifer they'd been keeping tabs on in the direction of the ranch buildings.

Her water had broken at the start of the evening and now she'd advanced to the stage where she was contracting. They'd been watching her for the last twenty minutes and things didn't seem to be progressing.

Shane shifted his horse so that the cow was between them and they could keep her heading where they wanted. It seemed to take forever and Brandee's nerves stretched tighter with each minute that passed. As many times as she'd seen calves drop, each birth held a place of importance in her heart.

They got the heifer into the barn and directed her into a chute. At the far end was a head gate that opened to the side and then closed after the cow stuck her head through. Once the heifer was secure, Brandee put on a long glove and moved to her back end.

"I've got to see what's going on up there," she explained to Shane, who watched her with interest.

"What can I do?"

"There's an obstetric chain, hooks and a calf puller over there." She indicated a spot on the wall where the equipment was kept. "Can you also grab the wood box propped up against the wall, as well?" Two feet square and four inches high, the box was used to brace against the heifer when she started pulling the calf out.

"Got it."

Now that they had the cow inside where it was dry and light, Brandee needed to examine the birth canal to determine the size and position of the calf. She was dreading that the calf was breeched. Most calves were born headfirst, but sometimes they were turned around, and if the legs were tucked up, it would mean she'd have to go rooting around an arm's-length distance to see if she could find a hoof and wrap the chain around it.

Brandee knew she was in trouble almost immediately. Chilled to the bone, exhausted and anticipating a hundred things that could possibly go wrong with this birth, she cursed.

"Problem?" Shane stood beside her with the equipment.

"Calf's breeched." She took the chain from Shane and indicated the puller. "You can put that aside. We're not going to need it yet."

She hoped not at all. If she could get the calf straightened out, the cow's contractions might be able to help her. Brandee just hoped the heifer wasn't worn-out from pushing the breeched baby.

"What do you do with that?" Shane indicated the chain. It was several feet in length with circles on each end, reminiscent of a dog's choke collar.

"I need to get this around the calf's legs so I can get

them straightened out. Right now its hind end is toward the birth canal and its legs are beneath it."

"Isn't this something a vet should handle?"

"Only if things get complicated." And she hoped that wouldn't happen. "I've done this before. It's just tricky and time-consuming, but doable."

"What can I do to help?"

Her heart gave a silly little flutter at his earnest question. Usually she had one of the guys helping her with this, but they were all out, tending to little miracles of their own. She could handle this.

She eyed Shane's beefy shoulders with a weary but heartfelt grin. "I'm going to let you show off your manly side."

"Meaning?" He cocked an eyebrow at her.

"You get to do all the pulling."

Her last glimpse of Shane before she focused all her attention on the cow was of his sure nod. He had his game face on. This aspect of ranching was one he'd never known, but he'd stepped up and she respected him for that.

Brandee made a loop with one end of the chain and reached in until she located the calf's legs. The snug fit and the way he was positioned meant that getting the chain over the hoof required dexterity and patience. To block out all distractions, Brandee closed her eyes and "saw" with her fingers. Before she could get the loop over the hoof, she lost the opening and the chain straightened out.

Frustration surged. The miserable night had worn her down. Feeling raw and unfocused, she pulled her arm out and re-created the loop before trying once more. It took her three attempts and ten agonizing minutes before she'd captured both hooves. She was breathing hard past the tightness in her throat as she turned to Shane.

"Okay, now it's your turn." Her voice was thick with

weariness and she struggled not to let her anxiety show. "We'll do this slow. I need you to pull one side and then the other to get his hooves pointed outward. I'll let you know which to pull and when."

Working together in slow stages, they got the calf's back legs straightened so that both were heading down the birth canal. Both Brandee and Shane were sweating in the cool barn air by the time stage one was complete.

"What now?" Shane asked, stepping back to give Brandee room to move around the heifer.

"We need to get her down on her right side. It's the natural position for birthing. I want as little stress on her as possible."

Brandee slipped a rope around the cow right in front of her hip bones and tightened it while rocking her gently to get her to lie down. Once the heifer was on her side, Brandee made sure the chains were still properly positioned around the calf's cannon bones.

"Good," she said, noting that the cow was starting to contract once more. "Let's get this done."

She sat down on the ground and grabbed the first hook. When the cow contracted, Brandee pulled. Nothing happened. She set her foot against the cow for leverage and switched to the second hook. With the next contraction, she pulled again without success. This breeched baby was good and stuck.

"Let me help." Shane nudged her over and sat beside her.

After alternating back and forth between the two chains a few times, Brandee dropped her head onto her arms as frustration swallowed her whole.

"Damn it, I don't want to use the calf puller." But it was very much appearing like she'd have to.

An uncharacteristic urge to cry rose in her. She wanted

to throw herself against Shane's chest and sob. Brandee gritted her teeth. She never got emotional like this.

"Come on," Shane said, bumping her shoulder with his in encouragement. "We can do this."

His focus was complete as he timed his exertions with the cow's contractions. Following his example, Brandee put her energy into willing the damned calf to move. The heifer groaned, Shane grunted and Brandee's muscles strained.

After four more contractions, they were able to get more of the legs out and Brandee felt some of the tension ease from her chest. There was still no guarantee that the calf would be alive when they were done, but at least they were making progress.

"Here," she said, shifting the wood platform and sliding it against the cow's backside between the calf's legs and the floor. Now she and Shane had a better brace for their feet. "He's starting to loosen. A few more contractions and we'll have him."

Then like a cork coming loose from a champagne bottle, the rear half of the calf was suddenly out. They scooted back to make way and then scrambled to their feet. With one final contraction and two mighty pulls from Brandee and Shane, the calf slipped free in a disgusting expulsion of amniotic fluid and blood.

Shane gave a soft whoop as he and a very relieved Brandee dragged the limp calf ten feet away from the cow.

"Is it alive?" Shane bent down and peered at the unmoving calf while Brandee peeled the sack from its face and cleared fluid from its nostrils.

"It sure is." She exuberantly roughed up its coat in a simulation of its mother's rough licking and watched it begin to draw breath into its lungs.

Shane peeled off the rubber gloves he'd donned and

turned them inside out to avoid transferring the gore to his skin. “What a rush.”

“It can be.” Brandee released the head gate and walked out of the birthing area. “Let’s get out of here so she can get up and smell her baby.”

The calf still hadn’t moved, but now the cow got to her feet and managed a lumbering turn. She seemed a little disengaged from what had just happened.

“She doesn’t seem too interested in her baby,” Shane commented, his voice low and mellow.

“Give her a minute.”

And sure enough the cow ambled over to the baby and gave him a good long sniff. This seemed to stimulate the calf and he gave a little jerk, which startled the cow for a second. Then Mama gave her baby another couple sniffs and began licking.

“What do you know.” Shane gently bumped against Brandee. “Looks like we did okay.”

She leaned her head on his shoulder. “We sure did.”

Within an hour the calf was on its feet and Brandee wanted very badly to get off hers. Several hands had swung by to check in and thumped Shane on the back when they found out he’d participated in his first calf pulling.

“I think we can leave these two for now,” Brandee said, pushing away from the railing. “I really want a shower and some breakfast.”

“Both sound great.”

Twenty minutes later, clean and dressed in leggings and an oversize sweater, Brandee pulled her damp hair into a topknot and padded into the kitchen, where Shane had already put on a pot of coffee and was staring into the refrigerator. He hadn’t noticed her arrival and she had an unguarded few seconds to stare at him.

He’d been a huge help tonight. She wondered if he still

disliked ranching as much as he had when he'd first arrived. Seeing his face light up as they'd pulled the calf free had given her such joy. She was starting to get how being partners with someone could be pretty great. Too bad there was a sinkhole the size of Hope Springs Ranch standing between them.

He must have heard her sigh because he asked, "What are you hungry for?"

He turned to look at her and she realized he was the manifestation of every longing, hope and fantasy she'd ever had. She had closed the distance and was sinking her fingers into his hair before the refrigerator door closed.

"You."

Eleven

Shane's arms locked around her as their mouths fused in a hot, frantic kiss. She was everything sweet and delicious. And sexy. He loved the way her hips moved against him as if driven by some all-consuming hunger. He sank his fingers into them and backed her against the counter.

If he'd thought she made him burn before, the soft moans that slipped out when he palmed her breast awakened a wildness he could barely contain. The big island in the kitchen had enough room for them both, but before he could lift her onto it, she shook her head.

"My room."

For an instant he froze. Over the last week, she'd made it pretty clear that her bedroom was off-limits. What had changed? He framed her face with his hands and peered into her eyes. She met his gaze with openness and trust. His heart wrenched and something broke loose inside him.

"You're the most amazing woman I've ever known,"

he murmured, dipping his head to capture her lips in a reverent kiss.

She melted into his body and he savored the plush give of her soft curves. Before the kiss could turn sizzling once more, Shane scooped Brandee off her feet and headed to her bedroom.

She'd left the nightstand lamps burning and he had no trouble finding his way to her bed. Setting her on her feet, he ripped off his T-shirt and tossed it aside. She managed to unfasten the button on his jeans before he pushed her hands aside and finished the job himself. Once he stood naked before her, he wasted little time stripping off her clothes.

Together they tumbled onto the mattress and rolled. Breathless, Shane found himself flat on his back with a smiling Brandee straddling him. Gloriously confident in her power, she cupped her breasts in her hands and lifted them in offering to him.

Shane's erection bobbed against her backside as he skimmed his palms up her rib cage and lightly pinched her tight nipples. He wanted what happened between them tonight to be something neither one would ever forget and tangled one hand in her hair to draw her mouth down to his.

Again they kissed with more tenderness than passion. The heat that had driven them earlier had given way to a curious intimacy. Shane kissed his way down her throat and sucked gently at the spot where her shoulder and neck came together. Her fingers bit into his shoulder as she shivered.

"You like that," he said, teasing the spot with his tongue and smiling at her shaky laugh.

"I like a lot of things that you do to me."

"Like this?" He brushed his hand over her abdomen.

Her thighs parted in anticipation of his touch, but he went no lower.

"Not like that," she murmured, pushing his fingers lower. "Like this." Her back arched as he slid a finger along the folds that concealed her intimate warmth. "Almost, but not quite…there."

Her shudder drove his willpower to the brink. Sensing she'd rush him if he let her, Shane eased down her body, gliding his mouth over the swell of one breast, and then the other. Brandee's fingers sifted through his hair as she sighed in pleasure.

But when his tongue drew damp patterns on her belly, she tensed, guessing his destination. His mouth found her without the preliminaries he usually observed. This time he wasn't here to seduce, only to push her over the edge hard.

Her body bowed as he lapped at her. A moan of intense pleasure ripped from her throat. The sound pierced him and drove his own passion higher. In the last week he'd learned what she liked and leveraged every bit of knowledge to wring his name from her lips over and over.

With her body still shaking in the aftermath of her climax, she directed him to her nightstand and an unopened box of condoms. The sight of it made him smile. She'd been planning to invite him to her room. This meant that her walls were crumbling, if only a little. Was he close to winning their bet?

The thought chilled him. If she fell in love with him and he took away the ranch that meant so much to her, would she ever be able to forgive him?

He slid on the condom and kissed his way up her body. She clung to him as he settled between her thighs and brought his lips to hers for a deep, hot kiss. Her foot skimmed up the back of his leg as she met his gaze. Then she opened herself for his possession. He thrust into her, his heart expanding at the vulnerability in her expression.

She pumped her hips, taking him all the way in, and he hissed through his teeth as her muscles contracted around him. For a long second he held still, breathing raggedly. Then he began to move, sliding out of her slowly, savoring every bit of friction.

"Let's go, Delgado," she urged, her nails digging into his back. She wrapped her leg around his hip, making his penetration a little deeper, and rocked to urge him on.

"You feel amazing." At the end of another slow thrust, he lightly bit her shoulder and she moaned. "I could go like this all night." He was lying.

Already he could feel pleasure tightening in his groin. He was climbing too fast toward orgasm. He surged into her, his strokes steady and deep, then quickening as he felt her body tighten around him. She was gasping for air, hands clamped down hard on his biceps as they began to climax nearly at the same moment. He'd discovered timing his orgasm to hers required very little attention on his part. It was as if some instinct allowed their bodies to sync.

But tonight Shane grit his teeth and held off so he could watch Brandee come. It was a perfect moment, and in a lightning flash of clarity, he realized that he'd gone and done it. He'd fallen for her. Hard. Caught off guard by the shock of it, Shane's orgasm overcame him, and as his whole body clenched with it, pleasure bursting inside him, a shift occurred in his perception.

This was no longer a woman climaxing beneath him, but his woman. He couldn't imagine his life without her in it. He wanted her in his bed. Riding beside him on a horse. Laughing, teasing, working. Yes, even working. He wanted to be with her all the time.

Stunned by what he'd just admitted to himself, Shane

lay on his back and stared at the ceiling while Brandee settled against his side, her arm draped over his chest, her breath puffing against his neck. Contentment saturated bone, muscle and sinew, rendering him incapable of movement, but his brain continued to whirl.

Brandee was already asleep, her deep, regular breathing dragging him toward slumber. Yet, despite his exhaustion, something nagged at him. As perfect as their lovemaking had been, there was a final piece of unfinished business that lay between them.

Leaving Brandee slumbering, Shane eased out of bed. He needed to do this while his thoughts were clear. He suspected doubts would muddy his motivation all too soon.

The first night he'd arrived, she'd shown him the two contracts. He'd taken both copies to his lawyer to make sure there was nothing tricky buried in the language. Turned out, it had been straightforward. If he signed the paperwork, he agreed to give up all claim to the land. If she signed, she agreed to sell him the land for ten million.

Several times in the last two weeks, she'd reminded him that his contract awaited his signature in her office. He headed there now. Turning on the desk light, he found a pen and set his signature to the document with a flourish.

As he added the date, it occurred to him he was declaring that he'd fallen for her. Opening himself up to rejection like this wasn't something he did. Usually he was the one making a break for it as soon as the woman he was dating started getting ideas.

Except Brandee wasn't like the women he usually went for. She was more like him. Fiercely independent. Relentlessly self-protective. And stubborn as all get-out.

Shane reached across the desk and turned off the lamp. A second after Brandee's office plunged back into darkness, her cell phone lit up. The text message caught his eye.

Pay up tomorrow or Delgado gets your land back.

Shane stared at the message in confusion. "Your land back"? Those three words made no sense. And what was this about "pay up tomorrow"? As far as Shane knew, Brandee owned the land outright. Could there be a lien on the property he didn't know about? Shane was still puzzling about the text as he sat down in Brandee's chair, once again turned on the lamp and pulled open her file drawer.

Her organizational skills betrayed her. A hanging file bearing his name hung in alphabetical order among files for property taxes, credit card and bank statements, as well as sketches for her upcoming clothing line. Shane pulled out his file and spread the pages across the desk.

His heart stopped when he saw the birth certificates going back several generations. He reviewed the copy of Jasper Crowley's legal document that made the Hope Springs Ranch land his daughter's dowry. After reading through the newspaper clippings and retracing his ancestry, Shane understood. Brandee intended to cheat him out of the land that should belong to his family.

Leaving everything behind, he returned to the bedroom to wake Brandee and demand answers. But when he got to the room, he stopped dead and stared at her sleeping form. He loved her. That was why he'd signed the document.

Not one thing his father had ever said to him had hurt as much as finding out he'd fallen in love with a woman who was using him.

Torn between confronting her and getting the hell away before he did something else he'd regret, Shane snatched his clothes off the floor and headed for the back door. He slid his feet into his boots, grabbed his coat with his truck keys and went out into the night.

* * *

Brandee woke to a sense of well-being and the pleasant ache of worn muscles. She lay on her side, tucked into a warm cocoon of sheets and quilts. Her bedroom was still dark. The time on her alarm clock was 5:43 a.m.

The room's emptiness struck her. There was no warm, rugged male snoring softly beside her. She didn't need to reach out her hand to know Shane's side of the bed was cool and unoccupied. After the night they'd shared, she didn't blame him for bolting before sunrise. The sex had been amazing. They'd dropped their guards after the difficult calf birthing, permitting a deeper connection than they'd yet experienced.

Part of her wanted to jump out of bed and run to find him. She longed to see the same soul-stirring emotion she'd glimpsed in his eyes last night. But would it be there? In her gut, she knew he felt something for her. No doubt he was as uncomfortable at being momentarily exposed as she'd been.

As much as she'd grown accustomed to having him around and had put aside her fierce independence to let him help, she was terrified to admit, even to herself, that she craved his companionship as much as his passionate lovemaking. But was it worth losing her ranch?

Brandee threw off the covers and went to shower. Fifteen minutes later, dressed in jeans and a loose-fitting sweater, she headed for the kitchen, hoping the lure of freshly made coffee would entice Shane.

And she'd decided to come clean about Maverick, Hope Springs Ranch and the blackmail.

Over a hearty breakfast, she would explain her fear of losing the ranch and see if he would agree to letting her keep it for now as long as she agreed to leave it to him in her will.

While she waited for the coffee to brew, Brandee headed to her office to get the document Maverick had sent to her as well as the ones she'd found during her research. Dawn was breaking and Brandee could see her desk well enough to spy the papers strewn across it. She approached and her heart jerked painfully as she realized what she was staring at.

With her stomach twisted into knots, Brandee raced from the room and headed straight for her guest suite. The room was empty. Next she dashed to the back door. Shane's coat and boots were gone. So was his truck. Her knees were shaking so badly she had to sit down on the bench in the mudroom to catch her breath.

No wonder he'd left so abruptly during the night. He knew. Everything. She'd failed to save her ranch. She'd hurt the man she loved.

It took almost ten minutes for Brandee to recover sufficiently to return to her office and confront the damning documents. How had he known to go into her filing cabinet and look for the file she'd made on him? Had he suspected something was wrong? Or had Maverick tipped him off early?

The answer was on her phone. A text message from Maverick warning her time was almost up. But how had Shane seen it? She gathered the research materials together and returned them to the file. It was then that she noticed Shane's signature on the document revoking his claim to her land.

She'd won.

It didn't matter if Shane knew. Legally he couldn't take her ranch away from her.

But morally, he had every right to it.

Brandee picked up the document. While the disclosure she'd been about to make was no longer necessary, the solution she'd intended to propose was still a valid one.

Brandee grabbed the document and her coat and headed for her truck. As she drove to Bullseye, the clawing anxiety of her upcoming confrontation warred with her determination to fix the situation. It might be more difficult now that he'd discovered she'd been lying to him all along before she had a chance to confess, but Shane was a businessman. He'd understand the value of her compromise and weigh it against an expensive court battle.

Yet, as she stood in the chilly morning air on his front steps, her optimism took a nosedive. Shane left her waiting so long before answering his doorbell that she wondered if he was going to refuse to see her. When he opened the door, he was showered and dressed in a tailored business suit, a stony expression on his face.

She held up the document he'd signed and ignored the anxious twisting of her stomach. "We need to talk about this."

"There's nothing to talk about. You won. I signed. You get to keep the ranch."

Brandee floundered. On the way over, she hadn't dwelled on how Shane might be hurt by her actions. She'd been thinking about how to convince him of her plan so they both got what they wanted.

"I didn't win. And there's plenty more to talk about. I know what you must think of me—"

He interrupted, "I highly doubt that."

"You think I tricked you. You'd be right. But if I lose the ranch, I lose everything." Immediately she saw this tack wasn't going to be effective. So, maybe she could give him some idea of what she was up against. "Look, I was being blackmailed, okay? Somebody named Maverick sent me the Jasper Crowley document."

"That's your story?" Shane obviously didn't believe her. "You're being blackmailed?"

"Maverick wanted fifty thousand dollars and for me to resign from the Texas Cattleman's Club." To Brandee's ears the whole thing sounded ridiculous. She couldn't imagine what would convince Shane she was telling the truth. "I should've done as I was asked, but I really thought it was…"

Telling him that she suspected Cecelia, Simone and Naomi wasn't going to make her story sound any more sympathetic. Shane liked those women. Brandee would only come off as petty and insecure if she accused them of blackmail without a shred of proof.

"Look," she continued, "I should've come clean in the beginning. Maybe we could've worked something out." She took a step closer, willing him to understand how afraid she'd been. "But when I proposed the wager, I didn't know anything about you except that for years you've been after me to sell. I didn't think I could trust you."

"Were you ever going to tell me the truth?"

The fear of opening herself up to rejection and ridicule once again clamped its ruthless fingers around her throat. "Last night…" She needed to say more, but the words wouldn't come.

"What about last night?"

"It was great," she said in a small voice, barely able to gather enough breath to make herself heard.

"You say that after I signed away my rights to *my family's* land."

Why had he? He could have torn up the agreement after finding out he owned the land, but he hadn't. He'd left it for her to find. Why would he do that?

"Not because of that," she said, reaching deep for the strength to say what was in her heart. "I say it because I think I might have fallen in love with you."

His face remained impassive, except at the corner of his

eyes where the muscles twitched. "Is this the part where I say I'm not going to pursue legal action against you?"

She floundered, wondering if that was what he intended. "No, this is me talking to you without this between us." She tore the document he'd signed down the middle, lined the pieces back up and tore them again.

"Is that supposed to impress me? Do you think that document would've stood up in court?"

Brandee hung her head. "It was never supposed to get that far."

"I imagine you were pretty confident you could get away with cheating me," Shane said, the icy bite of his voice making her flinch.

"I wasn't confident at all. And I wasn't happy about it. But the ranch is everything to me. Not just financially, but also it's my father's legacy. And the camp could have done so much good." Brandee ached with all she'd lost. "But I am truly sorry about the way I handled things. I didn't do it to hurt you."

He stared at her in silence for several heartbeats before stepping back.

"You didn't."

And then the door swung shut in her face.

Twelve

Five days and four long, empty, aching nights after Shane slammed the door in Brandee's face, he slid onto the open bar stool beside Gabe at the Texas Cattleman's Club and ordered a cup of coffee.

Ignoring the bartender's surprise, he growled at his friend, "Okay, you got me here. What's so damned important?"

Gabe nodded toward a table in the corner. A familiar blonde sat by herself, hunched over an empty glass. Brandee's long hair fell loosely about her face, hiding her expression, but there was no misreading her body language. She was as blue as a girl could be.

"Yeah, so?" Shane wasn't feeling particularly charitable at the moment and didn't have time to be dragged away from The Bellamy. He had his own problems to contend with.

"You don't think there's something wrong with that picture?" Gabe nodded his head in Brandee's direction.

There was a lot of something wrong, but it wasn't Shane's problem.

"Tell me that's not why you dragged me here. Because if it is, you've just wasted an hour of my time."

Gabe's eyes widened at Shane's tone. "I think you should talk to her."

"As I explained yesterday and the day before and the day before that, I'm done talking about what happened. She screwed me over."

"In order to keep her ranch," Gabe replied, his quiet, calm voice in marked contrast to Shane's sharp tone. "She stood to lose everything. How would you have behaved if the situation was reversed and you were about to lose Bullseye?"

It wasn't a fair comparison.

"I'd say good riddance." Shane sipped his coffee and stared at the bottles arranged behind the bar. "I would've sold it years ago if I thought it wouldn't upset my mom."

"You don't mean that."

"I do."

Or he mostly did. Ranching had been in his father's blood and Shane associated Bullseye with being bullied and criticized. Every memory of his father came with an accompanying ache. He'd never be the rancher his father wanted. In some ways it had been a relief when Landon had died. There, he'd admitted it. But by admitting it, he'd lived up to his father's poor opinion of him. He was a bad son. Guilt sharpened the pain until it felt like spikes were being driven into his head.

"I've never seen you like this." Gabe leaned back in his seat as if he needed to take a better look at his friend. "You're really upset."

"You're damned right," Shane said. "She intended to cheat me out of what belongs to my family."

"But you said the land was unclaimed..."

"And what really gets me—" Shane was a boulder rolling down a steep grade "—is the way she went about it."

She'd made him fall in love with her. There. He'd admitted that, too. He was in love with Brandee Lawless, the liar and cheat.

Shane signaled the bartender. Maybe something strong was in order. "Give me a shot of Patrón Silver."

She'd ruined scotch for him. He couldn't even smell the stuff without remembering the way she'd tasted of it the first night they'd made love. Or her delight when he'd introduced her to the proper way to drink it. And his surprise when she'd poured a shot of it over him and lapped up every drop.

Shane downed the tequila shot and signaled for another.

"Are you planning on going head down on the table, too?" Gabe's tone had a mild bite.

"Maybe." But instead of drinking the second shot, Shane stared at it. "You gonna sit around and watch me do it, or are you going to make sure she gets home safe?"

"I've already taken care of Brandee." Gabe nodded his head toward the entrance, where Chelsea had appeared. "If you feel like drowning your sorrows, I'll stick around to drive you home."

Shane rotated the glass and contemplated it. He'd spent the last four nights soaking his hurt feelings in alcohol and after waking up that morning with a whopping hangover had decided he was done moping. He pushed the shot away.

"No need. I'm getting out of here."

But before he could leave, Chelsea had gotten Brandee to her feet and the two women were heading toward the door. Despite how Brandee had looked staring morosely into the bottom of her glass, she wasn't at all unsteady on her feet.

Not wanting to risk bumping into her, Shane stayed where he was and turned his back to the departing women. He couldn't risk her or anyone else noticing the way his hungry gaze followed her. She'd ditched her jeans and was wearing another of those gauzy, romantic numbers that blew his mind. This one was pale pink and made her look as if a strong wind could carry her all the way to Austin. Gut-kicked and frustrated that she still got to him, he reminded himself that she was strong, independent and could take care of herself.

"Look at you three sitting here all smug and self-important." Brandee's voice rang out and conversations hushed. "Well, congratulations, you got your way."

Gabe caught Shane's eye and gave him a quizzical look. "Any idea why she's going after Cecilia, Simone and Naomi?"

With an abrupt shake of his head, Shane returned to staring at his untouched drink, but he was far less interested in it than he was the scene playing out behind him.

"I'm not going to be around to oppose you any longer. I've resigned from the Texas Cattleman's Club. It's all yours." Brandee didn't sound intoxicated exactly. More hysterical and overwrought than anything.

"We don't know what you're—" Cecelia Morgan began, only to be interrupted.

"Where do you three get off ruining other people's lives?"

The entire room was quiet and Brandee's voice bounced off the walls. None of the women answered and Brandee rambled on.

"You must have thought it would be great fun, but blackmail is an ugly business. And it will come back to bite you in the ass."

At the mention of blackmail, Shane turned around in

time to see Brandee push herself back from the table where she'd been looming over the three women. They were all staring at Brandee in openmouthed shock and fear.

Brandee punched the air with her finger. "Mark my words."

As Chelsea tugged Brandee toward the exit, the trio of women erupted in nervous laughter.

"I don't know what that was about," Simone said, her voice pitched to carry around the room. "Obviously she's finally snapped."

"It was only a matter of time," Naomi agreed, tossing her head before sipping her fruity drink.

Only Cecelia refrained from commenting. She stared after Brandee and Chelsea, her eyes narrowed and a pensive expression on her beautiful face. Moments later, however, she joined her friends in a loud replay of the clash. Around them, side conversations buzzed. News of Brandee's behavior and her wild accusations would spread through the TCC community before morning.

"She thinks those three blackmailed her?" Gabe glanced at Shane. "Did you know she was planning to resign from the TCC?"

"I don't know why she needed to. I signed her damned document giving up my right to the ranch." Yet, when Brandee had come to his house to apologize, he had refused her attempt to make amends.

"You said she tore it up."

"Well, yeah." Guilt flared. But Shane refused to accept blame for Brandee's overwrought state. "None of that had anything to do with me."

"That—" Gabe gestured at the departing women "—has everything to do with you." His features settled into grim lines. "Of all the times you should have come through and helped someone."

"What's that supposed to mean?"

Gabe looked unfazed by Shane's belligerent tone. "Everybody thinks you're a great guy. You make sure of that. You've always been the life of the party. But when it comes to helping out…" The former Texas Ranger shook his head.

Shane heard the echoes of his father's criticism in Gabe's words and bristled. "Why don't you come right out and say it? No one can count on me when it comes to things that need doing."

"Mostly you're good at getting other people to do stuff."

Shane recalled the expression on Megan Maguire's face when she'd spotted him helping out with Brandee's teen day. She'd been surprised.

And if he was honest with himself, Brandee's tactics to hold on to her land weren't all that different from his own way of doing things. He'd held back important information a time or two. And what Gabe had said about his getting other people to volunteer when there was work to be done…

Growing up, his father had accused him of being lazy and Shane had resented it, despite knowing there was a bit of truth to it. So, what was he supposed to do? Change who he was? He was thirty-five years old and far too accustomed to doing things his way.

"How is it I'm the bad guy all of a sudden?" Shane demanded. "And where do you get off making judgments about me?"

"I just want to point out that while Brandee may have manipulated you, it's not like you haven't done the same to others. She's not perfect. You're not perfect. But from watching you both, you might be perfect together."

And with that, Gabe pushed away from the bar and headed out, abandoning Shane to a head filled with recriminations and a hollow feeling in his gut.

* * *

It took until Brandee was seated in Chelsea's car before the full import of what she'd just done hit her. By the time Chelsea slid behind the wheel, Brandee had planted her face in her hands and was muttering incoherent curses.

As she felt the car begin to move forward, Brandee lifted her head and glared at her best friend. "Why didn't you stop me?"

"Are you kidding?" Chelsea smirked. "You said what half the membership has been dying to. Did you see the look on their faces?"

The brisk walk across the chilly parking lot had done much to clear Brandee's head, but she was still pretty foggy. When was the last time she'd had this much to drink? She didn't even know how many she'd had.

"All I saw was red." Brandee groaned and set her head against the cool window. "Take me to the airport. I'm going to get on a plane and fly to someplace no one has ever heard of."

Chelsea chuckled. "Are you kidding? You're going to be a hero."

"No, I'm not. No one deserves to be talked to like that. I run…" She gulped. Hope Springs Camp was an impossibility now that Shane knew he owned her ranch. "I had hoped to run a camp that gave teenagers the skills to cope with their problems in a sensible, positive way. And what do I do? I stand in the middle of the Texas Cattleman's Club and shriek at those three like a drunken fishwife." The sounds coming from the seat beside her did not improve Brandee's mood. "Stop laughing."

"I'm sorry, but they deserved it. Especially if any one or all three is Maverick."

"Do you really think it's possible they're behind the blackmail?"

"I think someone needs to look into it."

"Well, it isn't going to be me. I'm going to be sitting on a beach, sipping something fruity and strong."

"You'll get a new guy? He'll have it going on?"

Despite her calamitous exit from the TCC clubhouse, Brandee gave a snort of amusement as Chelsea twisted the Dierks Bentley song lyrics from "Somewhere on a Beach" to suit the conversation. Then, despite her dire circumstances and the fact that she'd just humiliated herself, Brandee picked up the next line and in moments the two girls were singing at the top of their lungs.

They kept it up all the way to Chelsea's house, where Brandee had agreed to spend the night. She couldn't bear to be alone in her beautiful custom-tailored ranch home that she would soon have to pack up and move out of.

Tucked into a corner of Chelsea's couch, wrapped in a blanket with a mug of hot chocolate cradled in her hands, Brandee stared at the melting mini marshmallows and turned the corner on her situation. It wasn't as if it was the first time she'd lost everything. And in the scheme of things, she was a lot better off than she'd been at eighteen, broke and living out of her car.

"I guess I get to re-create myself again," she said, noticing the first hint of determination she'd felt in days.

"I think you should fight for your ranch. Take Shane to court and make him prove the land belongs to him."

Brandee didn't think she had the strength to take Shane on in a legal battle. She was still too raw from the way he'd slammed the door in her face.

"I'll think about it."

Chelsea regarded her in concern. "It isn't like you to give up like this."

"I know, but I'm not sure."

"Brandee, you can't just walk away from a ten-million-dollar property."

"It sounds crazy when you say it, but that's what I intend to do. Legally I might be able to get a court to determine the land is mine, but I think morally it belongs to Shane's family."

"What are you going to do?"

"Sell everything and start over?" The thought pained her more than she wanted to admit, but in the last five days she'd come to terms with her loss. "I wasn't kidding about finding a beach somewhere and getting lost."

"You can't seriously be thinking of leaving Royal?"

The pang in Chelsea's voice made Brandee wince. "I don't know that I want to stay here after everything that's happened." Just the thought of running into Shane and seeing his coldness toward her made her blood freeze. "Look, it's not like I have to do anything today. It's going to take me a while to sell my herd and settle things on the ranch. With The Bellamy still under construction and taking up all his energy, Shane isn't going to have time to start developing the ranch right away."

"And maybe you and Shane can work out an arrangement that will benefit you both."

"Did you see the way he acted as if I didn't exist?" Brandee shook her head, fighting back the misery that was her constant companion these days. "No, he hates me for what I tried to do to him and there's no going back from that."

"Now, aren't you glad we warned you off of Brandee Lawless?"

"Did you see how she spoke to us?"

"I think she had too much to drink. And happy hour's barely started."

"I've said from the beginning that she has no class."

"She must've had a reason for going after you," Shane said.

He recalled what had happened to Wesley Jackson, and thought there'd been some buzz around the clubhouse that Cecelia had been behind it. An anonymous hacker had exposed Wes as a deadbeat dad on social media and it had blown a major business deal for him. What had happened to Brandee was in the same vein.

"She's been out to get us from the moment we joined the Texas Cattleman's Club."

"That's not true," Shane said, a hint of warning in his tone. "She just hasn't bought into what you want to do with the place. A lot of people haven't."

"But she's been actively working to drum up resistance," Naomi said.

"That doesn't make her your enemy." Shane shook his head. "Not everyone wants the clubhouse to undergo any more changes, especially not the kind you're interested in making."

"Well, it doesn't matter anymore. She resigned her membership."

"And with her gone, the others will come around," Cecelia said. "You'll see."

"Sounds like everything is going your way." Shane set his hands on their table the way Brandee had and leaned forward to eye each woman in turn. "If I find out any of you three were behind what happened to Brandee, you'll have to answer to me."

He loomed menacingly for several heartbeats, taking in each startled expression in turn. Instinctively, they'd leaned back in their chairs as if gaining even a small amount of distance would keep them safe. At long last, satisfied they'd received his message, he pushed upright, jostling the table just enough to set their cutlery tingling and their drinks sloshing.

"Ladies." With a nod, he headed for the exit.

Icy gusts blew across the parking lot as Shane emerged from the clubhouse. He faced the north wind and lifted his hat, not realizing how angry he'd been until he dashed sweat from his brow. Damn Brandee for making him rush to defend her. He should've left well enough alone.

The cold reduced his body temperature to normal as he headed toward his truck. A row back and a few spaces over, he caught sight of her vehicle.

"Great."

Now he'd have to make sure she wasn't driving in her condition. But the truck was empty. Brandee was long gone. Shane headed to his own truck.

As he drove the familiar roads on his way to The Bellamy, he tried to put Brandee out of his thoughts, but couldn't shake the image of her going after Cecelia, Simone and Naomi. The outburst had shocked more than a few people.

Brandee's public face was vastly different from the one she showed in private. Not once in all the years that he'd pursued her to sell the ranch had she ever cracked and lost her temper with him. Because of her cool, composed manner, he'd worked extra hard to get beneath her skin. From getting to know her these last two weeks, he recognized that she put a lot of energy into maintaining a professional image. It was why she was so well respected at the male-dominated Texas Cattleman's Club.

Today, she'd blown that. Her words came back to him. Why had she quit the TCC? Did she really think he had any intention of taking her ranch? Then he thought about how she'd torn up the document he'd signed, relinquishing his claim. The damned woman was so stubborn she probably figured she'd turn the place over to him regardless of what he wanted.

And if she did? What would she do? Where would she go? The ranch was everything to her. With her capital tied up in her land and her cows, she probably figured she'd have to downsize her herd in order to start over.

After checking to make sure everything was on track at The Bellamy, he headed home and was surprised to see his mother's car as well as a catering van in the driveway. Shane parked his truck, drawing a blank. He was pretty sure he'd remember if there was a party scheduled.

When it hit him, he cursed, belatedly remembering he'd promised his mother to help her make catering decisions this afternoon for the party being held in four weeks to celebrate Bullseye's hundred-year anniversary. He'd neglected to add the appointment to his calendar any of the four times she'd reminded him of the event.

He rushed into the house and found everything set up in the dining room. "Hello, Mother." He circled the table to kiss the cheek she offered him.

"You're late," she scolded, more annoyed than she sounded.

The way she looked, he was going to need a drink. "I'm sorry."

"Well, at least you're here now, so we can begin."

Until that second, Shane had been hoping that his mother had already sampled everything and made her decisions. Now he regarded the food spread over every available inch of table and groaned. The appetizers ran the gamut from individual ribs glazed in sweet-smelling barbecue sauce to ornate pastries begging to be tasted. Three champagne flutes sat before Elyse. She gestured toward the dining chair nearest her with a fourth glass.

"Vincent, please pour my son some champagne so he can give his opinion on the two I'm deciding between."

"I'm sure whatever you decide is fine," Shane said, edging backward. He was in no mood to sit through an elaborate tasting.

"You will sit down and you will help me decide what we are going to serve at your party."

If her tone hadn't been so severe, he might have protested that the party hadn't been his idea and he couldn't care less what they served. But since he'd already alienated Gabe today and ruined any hope of future happiness with the woman he loved several days earlier, Shane decided he needed at least one person in his corner.

It took a half an hour to taste everything and another fifteen minutes for them to narrow it down to ten items. Elyse generously included several selections Shane preferred that she'd described as too basic. He wondered if she gave him his way in appreciation of his help tonight or if it was a ploy to make him more pliable the next time she asked for his assistance.

And then he wondered why he was questioning his mother's motives. Was this what playing games had turned him into? Had he become suspicious of his own mother?

And what about Brandee? Was she solely to blame for the way she'd tried to trick him? If he'd been more like Gabe, honest and aboveboard, might she have come to him and negotiated a settlement that would have benefited both of them? Instead, because he liked to play games, she'd played one on him.

"I'm sorry I forgot about today," he told his mother as Vincent packed up his edibles and returned the kitchen to its usual pristine state.

She sipped champagne and sighed. "I should be used to it by now."

Shane winced. With Gabe's lecture foremost in his thoughts, he asked, "Am I really that bad when it comes to getting out of doing things?"

"You're my son. And I love you." She reached out and patted his hand. "But when it comes to doing something you'd rather avoid, you're not very reliable."

It hurt more than he imagined it would to hear his mother say those words. Realizing he wasn't his mother's golden child humbled Shane. "Dad yelled at me about that all the time, but you never said a word."

"Your father was very hard on you and it certainly decreased your willingness to help around the ranch. You didn't need to feel ganged up on."

From where he was sitting, he could see the informal family portrait taken when he'd been seventeen. His father stood with his arm around his beaming wife and looked happy, while Shane's expression was slightly resentful. He'd always hated it because he was supposed to be on a hunting trip with friends the weekend the photo shoot had been scheduled. The photo seemed to sum up how he'd felt since he was ten.

Mother and son chatted for over an hour after the caterer departed about Elyse's upcoming trip to Boston for her brother Gavin's surprise sixty-fifth birthday party. She and Gavin's wife, Jennifer, were planning a tropical-themed bash because Gavin was also retiring at the end of the month and he and Jennifer were going to Belize to look at vacation properties.

"I need to get going," Elyse said, glancing at her watch. "I promised Jennifer I would call her to firm up the last few details for Gavin's party." She got to her feet and deposited a kiss on Shane's cheek. "Thank you for helping me today."

"It was my pleasure." And in fact, once he got over

his initial reluctance, he'd enjoyed spending time with his mom, doing something she took great pride in. "Your party-planning skills are second to none and the centennial is going to be fantastic. Let me know what else I can do to help you."

His mother didn't try to hide her surprise. "You mean that?"

"I do. Send me a list. I'll get it done."

"Thank you," she said, kissing him on the cheek.

After his mom left, Shane remembered something else he'd been putting off. His keys jingled as he trotted down the steps to the driveway. He needed to pick up his stuff from Brandee's. He'd been in such a hurry to leave that he hadn't taken anything with him.

He didn't expect to see her truck in the driveway and it wasn't. It was nearly seven o'clock. The sun was below the horizon and a soft glow from the living room lights filled the front windows. Shane got out of his truck and headed for the front door, remembering the first time he'd stepped onto her porch two weeks ago. So much had happened. So much had gone wrong.

First he tried the doorbell, but when that went unanswered, he tried knocking. Was she avoiding him? Or had she come home, consumed more alcohol and passed out? Shane decided he needed to see for himself that she was okay and used the key she'd given him to unlock the door.

As he stepped across her threshold, he half expected her to come tearing toward him, shrieking at him to get out. Of course, that wasn't her style. Or he hadn't thought it was until he'd witnessed her going after Cecelia, Simone and Naomi today.

He needn't have worried. The house had an unoccupied feel to it.

A quick look around confirmed Brandee hadn't come

home. Shane headed to the guest suite and was surprised to find none of his things had been touched. Moving quickly, he packed up his toiletries and clothes. He kept his gaze away from the luxurious shower and the big, comfortable bed. Already a lump had formed in his throat that had no business being there. He swallowed hard and cursed.

What the hell had he expected? That they would live happily-ever-after? Even before he found out she'd been keeping the truth from him about the ranch, that ending hadn't been in the cards. All along Brandee had said she didn't need anyone's help. She'd never wanted a partner or a long-term lover. They might have enjoyed each other's company for a while, but in the end both of them were too independent and afraid of intimacy for it to have worked.

Eager to be gone, Shane strode toward the front door, but as he reached it, a familiar ringtone began playing from the direction of the kitchen. He stopped walking and, with a resigned sigh, turned toward the sound. Brandee had left her smartphone on the large concrete island.

Though he knew he should just leave well enough alone, Shane headed to check out who might be calling. Brandee always made a point of being available to her ranch hands and with her not being home, they would have no way of knowing how to get in contact with her.

Shane leaned over and peered at the screen. Sure enough, it was her ranch foreman. Now Shane had two choices. He could get ahold of Chelsea and see if Brandee was staying there, or he could find out what was up and then call Chelsea.

"Hey, Jimmy," Shane said, deciding to answer the call. "Brandee isn't around at the moment. She left her phone behind. Is there something you need?"

"Is she planning on coming back soon?"

Shane recalled how she'd looked earlier. "I doubt it. She

went into town and I think she might be staying the night at Chelsea's. Is there something wrong?"

"Not wrong, but we've got a half-dozen cows showing signs of calving and she said if we needed her to help out tonight to call. But it's okay, we'll make do."

As Jimmy was speaking, Shane's gaze fell on something he hadn't noticed before. A large poster was tacked on the wall near the door to the mudroom. It held pictures of all the teenagers and their dogs surrounding a big, glittery thank-you in the middle. It was a gaudy, glorious mess and Shane knew that Brandee loved it.

He closed his eyes to block out the sight. Brandee didn't have to give her time or energy to a bunch of troubled kids, but she did it because even small events like the one with the rescue dogs had the power to change lives. He'd seen firsthand how her program had impacted each of the teens in some way, and with her camp she was poised to do so much more.

"Why don't I stop down and give you a hand." The last thing he wanted was to spend an endless, freezing night outside, but he knew it was the right thing to do.

"That would be a big help." Jimmy sounded relieved. "But are you sure? Between the cold and the number of cows ready to go, it's going to be a long, miserable night."

"I'm sure. See you in ten."

The way Shane was feeling at the moment, he was going to be miserable regardless. And to his surprise, as he headed back to the guest suite to change into work clothes, his mood felt significantly lighter. Maybe there was something to this helping-others thing after all.

Thirteen

Brandee came awake with a jolt and groped for her cell phone. Jimmy was supposed to check in with her last night and let her know if he needed her help with the calving. Had she slept through his call? That had never happened before.

Yet here she was, six short days after her reckoning with Shane, and already she was disengaging from her ranch. Had she really given up on her dream so easily? She couldn't imagine her father being very proud of her for doing so. And yet what choice did she have? All her capital was tied up in the land and her livestock. With the land returned to Shane, she didn't have a place for her cows and calves. It only made sense to sell them.

When she didn't find her phone on the nightstand, she realized why. This wasn't her room. She'd spent the night at Chelsea's after making a scene at the Texas Cattleman's Club. Brandee buried her face in the pillow and groaned.

She hadn't been anywhere near drunk, but her blood had been up and she'd consumed one drink too many.

Thank goodness she'd never have to set foot in the clubhouse again. Of course, that didn't mean she wouldn't be running into members elsewhere. Maybe she could hide out for a month or so while she settled her business with the ranch stock and figured out what to do next.

Should she move away from Royal? The thought triggered gut-wrenching loneliness and crippling anxiety. She couldn't leave behind so many wonderful friends. Two weeks ago, she might have considered herself self-sufficient, but after living with Shane she realized she was way needier than she'd let herself believe.

After sliding out of bed and feeling around the floor, Brandee broke down and turned on the bedside light. Her cell phone wasn't beneath the bed or lost among the sheets. Feeling a stir of panic, she considered all the places she might've left it.

A quick glance at the clock told her it was six o'clock in the morning. Too early for Chelsea to be awake, and Brandee would not borrow her friend's computer to check on her phone's location without permission. She could, however, use Chelsea's landline to call her foreman.

He answered after the third ring. "Hey, boss."

"I can't find my phone. I'm sorry I didn't check in sooner. Is everything okay?"

"It was a pretty crazy night, but me and the boys handled it."

"That's great to hear. I'm sorry I wasn't there to help you out."

"It's okay. Shane said you were staying the night at Chelsea's."

A jolt of adrenaline shot through her at Jimmy's words.

"How is it you spoke with Shane?" Annoyance flared. Was he already taking over her ranch?

"He answered your phone when I called."

"Did he say how he'd gotten my phone?" Had she left it in the parking lot of the Texas Cattleman's Club?

"He said you left it at your house." Jimmy's voice held concern. "You okay?"

For a long moment Brandee was so incensed she couldn't speak. What the hell was Shane doing in her house? "I'm fine. I need to get my truck and then I'll be by. Maybe an hour and a half, two hours tops." Cooling her heels for an hour until it was reasonable to wake Chelsea was not going to improve her temper.

"No rush. As I said, we have everything under control."

To keep herself busy, Brandee made coffee and foraged in Chelsea's pantry for breakfast. She wasn't accustomed to sitting still, and this brought home just how hard it was going to be to give up her ranch.

As seven o'clock rolled around, she brought a cup of coffee to Chelsea's bedside and gently woke her friend.

"What time is it?"

"Seven." Brandee winced at Chelsea's groan. "I made coffee," she said in her most beguiling voice.

"How long have you been up?"

"An hour." She bounced a little on the springy mattress.

"And how much coffee have you had?"

She extended the coffee so the aroma could rouse Chelsea. "This is the last cup."

"You drank an entire pot of coffee?"

"I didn't have anything else to do. I left my phone at home and didn't want to use your computer. I think the boys had a rough night and need me back at the ranch."

Chelsea lifted herself into a sitting position and reached

for the coffee. "Give me ten minutes to wake up and I'll take you to your truck."

"Thank you." She didn't explain about how Jimmy had spoken with Shane or the anxiety that overwhelmed her at the thought of him giving orders to her hands.

An hour later, Brandee had picked up her truck, driven home, changed clothes and was on the way to the ranch buildings. A familiar vehicle was parked beside the barn where they kept the cows and calves who needed special attention. Brandee pulled up alongside and shut off her engine. It ticked, cooling as she stared toward the barn.

What was Shane doing here?

Brandee slid from the truck and entered the barn. She found Shane standing in front of the large enclosure that housed the breeched calf they'd brought into the world. He stood with his arms on the top rail of the pen, his chin resting on his hands.

"Hey," she said softly, stepping up beside him and matching his posture. "What are you doing here?"

"Jimmy said these two are ready to head to the pasture today."

"So you came to say goodbye?" The question didn't come out light and unconcerned the way she'd intended. Anxiety and melancholy weighed down her voice.

"Something like that."

Since Brandee didn't know what to make of his mood, she held her tongue and waited him out. She had nothing new to say and reprising her apology wouldn't win her any points. The silence stretched. She could ask him again why he'd come out to the ranch or she could demand to know why he'd entered her house without asking.

He probably figured he was entitled to come and go anytime he wanted since the land beneath the house belonged to him. Frustration built up a head of steam and she took a deep breath, preparing to unleash it. But before she could utter a word, Shane pushed away from the fence.

"I'd better go." He looked into her eyes, tugged at the brim of his hat in a mock salute and turned away.

Deflated, Brandee watched him go. She couldn't shake the feeling that she'd missed an opportunity to say or do something that would span the gap between them. Which was ridiculous. Shane hated her. She'd tricked him into giving up all claim to his family's land and he would never forgive her.

Her throat closed around a lump and suddenly she couldn't catch her breath. Tears collected and she wiped at the corners of her eyes before the moisture could spill down her cheeks. All at once she was twelve again and hearing the news that her dad was dead. Faced with an equally uncertain future, she'd gotten on her horse and rode off.

She'd ridden all day, tracing the familiar paths that she'd traveled beside her dad. At first she'd been scared. Where would she go? Who would take her in? Her mother's abandonment had hit her for the first time and she'd cried out all her loneliness and loss until she could barely breathe through the hysterical, hiccupping sobs. Once those had passed, she'd been an empty vessel, scrubbed clean and ready to be filled with determination and stubbornness.

She felt a little like that now. Empty. Ready to be filled with something.

Leaving the cow and calf, Brandee headed for the horse barn and greeted her ranch hands. They looked weary, but smiled when they saw her. Apparently the cows had kept them busy, but the night had passed without serious incident. Next she headed to the ranch office to look for Jimmy. Her foreman was staring blankly at the computer, a full mug of coffee untouched beside the keyboard.

"You should head off," she told him, sitting in the only other chair. "I can handle entering the information."

"Thanks. I'm more beat than I thought."

"I'm sorry I wasn't here," she said again, pricked by guilt.

"It's okay. We had Shane's help and everything worked out fine."

"Shane was here all night?" Brandee's heart jumped.

"He came right after answering your phone. About seven or so."

Shane had been helping out at her ranch for over twelve hours? Why hadn't he said anything just now? Maybe he'd been waiting for her to thank him. If she'd known, she would have. Damn. No wonder he'd left so abruptly. She'd screwed up with him again.

But this she could fix. She just needed to come up with a great way to show her appreciation.

Shane wasn't exactly regretting that he'd promised his mother he'd help with Bullseye's centennial party, but he was starting to dread her texts. This last one had summoned him back to the ranch on some vague request for his opinion.

He parked his truck next to her Lexus and took the porch steps in one bound. Entering the house, he spied her in the living room and began, "Mother, couldn't this have waited…" The rest of what he'd been about to say vanished from his mind as he noticed his mother wasn't alone.

"Oh good." Elyse Delgado got to her feet. "You're home."

Shane's gaze locked on Brandee and his heart stopped as if jabbed by an icicle. "What is she doing here?"

"Shane, that's rude. I raised you better than that." Elyse set her hands on her hips and glared at her son. "She came to see me about this disturbing business about her ranch belonging to our family."

"Let me get this straight," Shane began, leveling his gaze on Brandee. "You called my mother to intervene on your behalf?"

"She did no such thing."

"It was Gabe's idea," Brandee said, a touch defensive. "He said you'd listen to her."

It was all too much. First Gabe, now his mother. Shane crossed to the bar and poured himself a shot of scotch. As soon as he lifted it to his lips, he recognized his mistake and set it back down.

"I don't know what you want," he said, dropping two ice cubes into a fresh glass and adding a splash of vodka.

"I brought this as a thank-you for helping out at the ranch the other night." While he'd had his back turned, she'd approached and set a bottle on the bar beside him.

"I don't want your thanks." Mouth watering, he eyed the rare vintage. "Besides, you've ruined scotch for me." He lifted his glass of vodka and took a sip. It took all his willpower not to wince at the taste.

Her lips curved enticingly. "It's a thirty-five-year-old Glengoyne. Only five hundred were released for sale."

"You can't bribe me to like you."

At his aggressive tone, all the light went out of her eyes. Once again she became the pale version of herself, the disheartened woman hunched over an empty glass in the TCC clubhouse.

"Shane Robert Delgado, you come with me this instant." Elyse didn't bother glancing over her shoulder to see if her son followed her toward the French doors leading out to the pool deck. She barely waited until the door had shut behind him before speaking. "How dare you speak to Brandee like that. She's in love with you."

"She tried to cheat us out of our family's land." He tried for righteous anger but couldn't summon the energy. The accusation had lost its impact.

"I don't care. We have more than enough wealth and Bullseye is one of the largest ranches around Royal. Besides, that land was unclaimed for over a hundred years and she paid for it fair and square. If anyone cheated us, it was the person who claimed the land without doing due diligence on the property's heirs."

"So, what do you want me to do? Be friends with her again?"

"I'd like for you to give up feeling sorry for yourself and tell that girl how much she means to you."

"What makes you think she means anything to me?"

"From what I hear, you've been an ornery, unlikable jerk this last week and I think it's because you love that girl and she hurt you."

Shane stood with his hands on his hips, glaring at his mother, while in his chest a storm raged. He did love Brandee, but the emotion he felt wasn't wondrous and happy. It was raw and painful and terrifying.

"Now," his mother continued, her tone calm and practical. "I'm going to go home and you are going to tell that girl that you love her. After which the two of you are going to sit down and figure out a way to get past this whole 'her ranch, our land' thing. Because if you can't, she told me she's going to sell everything and leave Royal. You'll never see her again and I don't think that's what you want."

Shane stared out at the vista behind the ranch house long after the French door closed behind his mother.

When he reentered the house, Brandee was still standing by the bar where he'd left her. "You're still here."

"I came with your mother and she refused to give me a ride back to her house, where my truck is parked." She took a step in his direction and stopped. After surveying his expression for several seconds, her gaze fell to his feet. "Look, I'm sorry about what I did. Whatever you want me to do about the land, I will."

"I don't give a damn about the land and I'm certainly not going to kick you off and take away everything you worked so hard to build." He sucked in a shaky breath.

This was his chance to push aside bitterness and be happy. He'd lost his father before making peace with him and was haunted by that. Losing Brandee would make his life hell.

"What I want more than anything is…" He dug the heels of both hands into his eyes. Deep inside he recognized that everything would be better if he just spoke what was in his heart. Shane let his hands fall to his sides and regarded her with naked longing. "You."

Her head came up. Tears shone in her eyes as she scanned his expression. "Are you sure?" she whispered, covering her mouth and staring at him with a look of heart-breaking hope.

"I am." Shane crossed the distance between them and put his arms around her. For the first time in a week, everything was perfect in his world. "I love you and I can't bear to spend another second apart."

His lips claimed hers, drinking in her half sob and turning it into a happy sigh.

When he finally let her come up for air, she framed his face with her fingers and gazed into his eyes. "Then you're not mad at me anymore?"

"For what? Trying to save your ranch and your dreams?" He shook his head. "I don't think I was ever really angry with you for that. I fell in love with you and when I found the documents I thought you'd been playing me the whole time."

"I should have told you about the blackmail after we made love that first time. I knew then that I was falling for you, but I didn't know how to trust my feelings and then there was that stupid bet." She shook her head.

"You weren't the only one struggling. I lost interest in your land after the tornado tore through Royal. I only agreed to the wager to spend time with you. All along I'd planned to lose."

She stared at him, an incredulous expression spreading across her features. "Then why did you work so hard to win?"

"Are you kidding?" He chuckled. "The bet was for you to fall for me. That was the real prize."

"I love you." Brandee set her cheek against his chest and hugged him tight. "I can't believe I'm saying this, but I'm really glad Maverick blackmailed me. If it hadn't happened, I never would've invited you to move in."

Shane growled. "I'll buy Maverick a drink and then knock his lights out."

"We don't know who he or she is."

"I asked Gabe to investigate. He'll figure out who Maverick is." Shane scooped Brandee off her feet and headed for the master suite. "In the meantime, I'd like to see how you look in my bed."

Brandee laughed and wrapped her arms around his neck. "I'm sure not much different than I looked in mine."

There she was wrong. As he stripped off her lacy top and snug jeans, the shadows he'd often glimpsed in her eyes were gone. All he could see was the clear light of love shining for him. There was no more need for either of them to hide. This was the first step toward a new partnership. In love and in life.

With her glorious blond hair fanned across his pillow and her blue-gray eyes devouring his body while he peeled off his clothes, Shane decided she was the most incredible woman he'd ever known.

He set his knee on the bed and leaned forward to frame her cheek with his fingers. His thumb drifted over her full lower lip. "You're looking particularly gorgeous today."

She placed her hand over his and turned to drop a kiss in his palm. With her free hand, she reached up to draw him down to her. "You're not looking so bad yourself, Delgado."

And when their lips met, both were smiling.

* * * * *

Don't miss a single installment of the
TEXAS CATTLEMAN'S CLUB: BLACKMAIL.
No secret—or heart—is safe in Royal, Texas...

January 2017: THE TYCOON'S SECRET CHILD
by USA TODAY *bestselling author Maureen Child*

February 2017: TWO-WEEK TEXAS SEDUCTION
by Cat Schield

March 2017: REUNITED WITH THE RANCHER
by USA TODAY *bestselling author Sara Orwig*

April 2017: EXPECTING THE BILLIONAIRE'S BABY
by Andrea Laurence

May 2017: TRIPLETS FOR THE TEXAN
by USA TODAY *bestselling author Janice Maynard*

June 2017: A TEXAS-SIZED SECRET
by USA TODAY *bestselling author Maureen Child*

July 2017: LONE STAR BABY SCANDAL
by Golden Heart® Award winner Lauren Canan

August 2017: TEMPTED BY THE WRONG TWIN
by USA TODAY *bestselling author Rachel Bailey*

September 2017: TAKING HOME THE TYCOON
by USA TODAY *bestselling author Catherine Mann*

October 2017: BILLIONAIRE'S BABY BIND
by USA TODAY *bestselling author*
Katherine Garbera

November 2017: THE TEXAN TAKES A WIFE
by USA TODAY *bestselling author Charlene Sands*

December 2017: BEST MAN UNDER THE MISTLETOE
by USA TODAY *bestselling author Kathie DeNosky*

* * *

If you're on Twitter, tell us what you
think of Mills & Boon Desire!

“Could we start again, Tallie?”

He lowered his head, his lips almost touching hers. Then he was kissing her again. This time she felt his hunger and it drew her to him. His tongue moistened her lips before plunging deep inside the cavern of her mouth. She felt his hand at the back of her head, holding her to him as he continued to blow her mind. She heard him groan, then he was backing away, making the heat of the day drop to below freezing.

She wanted his arms around her. She wanted him to kiss her some more, make love to her. She was putty in his arms, encircled by the scent and strength and touch of him. But he was Cole Masters. *The* Cole Masters. Playboy of the western world. He knew what he was doing. He knew a woman’s body as well as his own, so under the circumstances she couldn’t agree. Eventually he would feel her enlarging belly and he would know. Then his professed interest would change into loathing because he would think she’d set him up; that she had gotten pregnant on purpose.

“I suppose we could talk.”

* * *

One Night with the Texan
is part of Lauren Canan’s
the Masters of Texas series.

ONE NIGHT WITH THE TEXAN

BY

LAUREN CANAN

HarperCollins
PUBLISHERS
Since 1817

First Published in Great Britain 2017
By Mills & Boon, an imprint of HarperCollins*Publishers*
1 London Bridge Street, London, SE1 9GF

ISBN: 978-0-263-92807-5

51-0217

Our policy is to use papers that are natural, renewable and recyclable products and made from wood grown in sustainable forests. The logging and manufacturing processes conform to the legal environmental regulations of the country of origin.

Printed and bound in Spain
by CPI, Barcelona

Lauren Canan has always been in love with love. When she began writing, stories of romance and unbridled passion flowed through her fingers onto the page. Today she is a multi-award-winning author, including the prestigious Romance Writers of America Golden Heart® Award. She lives in Texas with her own real-life hero, four dogs and a mouthy parrot named Bird.

She loves to hear from readers. Find her on Facebook or visit her website, www.laurencanan.com.

One

Cole Masters descended the steps of the hotel after his business meeting, bodyguards in tow, and walked toward the waiting limo that would take him to the airport and back to Dallas. The deal he was here to finalize had gone without a hitch. He'd actually been hoping the other party would voice some objections, stir things up a bit. But it had gone down as just another dull and boring merger.

Cole stopped and looked around him. The late-afternoon sun felt good on his face. New Orleans. The Big Easy. It had been years since he'd ventured into the French Quarter with all its laughter and music, but he remembered it fondly. Suddenly something snapped inside and he walked to the waiting car.

"Find out where there's a thrift store. Something like Goodwill."

"Sir?"

"Just do it, please."

The driver disappeared inside the car and returned minutes later with an address.

"Excellent. Can you take me there?"

"Yes, sir."

"Gene, you and Marco are dismissed," he said to the security detail. "The plane is waiting in Concourse D. Use it and fly home."

"Mr. Masters, I don't know if this is such a good idea."

"It'll be fine. Have the pilot back here by tomorrow afternoon."

Cole got into the limo. "Let's go shopping," he told the driver and they were off, leaving the two bodyguards standing at the edge of the street staring after him as though he'd lost his mind. And maybe he had. He wanted to be wild, live in the moment, free of obligations to anyone or anything. Blend in with the other pedestrians and enjoy the few hours he'd allotted himself.

He was tired. Tired of the yes-men who would agree with anything he said. Tired of people using him. Tired of the same corporate demands, the same schemes. He'd grown weary of knowing what questions would be asked and knowing the answers before words ever left the person's mouth. He was especially tired of being hostage to the family's business negotiations. The image he was required to maintain had come to feel like a chain around his neck. He couldn't free himself from it. He couldn't get a reprieve. Consequently he knew he had become hard and bitter. He heard words come from his mouth he didn't recognize as his own. People were starting to distance themselves from him and he didn't blame them. Cynical, suspicious, contemptuous;

he sometimes saw himself through others' eyes and didn't like what he'd become. As the CFO of a successful 8.2 billion-dollar family conglomerate, he took no pride in his accomplishments.

After purchasing jeans, T-shirt, jacket and a pair of scuffed shoes, he dismissed the driver, changed his clothes and hit the streets where hopefully no one would recognize him and subsequently no one would ask anything of him. He would let his soul get lost in the music and the ambience that is only New Orleans.

The man looked every bit as daunting up close as he had from a block away. The hard features of his wickedly handsome face bore the stamp of experience: a complete awareness of the world around him and those in it. Even in the increasing darkness, illuminated only by small twinkle lights strung over the outside tables at the bistro, that much was obvious. The dark, chocolate-brown hair with lighter highlights seemed to accent the golden brown of his eyes. Eyes that tempted her to look closer. To come closer without any rational thought of the consequences.

His lips were full, sensuous, made for seduction. She couldn't stop herself from imagining what it would be like to feel them moving over her own; feel his hands caress her body as the heat between them intensified. His skills in bed would be amazing. How she knew, she couldn't answer. But she knew.

Tallie Finley sensed he would be a formidable opponent. He was tall, powerfully built, dressed in a pair of jeans that had seen better days, a black T-shirt with some faded design on the front and a black jacket that appeared too large—an amazing feat when one considered the breadth of his shoulders. He impressed her as a man who had at one time owned the world and lost it. But not without a fight.

"What's next?" Kate "Mac" McAdams asked, polishing off the last of her glass of wine.

"Beads. We cannot go home without earning our beads," Ginger Barnes stated.

Leaving the stranger behind—again, because it seemed that everywhere she went tonight, he was there—Tallie followed her two friends out to Bourbon Street to experience the "Beads for Boobs" tradition, knowing it was one she would pass up.

Once they'd climbed the stairs to their second-story hotel room, Tallie made her way out to the balcony railing and looked down into the crowds below. The people in the adjacent apartment were already vying for their beads. Guys on the street held up ropes of the shiny multicolored necklaces for display, tempting the girls on the balcony to remove their tops and show all.

Street musicians vied with the jazz and R & B pouring out the open doors of bar-and-grills in a manner you'd think would clash. But not here. Not in this amazing city. The air was full of laughter, drunken wolf whistles, woots and cheers, the flamboyant colors of the clothes and the scent of spices and food cooking over open grills. It was a world like none other and Tallie was front and center. She would miss it when it was time to leave and begin her new research appointment in Texas.

"Don't just stand there," called Ginger, her closest friend and roommate for the past six years during college and grad school. "You've got 'em, girl. Use 'em!"

"Right on," Mac encouraged. She made up the third of the trio. She'd flown to the Big Easy just to celebrate with her best friends.

"I don't think so," Tallie refused. "But don't let me stop you."

"Oh, you won't," Mac answered with a wink. "If you're chicken, I'll go first. I've got to get some of those beads."

"You do know you can buy them in the local stores?"

"Yes, but where's the fun in that?"

With her hips gyrating to the heavy beat reverberating off the walls, the blonde teasingly danced her way out to the balcony edge and began to unfasten her shirt, button by button. The crowd below began to clap and yell even louder.

If you blinked, you missed it. But apparently it was enough because men quickly threw strings of various colored beads up to her. Tallie watched in disbelief as Ginger did the same thing. Then both her friends looked at her.

Tallie shook her head. "I'm gonna pass. This just isn't my thing. And frankly, I'm surprised at the two of you doing something this…bizarre."

"Do you mean to tell me you're going out in the world—about to start your new career with a Ph.D. in your pocket—and you're going to let this amazing memory slip by?" Ginger had to yell to be heard over the crowd and the music. She giggled and downed the rest of her drink.

Tipsy. They were both tipsy and headed to full blown smashed.

"That's exactly what I'm saying," she laughed. No way would she ever be so intoxicated she would shake her boobs in front of a hundred people from a second-story balcony. What had gotten into her studious, straight-laced friends? She could understand blowing off steam after all the hard work they'd done to get their degrees, but still. "Come on. There has to be someplace we haven't been yet." She led the others down the stairs back to the street. "I feel like dancing."

"I could do some dancing," Ginger agreed. "Give me a sultry, sexy tune anytime. Here—" Ginger looped several strands of beads over Tallie's head "—you gotta have some finery if you want to be asked to dance."

"She's right," Mac added as she draped more strands of beads around Tallie's neck. "Now it looks like we're all daring and ready to get down."

Get down? Tallie could only imagine.

"Anybody have a suggestion? I'm guessing this being a Friday night, the better pubs and lounges are full," Ginger sighed.

"I saw lines of people waiting to get in a couple of places on our way back here," Mac added. "But there has to be someplace we can go."

"Wait, wait. I heard some people talking at the bistro about a place on the outskirts of the Quarter they thought was good. The Gator Trap Bar and Grill. It's on Bourbon Street down toward St. Ann. I want to try a drink they mentioned called the Horny Crock." Ginger giggled. "Or the Swamp Itch."

"That sounds bad," the other two chimed in.

"I didn't name them. But I could sure drink one. Or two!"

After agreeing on the next destination, they refreshed their drinks at a street vendor and headed down Bourbon.

If there was a bar in New Orleans moodier and more atmospheric than the Gator Trap, Tallie couldn't imagine what it must be like. The place was dark. There were candles on each table and lights heralding the yuletide season that had ended five months ago still hung over the large mirror behind the bar. They provided the only light. The soulful sax, trumpet, piano and bass coming from the quartet in the back of the room pulled you in.

While Ginger and Mac headed for the ladies' room Tallie slipped onto a seat at the bar.

"What can I get you?" the bartender asked as he removed two dirty glasses from in front of her and wiped the countertop. Tallie gave her order.

"Make that two," said a man to her right as he tossed some bills on the counter. "I couldn't say I've experienced New Orleans without sampling a Swamp Itch."

Laughing, Tallie swung around, her eyes growing wide as she recognized the mysterious man she'd been seeing at various places most of the evening. His golden eyes were gleaming with humor as he acknowledged her. "We seem to have a lot in common."

"You mean like the aquarium?" The first time she'd seen him was as she was leaving the aquarium.

"And the artists on Jackson Square."

"Yes. Some were brilliant, didn't you think? We didn't make it to the paddle boats or the zoo," she said. "Did we?" She wondered if he had gone there.

"No, we didn't. We'll have to save those for next time."

His voice was deep and crusty and well over the line to absolutely sexy. As their drinks were placed before them, he offered a toast. "Here's to new experiences."

"To new experiences." Tallie grinned. This entire evening had definitely been that and more. She'd gone to school here but had never let herself get drawn into the nightlife. Money was tight and she'd taken her studies seriously. Archeology wasn't just a degree for her. It was a passion.

Ginger had been right in her speculation that the

drinks would be good here. Between the warm, humid air filling the room and the man's close presence, Tallie all but guzzled the entire glass.

"Two more," the man said, holding up some money. He laid it on the counter and looked back at Tallie. "Dance with me."

It wasn't a question. But when he took her hand in his much larger one she didn't protest. He led her to the small dance floor, placed her hands on his shoulders and held her close with both arms around her. As expected, he was all hard muscle and iron strength. She was five seven, but the top of her head barely reached his collarbone. Rather than talk, he seemed content to hold her close and move to the soulful music. It worked for her.

She caught a glimpse of Ginger and Mac as they passed by. Both grinned and winked, giving her a thumbs-up. After three songs her mystery man led her back to the bar where their freshened drinks awaited. Like before, she wasted no time emptying her glass.

When the bartender approached, the man ordered for both of them. In French. "You'll like this drink. It's a specialty of the house."

And it was delicious.

"So, do you live here?" she asked, mesmerized by the way his Adam's apple moved when he swallowed his drink. Was there anything not sexy about this guy?

"No. I live…in various places. No one place I'd call home."

"Oh," she replied. "That's sad."

"Sad? You think it's sad to live all over the world?"

"I think its fine to travel on occasion, but you need a home base. At least, I would. A special place you long to return to. Somewhere you can kick off your shoes, turn off the phone, sleep in your own bed and know you're...well...home." Tallie patted his arm. "But don't worry. You'll get through the hard times and find a home. I guarantee it."

"I'll take your word for it." He pursed his lips as though he found her remark funny.

She finished her drink and he ordered two more. "Where is it you call home?"

"Texas. Far northeast. That's where I grew up, where my family lives. I've been going to school at Tulane. In the morning I head home."

The band kicked off another song just as the bartender set the two new beverages on the counter. The sexy stranger watched in obvious amusement while she took a sip. "This is really, really good."

"I'm glad you like it," he said, standing. "Ready?"

"Yes."

The tune was slow, moody and the perfect tempo. He once again enclosed her in his powerful arms and she rested her head against his shoulder and swayed to the music. She could smell his essence, feel the heat of his body. His hands moved up and down her back, easing her still closer. Then he cupped her face, brushing her hair back over her shoulders. She couldn't see much in the dim light, but what she saw was mesmerizing. His amber eyes seemed to glow, but it was his lips that beckoned her. What must it be like to kiss him?

Before the thought could leave her mind he lowered his head and his lips covered hers, warm, gentle, enticing.

Tallie was struck by the soft pliability of his mouth, which was a complete contrast to the hard-muscled body that pressed against her. But the kiss was so brief she wondered if she'd imagined it. He watched her as though looking for any sign she didn't want to be kissed.

She smiled, conveying a silent approval. Apparently satisfied, he again bent his head toward her. "You are so beautiful." His breath was warm against her ear, sending shivers racing across her skin. He returned to her mouth and drew his tongue across her lips, enticing them to open. Without conscious thought, she complied. His tongue swept inside her mouth, deep and decisive. He tasted of a dark spice, with a hint of the drink they'd been enjoying, along with his own unique all-male flavor, and she couldn't get enough.

She gently suckled his tongue and he moaned, filling her mouth, going deep, as though he needed to taste all she had to offer. Tallie had never been kissed like this, with such expertise, such blatant sexuality. It was so far removed from the stilted good-night kisses she'd experienced in the past, and she knew now that she'd never really been kissed. Too soon, his lips left hers as he licked and kissed across her jaw to her earlobe. Then, as if he had no choice, his mouth returned to hers and she was once again sinking in a dizzying storm of emotions as his lips, his scent, the feel of his skin and the power of his body, consumed all rational thought.

He made a slight adjustment and she felt his desire press against her belly. Her body's natural instinct was to push against him. In response, he moaned, low and deep. His lips again covered hers in another deep, drugging kiss laced with pure fire.

The way he held her and kissed her was so primal, so captivating. She could sense his strength even though he held it at bay. He gave her no time to think as he returned to her lips, both hands cupping her face as he pushed any other thought from her mind. Then one hand came around her waist, holding her close while the other entangled in her hair, drawing her head back as the kiss deepened, intensified. She gripped the front of his open jacket and held on as the feel of hot lava ran through her veins, pooling below her belly.

It was amazing how their bodies fit together so perfectly. Her breasts pressed against his broad chest. His muscular thighs and his erection pushed hard against her. A cloud of heat surrounded her and sexual instincts overtook logic as she moved against him. Had they stopped dancing? Were they still on the dance floor?

Tallie didn't want to open her eyes for fear it might break the spell.

Two

The world around them disappeared. Tallie knew only the warmth and taste of this stranger's lips and tongue and the incredible way he made her feel. His scent was pure male. His actions screamed experience. Lots of it. And she never wanted this to end. There was something in his voice, in his body language, that drew her to him. Maybe it was a rush of pheromones? Whatever the cause, it was definitely past time to take some risks in her admittedly sheltered life. This man looked like he'd seen both the worst life had to offer and the best. What tremendous hardships had he weathered? No home. Old clothes that didn't fit. Every time she'd seen him over the course of the evening he'd been alone. She didn't want him to be alone.

Slowly their lips parted and his strong arms surrounded her, holding her close.

"The music stopped," he said, his voice deep and raspy. "I could use some fresh air. How about you?"

When she nodded her agreement he took her by the hand and headed for the door. Outside he continued to lead her down the worn sidewalk, where they were surrounded by revelers who didn't seem to have a care in the world.

Tallie hated for the evening to end. This was one night she would never forget. "Thanks for dancing with me. I love to dance and don't get to do it very often."

"It was my pleasure. Let me walk you back to your hotel."

"Thank you. It's this way." She pointed then frowned. "Oh. No, it's that way." She looked back at him and detected humor in his eyes. "I can't remember how I got here. But I'll figure it out. You don't have to stay out here because of me."

"What's the name of your hotel?"

Surely she could remember. But she finally had to admit she didn't have a clue. "It's something in French." She absently chewed her bottom lip, shook her head and once again looked around where they stood.

"How about coming to my place? We can have a bite to eat, make some tea and I'm sure your memory will come back."

The delicious drinks were clouding her mind. Even outside in the evening air, her head was still spinning.

"You know you really are a very nice man."

"Don't think I'm too nice," he said, taking her hand and leading her down the darkened street. "Not when I have a beautiful woman in my arms."

Since she had never been considered beautiful in her life, his words struck her as funny. Tallie couldn't stop the giggle from leaving her throat.

She felt light on her feet, as though she was floating on air. Then she realized that he'd picked her up and was carrying her in his arms. After that, everything was a blur. A bell dinged and doors opened in front of them. She rested her head on his shoulder thinking what an incredible night it had been.

She caught a glimpse of his face through the darkening shadows. So very male. The deep indentions on both sides of his mouth seemed to make him that much more delicious. But it was those golden eyes that consumed her.

She had a vague realization that they were in a private apartment, although there was no light in the room. He set her on her feet.

"I'll put that tea on," he said and stepped back from her.

Tallie stepped forward, her hands running down the front of his shirt. Standing on her tiptoes, she placed her lips on his. The passion between them surged.

He pulled back. "Be very careful of what you ask for, darlin'. You're playing with fire and you're likely to get burned. I don't do relationships."

"What do you do?" Tallie was acting out of character, but it felt good. For the first time in her life she was actually flirting with a man.

"I think I'd better make the tea."

"Do you really want tea?"

He stared at her in silence. She had her answer and suddenly she felt foolish. She could feel the blush crawl up her neck and cover her face. "I'm not looking for a relationship, either," she said, turning away and picking up her purse. "And I know when I'm not wanted. Thanks again for the dance. Good night."

Tallie walked toward the door.

Before she could open it he was in front of her, ensuring the door remained closed.

"Where are you going?"

"Back to my hotel. I'm just having a little trouble remembering where it is." The humiliation burned inside like acid, acting as anti-venom for the passion she'd felt only moments ago. It stopped her from doing anything else stupid but couldn't reverse the damage already done. She should never have accepted his offer to dance. "I'll get a taxi."

"And tell them to go where?"

He took her purse from her hand and tossed it behind them on the sofa. Then he picked her up again and carried her to a bedroom, setting her down gently next to the bed. His lips found hers again in a smoldering kiss. She was dimly aware he was unbuttoning her blouse. She sensed coolness against her back and a freedom from any restrictions and hazily realized he had removed her blouse and her bra. She ran her arms across the cool, silken sheets. The scent of incense hung heavy in the air around them. With one fluid movement his jacket and T-shirt hit the floor and she heard the zipper on his jeans.

His body was magnificent and Tallie knew they were about to cross a line, one that seemed to be growing blurrier by the second. If she didn't say no immediately, he was going to make love to her.

As if sensing her apprehension, he raised his head, watching her through the dim glow of the subdued lighting, his eyes almost black with desire.

Her gaze moved over his face, finally coming to rest on his mouth.

"Are…are you married?" she whispered, running one finger across his bottom lip.

"No." He lightly bit the tip of her finger before sucking it gently into his mouth and then releasing it. A shot of pure heat speared through her. "I'm going to make love to you. But I need to know you're okay with this."

"Yes," she said. More than he might ever know. Any other time her timidity would step in and she wouldn't think of admitting such a thing. She wasn't sure if it was the alcohol she'd consumed or the man.

"I was hoping you would say that."

Bracing his weight on both his arms and one knee, he hovered over her, kissing her cheek and trailing his teeth across her jawline, causing a surge of heat to flood her lower regions.

Oh, yes. She was very sure she wanted this. To hell with caution and rational thinking. She reached out to touch his face and felt the coarse five-o'clock shadow. In his arms she ached, overwhelmed with the feeling she was incomplete, needing him to make her whole. He kissed the palm of her hand then proceeded to suckle her fingers one finger at a time. His heavy body settled over hers. She felt his erection, hard and unyielding against her core, and heard him emit a deep growl. Pure liquid heat ran through her veins and Tallie was lost. Her head fell back on the pillow as the world spun. She pressed against him out of pure instinct, needing more, her body demanding it.

This incredible man was about to make love to her. And she was going to let him. A complete stranger. She'd gone around the bend to insanity. She inhaled a deep breath, the need for him destroying the last of her common sense. Her body was on fire. Was she dreaming? Or was this her prince charming in disguise? In this moment it didn't matter. She was his. And she really couldn't imagine anything better.

He stripped her of her jeans and panties in short order. She heard his own jeans hit the floor and then he was back. The strands of gold, blue and red beads fell around her breasts. They felt cold compared to the heat that was raging through her. His hand slid down over her stomach and farther, testing to ensure she was ready for him. He adjusted his body over hers. She knew a moment of panic as she noted the immense size of him. She wouldn't be able to compete with his overpowering strength. She suddenly felt small and helpless as she realized she would have no control.

"This is your last chance to say no," he told her, as if reading her mind, his voice both deep and hoarse with emotion. His breathing was shallow. She felt the blunt end of his sex positioned at her core. "Once I'm inside you, I can't guarantee I'll be able to stop."

All Tallie could do was nod her head and hope her instincts about this man were right. She wanted this. Just once in her life she wanted to be with a man who could give her the experience she'd previously only heard about. Just once.

In what seemed to be slow motion, his lips again descended, finding and suckling her breast. His large hand kneaded the other, gently pinching her swollen nipple, making her arch her back as she swelled under his touch. Then he cupped her head in his hands, as though holding her where she needed to be. She inhaled the raw scent of him, lost in the heady potency that surrounded him. She felt her body relax, her mind clear of all thought, accepting what was to come without any thought of denying him what she knew he was about to take. The breath left her lungs on a sigh as the world grew dark and he was all that existed.

He pushed inside and the last remnant of her mind disappeared. Even though he went slowly, careful not to hurt her, she'd never been filled to such a degree. She hadn't realized how muscular he was; how much bigger his body felt against hers. She inhaled a shuddering breath. As if understanding, he stopped.

"Take it easy, hon," he whispered against her ear. "Just let yourself relax."

Seconds passed and the pressure turned to incessant need. When she pushed against him, he began to move. Deeper. Harder. It sent her spiraling and, almost instantaneously, with a cry, she exploded. He held her close, encouraging, speaking words that made her climax go on and on.

She heard the foil packet being ripped open and seconds later he returned to her. He raised her hands above her head and kissed her neck and breasts as he entered her and once again began to move. This time more forcefully, almost urgently, his strength obvious in the way he held her; the way he took her. He pounded into her until it was both too much and yet not enough, bringing her to the edge then backing off, over and over until she wanted to scream.

She whimpered her frustration.

"What is it you want, sweetheart?"

"Please," she whispered, straining against him. "It's so hot."

The excessive heat between her legs burned and there was only one person who could give her relief.

He began to move again and this time it was with one intention. She became separated from reality, her body one with his. She couldn't open to him enough as he fulfilled her every need, bringing her to orgasm then joining her. The groan he made as he found his release was the sexiest sound she'd ever heard.

He fell to her side and pulled her next to him, her head on his shoulder. She experienced the feeling of a warm, cozy cocoon, his heavy arms around her, holding her close. Later in the night she was awakened and, once again, knew mindless passion. Then, once again, she slept.

"Tallie!" a woman's voice called out, followed by a knock on the door. "Tallie, where are you?"

She opened her eyes and looked around the room at the strange surroundings. "I'm in here," she responded in a sleepy voice. The door opened and Ginger and Mac sailed into the room.

"When you never came back to the hotel, we got pretty worried," Mac said, walking around the room. The soft morning sunlight attempted to enter through the edges of the lush, thick draperies. "Then early this morning some man called from your phone and left a message saying you were okay and where we could find you. He must have seen our panicky texts."

Tallie sat up, immediately realizing she had on no clothes. Covering herself with the sheet, she rubbed her eyes and yawned. "What time is it?"

"Almost eight, you wicked, lucky girl." Ginger smiled and winked at Tallie. "Who would have ever thought that, of the three of us, Miss Quiet Mouse would be the one to get lucky?"

"Eight…in the morning?"

"Yep. We need to get back to the hotel and pack. Our flight is at noon," Mac reminded her. "And you will have two hours to tell us every naughty luscious tidbit of last night's little escapade." She tossed Tallie her clothes. "And this is one you're not getting out of."

"Are you going to see him again?" Ginger asked. "I couldn't see him very well in the bar. Is he cute?"

Tallie didn't know what to say. Cute was not an adjective she would use to describe him. Sixteen-year-old boys were cute. This was a man in every sense of the word. As far as his looks, she hadn't gotten a very good look at him—everywhere they met, it had been dark. Would she recognize him again? Possibly. Possibly not. "I would have to say he was handsome," she told Ginger. "And definitely sexy."

"Yeah, we kinda got that."

"He had a sexy voice when he called," Mac added.

As Tallie moved to get out of bed she felt sore in places she never knew she had. She smiled to herself. He had been an exceedingly patient and proficient lover. Amazing. Just as she put her feet on the plush carpet a sight caught her eye. A folded store receipt. On the back was written "You are the best. Thanks, C—"

"What is that?" Ginger asked.

"Did he write you a note?" Mac asked, walking toward the bed. "I hope you got his phone number!"

Still staring at the receipt in her hand she slowly shook her head, still stunned that she'd lost all control last night.

"I don't even know his name."

Three

Three months later

Tallie looked around her at the open farmland extending as far as her eyes could see. A river snaked through the golden, knee-high wheat, feeding huge trees that grew sporadically in giant clumps near its edge. An old trapper's shack that a sneeze could probably blow down sat under the branches of a giant, towering oak. To the east were cliffs, their dark red composite a vivid contrast to the white-gold of the wheat. Dark impressions on the face of the cliffs gave indication of caves, which could have at one time been home to ancient people.

It had taken her an enormous effort to get the huge bulldozers and other machinery to shut down on this site. But she'd finally ascertained which man was the head of this operation and waved the court document under his nose. Now, with the motors of the huge machines turned off, only the sound of the wind blowing through the wheat and the occasional call of a bird remained.

Somehow in this mass of timber, cliffs and cultivated soil that went on for miles she was supposed to find confirmation that an ancient people had, at one time, existed. A tribe of Native Americans never referenced in any record book in history. Never mentioned by scholars or spoken of in the homes of the people. Except one: her paternal grandmother's. The day before she'd died.

When a person so dear to her heart asked Tallie to find her people and, with trembling hands, opened her palm and dropped a tiny token into hers, Tallie had no other option but to promise she would do as asked. A sense of calm had overtaken her *ipokini* and, with a smile, she'd handed Tallie one other item: a doeskin about two feet square, rolled and tied with a braid of leather.

On the inside of the doeskin was a crude, hand-drawn map. One large area, marked in faded red powder, must relate to what her grandmother had asked her to find. It encompassed an area from a river on the west where the water washed the roots of a massive oak tree to just beyond cliffs to the east. At various points inside the red circle were rudimentary images similar to those found in caves. A horse. A deer. A warrior with a lance. A teepee village. At the top, a cryptic design indicated mountains. Across the bottom the word *Oshahunntee.* The tribe of no existence. Like many of the words taught by her grandmother, it was also unknown to all but a few.

Her *ipokini* was not a wealthy woman. Her gold was encased in a heart as big as Texas and spread among all the people she'd helped for almost one hundred years.

For her to give Tallie something that must have been so special to her was a great honor. Tallie had promised her then—and in her heart now—that she wouldn't let her down.

She had been surprised when her boss, the chief curator at the museum where she'd worked the past three months, not only okayed her request to do this search but had, in fact, become quite excited when she'd showed him the map. Instead of making her take a leave, Dr. Sterling had endorsed it as an approved dig for the museum, though Tallie would have to cover her own personal expenses. Dr. Sterling had even been able to point her to the part of Texas the map seemed to describe. Now, with the court's backing to explore the site, only one thing might stand between her and discovery. She was pregnant.

Dr. Sterling had voiced his concern about her condition and made her promise to check in regularly. He couldn't spare another associate to send with her and had made it clear she would be on her own. She'd convinced him she was fine. And she was. Or soon would be. Beginning her third month of pregnancy, she was almost over the morning sickness. At least, she hoped so.

Discovering she was pregnant from her night in New Orleans had been a life-changing moment. Her memories of the encounter were so hazy, it was almost as if she'd been in a blackout. But she was left with a very real reminder of what had happened. She had no hope of finding the father, and initially, her dreams of the future had gone out the window. She couldn't imagine traveling the world on archeological expeditions with a baby. Yet as the idea of having one settled into her mind and filled her heart, she made peace with it. Other single mothers worked and raised their children. She could, too. Admittedly, she would have to halt travel to remote sites until the baby was old enough, but just because she didn't have a regular nine-to-five didn't mean she'd have to throw away years of study just to be a mother.

But right now she would concentrate on the present and take the future one step at a time. She was healthy and happy and determined to find the proof of the lost tribe as she'd promised her grandmother she would. At least, she had to try.

A chill went down her spine at the thought that the lost tribe might actually prove to have existed. But why had her grandmother waited until she was dying to tell her? And where had the map been all these years? She'd spent a lot of time at her *ipokini*'s house as a child and had never seen it or anything like it. Tallie could only suppose her grandmother had her reasons and all she could do now was accept that some things would never be explained.

Clutching the court-issued injunction in her hand, she took another look around. The paperwork required the owner of the property to halt all operations for ninety days so that she could search for relics. She would concentrate on the present and take the future one step at a time.

Suddenly the wind kicked up, blowing her long hair in every direction. She fought to catch it at the back of her head and then pulled a band from the pocket of her jeans and secured it in a rough knot on her crown. The sound of a helicopter in the distance shattered the silence. It was coming toward her and not wasting any time, soon landing a safe distance from where she stood between the old trapper's hut and the river. She didn't have to be told who it was. Cole Masters, billionaire eight-times-over and owner of this land, had arrived. Dr.

Sterling had mentioned she might receive some resistance from this man, whose reputation for doing things his way preceded him.

The man who emerged from the chopper was big. Broad shoulders, his biceps bulging beneath the rolled-up sleeves of the white-silk dress shirt. A blue tie had been loosened at the neck to accommodate the unbuttoned top of his shirt. Honey-brown eyes were emphasized by dark lashes. His short, dark brown hair and his thick beard gave him the look of a warrior. His chiseled jaw was set for a fight. His full lips were drawn into a line of disapproval and those eyes were fixed on her as he marched to where she stood. So this was the great Cole Masters. Alive and in person.

In spite of her professional approach to matters such as these, the closer he came, the more she felt her years of study and experience fading to nothing. On that realization, she took a deep breath and concentrated on why she was here. This dig was a one-shot attempt to prove something incredible. She wouldn't allow herself to be swayed by his sex appeal or intimidated by his rumored bitterness and arrogance. She'd somehow maintain the professional attitude the situation called for.

"Cole Masters," he introduced himself, extending his hand.

"Dr. Tallie Finley, archaeologist with the North Texas Natural History Museum," she said as she accepted his hand. It was twice the size of hers and exceedingly warm. A slight electric current tingled between their grips, traveling some distance up her arm. She could tell by his frown he'd felt it, too. She quickly withdrew her hand.

"It's *you*." His brows raised in surprise and his demeanor became less in your face.

"Ah…yes. I'm me and I'm guessing this is what you want to see." Something about him seemed vaguely familiar but she couldn't quite place him.

She handed him the court document. "It allows an intrusive and extensive survey of the area indicated on the map as presented to the court."

"*You* are Dr. Finley?"

Something had suddenly removed the harsh tone from Mr. Masters's voice and replaced it with a slight hint of congeniality. Because she didn't know what had caused the change, she was more off kilter than when she'd initially faced his hostility. Good grief. Had she failed to button her blouse? Was she wearing the oatmeal she'd had for breakfast?

"I am."

"Dr. Finley…" he said again, and handed the paper back to her. He cleared his throat. "Do you see that heavy equipment over there?" He swung around and nodded at the bulldozers, cement trucks and other pieces of large equipment she couldn't name. "We are in the middle of a project. The planning alone has taken years. These guys are here today to pour the foundations, all twenty-five of them. As you can see, the roughed-in plumbing is already installed. How are we supposed to do our work if you're in the same area looking for whatever you think might be there?"

Her eyes were drawn to his lips. So full. So enticing. She swallowed hard. She again had that vague feeling of having met this man before but the only face that came to mind was the mysterious stranger who had seduced her. No way could the two men be the same.

"I understand this might be an inconvenience for you, Mr. Masters. But the reason I'm here is equally important. Possibly more so." He drew back, shaking his head. "What I'm seeking could potentially be under the spot where you plan to pour concrete, which would be a problem. If there are artifacts there, they could be damaged by your construction. If you'll tell your workers to move their equipment out of my work area, I'll conduct my research as expeditiously as I can to get out of your way."

"That's it?" His eyes locked with hers and she felt a tingle run down her spine. Where had she seen those eyes before? Suddenly a feeling of deja vu ran rampant. "We halt our operation and get out of *your* way? On *my* land." His frustration was coming back. She could see the muscles in his jaw working overtime. Something about his voice touched a nerve. She'd swear she'd heard it before, which was ridiculous. She didn't run in the same circles as billionaires.

"I would assume the judge knew who owned this land when he signed the order. I would have to say he's probably not going to change his mind. If you should decide to take your case before a higher court, it would take longer than I'll be here." Unless she found proof an ancient civilization existed, which would make the ninety-day limit moot, but she would be throwing gas on the fire to bring that up now.

"Yeah. He knows me. And I know that judge. My attorneys will handle this."

"Of course. That's entirely your right." The man sure didn't mind throwing his weight around. She'd never seen a court-ordered, ninety-day search permit overturned. But to smile, as she wanted to do, might provoke him further. She fought the urge. Neither of them needed that. Just the fact that he was here and causing a delay was bad enough.

He called out to one of his men. "Harvey, this is Dr.

Finley." His eyes flashed to hers then back to his foreman. "She has a map detailing an area in which she needs to work and has been given the authority to do so by the court. Temporarily. I want the area flagged. Call Michaels at the land surveyor's office, if need be."

Harvey didn't look at all convinced he could do as asked, but he wasn't going to tell his boss that. "Yes, sir."

"And you'll have to move the equipment. Find a rise, in case we get a storm, and make sure it's all outside of her...*work* area. The concrete trucks need to go back to Latham's Equipment." He received another nod from his foreman. "Just what is it, exactly, you're looking for, *Doctor*?" His hands rose to his hips. "Some kind of Indian relics?"

"Something like that." It was a heck of a lot more than that. But because of his in-your-face attitude, she was hesitant to enlighten him further. He wouldn't care and it was her experience the more a land owner knew, the worse they could make it for the archaeology team. "Actually, I'm looking for artifacts establishing my own family line. The recovery of such relics will be of great scientific value to the Native American Historical Society as well as to the National Historical Association. Do you keep cattle here? I need to know so I can take precautions if the answer is yes," she continued.

"No," he replied. "No cows or any other livestock allowed on this part of the property."

He stared at her. His eyes narrowed as he looked, really looked, at her face. He couldn't stop his eyes from roaming from her eyes and lips down her body, all the way to her toes. He ran one hand over his lower face as her identity confirmed in his mind. It hit him like a blow to his solar plexus. His expression changed to a smile he tried to hold in check.

Tallie Finley was the beautiful woman he'd spent the night with in New Orleans. No doubt.

Apparently she hadn't recognized him. Yet. He currently wore a beard and was dressed in a suit and tie. He was certain she had a completely different perspective of him now than she had then. But he knew her. He would never forget those beautiful, voluptuous curves, that stunning face, the long, silky, ebony hair and that deep Southern drawl.

She was the vision he'd dreamed about and thought about for almost three months. While striking, in the darkness her eyes hadn't been such a vivid green. Now they blazed emerald fire.

"Your eyes are so green." It just came out. And right now they were spitting green daggers.

She stared like he'd gone daft then turned away, suddenly angry. "Is the color of my eyes of great importance?"

"No. No. I just...it surprised me, that's all."

"Yeah, well, a lot of things surprise me."

Yeah, Cole thought. And she was going to face a whopper of a surprise just around the corner. He would wait to see how long it took her to figure it out.

She reached up and pulled the band from her hair. With a quick shake and a finger-comb it was floating on the breeze like a dark, wispy cloud.

Damn, she was a beautiful woman. Tall and slender. Still a head shorter than his six foot four, she appeared both fragile and resilient. He had firsthand, intimate knowledge she possessed both those qualities. Her eyes demanded respect. Her hair was long, past her waist, and so black it looked blue under the direct sunlight. He could see the determination in her stance; in the way she carried herself. High cheekbones and those brilliant green eyes stood out in her slightly bronzed face. A man could get lost in those eyes. Easily. But he saw the determination in them. She wasn't here on a fool's mission. She would fight for the right to work on this dig and uncover evidence of her Native American ancestors' lost tribe. How did a man compete with something like that? *If* she was legit. If she was really here to find artifacts.

"Is there anything more I can do for you, Mr. Masters?"

He stepped toward her until less than a foot separated them. "That is the question."

He was close enough that he could feel the warmth of her body.

She stepped back. "If not, I need to get busy."

He'd never thought he would see her again, although he'd hoped to. He'd kicked himself a hundred times for not getting her name and contact information before he'd left that Saturday morning. He began to relax. With her hair piled up on top of her head at first and the green coveralls that hid every luscious curve, he was surprised he'd recognized her. But he had and she was here. His project was going to be delayed for a while but now it had a silver lining.

He could only stare as she began to work her locks into a long, silken braid. Suddenly it felt as though they were the only two people on earth. In this setting it wasn't hard to imagine. The sight caused every cell in his body to spring to readiness. A liquid heat ran rampant through him, pooling in his groin. It was New Orleans on steroids. And he wanted her until it hurt.

Images raced through his mind; images of her in bed,

sheets tangled from their hot, sensual lovemaking. On her face were satisfaction and the need for more of him, which he gladly gave. Her ebony hair draped over his chest as he held her hot, damp body in his arms, fighting to slow his breathing. Tallie left the rest of the women he'd known in the dirt. How long until he could hold her in his arms again? There was no thought of never.

Cole took a deep breath and blew it out. He needed to push his wayward thoughts to the back of his mind and get away from this woman with all possible speed. Making a concentrated effort, he snapped himself out of the daydream. *Get a grip.*

"I—" He cleared his throat. "I'll leave you to your work." He nodded, turned and walked back toward the chopper, his clarity of mind shot to hell.

He hadn't gone ten feet before he stopped and turned to face her. "Have you ever been to New Orleans, Dr. Finley?"

She squinted her eyes and tilted her head, no doubt finding the question odd.

"It's where I went to school. So, yes. I spent six years there. Why?"

He shrugged. "You just look like someone I knew once who lived there." He planted the seed. Now to see how long it would take her to come to figure things out.

A long moment passed between them before he turned toward the helicopter, boarded, started the massive engine, lifted off and flew away.

"Thanks for welcoming me to the neighborhood," she muttered to herself as she turned toward her old, battered Ford. What an odd man.

And she couldn't get over the fact that her mind was screaming, *You know him!* It was an absurdity. He traveled the world, was worth billions with a capital B, while she worked in the dirt and had barely a thousand bucks in the bank. Still…she couldn't seem to shake the feeling they had met before. And what was with that question about New Orleans? She'd gone to school there but she surely would remember if she had ever met him. She never ventured far from campus and knew very few that weren't associated with the college.

In fact, the only real outing she'd had was when she, Mac and Ginger had gotten together after graduation. She'd met a handsome stranger that night. But no way could that man have been Cole Masters. The stranger was nice and showed no arrogance at all. If the stranger had even one penny for every hundred thousand Masters had, he would be doing all right. He could even buy himself some new clothes. They were almost the same size. No doubt that's what kept bugging her. Pushing the thoughts from her mind she began to unpack the old Ford wagon. Maybe it would come to her eventually.

It took her a while to unpack. Most of her things could be stored inside the trapper's cabin. It was on the land covered by the court order, so she had no qualms using it. If Cole Masters didn't like it, she could always set up her tent. A closer inspection confirmed the one-room shack was sturdier than she'd originally thought. It contained an old wood-burning stove and a twin-size bed. The mattress, once white, was now the color of the dirt outside and so old it had been stuffed with peanut shells and cotton. There were holes in the roof and floor and the only window didn't have any panes. She had camped in worse. She just couldn't remember when. Her sleeping bag would provide some insulation and the rusty legs of the bed would keep her off the floor, so there was that at least.

She was used to roughing it, but her pregnancy added an extra wrinkle to the situation. Before she'd come here, her doctor had given her the green light—she was in excellent health and should be fine to do her job. But he'd warned her to take care of herself. The cabin would do for now, but she was going to have to keep a close eye on how she was feeling and make sure she didn't overdo it.

By the time she had unpacked most of her things, the bulldozers had been moved and an area had been marked off by little red flags. It was actually a larger area than she'd first imagined. She would have to thank Mr. Masters for that the next time he came snooping, which, if he was like other land owners, should be in about three days.

Tallie eyed the area to determine the best place to start. Over toward the cliffs, she decided. She would map out a grid and go from there.

She returned to her car for the last of the gear. Her old tent was on the bottom of a pile of equipment. She probably should drag it out and spend some time patching the rips and holes. She hadn't taken time to patch it after the last dig when the wind had blown it into a huge cactus patch. But she was anxious to start the dig. She would leave it for now and just use the old trapper's cabin. It was easier to ask for forgiveness than permission anyway. If Mr. Masters wanted her out of the ramshackle building, all he had to do was tell her.

She picked up the bolt of orange string, a handful of wooden stakes and a hammer, and chose a spot most favorable. She wouldn't finish before the sun set, but every step she could complete today would be one step closer to finding the proof of the lost tribe for her grandmother and the faster she could get back to the museum.

She wasn't used to working alone, but the silence was nice. She just hoped Masters found other things to occupy his time than coming out to bother her. She didn't need the veiled threats—or the sexual magnetism that made her heart speed up and her rational thinking, for which she was known, take a high dive off the nearest cliff.

With a sigh she hammered the first stake into the ground. Then another. By sunset she'd marked off an area of about one hundred and twenty square feet, and divided it into smaller sections. She'd been able to examine the first four grids. Tomorrow she would set up the sifting box and, with shovel in hand, she would be on her way to discovery. She hoped.

Grabbing her tools, she returned to the trapper's cabin, dropped the hammer and remaining stakes on the floor just inside the door and stared at the bed, such that it was. It was going to be a long night.

Cole walked from the helipad toward the house, still in disbelief, livid that Tallie Finley's dig was allowed to supersede his project and slow things to a crawl. It was ironic that on the day...*the day*...they were to pour the foundation she had received her permit from Judge Mitchell and shut Cole down. Unbelievable. Even more incredible was that he'd checked with his lawyers eight ways from Sunday and there was nothing he could do about the court order. The only silver lining was that he would have the opportunity to get to know this irresistible woman much better.

Since the day he'd left college his efforts had focused on company business, improving and doing his part to make Masters Corporation, LLC, one of the leading real-estate companies in Texas if not the entire United

States. Days turned into nights that turned back into days as he'd worked. He'd flown countless miles, attended innumerable meetings. But it had always been for the family business; he'd never ventured out on his own. This project to build a world-class corporate retreat where Fortune 500 companies could send their executives for training and relaxation was special in that it was his. It was his chance to accomplish something important without company backing. He would prove his worth to his brothers and, more importantly, to himself. At the age of thirty-four he would finally be able to say, *I did that.* It wasn't about the money or acclaim. It was the sense of accomplishment and the pride.

The planning had taken years but the end was in sight. The announcement and a brochure detailing the project had gone out to the business leaders and entrepreneurs on almost every continent in the world. An invitation to tour the site had been sent to several prominent CEOs in the U.S. with the hope they would invest in the project. How uncharacteristically naive of him to think at this stage nothing would go wrong.

He'd never seen it coming. Just like before, when he'd found out about his ex-wife's cheating, he'd once again been caught with his pants down. If anyone had told him a month ago that a one-hundred-and-twenty-five-pound woman could shut down a multimillion-dollar project with a piece of paper and some orange string, he would have laughed in their face. He wasn't laughing now. He had to wonder if she was a part of a bigger plan by one of his corporate enemies to sabotage his project. If not, he had to be open to the possibility that she was working on her own in an attempt to gain some of his wealth. Did she know who he was and was she only acting a part? He'd learned three years ago just how deceptive a woman could be.

Even after the sheer hell he'd been through with his ex-wife, until today he thought he'd heard and seen it all. False pregnancy claims, varying attempts at blackmail. But claiming to look for some relic on the same spot as his future lodge was a new one. This must have taken some planning. How much was she being paid to sabotage his project and who was paying her to do it? What was the full game plan? Was she planning to fake an injury, as well? Had she set him up in New Orleans? Or was she legit?

As soon as he stepped into the house at the Circle M Ranch, he grabbed his cell and called the head of the security division at the home office in Dallas.

"Jonas? Yeah. I want someone checked out. I want to know when she lost her first baby tooth, the names of her friends in second grade, who she dated in college… I want you to turn over every rock no matter how small. Her name is Dr. Tallie Finley. She's supposedly an archeologist with the North Texas Natural History Museum. That's all I have."

"That should be plenty. I'll get right on it," said the voice on the other end of the line. "When I finish, I'll notify you by email?"

"Call me as soon as you have the full report. You can reach me at this number."

"Consider it done."

Cole hung up and slid his phone into his pocket. There had to be more to this than just a search for artifacts. No, she had to be after something more than a relic. It would be interesting to see what it was and how she went about trying to attain it.

For the first time in years, he thought of Gina. When

they were newly married, he had trusted her, and she'd had his father's blessing. But less than a year into the marriage the warning signs had begun to appear. Lying. Disappearing for an afternoon or evening, money in her private account—tens of millions of dollars—vanishing at an alarming rate. His father's odd advice to not worry about it had sent Cole scurrying to the company's head of security, who'd provided a report that told it all. She was involved with another man. And she was pregnant. The father of the baby remained a mystery. Cole had had reason to doubt it was his.

But then tragedy had struck and that unborn baby had never gotten to see the world. Because he'd died with Gina the fateful night she'd spun out of control on a rain-soaked road, her car going over a steep embankment and exploding in flames at the bottom of a deep ravine. The night Cole had told her to get out.

There was just something about all the coincidences surrounding Dr. Finley's arrival that reminded him of his late wife's deception. Was Dr. Finley trying to play him, too? He damn sure didn't want to believe something bad about his new mystery woman, but neither did he intend to sit back and watch her destroy his plans.

Four

Three days after meeting her face to face, Cole still couldn't get over how Dr. Finley had taken over his land. He knew she'd settled into the trapper's cabin, and he was fine with that. The rough conditions in there would probably hasten her departure. He'd sent ranch hands out to spy on her at varying times. The reports were all the same. During the day, she worked. At night, she soaked in the river then disappeared into the little shack. They had to be missing something. Maybe she was sneaking around at night, looking for who knew what. He decided he would go out to assess the situation for himself.

Frustrated, Cole watched her through the lenses of his binoculars and confirmed what the ranch hands had reported. She worked from sunup to sundown, went for a dip in the cool waters of the river—he had trouble taking his eyes off her voluptuous curves—and finally trudged back to the old trapper's cabin where she presumably slept through the night. She was a damned hard worker, he'd give her that. But after three days of this nonsense, it appeared as though she'd found nothing, at least nothing she cared to share with him, and his heavy equipment still sat idle.

The next day his head of security called with the findings about Dr. Finley. Nothing out of the ordinary and nothing he could use to get rid of her. There was not one single thing she'd ever done that was suspicious. No black mark against her. Not even a gray one. She'd worked to put herself through school. Her grades had been top-notch. She'd made the dean's list in her junior and senior years of college before going for her master's degree then her doctorate at Tulane University. Her mother's family was Irish. Her father was Choctaw. Her mother taught seventh and eighth grade. Her dad had been an archeologist before he was killed on a dig in Brazil four years ago. Dr. Finley had broken up with her boyfriend, an English literature professor, a year before.

But how could anyone in this day and age be that squeaky clean? How was it possible?

He zeroed in on how she'd gone to Tulane. New Orleans was a city Cole loved. In fact, the night he'd spent there was the first time in years he'd taken the opportunity to enjoy the city. Then, out of all the people who swarmed into the French Quarter on that particular Friday night, he had ended up spending it with the most beautiful woman he'd ever set eyes on. That was one night, one memory, he would not soon forget. He would have never believed the next time he saw the woman she would be on his property, calling a halt to his pet construction project. It was uncanny. The chances were a billion to one. But as delighted as he was to see her again and this time to learn her name, he still would not wait ninety days to get his project back on track. Something had to give and it wouldn't be him.

Maybe if he talked to her, reined in his temper and kept it unemotional, just business, he could make her understand how many problems she was causing. And there was no time like the present. He jumped into a pickup and headed back to the site. He easily spotted her and walked to within a couple of feet of where she worked, moving the soil with a little brush. She glanced at him briefly in acknowledgment and continued to work, all but ignoring him. She was working about halfway through the grid, slowly, methodically, gently raking the dirt then brushing over anything that might be promising.

On hands and knees, she was leaning forward over her digging spot, her butt in the air. He wouldn't be a man if he didn't take another long look. She had a damn fine backside. Her hair was pulled up into a messy knot that made her look sexy as hell. Her face was smudged with dirt. He didn't know many women who would still look attractive in such a state. But it showed the commitment on Dr. Finley's part, which was something he had to admire.

"Dr. Finley, how are you doing today?"

"Just fine," she said, eying him suspiciously.

He cleared his throat. "I understand your dig, your search, is important to you." Admittedly he wasn't used to talking to someone's backside. "But the fact is, while you are out here playing with your rake in the dirt, I'm losing thousands of dollars a day."

"I'm sorry. That's too bad."

She didn't sound sorry. "Well, the thing is, I need to finish what I've started."

"If postponing your project is costing that much money, perhaps you should move it to another location," she suggested matter-of-factly, never taking her eyes off the section of ground she was working on.

"Impossible," he snorted. "I already have the plumbing roughed in. The forms are set. Other aspects of my project feed off of this location. It isn't that easy to just pick up and move."

"And if I find evidence next to one of your twenty foundations, that foundation will have to be torn out. You only have to stand down twelve weeks, maybe less." She looked up and caught his gaze. "Surely your business dealings have taught you that sometimes you don't get your way."

Cole could feel the anger rising in his chest. Even more frustrating, he couldn't escape the sheer physical pull of attraction he had for this woman.

"We have every reason to believe there may be remnants of an ancient civilization here," she continued. "I wasn't around several thousand years ago to warn them that in the twenty-first century someone would want to build…whatever you're building here."

She picked up a soft-bristle brush and began fanning over a small area.

"Dr. Finley," he mumbled. "There are museums full of paintings and crafts of all kinds. Why is this any different? What's so damned important that it's costing me a ninety-day delay? If what you're looking for is thousands of years old, what's another three months until you find them? It. Whatever you're searching for. Or is there something you're not telling me?"

Suddenly she dropped the little brush and stood. Pulling off her gloves, she slapped them against her jeans-covered leg. "I've already told you why you need to stop construction. Twice, if I recall. Why would you think I'm hiding something? What? Do you think I'm digging for gold? Some hidden Spanish treasure? A cache stashed by Jesse James?"

Now she was being snide.

"I assure you I'm not. Any of those things would be turned over to you immediately to do with as you pleased. Well, you and the IRS. And the longer you stand here harassing me, the longer I remain idle, causing further delays. Believe me when I say it's irritating for both of us."

"Fine." He glared at her. "Have it your way. But don't expect any help from me or my employees." With that said, he turned and walked back to his truck.

A cool breeze came in through the broken window. She hoped it continued through the night. But as she got into the tiny bed she heard a scurrying of animal feet underneath it. Either rats or gophers. Maybe a raccoon. She quickly stepped to the opposite side of the cabin. "Go on. Shoo!" She beat against the rusted bed legs with a stick she'd found in the corner. Two skunks made their escape through the open cabin door, thankfully without releasing their odor. Bending over, she checked under the bed for any more night visitors. All clear.

With a shiver and a sigh, she went out to her Ford wagon in the hope she could find something to prop against the cabin door to keep it closed. She'd gone only a few steps when her foot got caught in a small indention in the ground, causing her to lose balance. She groped for anything that would keep her from falling and grabbed onto a low-hanging tree limb. But she immediately realized she'd become ensnared in a spider's web. The idea that the inhabitant might be looking for a new home somewhere inside her clothes slammed her panic button. As she frantically brushed at her clothing and hair, she heard a rustling of the underbrush a few feet away. It was then that she felt something crawling on her back. Under her shirt.

She screamed. There wasn't a lot in life that bothered her, but she'd been afraid of spiders since she was a kid. In complete panic, she tore off her shirt and began to brush at her back. Then something moved just under the waistband of her jeans, heading south. Another scream pierced the air as she frantically unbuttoned her pants and pushed them down her legs. About the time they cleared her behind, she lost balance, falling into a thick layer of last year's autumn leaves. Rolling onto her back, she continued to kick and fight off the jeans that had bunched around her ankles.

She'd just freed her feet when Cole appeared next to her, coming down on one knee, a gun held with both hands as he scanned the immediate area. "What is it? What the hell is going on?"

"It's a…a spider."

"*What*?"

"A sss…spider," she sobbed, becoming aware that she was sitting on the ground, almost naked, her T-shirt hanging from a tree limb and her pants flung to the side. She wasn't immediately sure what had happened to her shoes.

He took a deep breath and blew it out. Shoving the gun into the back of his jeans, he rose. "Stand up," he ordered, catching her upper arm and pulling her to her feet. Extracting a small flashlight from his pocket, he checked her hair. Then she felt his large hand move lightly across her shoulders and down her back. Turning her to face him, he shone the light on her face, down her neck and over her breasts, which thankfully were still clad in her bra. His face remained void of expression, even as he shined the light on her stomach and legs.

"I don't see anything," he said, a trace of annoyance in his tone. "How about you stay with me tonight? There's plenty of room."

He reached up and disentangled her shirt from the overhead branch, then picked up her jeans, shook them out and handed them back to her.

"Where are your shoes?"

"I...I'm not sure."

Without another word, he scooped her into his arms and began walking through the dried leaves in a direct line to his truck. Nestled against his broad chest, Tallie's arms instinctively came around his neck. He was so muscled, his chest and shoulders hard and unyielding. She'd only felt one other man with as much strength and power as this man had. Maybe that was the reason Masters reminded her of the guy in New Orleans. Like that other man, he moved gracefully, and carried her as though she weighed nothing at all. The heat rolled off his body, a warm caress against her back, arms and legs. He smelled faintly of hickory and something else she couldn't immediately define, but it was spicy and very appealing. And that was something she didn't need to notice. And there was still, at the back of her mind, the feeling she'd met this man before. But how was that even possible?

With the spider out of the picture and adrenaline no longer pumping through her veins, she felt more than a little foolish. She shouldn't let her phobias overrule her common sense.

A couple of feet from his truck, Cole paused. Tallie waited for the reprimand to come, for him to call her every kind of fool. But no words came.

She watched his eyes as he scanned her face, his intense expression a mixture of concern and something else she couldn't quite put a finger on. His lips, full and sensuous, were so close. For one crazy minute she thought he was going to kiss her and her breathing all but stopped. Then he turned away, pulled open the door and set her down on the passenger seat. Tallie sat, holding her shirt and jeans against her chest.

Within minutes Cole pulled up in the parking area near his house. They both got out of the truck and headed inside, past the enormous pool and waterfall.

The house was massive. The den was big enough to land one of his helicopters with room to spare. The walls were natural wood up to the third-story ceiling with an impressive natural-stone fireplace serving as the wall between the den and the kitchen.

Tallie followed him up a curving staircase. On the second floor they walked silently down a long hallway until he stopped and opened a door on the right. At that point, she lost the ability to describe the beauty of the room in front of her. It was carpeted in soft cream with walls painted to match; all of the accents, including the crown molding, internal doors and the fireplace mantel were mahogany. The king-size poster bed with its intricate scrollwork matched perfectly.

"The towels are in the cabinet, as are the shampoos and bath salts. Come downstairs when you're finished. Andre is just starting supper, so take as long as you want."

She nodded, noticing the sparkle in his eyes that lit

his handsome face. His full lips were pursed as though he was holding back a grin.

"Thank you," she murmured.

The bathroom boasted a huge whirlpool tub and a brown marble shower that could probably fit ten people. She had read about these thermostatic shower systems. This one had six shower heads plus a bench and steam jets that could turn it into a sauna. There were dual sinks in the same brown marble. The cabinets contained all the basic necessities: towels, washcloths, shampoo and soap. A lower drawer held an assortment of clean black and navy T-shirts, all size XXL.

Selecting one of the washcloths and a towel, she managed to turn on the water in the shower. Quickly stripping off her bra and panties, she stepped under the warm spray, languishing in the wonderful feel of it cascading down over her shoulders and back.

As much as Tallie would have liked to prolong this moment, she didn't intend to outstay her welcome. She washed, lathered then rinsed her hair, and turned off the water. Stepping out of the shower, she quickly dried herself. She hated putting on the same dirty clothes, and still wasn't convinced the spider had vacated her pants. Could she borrow one of Cole's tees?

She pulled a navy blue T-shirt from the drawer and quickly pulled it on over her head. It reached to her knees. Feeling adequately covered, she gathered her dirty clothes into a bundle, hung the towel to dry, combed her hair and went downstairs to the den.

Settling on the oversize sofa, she closed her eyes and tried to relax. It was then the nausea hit, hard and fast. She ran back up the stairs and into the bathroom she'd just used, not stopping until she was standing in front of the toilet. She hated the daily sickness. Hopefully when she went into her second trimester it would stop. She thought back to how Dr. Sterling had tried to talk her out of coming here, concerned about her safety. But Tallie wouldn't break the promise she'd made to her grandmother. She reasoned that wherever she was, she would still be sick.

The bout of sickness over, she rinsed her mouth then took a cooling sip of water. Better. She grabbed a new toothbrush from inside the cabinet and brushed her teeth, hoping it was over for the day.

She couldn't blame anyone but herself for her condition. When you got tipsy in New Orleans and were approached by the man of your dreams, this was what could happen. And in her case, it had happened. But even when the doctor had confirmed her condition, she'd still had a tough time grasping it. A baby. A tiny new soul.

The one thing that still angered her was how the man had just disappeared before the sun rose the next morning, not giving her a chance to learn his identity. Just who in the hell did he think he was to degrade her in such a manner?

Cole was waiting for her when she returned to the den.

"Can I get a ride back from you?"

He stood staring at her for the longest time. "Are you ill?"

She shrugged and prayed he couldn't see the blush that crossed her face. "Just a bug I picked up somewhere. It's better now."

"Are you sure you don't want to stay here? We have plenty of room."

"Thank you, but I would prefer to return to the little cabin. I can walk if you don't have the time."

"Walk? Through a mile of trees and wheat until you find another spider or stumble over a snake?" He shook his head at the idea. "If you insist on going, let's go."

With a small white bag holding her clothes, she followed Cole out to his truck.

"You do know that attempting to live in that old shack puts you in every kind of danger. Why don't you just pack it in for now and come back in the fall when the weather is cooler and there are a lot fewer bugs? The camping conditions will be better."

In the fall Tallie would be caring for her newborn baby.

"I'm afraid I have other commitments then," she said. "Besides, by then I won't have access to the area. We both know as soon as I leave construction will commence."

He didn't argue with her. Masters just wanted her gone and apparently he would say or do anything to achieve it.

The next morning she had just finished dressing when she heard the sound of men's voices coming from the direction of the dig site. She stepped outside onto the cabin's porch and, sure enough, there were three men with shovels standing around the dig. She pulled on her boots and headed in their direction. Before she could close the distance, the men put their shovels to good use.

She broke into a jog. As she grew closer she saw where they had already churned her carefully laid out site in three different directions.

"Stop! Please stop!" she called out as she got to the

men, who immediately halted their digging. "What are you doing? Who are you?"

One of the men removed his hat. "We work for the Circle M Ranch. Cole sent us up here to help you out. He said take some shovels and dig at the spot you had marked out."

"If you aren't careful, you might destroy something that's hundreds if not thousands of years old. What I'm looking for…it's very old and fragile."

The man who'd spoken looked at the other two and they all shrugged. "We're just doing what we were told to do, ma'am."

"And unless we hear differently from our boss, we have to keep digging," the second man chimed in.

"That's ridiculous." She faced the third man, who appeared to be the oldest of the three. "I'll go and speak with Mr. Masters. Until this is straightened out, please stop digging."

The first man put his cowboy hat back on and looked at the other two. "I'm not sure Cole is here. He was going to fly into Dallas. You may have missed him. But we'll wait an hour or so to give you a chance to talk with him. After that, we pretty much have to follow his orders."

She turned and hurried up the hill to her Ford wagon. She would tell Masters exactly what he could do with his orders. Normally a careful driver, she slammed her foot down on the accelerator and the old vehicle fishtailed several times before she reached the paved road leading to the mansion on the hill. How could he do this?

When she reached the parking area she hopped from her old Ford car and jogged toward the mansion.

After several frantic rings of the bell, a housekeeper

answered the door. “I’m sorry,” she said. “Mr. Masters just left. He’s headed for the airstrip some distance behind the barn. Don’t know if you can catch him, but it’s that way if you want to try.” She pointed toward the large barn and stables.

With quick thanks thrown over her shoulder, Tallie got back in her vehicle and headed out of the parking area. Following the directions, she almost immediately spotted the private air strip and the giant warehouse that housed the planes. There appeared to be only one thing in motion: a helicopter on the far left of the airfield with MASTERS CORPORATION on the side. As she got closer she could see Cole at the controls. He was writing something on a notepad and hadn’t seen her approach. Tallie pulled up close to the helipad just as the rotor blade increased its speed. Knowing what was at stake, she leaped from her wagon car, ran to the chopper and pulled open the door.

The look on Cole’s face was a mix of surprise, frustration and anger. Tallie silently glared at him. If looks could kill, he’d be a dead man. With obvious reservations he shut off the motor and the blades slowed. Pulling off the headset, he tossed it on the seat next to him and got out of the chopper. He was not happy. But neither was she.

“What in the hell do you think you’re doing?” he bellowed as he reached her side of the helicopter.

“I might ask you the same question.”

“You could have been killed.”

“So what would you care?” Tallie was so furious her hands were held in tightly formed fists at her sides. “You send three of your ranch hands to my dig to destroy it. Then you sneak out so I can’t contact you. You’ve reached a new low, Masters.”

"I was trying to offer you some help," he argued. "And I've never *snuck* away from anything."

She could tell that her accusation had hit the target. She had him on the defensive, which was good. "I've already told you it takes time and patience to extract the soil. You chop up a five-thousand-year-old artifact and it's game over. If that happens, this would all be for nothing. My time here meaningless. And the delay to your project pointless, as well."

"It appears to me that's already the case."

"You just don't get it. Is it that you don't want to understand or are you incapable of understanding?"

"Dr. Finley—"

"You did this on purpose. You might have destroyed an invaluable historical object. You didn't even tell your employees what they were doing. Just to dig. I hope you aren't that sloppy directing your companies."

That appeared to hit the nail squarely on the head. His eyes narrowed while his jaw muscles worked overtime; no doubt he was biting his tongue.

"So, what do you want, Dr. Finley? I'm late for a meeting in Dallas."

She coughed out a sarcastic laugh. "You have to ask? You have three cowboys with shovels digging up my site. Figure it out. Tell them to stop. Tell them to go away. Would you like for me to write it down for you? Do I need to lead you by the hand? Tell them to go mend a fence or shoe a horse or something."

Cole shook his head, not bothering to try to hide his frustration. "Fine. If you will kindly step back from the aircraft, I'll tell them to stop digging."

"I'll be watching."

"I'm sure you will." The sarcasm was heavy in his tone. She didn't care. Not knowing if she could trust him after this stunt, she returned to the wagon and backed away from the helipad but waited to see which direction he would go. Within minutes the chopper lifted off and made a beeline for the dig site where it made a perfect landing. Cole was talking to the men as she pulled up next to the old shack.

He saw her and walked to the helicopter before she could get there. It lifted off and headed south toward Dallas, the rotors slapping the air like thunder in the sky. The men were already putting their shovels and other tools back in their truck. "Ma'am," the older cowboy said and nodded before he turned and walked to their pickup. Soon Tallie was left alone with only the birds to keep her company.

She didn't believe for a second that Cole had done this to help her. He'd thought he could sabotage her into leaving. He could think again. He had started a war and made it worse by making her miss her morning tea, and that was an unforgivable offense. She picked up her shovel and began the daunting task of checking for any destruction and ensuring no artifacts were embedded in the churned soil.

After many hours, she was convinced she'd been lucky. She emptied shovelful after shovelful into the sifter. There were arrowheads, broken pieces of pottery, a few beads made within the past few hundred years and not evidence of the lost tribe she was looking for, which was much older. The digging didn't seem to have caused any damage, though. She logged each one, took a picture and noted the day and time and other facts about each piece in her journal. She might be wrong about the date of the pieces but she didn't think so.

The sun was setting behind the far hills when the last sifting was completed. She would have to wait until the morning to outline a new grid. Trudging back to the cabin she fell onto the rickety old bed and kicked off her boots. Exhaustion propelled her to sleep with one last thought: what would Cole Masters try to pull tomorrow?

Five

It was a feeling rather than a sound that woke Tallie from a deep sleep. Her eyes opened just enough that she could tell it was before dawn. She felt eyes on her. Slowly sitting up, she looked out the door opening. A cow was standing in the doorway. Before she could pull on some jeans, another cow poked his head in over the first. Then a third came in low, as if to see what the other two had found.

"Shoo!" she screeched, stomping her foot at the heifers in the doorway. Her actions had no effect.

She swung a piece of cardboard at them and finally they took the hint and moved back. How many cows were there? Ten—at least—standing around the old shack. Slipping on her jeans and boots, she readied for war. Reaching back to her bedroll, she grabbed the white sheet from inside. Waving it and shouting "shoo" and "get out" finally caused a reaction. The entire group headed away from the cabin toward a fence with a wire gate half off its hinges. The cows kept going. When all were through the partial opening, Tallie quickly closed the gate. She hoped they weren't hurt by the wire but dreaded to see the damage they had caused to her camp and the dig site.

An hour later she was still picking up pieces of garbage from the bright blue barrels that had been overturned on the porch. She didn't know how much time it took to clean up all the mess. Only one thing she knew for sure: this was Cole Masters's doing. He was behind it. She couldn't prove it, but she knew it all the same.

She was sitting on the ramshackle porch still rolling up the last of the orange twine when she heard a pickup come down the path.

"Good morning, Dr. Finley," Cole said as he exited the truck.

She glared at him. If she opened her mouth she would chew him up and spit him out.

"So, how is your day?"

She shrugged.

"I don't know if you saw them, but about a dozen heifers with cuts and scratches showed up at the barn. Looks like they were run through a fence. I don't suppose you would know anything about that?"

She shrugged again. "Can't say I do. I've been right here, on the property, all morning. No cows are allowed in this area, isn't that what you told me?"

His jaw worked overtime. He'd been caught in a trap of his own making.

"Yeah." He stared, suspicion marring his handsome features. "That's what I said."

"If I see a cow within the borders of the dig site, I'll be sure to let you know."

"You do that." He sounded skeptical. "What happened to your string?"

She shrugged her shoulders. "Part of it unraveled." She stated the obvious. Of course, it had had a bit of help. "Are you on some sort of leave? I mean I haven't seen you go to work but a couple of times since I've been here."

"You think I need to go to Dallas and work?"

"Well, Dallas or New York…wherever you have offices." She shrugged again. "It just seems odd to me that you're spending so much time out here worrying about cows and directing your ranch hands to 'help' me. That can't be very profitable."

She set the roll of string aside, leaned back against one of the posts supporting the roof over the porch and looked at him.

"I originally intended to use this period to oversee the initial phase of construction on my project and, as you know, that has been…postponed. So now I have free time to check on you and your progress. I see you sitting back rolling up a ball of string and I get curious. Shouldn't you be grabbing your little rake and brushing at dirt?"

Tallie's nostrils flared in anger. She wasn't a violent person, but in her mind's eye she could see her hand popping him on the back of his head for all of his lamebrained failed attempts to make her leave. "All in good time. It sounds like you're preoccupied with shutting me down." She looked at him and forced a smile. "I wouldn't go to too much trouble. I'm pretty stubborn as well as resilient."

He muttered something she couldn't understand before turning and walking toward his truck. And Tallie patted herself on the back for winning another round with the stubborn billionaire.

* * *

The days stretched into weeks and Tallie still hadn't found any proof of an ancient tribe. She was frustrated and tired of being sick. Every day. The morning sickness visited her in the afternoon now.

One morning during her fifth week on site, Tallie stretched and yawned as the sun rose over the distant hills. The past month had reminded her of both the positive and negative aspects of being on a dig. She felt soreness in her entire body. Concern for the baby made her slow down and take short breaks more often. Even if she ran out of time and found nothing, her *ipokini* would have understood.

Grabbing a stick leaning against the base of the old wood-burning stove, she clanged it against the metal and yawned again. By the fourth ding, the two skunks waddled out from under the bed and headed for the front door.

"You guys need to find a day job."

Normally she wouldn't allow houseguests but she'd been so tired the past few days, she just came inside after her bath in the river and dropped. If they didn't bother her or bite her toes, she would pay them the same courtesy. Her food was locked up in the Ford so there was nothing in the cabin to entice them. She figured they rummaged all night in places unknown and joined her in the shack just before daylight. Where they went now was anyone's guess.

She had just finished her morning tea when the sound of an engine—or engines—shredded the air. Stepping out onto the porch, she was shocked to see about a dozen four-wheelers top the rise near the cabin and continue on, making a large loop that took in the hills and valleys…and her current dig site. They didn't ride over the string that clearly defined the current grid but came close to it. A man in a pickup rode behind them, stopping on occasion to post a numbered sign.

What had Masters done now? With her mouth drawn into a straight line, she set her teacup down on the porch and angrily walked in that direction.

"Excuse me," she said, dodging two more riders as they topped the hill. "What is this?"

"Good morning, ma'am," the man replied, tipping his hat. "This is the day we have our Wheels for Wishing charity event. There are various skill levels and, by the end of the day, the rider with the fastest time will win the trophy and the grand prize. Of course, all the money including the grand prize will go to the charity. This year it's for the orphanage in Calico Springs. The owners of the Circle M Ranch always let us hold it on their land. Different locations each year, so no one has an advantage over the new contestants."

"And this year it's here."

"Yes, ma'am." He nodded. "But don't you worry. Cole told us you were working in the area and cautioned us to be sure to stay clear of your archeology site."

"Oh, he did?"

"We drew out the course together, just to be sure."

A calm seemed to come over her. She had to give Masters kudos for his determination. This time, however, she wasn't going to lose her temper. She was not going to ask him what he thought he was doing. He knew full well what he was doing. And she had no intention of leaving. No, this time she was going to give him a taste of his own medicine.

"Where is Mr. Masters?"

"He had business in Dallas, but he'll be back late this afternoon."

That should be just about right.

The people at the copy store in town were more than willing to lend assistance, helping her to put on paper an eye-catching announcement. Buzzy and his friends who, excited at getting five dollars for their efforts, began to spread the several hundred flyers all around the small town.

The ground below was carpeted in every size, make and model of vehicle produced in the past twenty years. It was a virtual smorgasbord of metal roofs and hood tops in every color under the sun. It would be an amazing sight to behold if it hadn't been on the grounds surrounding his house. Cole flew in close, making a small circle above the cars and trucks, curious what in the hell these people were doing.

It looked like they were making toasts: people were coming and going in and out of the house holding glasses up toward him. Those who swarmed the swimming pool clapped. And he could hear what sounded like rock-and-roll music above the sound of the helicopter's engine. In the far distance there were more parked cars surrounding the circular route chosen for the four-wheeler competition.

Cole quickly landed the chopper and stormed toward the house. His cell in his hand, he tried to contact his security team. The phone was finally answered with, "Hey, Mr. M. You're just in time. The second round of pizzas was just delivered."

"Is this Marco? Meet me in my office in two minutes." He ended the call.

As Cole made it through the back lawn and pool area, he was greeted with shouts of "Thank you" and a drink was pushed into his hand—perfect timing. The crowd parted, opening a path to his back door. Before he ever got to his office he'd ascertained what was happening and knew without any doubt whatsoever a certain archeologist was to thank for all her trouble.

After meeting with his security detail, he strolled outside, letting his eyes search the crowds around the pool. He spotted several ranch hands and more than half the residents of the town and, in the middle of it all, there she was. Miss Let's-Throw-a-Party, kicked back in a lounger wearing the tiniest hot-pink string bikini he'd ever seen in his life. How did one approach such a sight and keep his anger in the foreground?

"Dr. Finley," he said, his hands on his hips. "Great party you're hosting."

She looked up over the sunglasses perched on her nose. "Oh, it isn't my party. It was a work day until the four-wheeler festivities began." She laid back and pushed her glasses farther up her nose. "What's the old saying...if you can't beat 'em, join 'em?"

About then someone did a belly flop into the pool, sending a wave of water directly toward Cole's backside.

"Hey, see if you can find a chair and enjoy the perfect weather."

His jaw muscles worked convulsively. *If you can't beat 'em...* He looked around and spotted an empty lounger. Within a few seconds he had dragged the chair next to Tallie and sprawled out beside her. If his action surprised her she hid it well.

"You're gonna get too hot in those clothes."

"How nice of you to notice. Maybe you would like to help me take them off?"

"So glad you could make it for the celebration," she said, ignoring his question.

"Actually the party is over. The security detail will

be making the rounds shortly. I couldn't pass up the opportunity to share a couple of moments with a gorgeous woman."

She tensed. "Why do men see only the outside?"

"Because we're men." He looked over at her. "That's just what we do. But...give us the chance to get to know a woman and it's amazing how fast the old heart can start tripping all over itself."

"You talk as if you know that from experience."

He nodded. "Maybe I do. Have dinner with me tonight, Tallie. You've lost the entire day, might as well waste the evening, too."

She turned and stared at him. "You want me to have dinner with you?"

"Absolutely." He sat up from the recliner. "Unlike some among us, I don't hold grudges."

"Can't say I know what you're talking about, but I have to work tonight. Catch up the discovery log. And I don't really want to get into another...*discussion* of why I can't just leave now."

"But here's something you might keep in mind. I can make a large contribution to the museum if certain needs are met."

"And what would those needs be?"

"Postpone your dig."

"Not happening."

"You're sure about dinner?"

"I'm sure, and here's why. You are a spoiled egomaniac who thinks he's a hotshot. But you want to kick back, lose the bad boy, hottest-man-of-the-year reputation and be a real guy for a change. And my weakness is falling for guys like you. My strength is saying no to them. Now, if you'll excuse me."

Cole reflected on the irony of what she'd just said.

Tallie *had* fallen for him, in a big way, in New Orleans. It was a small miracle that she still didn't recognize him—or was that just an act? He needed to figure out what she was up to.

She stood from her chair and smiled. That perfect little grin that made him crazy. He would remember this. He hadn't been played this well in…maybe forever. Still, paybacks for Dr. Finley would be priceless. She wouldn't get away with this.

But why did that little voice of reason in the back of his mind keep repeating, *Yeah, she will…*

Tallie swung her feet to the floor and got out of bed. She had a long day ahead of her. She quickly got dressed, grabbed the bottled water and headed to the wagon to get her tea. But the can was empty. She dug down inside the boxes of rations. No tea. In fact, she realized she was out of almost everything.

In the past few days, she'd made real progress on the site. She had just begun to find tiny pieces of pottery she was almost certain came from the 1500s or earlier. She hated to interrupt her work now. But she'd learned long ago, no tea, no clear head. No clear head, no work. So, to the store she would go.

The small town of Calico Springs was only about ten miles from the dig site. Returning to civilization always felt good but odd. It didn't take her long to find what she needed, including her tea. To be safe, she grabbed two more cans. She added a can of insect repellent that hopefully was better than the first she'd bought and a box of mothballs to the items in her cart. Somebody had long ago told her skunks wouldn't tread over mothballs. She didn't have anything to lose.

Once she'd purchased the supplies, it was back to

the dig site. On the way she called in to Dr. Sterling at the museum. He was excited about the slivers of pottery she'd found in the past few days. He encouraged her to keep at it as long as her condition would allow, apologizing again for not having enough staff to send someone to help her.

The remaining seven weeks would go fast and, before she knew it, she would be out of time. That was one thing her boss didn't need to remind her of. She had Cole Masters for that.

Only a mile from the cabin the car began to pull hard to the left. *Crud. Not a flat. Please.* But when she got out and checked, that was exactly what she had. She looked around at the same rolling hills she'd been gazing at since the day she'd arrived. No human in sight.

Tallie walked to the back of the vehicle and began taking boxes of groceries out to get to the spare tire. The spare tire rack had long since stopped functioning so the tire had to be stored in the back along with everything else. She crossed her fingers the jack was with it and the spare had some air.

She was in luck. She found the jack and when she bounced the spare out of the vehicle she was pleased to see that it had plenty of air. But then she popped off the hubcap only to find the lug nuts were rusted onto the bolts. She stood, arched her back and considered her alternatives. It would take a dozen trips to carry her supplies to the camp. She might have phone service but no clue whom to call. It looked like this would cost her a full day of digging.

She heard a pickup coming down the private road, turned and saw Cole Masters behind the wheel. Of all the possible white knights, why did it have to be him?

She didn't want to be indebted to this surly man for anything.

He pulled up next to her and got out of his truck. "Give me the lug wrench."

"I can do this myself. Thanks anyway."

"There might be a spider lurking behind the tire."

She glared. "It must be nice not to fear anything."

He snatched the tool out of her hand, lowered the car until the wheel was firmly back on the ground and loosened the rusty bolts in less time than it would have taken her to remove one brand-new one. As she watched him work, she was again struck with the feeling that she'd met him before. Something about him seemed familiar. It was then that she saw it: a small tattoo, partially revealed in the vee of his shirt collar where it was unbuttoned.

"You have a tattoo," she ventured. "What is it, if you don't mind me asking?"

He froze. Then he turned the last lug nut, pulled off the tire and stood. "You've probably seen one like it at some point." He pulled aside the collar on the shirt.

"That's cool. You know I do remember seeing one like it." She frowned with a shrug. "I just can't remember where."

He merely smiled. It was a humorless smile that only amplified the little warning bells going off in her head. What was he up to now?

Today he was wearing black jeans and a black shirt. His hair had grown out since she'd first arrived at the ranch and it looked shaggy and wind-blown. If you took away his beard, he'd look exactly the way the stranger had looked that night in New Orleans.

She stepped back from him, her heart thundering in her chest and her eyes growing wide. It couldn't be.

It. Could. Not. Be. Was Cole Masters the man she'd… *met…*in New Orleans? She shook her head in denial. It was impossible. The man who had taken her to bed was nice. He wasn't arrogant. There might be an uncanny resemblance, but the two men were completely different.

But everything fit; all the pieces suddenly slammed together. Cole would be the kind of guy to have treated her the way he had. He probably either borrowed the clothes he'd worn or visited a thrift store. *So no one would recognize him.* He didn't live under a bridge or in a run-down apartment in New Orleans. He lived in multiple mansions around the world. She recalled a couple of news articles she'd read after Dr. Sterling had warned her to be wary of Cole Masters.

Dr. Sterling had no idea just how right that warning had been.

Six

She took a step back as the truth washed over her. "You knew. All this time. You knew and you didn't bother to tell me?"

"I was curious how long it would take you."

Her emotions were all over the place. She pressed her hands against her forehead. She could feel the blood surging to her head while her heart pounded in her chest.

"You are an arrogant, sneaky, sabotaging, lying, two-faced billionaire." She turned to march back to her truck. "Is this how you get your kicks? You…you play with people's emotions?"

In her mind a war raged. Was this the same guy she had met and shared a bed with or was he trying to mess with her? The man she'd met in New Orleans might have been a derelict but he was a nice derelict. She could feel the blush run up her neck and across her face. Even the tips of her ears felt hot.

Her mind was whirling. She couldn't stop staring at Cole as she desperately tried to dispel the notion that he was the sexy stranger who had so easily and proficiently taken her to bed. A stranger. One who did magic things with his hands, his mouth, his body. The memory of that night would stay with her forever.

"You lied to me."

"No, I didn't."

"Yes, you did. If you'd been honest, you would have told me as soon as you knew I didn't recognize you. And I wouldn't have recognized you without the tattoo. And the dark shirt. And the jeans."

What was he grinning about?

"I've never done that before, just so you know," she added.

"Done what?"

"Gone to bed with a complete stranger."

"It was a great night. Why are you apologizing?"

"I'm not apologizing," she retorted. "I just wanted to set the record straight."

"It doesn't matter."

"It matters to *me*."

He stood and rubbed his hands together. "I didn't do anything you didn't want me to do. You worry too much. We both had a great time. That's all that counts. It just isn't a big deal."

The more he shrugged it off, the angrier she got.

"So picking up a stranger in a bar is the norm for you? How very sad."

"No." He rested his hands on his waist and held her gaze. "As a matter of fact, that was a first for me, as well. But I can't say I'm sorry."

"I wouldn't be so sure about that."

He frowned, obviously not understanding.

"You left me there," she continued. "You left me to wake up alone without even knowing your name. Who does that?"

"Look, Tallie—"

"No. Don't 'look, Tallie' me. What if you had a disease? For that matter, what if I had a disease?"

"I took precautions. Anyway, we both know it's all right now."

Oh, how she wanted to tell him how it wasn't all right. Before she could gather the words Cole spoke.

"Tallie, I admit I could have handled it better. But everywhere I go, at least several times a month, I come in contact with a woman or a tight little group who sends in a woman to try and entrap me. If we have sex, a false pregnancy claim will shortly follow. If we arrive at a restaurant, you can set your watch by how soon she will accidently fall. Or step in a hole walking up to my front door and sprain her ankle so that she can sue. In New Orleans, when I told you I wasn't into a long or permanent relationship, I meant it. If I recall, you said the same thing. I'm not a family man. I never will be. I don't want a wife and I don't want kids. For all I knew, you could have been like any of those other women. I never thought I would see you again, so why bother with formalities?"

He tossed the tire iron in the back of her vehicle and walked toward her.

"You could have asked me my name. I know my own name and I wouldn't mind sharing it. Especially… especially under the circumstances."

"At the time I wasn't thinking. I don't think you were, either."

She couldn't argue with that. She was still trying to

swallow the fact that Cole was her dream man. And it had nothing to do with money. Their coming together in New Orleans was like something out of a movie or a romantic novel. At least it had been until she'd confirmed she was pregnant.

But now she had her answer. If she told him she was carrying his child he would accuse her of all sorts of awful things. Tears welled in her eyes at the complete finality of the situation. Any dream that he would believe her and maybe even ask her to marry him was gone. She would raise the baby herself. She now knew without any shadow of doubt that was what she must do. He'd made it clear he wasn't a family man. He wanted no kids.

Considering how unconcerned he was about their time together in New Orleans, he wouldn't care two hoots about a baby. Or he would accuse Tallie of getting pregnant on purpose. She could think of a half dozen scenarios and none of them was pleasant. Tallie refused to bring a child into this world and subject him to a father who was never going to show up. Every child deserved better. Hopefully, someday she would find a good man who would raise her baby as his own and Cole would never be the wiser. And her baby would not lack for anything in spite of the fact that she had no money to speak of. Love was more important than money. As long as she could provide a roof over their heads and food on the table, they would be fine.

In minutes, Cole had replaced the flat tire with the spare. He handed her the jack and tossed the flat into the back of his truck.

Tallie tried to maintain a grip on her emotions. She inhaled deeply to clear her mind of what she'd just learned. Better save it for later; she could work through all this devastating information when she was alone.

"I think the tire is fixable. I'll take it to the local garage and have it repaired."

"Thank you, Mr. Masters. I am in your debt," she choked out. He looked at her as though he just now realized her words said one thing but her body language said quite another.

"I think we're past the 'mister.' My name is Cole."

"I don't care what your name is, *Mr.* Masters. If I wasn't worthy of knowing it three months ago, I don't want to know it now."

"Tallie, you're being stubborn."

For the briefest of seconds she struggled with his comment. She did not want to be on a first-name basis with this man. He was not the same man she'd met in New Orleans, although she had to admit his current attitude matched the first glimpse she'd had of him: dark and ruthless. Dangerous. Being on a first-name basis was the first step to a relationship. She didn't want a relationship that had nowhere to go. It wasn't on her bucket list.

But neither was bearing his child.

Why did she have such bad luck with men? Her last relationship was a case in point. John Mosby, a guy she'd dated for a year, had been an egocentric control freak. She'd done everything he'd asked her to do and still he'd dumped her, sneaking his stuff out of her apartment while she was away on a dig. It hurt. Eventually she'd decided it was the best thing that could have happened to her. Like she'd had a choice. He hadn't even bothered to leave a note. She'd had the humiliating task of asking her girlfriends if they'd known what had happened to John.

But at least she was free of his constant, overbearing, fault-finding harassment. She wasn't about to jump from that frying pan into the Cole Masters's fire.

"Go ahead and I'll follow you to your camp site just to be sure nothing else happens."

"No."

She turned to go back to her vehicle when he seized her shoulders and spun her around. She opened her mouth to ask what he thought he was doing and his lips came down over hers. For seconds she struggled, but his lips, the taste of him, were potent, overcoming her stubborn resolve to not make another mistake with this man. As soon as she relented he kissed her long and deep, and moments later raised his head, leaving her lips swollen. Leaving her wanting more.

"I want to start fresh, learn more about you other than how insanely phenomenal you are in bed." His deep voice was raspy. Her body immediately responded.

He lowered his head, his lips almost touching hers. "Could we start over, Tallie?" Then he was kissing her again, and this time she felt his hunger and it drew her to him. His tongue moistened her lips before plunging deep inside the cavern of her mouth. She felt his hand at the back of her head, holding her to him as he continued to blow her mind. She heard him groan then he was backing away, making the heat of the day drop to below freezing.

She wanted his arms around her. She wanted him to kiss her some more, to make love to her. She was putty in his arms, encircled by the scent and strength and touch of him. She'd often dreamed of the night they had spent together, burning the sheets and making love until most sane people would have been satisfied. Not them. Every climax he'd given her would satisfy her for a while then he would say something to her in that remarkable voice or kiss her and nibble her jawline or find her breast with his hand and lips and she would be lost again.

But he was Cole Masters. *The* Cole Masters. Playboy of the western world. He knew what he was doing. He knew a woman's body as well as his own, so under the circumstances she couldn't agree to starting over. Eventually he would feel her enlarging belly and he would know. Then his professed interest would change into loathing because he would think she'd set him up; that she had gotten pregnant on purpose.

"I suppose we could talk." That was the most she was willing to do.

"If that's all you can give me right now, I'll take it. Maybe I can convince you otherwise. Go ahead and get in your car. I'll follow you to the cabin."

She got into her wagon, started the engine and looked in her rearview mirror. She had to grudgingly admit it had been nice of him to stop and help her change the tire. She had no experience with millionaires, let alone billionaires, but she doubted if anyone else of his social status would do what he'd done, especially after all the times they'd butted heads over the past several weeks.

After a twenty-minute drive, she pulled up next to the shack. By the time she got out of the truck Cole was already opening the back door to her wagon, asking where she wanted things to go.

"Okay, that's everything," Cole said as he closed the doors to her vehicle.

"I appreciate all you've done. I really—"

Cole pushed her against the side of his truck and, in the glow of the setting sun, kissed her again.

Tallie tried to push out of his arms but Cole was determined. It didn't take very many seconds until she was kissing him back. Her belly tightened as the heat ran rampant through her veins.

His hands moved to cup her face, holding her to him and sending sparks of pleasure along her spine. Finally she placed her smaller hands over his and he allowed her to push him back.

"Cole." She was breathing hard. Her lips were inches away from his, moist, swollen from his kisses, slightly open, wanting more. His member was rock-hard, just like before. And there would be no relief for either of them until he took her to his bed.

"Tallie, are you involved with anyone?"

Was it any of his business? "No."

Then he was kissing her again with an intensity that proclaimed his ownership. He pressed his erection against her and growled his claim.

She felt the intense heat from his body and fought the urge to slide her arms up over his shoulders and pull him closer to her. As she turned away, her breasts brushed against the hard contours of his chest. Her nipples jumped to full attention, sending an electrifying sensation through her entire body. She could sense the sexual charge between them when his body responded. She didn't move. She didn't have to. The awareness of her arousal was noted and returned.

"Tallie," he murmured as his mouth came down over her lips once again. The kiss was amazing, his lips soft and pliable yet firm at the same time. She wanted to melt into them. Into *him*. With a small whimper, she turned away but she'd had a reminder of just how seriously sexy, how potent, Cole Masters could be. It was enough to leave her wanting more. A lot more. She could sense his desire. They barely knew each other yet her body was throwing off hormones like fireworks on Independence Day. Fighting her own desire as well as his, she pushed out of his arms.

"I told you before, with the exception of our night in the French Quarter, I don't sleep around."

"Then why me?" he asked. "Why did you let me seduce you? Why was our night together different?" He looked at her long and hard before dropping his hands to his sides. It might be the first time in his life Cole Masters had been turned down.

"I suppose I drank too much. I lost track of who I really am."

"No. I think you found out who you really are. A beautiful, passionate woman who let her attraction to a man overcome her staid impractical beliefs."

With John it had taken months of knowing him to even get remotely close to the state Tallie was in right now if, in fact, she ever did. John had never cared enough to make the effort to turn her on. He was only in it to please himself.

But Cole didn't need to make any effort to turn her on. She felt her response to him loud and clear. His hard body was erect and ready. And all she had to do was say yes. The heat surged through her at the thought. But with determination she stepped back and this time he let her go.

She didn't know if he was trying to seduce her because he found something about her he liked, or if he was trying to seduce her into making her leave. It had to be one or the other. She had her doubts about the first possibility, though. In a lot of ways, she was still that gangly, naïve girl who had grasped hold of any attention John had offered and done what he'd wanted her to do because he was the only one who had ever showed any interest. So what would a man like Cole Masters see in her?

Then again, if he was trying to seduce her to have his way over the dig site, it could backfire on him. Seducing her, if she allowed it, would not make her leave any faster. In fact, it could very well further complicate the entire situation.

It was more than likely he saw her as weak and vulnerable. She had the education but she'd never experienced the level of sophistication he was used to. She'd never had a man of Cole's wealth and status coming on to her and she would be the first to admit she was completely out of her depth. He was probably taking advantage of any opportunity to talk her into abandoning the dig. He was a master manipulator who would warp any love session into forcing her to leave. She'd be stupid to discount that option; the most probable one under the circumstances.

"Good night, Cole." She turned and walked toward the front door of the shack. Stepping inside, she sat on the sleeping bag, absently watching as the lights from his truck shone through the holes in the sides and top of the cabin as he turned around then drove away.

She didn't know the man and he didn't know her. She didn't know how to get to know him without precariously dangling her heart on a string. If she were more worldly, she might say yes and see where it would go. But her experience with John painted a pretty clear and dismal picture of how men acted.

And she would never put herself in that situation again.

* * *

It was four o'clock in the afternoon the following day when the garage called about Tallie's tire. It couldn't be saved.

"Fine. Put a new one on my account." Cole started to end the call but thought better of it. "Ray? I need the new tire to look like the old one. Roll it in the mud a couple of times and walk your dog."

"Walk my dog?"

"Yeah. You know. *Walk your dog.* Let him do his business on the tire, then roll it in the dirt again."

"Cole, you ask for some strange things."

Cole couldn't help but laugh. "Thanks, Ray."

Clearly the man didn't understand the why of the request but he would do it. Cole suspected Tallie would insist on paying for the fix. She wouldn't be happy about an entirely new tire and he would have to listen to a long argument over a hundred bucks. No thanks. With any luck, he would accept her ten dollars for the "repaired" tire and that would be that.

By five o'clock the new tire was delivered. It looked pretty bad. Cole was impressed. He threw it in the back of his truck and headed for the dig site. *Damn.* She even had him calling it a dig site. Whatever, it was a good excuse to check on her progress, as if he needed one. She'd been working on the last section of her initial grid this morning. He couldn't help but wonder where she would go next.

He drove out to the site, pulled the new old tire out of the back of his truck and rolled it over to her vehicle. He was almost finished changing it out when she came around the corner.

"How much do I owe you?"

"Ten dollars."

"Ten dollars? For a new tire?" She gave him a look that clearly said nice try.

"I'll put it on the tab."

"Fine. I'll settle up before I leave."

And Cole believed she would. At least she would try.

Seven

It was not fully light the next morning when Tallie was awakened by an odd sound. It was as though someone had turned on a giant sprinkler. She looked toward the dig site. There was just enough light to see an irrigation system, silent and unused until now, watering the wheat. One of the sprayers appeared to be centered on the area she had planned on digging that day.

No way. This could not be happening. She quickly pulled on her jeans, a clean shirt and her boots, grabbed a sheet of plastic they used to preserve a site during a rain storm and hurried to the dig. Water was spewing at full throttle. She made an attempt to cover the ground where she'd planned to work. The soil had already become saturated.

She took a step forward and realized, belatedly, that her boots were stuck more than ankle deep in the reddish-brown mud. About then a blast of cold water hit her smack in the face, causing her to lose her balance. She fell to the left, her right foot sliding out of the boot. Turning onto her back, which seemed to be the only way to right herself, she sat up, struggling to pull her boots out of the now almost shin-deep mud. She succeeded in freeing one boot before another blast of water knocked her down again, this time face-first. At that point, a slow crawl was the only remaining option to escape.

Lumbering toward the end of the sprinkler, she attempted to turn it off. The thing was controlled remotely. As in, from the ranch. She didn't have to ask who'd done this.

As she sloshed back toward her Ford wagon, her anger grew with each step. It would be days before that area could be excavated. And the longer the sprinklers were on, the worse it would get. Cole Masters was behind this. The man just would not give up, but she had to admit after this stunt he was getting closer to inspiring her to pack her bags. Reaching the vehicle she started the engine and headed to Cole's ranch house.

She passed the Circle M Ranch sign over the entrance to the driveway. The blacktop road continued on, rising at a steady elevation until she arrived at the house. She got out of her Ford and followed the flagstone path up to the door. She rang the bell then knocked.

She would give him thirty seconds before she walked in. Her blood pressure was sending off warning signals, her ears were ringing and she prayed the horrible man would get to the door before she stroked out. There were few times over the course of her life she'd ever been this furious.

Just seconds before she reached for the knob, the door opened. Cole took one look, his eyes growing big at the sight of her. She knew what she must look like, wet and covered in dark red mud head to toe, with one boot on and the other still stuck in the mud back at camp. She glared at the preposterous man and then noticed another man rise from the sofa in the den behind him and slowly walk toward the open door where she stood.

"If you think, for one second, your little schemes will drive me away, you'd better think again." Her voice was quivering in anger. "Shut that irrigation system off. Now."

"Irrigation? The irrigation system is not scheduled to come on in that area. The wheat is about to be harvested. Because of both your dig and my project I had it shut down."

"Convince me."

"Tallie, I didn't do this." Cole held up his hands, palms forward in a gesture of surrender. But he pursed his lips as he tried to hide a grin. "I don't know what happened but I'll take care of it." He paused, allowing his eyes to roam over her from head to foot as if he couldn't believe what he'd seen the first time.

"You have fifteen seconds." She pinned him to the spot with her eyes, her finger poking at his chest. "This little gimmick will set me back days, but I'm not leaving. I refuse. You cannot run me off, Masters. Believe it. Deal with it."

"Come inside. Please."

She stepped inside, hoping to leave as much mud as possible. She nodded to the other man. He nodded back and also pursed his lips as though fighting not to laugh. "I'm Cole's brother, Wade. And you must be Dr. Finley."

"I would shake but..." She held out her mud-covered hand.

Cole reached for the phone and hit a speed dial number. “Yeah. Griff? I thought I instructed your boys to kill the watering on the east part of the forty thousand acres for a while.” He listened quietly. “Well, whatever you did, it didn’t work. The irrigation is going full-blast and has apparently destroyed Dr. Finley’s excavation site. Shut it down now then find out who turned it on or fix what’s wrong and call me when you make a determination.” He ended the call.

“I’m sorry, Tallie, but I had nothing to do with this. Perhaps you can relocate to another area until that section of the site dries out. It would appear,” he said as he once again let his eyes rake her from top to bottom, “that the site is too muddy to work.”

“Ya think?” Fool that she was she believed him when he said he had no part in what happened, but he still had no appreciation for what she was trying to accomplish. “Do you even know or care what I’m trying to do out there?”

He shrugged. “Look for pieces of old pottery? I guess I really don’t know. Should I?”

“No. No, you’re right. It has nothing to do with you except to delay your project.”

Shaking her head, she turned around and limped back outside to her vehicle. She had to go back and try to retrieve her other boot from the mud once the water was turned off. Pulling out her phone, she wiped the dried dirt from the screen and punched speed dial to the museum curator’s private line.

“Tallie? Great to hear from you,” Dr. Sterling said. “How’s it going?”

“Excuse me, sir,” said one of the house staff. “You are wanted on line one.”

“Take a message.”

"I'm afraid he's rather insistent. It's Governor Mitchell."

Cole snatched up the phone. "Governor?"

The man sounded angry. Cole caught two words: "attack" and "hose."

"What?"

The governor repeated himself.

"I most assuredly did not attack her with a water hose!"

"This is getting too good," Wade muttered from the sofa in Cole's home office.

Cole sat forward in his desk chair. "It was a problem with the irrigation system and it's being repaired as we speak."

"I shouldn't have to tell you that Dr. Finley is there on a very important assignment. I would expect you to assist her in any way you can. From what I was told, you also tried to sabotage her dig in other ways." Governor Mitchell paused. "Cole, I've known you boys for a lot of years and, frankly, I'm surprised and disheartened by the reports I'm getting from the director of the museum where Dr. Finley works."

Cole was seething. He found himself out of his chair and pacing around his office. *She* did this. Governor Mitchell had been a family friend for most of his lifetime. But apparently Cole wasn't the only one in the picture who carried some weight. And right now Tallie's side was winning.

"It was all a misunderstanding, Ted," Cole said in what he hoped was a convincing tone. "I was attempting to lend assistance not destroy her work."

"I'd have to say your assistance blew up in your face," the governor replied. "As I understand, she only has another six or seven weeks. Try and work with this woman, Cole. She's highly regarded in the academic community. Graduated with the highest honors and is well on her way to becoming one of the top researchers in her field. It would not bode well for either of us if she botched this dig and you were the reason behind it."

"I understand."

"I hope you do," he returned. "So, how are Chance and Holly? Is married life treating them well?" Cole's younger brother, Chance, had just gotten married a little over a year ago.

"Yes. They're doing great." A lot better than he was. "They just moved into their own house here on the ranch. It's kind of you to ask."

"You tell them both I sent my regards. To Wade, too," the governor said.

"I certainly will, Governor. Thanks for your call."

Cole hung up the phone and felt the room spinning around him. He looked at Wade, who sat five feet away still trying not to laugh. "Governor Mitchell sends his regards."

"I take it that call was about our little archeologist?"

"Don't say a word," Cole warned his brother.

"The two of you make a cute couple."

"Wade, I'm warning you."

"When did you meet her?"

"What does it matter?"

"Exactly."

"New Orleans. That weekend I stayed over after the Coleman merger."

"New Orleans? Interesting."

"Shut up or leave."

"This just gets better and better."

"I think she's in cahoots with someone who doesn't want me to finish my project."

"Maybe if you offered to help her, she would complete her mission faster and get out of your way."

"Tried. Failed."

"What did Mitchell want?"

"The irrigation thing. Someone told him I attacked her with a garden hose," Cole said.

"And you would never do that."

"I didn't!" Cole's anger returned. "Okay, I did have Red and a couple of the boys go digging on her site."

"Bro, you are bad. What else?"

"I asked Stuart to turn some heifers loose in the pasture. She ran them right through the damned fence. Not only did I have to have somebody put up a new fence, Holly spent a week bandaging cuts and giving tetanus shots. But the damned sprinkler system wasn't me."

The most irritating part of the whole thing was that, despite everything, Cole still found her exceedingly attractive. He had even envisioned helping her clean the mud from her body, making certain to check every square inch. The thought had come to him while she'd stood there miserable and soaked to the skin, pointing her finger at him, and he still couldn't shake the image from his mind.

He wished they had met under different circumstances. But when he thought about it, they actually had. If only he could rewind to what they'd shared that weekend in New Orleans. He would have liked to get to know her and see where it would go from there. But with their current situation, it wasn't in the cards. She couldn't stand him for reasons that were obvious. And she made him crazy. He didn't exactly know how to get around that. He refused to grovel. So he would move on, suppress his feelings, and no one would be the wiser.

Eight

"Cole?"

It was Debra Davis, his secretary, a middle-aged woman who'd been his right hand for almost ten years. Hopefully she was calling him to give him the good news that something—a loophole, a favor, money—*something* had been found that would remove the good doctor from his land once and for all.

He knew he was on shaky ground. Tallie was just too damn tempting. In fact she was the first woman in all the years since Gina's death who'd touched him on a level he never thought he would feel again. He needed to keep his eye on the ball, to stay focused on building the corporate retreat. Every time he came in contact with Tallie he lost his mind. He wasn't getting much sleep. Had no appetite. And her beautiful face was always in his thoughts. It was all he could do to stay away. This last-ditch effort to remove her was as much for self-preservation as it was the project.

"Talk to me, Debra."

The silence on the other end of the line was not a good sign.

"There's nothing," his secretary finally said.

"What do you mean there's nothing?" Cole asked, sitting forward in his chair, ready for some serious explanations. Debra was the best. She could find information where there wasn't any. She could make things happen that seemed impossible. She was Cole's genius at the controls. No one could best Debra. This was not the answer he'd anticipated but after receiving the report from his security division, he wasn't surprised.

"I checked with Jeremy—" the lead counsel at Masters Corporation "—the court, Dr. Finley's boss at the museum. There's no way around it. Sorry, Cole, but it looks like you're stuck with her for fifty-one more days."

This was not happening. He'd dealt with bureaucratic red tape before but this was pure insanity.

"See if you can get him on the line, Debra."

"One moment." And it literally only took Cole's assistant one moment to get Tallie's boss on the phone.

"This is Henry Sterling."

"Dr. Sterling? Cole Masters. Thank you for taking my call."

"Of course, Mr. Masters. How can I help you?"

"As I'm sure you know, one of your archeologists, Dr. Finley, is working on some land I own in Calico County."

"Yes. We are all most excited about the possibility of what she may discover." He caught himself, apparently realizing that would not be why Cole was calling. "Your administrative assistant called earlier, asking if the dig could be postponed or cancelled. I'm afraid I couldn't accommodate her."

Cole had to make the man understand his need for Tallie to leave. "I don't know if you are aware but I am in the process of developing that land. In fact, I have cement trucks standing by to pour the foundations for both the main lodge and thirty cabins. Then a pool will be constructed along with other amenities. The dig, as she refers to it, is causing me a serious delay."

"That is regretful."

"It's more than regretful."

Cole felt his frustration rise to the surface. "I'm sitting around twiddling my thumbs while she scrutinizes dirt." Which wasn't entirely true. He had plenty of projects needing his attention, but this was *his* project. Other than the sheer indignity he would suffer if this venture fell apart, his brothers would never let him live it down, all in good-natured joking, but still… Plus, he needed Tallie off his land for a very personal reason. The longer he was presented with the temptation of this woman, the harder it was to keep a hold on his sanity. "Why is there no one helping her?"

"Unfortunately all of the archeologists and even the approved volunteers from both the museum and the university are tied up on other projects. Dr. Finley was scheduled to join a dig in Brazil that is also short on manpower as soon as she finishes at your property."

"Was?"

There was a long pause. "You understand I can't discuss Dr. Finley's employment or any health issues she might have. Let me just say that her participation in the Brazil dig is still to be determined."

"Of course." It struck Cole as odd that Dr. Sterling would bring up her health. What medical condition could she possibly have? He hoped it wasn't cancer or some equally horrific disease. His heart did a flip-flop in his chest. Guilt at giving her such a hard time almost overwhelmed him. "Why don't you hire more people? That would seem to be the obvious solution."

"Primarily the problem is a severely limited budget. We just don't have the resources to fulfill the needs of all the sites allotted to us. Pretty much par for course, unfortunately. Dr. Finley is donating her time and some of her own money to see her project finished. Perhaps you can—"

"So what if my corporation made a donation? Enough for you to hire, say, a dozen people for a year?"

"We are always delighted to receive donations, but I must tell you that isn't the way it works here. Donations are handled through the museum's board of directors. They decide the allocation of funds. There are many other programs that are waiting for backing besides archeology-related projects."

When Cole made no response, Dr. Sterling added, "I am genuinely sorry for your inconvenience, Mr. Masters. If it's any consolation, Dr. Finley is one of our more highly educated specialists with dual degrees in both archeology and biological and forensic anthropology. I have no doubt she will work as hard as possible to complete the dig as soon as she can."

"Are you telling me there is no one I can call and offer to pay them to help her?"

"Not as far as I know. You might try calling the State Archeology Program Center. Perhaps they know something I don't. Would you like that number?"

This was insane. "I'll pass on the number. Thanks for your time." Cole ended the call.

Before he could stand, his private line rang.

"Yes?"

"Cole, I forgot to remind you…" Debra sounded a bit hesitant. Again. What could it be this time?

"The ground-breaking ceremony for the retreat is next week. On Friday. I was afraid you might have forgotten under the circumstances."

He had indeed. "You'll have to cancel it."

Another hesitation. "I can't. The RSVPs have been confirmed with a card from you, thanking them for coming to this—"

"I know what the cards say," he snapped. *God damn.* Some twenty potential investors would be arriving on Thursday. And on Friday they would be escorted to the site where the main lodge would be constructed. Would they see a foundation? Oh, no. Hell, no. They would see one little red flag among two hundred other little red flags and a woman crawling around in the dirt in the middle of it all.

"The limos are set and ready to meet each flight, pick up the guest at the airport and escort them to the hotel then bring them to the project site." Debra stopped talking and the silence was deafening.

"Cole?"

"I'm here." But he sure as hell didn't want to be.

"Have you used your…skills?" He could picture Debra with that irritating smirk on her face. The one she used every time she caught him in some peculiar situation. He appreciated her humor and positive thinking. Except at times like this. "You can be pretty persuasive when you set your mind to it. *Dallas* magazine didn't name you Bachelor of the Year three times for nothing."

This nightmare just would not end. He wasn't about to confess to Debra that the good doctor had already turned him down flat. "I'll consider it. Thanks, Debra."

"I'll talk with you tomorrow. Chin up."

Cole ended the call. What in the hell was he going to do?

He let himself consider seducing Dr. Finley for two seconds longer than he should. He knew he couldn't do it. Not only would it feel wrong to him, a woman with her intellect would never let it happen and he would end up looking like a love-starved idiot. Again. In the short time he'd known her he knew what she would and would not accept in certain situations. And a love affair was probably at the top of her list of things to avoid.

There would be no flattery, flirting or sucking up with Dr. Finley because if he tried he knew she would call him on it. He was drawn to her, his body responding immediately and decisively every time he got close. At those times she could ask him to fly to the moon and he would do it. He had to get a grip on the attraction, step back from her and the situation.

He sat back in his desk chair, took a deep breath then rubbed his hands together, an old habit he had any time he was perplexed about something. Somehow he had to get her out of there, at least for the day of the groundbreaking. Surely she would agree once she understood the necessity.

He could offer to extend the ninety days in exchange for her agreeing to disappear next weekend. It would delay his project even further but at this point, what was another few days? The impression he made next week was vitally important. His plan had been to have the foundations poured and some of the framing completed on the main lodge structure. So much for that idea. All he could do now was pick up the pieces and go from there. And the last thing he needed was Tallie there distracting him when so much was on the line.

* * *

The next day when Cole pulled his truck up to the site, she kept working. For a man who wanted her off his property he certainly spent an exorbitant amount of time at the dig.

"Good morning," he said, smiling.

Tallie couldn't tell if his greeting was forced but she had an inkling he was after something. What was it this time?

"You moved where you're working."

She didn't give the man the benefit of an answer.

"Didn't you?"

With a huffed sigh, she embedded the shovel into the ground and faced the horrible man. "Yes. I moved out of the mud."

"I hope your instincts are right," he said. "Too bad if you spent all this time for nothing."

Tallie chose to remain quiet.

"What's this?" Cole walked over to the sifter, obviously choosing to ignore her cold shoulder. "Is it broken?"

"That's my sifting box and, no, it isn't broken. I normally use it in a plowed field but I decided to try it here. It speeds up the process especially since someone kindly provided me with thoroughly churned dirt. The negative is I run the risk of damaging a relic."

She demonstrated by jabbing the narrow shovel into the earth, used her foot to send it a bit farther into the red soil then dumped her load into the sifter. "Now you shake it and look for anything unnatural left in the tray. Anything you think shouldn't be in there. It could be unusually shaped rocks, onions or other roots from a past garden, or of course, painted pottery, arrow heads, jewelry..."

"Jewelry?"

"Just because people lived five or six thousand years ago doesn't mean the ladies didn't want to look their best."

"Five *thousand* years?" Cole was surprised. "You're attempting to find something from a culture that old?"

"That's the plan. According to my grandmother, our ancestors' tribe dates back that far. But it doesn't matter because it's none of your concern," she replied, keeping her voice calm even though she was flustered. She seemed to constantly be flustered around this man. Thankfully, the little butterflies in her stomach remained on the inside out of sight. "Anyway, how can I help you this morning?" If she had a door, she would help him through it.

He seemed to hesitate; his hands coming to rest on his hips while he appeared to stare into space. "I need a favor," he said, shifting his gaze to her face.

"A favor? From *me*?" She couldn't keep the sarcastic tone from her voice. "This should be good."

"There's a ground-breaking ceremony scheduled for next Friday. I have CEOs from various companies coming in from all over the country. They are interested in investing in my project and want to see it. What little there is of it."

"And you need me to disappear."

His eyebrows rose in surprise, as though he hadn't expected her to understand so quickly. "Friday, if you wouldn't mind?"

She stopped shaking the sifter and faced him, one hand on her hip. "You need to make up your mind. You call my boss and insist I work faster. Now you're asking me to stop working altogether." She shook her head. "Can I know why you want me to stop my work? I mean, what I'm doing is perfectly legal. It's certainly nothing to be ashamed of. In fact it's been my experience that most people are fascinated by what we do. Normally we lose a couple of hours a day from having to stop and give demonstrations or explanations of exactly what we hope to find and how we go about finding it."

"So, you're refusing?"

The bullheaded man obviously hadn't heard one word she'd said. She shook her head and absently pulled the banana clip from her hair. She finger-combed her locks, twisted the length back into a scruffy knot and replaced the clip.

"I'll try and work in an area as remote and out of sight of your guests as possible on that day. But I can't stop working completely. I'm sure it never occurred to you, but I want to go home as badly as you want me to. But this isn't over until I find proof of what I'm looking for or run out of time."

"Even if I extended your ninety days by another four days to make up for it?"

She shook her head. "The day after I finish here I'm on a flight to Brazil." At least that had been the plan before an egotistical, drop-dead gorgeous male had gotten her pregnant. "I just don't see any need to stop if I stay out of the way." She pointed to an area on the other side of a shallow ravine. "I'll work over there while your group is here, but that's all I'm willing to do. I cannot lose a full day of work."

"How about if I call you before we get here and you disappear for an hour or so?"

That would work. She nodded her head and provided him with her cell number.

Today Cole wore a T-shirt, his biceps stretching the short sleeves; a slight smattering of dark hair peeked over the top of the neckline. The jeans he wore were not skintight but it was still easy to see the muscles. They made his legs appear slightly bowed, which seemed to emphasize his sexuality. Well-worn Western boots completed the effect. Which was all undoubtedly part of his plan. Dress down. Talk to her on her lower level. She could appreciate the effort but it didn't work. God! If he would just stop the stupid sneak attacks and be open and straightforward about things.

But she had to admit, whatever he wore, he was temptation run amok. With his almost golden eyes, thick, dark hair and full lips begging to be kissed, he could easily have most women falling at his feet. He could never know how close she was to giving in and running into his arms. She wanted that and more. And how stupid would that be? Cole Masters made her ex look like an amateur by comparison.

Good grief. She pushed such thoughts away. She had to focus on her work and keep her imagination at bay. Still…it was next to impossible to not imagine his arms around her, his lips on hers as he explored deeper inside her mouth, his touch scorching her skin. She envied the beautiful women who drew him like a hummingbird to nectar. But she would never be one of those women. She'd be wise to remember that.

A week later Tallie still hadn't found anything. That morning she slept in. Not that she did it on purpose. She'd always used her internal clock, which was amazingly accurate but apparently had failed to work this time. Cole Masters had turned off the alarm. Her dreams had been filled with him and that bothered her.

Yawning, she thought about her next steps. Toward the cliffs. She just had a feeling if there was ever a tribe in this immediate area, it would be within a fairly small radius of the cliffs. Prepared for surprises, she always began her digs at the furthermost spot and worked her way in. Now, with time growing ever shorter, she needed to move faster, take bigger steps to where the heart of the village might have been. The area where she would stake out yet another grid was still within the field of wheat but would edge her much closer to the sharp incline at the foot of the mesa. If there had been caves in the cliffs at some time in the past, there had to be remnants of a society below.

An hour later, after finishing her tea, she was on her way to the site to set up another grid. It took a couple hours before Tallie tossed her first shovelful of soil from the new area into the sifter. And an hour later still, all she'd found were rocks and some pottery splinters. They were definitely old and came from deeper in the ground than the other remnants she'd found, which was promising. Unfortunately she didn't have the equipment or the software to determine age. That would require a lab. All she could do was make a best guess.

As she began to shake the dirt from the wire screen, a flash of light caught her attention. Glancing over to the tracks behind the cabin she saw a line of limos turning into the gates of the property, headed in the general direction of the cabin. *Crap.* Was this Friday? As usual she'd lost all track of time.

Why hadn't Cole called? That was the plan. Cole was to give her a one-hour heads-up. Reaching into her pocket she pulled out her cell. No bars. She had no reception. She stared at the phone in shock. Cole's guests had arrived. And even after the stunts he'd pulled, she believed in keeping her word. She'd told him she would disappear for a couple of hours and she would do it.

She glanced around her, making sure all of her equipment was out of sight. She was lower than the trapper shack, giving them a better view of her than she had of them. Thankfully everything looked to be as camouflaged as was possible. The sifter was the only obvious tool and there was no time to tear it down.

The cars were slowly approaching the gate to the property fifty yards from the shack. *The shack.* She'd forgotten to clear her things out of the old cabin. Would they look inside? She did a quick mental calculation. She might have time to remove her belongings before the motorcade got to Cole's project site. She'd also have to move her old Ford wagon, which was parked right next to the shack. If they even slowed down, they would know someone was working in the area.

She tossed the shovel into the hole and hurried to the old trapper's cabin. Sprinting up the steps and into the building, she grabbed an armful of clothes and headed back out to throw them into the wagon. The bedroll and pillow were next. She had just cleared the last of her personal items from in and around the rickety old building and shut the Ford's door when the first limo drove past. She darted back inside the shack, having no clue what to do now. Maybe no one would come over. They had no reason to. Backing into the corner next to the window opening, she silently watched as several more limos eased past. Could she slowly back her vehicle out of here without anyone knowing?

The dig was in the opposite direction from the shack and his project site. If she could sneak out the door and get to the oak tree, maybe she could nonchalantly stroll back to her dig? The current excavation was deep enough to provide cover if she could make it there. But she immediately nixed that idea. Better not to take a chance. She would stay where she was and hope no one noticed.

Tallie could hear Cole's voice as he explained his vision for the corporate retreat center he was planning, answering questions and fielding concerns. Then there were a few chuckles, which should be a good sign, but nothing in Cole's voice indicated he was laughing. More to the point, it sounded as if he'd been put on the defensive. Dare she peek at the small group to see what was happening? Curiosity overcame her. Easing over to the doorway, she peeked out in time to see several people in the group pointing toward her dig.

Oh, man. She withdrew inside the cabin. Everything outside got quiet. What was happening? She didn't want to sabotage Cole or his project. She didn't have the same ruthless character he did. His project was as important to him as her dig was to her. She went back over the actions she'd taken since first seeing the limos start to arrive. She was certain no one had seen her dumping clothes and tools in her wagon. She was done before the first car had topped the small rise. So what was going on out there?

She again stepped over to the door, peered around the corner and came face-to-face with Cole. He was definitely not a happy camper. Though his features were still handsome, his eyes narrowed, honing in on her. She pulled back then took a couple of steps further inside the cabin. She felt like an animal caught in a trap. When he stepped inside, the space in the small room seemed to evaporate. His shoulders were so wide he had to turn slightly sideways to enter; his head was mere inches from the ceiling rafters. His full lips were pulled into a straight line. She never thought she would see him angrier than he'd been that first day. She'd been wrong.

"Your presence is requested outside," he said. "It appears digging a hole is more interesting than any project I could come up with. Would you mind coming out and addressing the group of investors?"

"You're kidding." Her voice was gone; a whisper was the best she could do. "Tell me you're joking! Everything is stashed out of sight except…"

"The sifter," they both said at once.

"Why didn't you leave?" he asked in an angry whisper.

"Because I never got your call," she snapped, equally mad. "You should have known there would be no cell service down there."

"Me?"

"Yes, *you*!"

"You're the one digging over there."

"It's not my land."

"You couldn't prove that by me," he huffed. "Come on. Might as well give them some reason for being here."

She took a deep breath and blew it out, shaking her head at the irony. One small sifter on forty thousand acres and that's what they wanted to see. She glanced down at her bare legs and shorts. The worn T-shirt added to the effect. "I'm not appropriately dressed."

Cole's eyebrows went straight up. "Dr. Finley, that is the least of your worries." He walked back outside and turned around. "Are you coming?"

Nine

Tallie didn't want to go out there and address his potential investors, and the temptation to be stubborn almost won out. But, taking a deep breath, she removed the banana clip from her hair and quickly brushed it out. When she stepped outside there were approximately twenty people, men and women, all standing under the giant oak tree, and everyone was smiling. Everyone except Cole Masters.

"This is Dr. Tallie Finley, archaeologist with the North Texas Natural History Museum. She has degrees in biological and forensic anthropology. She's agreed to take a few minutes and answer your questions."

Without any hesitation the questions started coming hard and heavy but she'd heard them all before. Many times. They were talking her language now and she felt herself start to relax. Most people were intrigued by the recovery of ancient artifacts but very few got to visit an actual dig. She could feel the investors' excitement building.

"We're looking for relics dating back about five or six thousand years. We received some evidence that a tribe once lived in this area. Mr. Masters was...*gracious* enough to let us come in and search, even though doing so delayed his own project."

Tallie didn't dare look at Cole, who stood next to her. "If we find what we're looking for, it could change the way we understand Native American history and culture, including my own lineage. We, at the museum, are holding our breath, we're so excited about this site."

Excitement spurred the crowd to ask more questions. Eventually someone asked to see where she was now digging. They followed Tallie down the small incline to the two large square holes.

After explaining the various tools and how they were used, Tallie reached down and picked up a tea can, tumbling a few objects onto the sifter so all could see. She picked one dark gray rock and held it up. "So far I've found several of these. The arrowheads were attached to sticks or poles and used for hunting." She put down the rock and picked up several pieces of pottery. "This is evidence that a village was here. We can scan these pieces and, with today's technology, the computer can give us a realistic idea of the size of the actual pot and, in some cases, what it was used for."

"Isn't that what you're looking for?" someone asked.

"No." She smiled and shook her head. "These are relatively new. Only a few hundred years old."

Everyone chuckled. Except Cole.

Tallie tossed the pieces back into the sifting tray and walked over to an odd-shaped rock, round on one end with a long, narrow stem on the other, sitting near a small shrub. "This we found yesterday." She was careful to use "we" instead of "I," implying a much bigger operation. "It was used to grind corn and wheat." She held it up for them to see. "And, yes, this, too, is only a few hundred years old."

The questions continued: How did she know the age of the samples? What kind of artifact did she hope to find that bore evidence of something five thousand years old? How long would this dig go on? What part did Cole play in all of this?

"If it were not for Mr. Masters, we wouldn't have any chance at obtaining the necessary proof." That much was true, even if it had taken a court order to search there.

She glanced at Cole. His face was unreadable. But his lips were pursed as though he was holding back a grin. Why would he do that?

The questions continued for several more minutes then eventually died off.

"If no one has any more questions, let's return to the house where a late luncheon is waiting." Cole directed them up the slight hill and back to the limos. Before following, he stepped over to Tallie. "You and I are going to have a talk."

"No problem. Name the place and the time." If he thought he could intimidate her, he could think again. He was not so different than John, who walked into a room as though he owned it. The only difference was that Cole actually did own this property.

"I'm curious. Where did you learn to lie so well?"

"I didn't lie." She shrugged. "I just didn't go into too much detail in my answers. And it just seemed like the right thing to do. Have a good afternoon."

Lively sparks lit his brown eyes and that said a lot.

Just what, exactly, she didn't know. But she was ready. She had formed tough armor long ago when she was in school. *So bring it on.*

He looked at her for another few seconds, pursed his lips again and shook his head before turning and walking away.

Tallie finished a quadrant and hung her head. Sitting back, her elbows bracing her shoulders, she asked herself what she was doing wrong. The top few layers of soil had not given up any secrets. Not surprising. Most of what she was searching for was so old it would be covered under several layers of dirt. Erosion, windstorms, flooding, any number of weather-related changes could move soil up or down or to a different location, making it harder to find what she was looking for. It was like stirring batter in a mixing bowl. The question was: where to go next? And how? Lately, she was starting to feel uncomfortable lying on her stomach. She certainly didn't want to do anything to hurt her baby.

She rose, looking at the red earthen cliff less than a hundred yards away. Shielding her eyes from the lowering sun, Tallie again scoured the embankment, alert to any signs of caves or stacked rocks. There were a couple of places that piqued her interest but getting to them wouldn't be a walk in the park. She would continue her search down here. She reasoned if anyone had lived up in the cliffs, they would have surely had to throw something down at some point. So she would keep looking on the ground.

The sun was setting on another day. She would move her exploration to the north, just below the dark spot on the cliff face. How she wished her grandmother was here so that she could ask her any number of questions. When she got back to camp, she would study the map again. Maybe she'd missed something.

She felt sick. She hurried away from the grid and dropped to her knees. She was so tired and the daily sickness seemed to zap the last bit of strength from her. A small part of her wanted to break down and cry—but she clamped down hard on those emotions.

As she walked back to the cabin her thoughts were of Cole. Sooner or later she would have to tell him about the baby. It was beginning to be impossible to snap her jeans, so she'd need some new clothing that would doubtlessly show her pregnancy. How would he take the news? What would he do? Would he accuse her of getting pregnant on purpose or would he be happy?

A sadness in her heart told her he probably wouldn't. Would he deny it was his? She almost wished he would. She'd loved the night they shared. She didn't want to have the memories of that night tainted by ugly accusations and anger. She longed for him to accept her; to accept the baby. But it was not reality. The most she could hope for was to complete her assignment as quickly as possible then leave with him being none the wiser.

Deep inside where no one could see, she'd given the mysterious stranger in New Orleans a small piece of her heart. Now, knowing the true identity of the man didn't change that at all. She remembered the sparkle in both of her parents' eyes when they were together. It was pure devotion; there was never a thought of anyone else. She doubted that dream would ever be hers. Especially with someone like Cole Masters. He was too handsome, too powerful. The epitome of a perfect male. He was everything she'd ever dreamed of. Her and a million other women. She needed to find the proof she was after and leave before she fell in love with a man who would never, *could* never, love her back.

The meeting had gone exceedingly well and while Cole was reluctant to admit it, in large part it was thanks to Tallie. Watching her address the guests, her long hair flowing down her back, and that incredible smile on her beautiful face, he realized she'd been right when she'd said people were curious about her work.

The conversation over lunch was lively, the topics ranging from his project to her dig to Masters Corporation. Cole avoided these last questions, needing the prospective investors to know from the get-go that his project had nothing to do with the family business. Most understood, or said they did, and were okay with it. Then Tallie's search for pottery or whatever she was looking for inched its way back into the conversation.

Several investors told him before leaving that if he was willing to go to such lengths to bring history alive, they had every confidence in his ability to bring his own project to fruition. And they'd all pledged they were on board. In one afternoon, Tallie had helped make his anxiety vanish. And for that, Cole was in her debt.

Tallie Finley was living in dangerous conditions. She could joke about finding the grass snake in her shoe but what would happen when she woke up one morning to find a rattlesnake coiled in the corner of the small shack or under the rusty old bed? He didn't like the odds of her coming away from this dig unscathed. And although signed disclaimers said differently, he felt ultimately responsible. If she wouldn't see reason and leave, it was up to him to ensure her living environment was as safe as he could make it. Staying at the ranch house was the ideal solution. If he was honest with himself, that idea had as much to do with his libido as it did with her safety, but he'd see to it safety concerns were addressed nonetheless.

He'd told her they needed to talk after the investors left. And he wanted to see her; to thank her for her participation and the positive way she'd handled the situation.

Once everyone was gone, Cole bounded up the stairs and changed into jeans and a plaid shirt. He was going to drive out and personally thank Tallie for her assistance. She'd made the difference. When he was dressed, he walked outside and jumped in the truck and headed for Tallie's dig.

It was a beautiful evening for a ride. He should have taken one of the horses, but he'd been in a hurry. A sensation akin to panic urged him to get to her as quickly as possible. He didn't question the why of it.

When Cole drove up to the little cabin he didn't immediately see her. Once more, a little twinge of concern nipped at his senses although why he didn't know.

He walked around to the front of the shack and peeked inside. She wasn't there. He took in the bedroll spread over a nasty mattress on a rusty bed that should have been thrown out years ago. A bird darted out the window. The rays of the setting sun lit the holes in the ceiling. He still couldn't believe she'd been living in this pathetic excuse for a shelter. Glancing toward the river, he spotted two jeans-clad legs under a tree. Sure enough, Tallie leaned against a giant tree trunk, sound asleep. Her hands were pressed together, palm to palm, making a pillow for her head.

When he got to her, Cole couldn't resist reaching out and smoothing her hair back from her brow. She felt hot. Not surprising, given the triple-digit temperatures. But dehydration was not something to be taken lightly.

"Tallie?" He squatted next to her. "Tallie?"

She responded by sitting up and stretching while taking a deep breath. Every nerve ending in his body sat up and took notice. Damn, she was hot. In more ways than one.

She gazed at him, blinking twice then shooting up like he'd thrown cold water in her face. For a few seconds she staggered, fighting to keep her balance and wake up. The surprise showed clearly in those radiant green eyes. Then she looked away and rubbed her hands over her face.

"Have you been drinking plenty of water?"

She nodded. "Yeah. I'm just really tired and I guess I fell asleep. I came down here because it's so hot at the dig." She chanced a glance in his direction.

Cole stood. Her voice was husky from sleep, a definite turn-on.

"But I'm making progress. I—"

Suddenly she staggered a short distance away from him, fell to her knees and proceeded to be sick. Cole honestly didn't know what to do. He walked over to her and pulled her long hair back from her face. By the time the nausea passed, she was trembling.

"Do you need a doctor?"

"No. I mean it's okay. I must have picked up a bug." She sat back, resting her head on her raised knees. "I'm sorry about that."

"No apologies necessary. Let's get you to the house. You need a few hours out of this heat. No arguments."

Her slender nose flared and the muscles in her jaw tightened as though his suggestion made her angry.

What had he said? She quickly brought whatever had bothered her under control.

"Thanks, but I really should stay with the dig. I'm now behind several hours." She turned toward him, still not meeting his eyes. "I really am doing my best to get out of your way. I can't quit. What may be here is too important."

"I promise I won't hold it against you if you take the afternoon and evening off. You've been at this solid for weeks."

She nodded.

"Come to dinner. Take a refreshing shower or soak in the tub—whatever makes you feel better. Get out of this heat for a while and put something in your stomach besides Cocoa Puffs and peanut butter and crackers."

That earned him a glance. He found himself holding his breath.

Finally she nodded. "Okay. If you're sure. That would be great. Thanks."

No woman he'd ever met could pass up a hot bath. And food was probably an equally important enticement under these circumstances. It was not helping his cause to feed and care for the enemy. But he couldn't let her work herself to death. He believed she was giving it her all. And he owed her for making him look good in front of his investors.

"Grab some clean clothes and anything else you need to take and let's go."

"Now?"

"Now," he confirmed. "Before you change your mind."

When they got to the mansion, they parked in the allotted area and headed to the French doors in the back.

The coolness of the air-conditioned room was a welcome relief as were the cold marble tiles under her feet. It was such a great feeling she didn't want to go any farther.

"Do you remember the way to the suite you used the last time?" he asked softly.

"Yes, thank you."

Looking around, she remembered the enormous, eight-foot-wide, natural-stone fireplace that rose to the ceiling of the three-story home. Huge log beams crossed the room just below the ceiling. The entire bottom floor was open, which made it seem even bigger. But it was the kitchen that really took her breath away. A bronze exhaust fan overshadowed the five-burner stove and copper pots and pans hung from a rack above the enormous marble-topped island in the center of the room. An oak table sat in a large area off to the side of the kitchen. The view out the floor-to-ceiling windows was incredible. It was a sight similar to the one she had from the trapper's shack, only from an elevation and a lot more dramatic.

After a wonderful massage in the jetted tub, shampooing her hair and putting on fresh clothes she felt invigorated. Gathering her dirty T-shirt and jeans into a bundle, she brushed out her hair and headed downstairs. The aroma of the food was the next thing to heaven. Cole met her as she entered the kitchen, holding a plastic bag for her laundry. With the light still dancing in his eyes, he handed her a glass of wine.

"You look like a new person," he said as his eyes roamed over the sundress she'd put on. "Very nice."

She knew it was stupid but she hadn't wanted to wear her work clothes. She'd wanted to dress up a little. And it was just a *little*. She'd brought plenty of shorts and jeans and, for reasons she would never understand, she'd thrown the white-lace sundress into the bag along with her sandals. Now here she was, standing in the home of a billionaire in a twenty-dollar dress she'd picked up from a discount store. She supposed stranger things happened to some people but this was it for her.

"Thanks," she said. "That bath was amazing. It's not often we are invited by the local residents to come into their home and experience some twenty-first-century innovations."

"You mean like indoor plumbing?" His eyes sparkled with humor.

"Exactly. I'm almost afraid to ask, but how did the meeting go? Hopefully they all signed up to give their support."

"They did, as a matter of fact. And it was in a large part thanks to you." He caught her gaze and held it. "I appreciate it, Tallie."

"Excuse me, sir," the chef interrupted. "Your dinner is served in the breakfast nook, as requested."

Cole nodded to Andre and turned to her, asking, "Are you hungry?"

"Not really, although it smells delicious." She placed a hand over her stomach. Then, realizing it would draw attention, she quickly let her hand drop to her side.

"Still feeling sick?"

"Maybe a little."

With a hand on her lower back that felt both comforting and strange he guided her through the great room, kitchen and finally to the dining area.

Tallie was surprised to see the room lit only with the glow from a large candle in the center of the table. Suddenly she wished she hadn't accepted the invitation to come to dinner. This had seduction written all over it and she would never fall into that trap again. She couldn't even imagine what a woman would feel on the day Cole Masters decided he wanted to move on. Especially if the woman imagined herself in love with him. But more than likely all Cole wanted was to find out more about the dig and any loopholes that he could use to make her leave. It had nothing to do with her personally.

Remember that.

Cole held out her chair. From this angle she could see the waterfall and the floral display highlighted by hidden lights. Lowering himself into a chair next to hers, he smiled as though glad to have her there. She attempted to smile back. But this wasn't some nice neighbor like old Ben Weatherly down the street where she lived.

She appreciated the bath. She would certainly appreciate a few bites of the delicious food that had just been set in front of her. But she was not stopping her dig. If that was his intention with all of this, he could have well saved his efforts. It would take a lot more than a gourmet dinner and some kiss-up dialogue to make her change her mind.

"So, have you discovered anything remotely interesting as yet?"

She shook her head, trying to keep her eyes from rolling at the question. "Not yet."

"I'm curious. Don't they usually send more than one person on an important dig like this?"

"Yes, they do. I'm here by myself because of budget constraints and because I was the one who provided the map."

He looked surprised. "You found that map?"

She nodded.

"Do you mind if I ask where?"

"It was given to me by my grandmother. Just before she died."

"So she isn't here to provide any answers."

"Exactly. I don't know why she waited. I don't know if she had any more information about where to look. Or specifically what I'm looking for. Everything but the map died with her."

"I'm sorry for your loss."

He was quiet for a while. Tallie knew he was debating if he should ask any more questions. She hoped he didn't. She didn't exactly know what she could tell him.

"This is really delicious," she said, making a valiant effort to change the subject.

He produced a smile that lit up his face. "Thanks. Beef stroganoff is one of my favorites, although I tend to like German food the most. What's your preference?"

"Cocoa Puffs and peanut butter," she answered with a completely straight face.

He laughed. "I guess that puts this a few notches down on the list."

"Well, like steak or lobster, it'll do in a pinch."

"Next time, I'll know what to serve."

Next time? Would there be a next time? She very much doubted it. This was his chance to use his persuasive powers to make her give up the dig. Most likely he wouldn't show her such hospitality again. She just had to get through tonight and perhaps he would leave her alone for a while.

"I feel good about the grid I'm working now. It's close to the cliffs and it looks like there may have been caves in that area at one time."

"And that's important?"

She nodded. "Ancient people often lived in caves. They were nature's way of providing the best refuge against the elements, wild animals and other tribes. I scanned the cliff face with the binoculars but couldn't see anything resembling an opening, even a small one."

"I hope for your sake you find something soon."

He must have seen the disbelief cross her face.

"No. I mean it. The temperature isn't getting any cooler. I can't believe they expect one person to pick her way through acres of land to find a piece of pottery or whatever it is you're hoping to find. You've been here for almost two months. I know you have to be getting anxious to get back to your home."

Tallie hoped he was a better negotiator over a conference table. He apparently didn't know the definition of the word subtle.

"Most of the digs I'm assigned take six to eight months. The number-one requirement for an archeologist is patience. Nothing ever happens fast or on a schedule."

"You must really love what you do."

"I'd better, huh?" She grinned at him and he looked stunned, as though someone had held up a cream pie and threatened to smash it in his face. "The hope of what you'll uncover in the next grid is such a rush. And once you start finding things, you just have to go for the next and the next. I guess to some people it's addictive."

"Are you addicted, Tallie?"

His question in that deep, raspy voice caught her by surprise and drew her gaze to his. It was almost as though he hadn't meant to ask it out loud. He sat back in his chair, one arm resting on the other, and idly drew his thumb back and forth across his bottom lip while he waited for her answer. Her gaze dropped to the movement and his mouth. What would it be like to give herself to him completely now that they knew each other?

Now that she knew who he was? What would he do? What *wouldn't* he do?

A picture flashed in her mind of pure, red-hot passion, tangled sheets and Cole's lips lingering a breath above hers as he moved deeper inside her. Tallie felt the singeing warmth flooding the area between her legs at the thought. The image became so clear, her stomach tightened in knots. Everything about him was so sexy. His handsome face alone would cause most women to feel the overwhelming need to be with him. He looked at a woman with those golden eyes and it made her want to toss any thought of saying no out the window. He was sex personified. All he needed to do was breathe.

Suddenly realizing what she was doing, she quickly looked away. Had he intended her to gaze at his lips? While the entire experience could not have lasted a full minute, her heart was beating out of her chest and her breathing was almost nonexistent. Laying her fork on the edge of her plate, she tried to control her eyes, not wanting to see if he was smiling or mocking her. Even though she didn't know him well at all, the thought that it might be the latter would be hard to take.

She blotted the linen napkin against her mouth. "This was really delicious. And the bath was great. Thank you, Cole."

"Stay, Tallie," he said as she moved to get up from the table. "Stay here tonight. Sleep in a clean bed. No bugs, raccoons or skunks. No heat." He dropped his napkin on the table and looked directly at her. "Unless you want there to be."

Tallie swallowed hard and felt a blush roll up her neck and over her face. She knew what he was suggesting but she didn't know if he was serious or teasing. And she didn't know how to answer.

"I'd better get back to the site," she said as she stood. "But, again, thanks for sharing your home. I feel much better."

Cole rounded the table to stand in front of her. "Why do you insist on sleeping in that shack? You can't possibly be resting well. No one could. Stay here, your choice of bedrooms, and drive to your dig each morning. It makes sense. It's a big house, so neither of us will be tripping over the other." He reached out and tilted her chin to meet his gaze. "It makes sense, Tallie."

She saw a glimmer of passion in his amazing eyes. She'd seen that glimmer before. She wanted to stay. She wanted him. Clearly he was only too happy to oblige. He leaned over and placed his lips on hers. She didn't move away. Encouraged, he encircled her with his arms and pulled her closer. She could feel his erection against her belly and that sent a stream of heat rushing to her core.

"I need you, Tallie," he whispered against her ear. "God help me, I can't stay away." He advanced, pushing her against the wall, threading her fingers with his behind her back. "Give us a chance. This time, no games. We'll both be up front. Make love to me."

Cole knew exactly where to touch, how to kiss to make her entire world spin out of control in a way that was good and wild and exciting. He was temptation run amuck. And she craved it. She'd heard stories of hot, steamy sex, of the climax that made you feel you were flying up to the stars, but she had never felt that sense of completion until one sultry night in New Orleans. "I'm flattered, really. But I'd better get back to my dig." She let go of his hands, breaking the physical tie between them.

"My intentions are not to flatter you. Take me off the damn pedestal, Tallie. I'm just a man. A man who wants you. Who needs you. You make me feel like no other woman ever has."

It was hard to argue with a man who towered over her with a look on his face of pure sincerity and a voice to back it up. Tallie closed her eyes, inhaling the scent of pure male, and her body responded accordingly, leaving her wanting to ask only where he wanted her.

Her eyes fluttered open and she stepped away. She'd almost done it again: succumbed to him and his desire. He was merely taking advantage of a situation that had landed in his lap. She believed he meant no harm, but the man had a reputation with the ladies and in business circles she'd heard he could be ruthless. If she took him up on the offer, she would feel awkward to still be stuck with having to deal with him until the ninety days on the site were up.

Without any warning, the room began to spin. She reached out for something to steady herself and found Cole's arm. "I...I think I'm going to—" Blackness surrounded her.

Ten

Tallie awakened on the sofa in the spacious den. A cool, damp cloth was being pressed against her forehead.

"Hey." Cole's voice called to her. "There you are."

Tallie didn't have time for small talk. Nausea was hitting hard and fast.

"Bathroom." She sat up. "Where is…?"

Cole stood, clearly looking concerned. "Down that hall on the right."

Tallie prayed she would make it in time as she lit out like a bottle rocket. When the worst was over, Cole stood ready to hand her a damp washcloth. Tallie dropped to the bathroom floor, too weak to move.

"Let's get you to a place you can lie down." Without another word, he scooped her up into his arms as though she weighed nothing.

"I'm so sorry I upset the dinner. I lost that great dinner."

"Don't worry about it."

He laid her gently on a huge bed in one of the bedrooms. The en suite bath was close by.

"Thank you," she said and closed her eyes. She couldn't think about the embarrassment of what had happened. She would have to face that tomorrow.

She must have dozed. She awoke sometime later with a kind-looking, gray-haired man sitting in a chair next to the bed. Cole hovered in the doorway.

"Tallie, I am Dr. Jenkins," the man introduced himself. "Can you tell me what happened?"

"We, uh, we had dinner. I stood up when we were finished and the room started spinning. Next thing I knew it was lights out. When I woke up I was exceedingly nauseous. I feel better now, though still a little queasy. It's probably just a two-day bug or something. No reason to bother you."

"You are most likely right about the virus, but since I'm already here, let's find out, okay?" He smiled. He was so gentle and reassuring Tallie couldn't help but agree. "Cole," the doctor said without looking toward the door, "please close the door on your way out."

The door was closed without any protest.

"Now, let's start with your lungs. Can you sit forward and take some deep breaths?"

He checked her lungs, looked in her eyes and throat. "Have you been feeling sluggish?"

"No."

"Any fever?"

"No. Not that I know of."

"Any other stomach-related virus?"

"No."

"Okay." The doctor returned his instruments to his

bag. "One last question," he said. "Could you be pregnant?"

Tallie could feel the blood drain from her face. She should have anticipated the question. She had been with one man. And that man was no doubt standing on the other side of the door.

"I didn't mean to upset you, my dear," the doctor said, concern covering his face. "It's definitely a personal question. I mention it only because all the symptoms you described fit. How about you come by the office tomorrow and we can run a test and be absolutely certain?"

"Okay," she agreed. But Tallie knew he was right. She had already seen an OB-GYN. Today wasn't the first time she'd felt that wave of nausea. She was pregnant and Cole was the only man who could be the father. And she knew he would not be pleased. And that was an understatement.

"Dr. Jenkins," she said, "please don't say anything to Cole about your suspicions. I'm an archeologist here for a limited amount of time. If he thought I was…well, he might make me leave and my work here is highly important." There was no way she would tell anyone who the father was, especially Cole and his doctor. Schemer. Tramp. Gold digger. Con artist. The insults she'd face would be endless. She just had to wrap up her work as quickly as possible and leave.

"I would never discuss a patient's health with anyone without prior written approval," he assured her. "But I must advise you, if you are with child, working outdoors in this heat could cause complications. It's a very realistic possibility that you could lose the baby."

That didn't help to calm her racing heart.

"Shall I let Cole come back in? I know he is worried."

She nodded; after all, she would have to face him sooner or later. "That's fine."

As soon as the good doctor left the room she was out of the bed, had her shoes on and was ready to walk out behind him. Cole met her at the door.

"I'm fine," she said, unable to look him in the face. "Sorry I caused you so much trouble."

"Where are you going?"

"Back to the dig site. I imagine it's late and everyone wants to get to sleep."

"I'm everyone. And I don't want you going back out there tonight. If you want, I can have some men stand guard over your things, but you need to have some time to hydrate and chill out under the air conditioning."

"I'll be fine."

"Did the doctor say what he thinks it is? Why you collapsed? Why you got sick?"

"He wasn't sure. Probably a virus I picked up somewhere."

Cole was looking at her with suspicion written all over his face. She had to get out of there and go somewhere she could be alone and sort all this out.

"I insist you remain here at least for the night. We can talk about future accommodations later."

She was torn between wanting to be away from him and wanting to stay in his home. To say it was very comfortable was an understatement. To sleep on fresh, cool, silk sheets atop a mattress as soft as a cloud was beyond tempting. But the longer she remained in his presence, the more tempting it was to come clean about the baby.

"Tallie, it's the right thing to do and I think you know that."

"Fine. Okay," she said. "But just for tonight."

"Good. No more badgering then, but we are going to discuss this. You need to sleep here from now on."

"I appreciate the loan of the shirt," she said, choosing to ignore his other statement.

Later, as she lay in bed inhaling the rich, relaxing scent of the linen spray, she wished she could remain here. But Cole would discover her secret soon enough without pushing it in his face. She would, therefore, remain at the old shack and hope she would find the relics she needed sooner than later.

She was up early. Dressed in the white sundress, she headed down the stairs. A woman in a maid's uniform met her in the kitchen.

"Good morning, ma'am. Would you care for a fresh cup of coffee or tea?"

Do bears have hair? "Tea would be wonderful. Is it possible I might also get a piece of dry toast?"

"Certainly, ma'am," the woman replied as she poured the tea into a large mug.

Tallie slipped onto a bar stool and added sugar and cream to the tea. She took a sip; the tea was amazingly good, better than what she could make for herself. Maybe before she left to return home she could find out the brand. It was definitely worth asking.

"She found the tea." Cole's voice came from behind her. She turned in her chair to face him. "How are you feeling this morning?"

"Much better, thank you. Cole, I am so sorry that I—"

"Stop. I'm just glad it was nothing serious."

Tallie swallowed hard and nodded her head. How serious was being pregnant? She knew in that moment she should tell him but couldn't bring herself to do it. Not here. Not now.

Cole slid into the chair next to her and sipped his own tea while Tallie ate her toast. She needed to get back to the dig while the temperature was still cool.

"I need to fly to Houston this morning," Cole told her. "I'm going to trust that you won't work so hard that your body overheats again."

"I won't."

"Good."

"I'll be back by six or seven. Consider moving into the big house. I don't want you sleeping out there with no telling what. Raccoons, at the very least."

"I'll be fine." She smiled at him. "I certainly don't want to intrude in a bachelor's domain."

"You would only make it better." He leaned down for a kiss and, with renewed promises he would see her later, finished the last of his tea and walked with her to his truck.

While Cole was in Houston, she wanted to get back to work. That was the only thing that seemed real and solid.

Half an hour later she had changed into shorts and a T-shirt and was busy mapping out a new grid. She loved working with the soil, the rich scent of the earth a heady reminder of what might be buried below. It was easy to get lost in her work and lose track of time, even when she wasn't really finding anything. The next thing she knew, when she paused and looked up from the dirt she was sifting, the sun was already low on the horizon.

She'd just stepped inside the old cabin at the end of the day when her cell phone began to ring. Her eyebrows went up in surprise to see Stan Bridger's name flash across the screen.

"Hey, you," she said, smiling. "It's about time you came home." Stan had been on a dig in central Mexico for the past three months.

"You will get no argument from me," he replied.

Stan was a good friend who had initially been the deciding factor in her choice to major in archeology. Several years her senior, he had helped her attain her Ph.D., cheered her on when she'd landed a job with the museum and stayed with her during most of her first dig. He'd taught her about all the documents required and the basic day-to-day operation on a dig. She had a sneaking suspicion he'd been partially responsible for her getting the job, but he wouldn't admit it and she couldn't prove it. As the months passed she'd let it drop. It no longer mattered. But they would always have that bond of friendship.

"Wondering if you would care to meet me in your little town for dinner?" he asked. "I'm dying to come out to your dig, but Sterling warned me off. A simple, 'where's Tallie?' landed me in the principal's office. So now I'm more curious than ever."

Tallie laughed. "I would love to. I've been thinking about a trip into town anyway."

"How about seven?"

"Perfect. I've been told there's a little family-run diner that has great food. Everything from sandwiches to steaks. It's called Frieda's Sandwich Shoppe. Apparently there is more on the menu than the name would imply."

"Sounds great. I'll see you then."

Tallie realized her stomach was much better today and she was hungry. That was happening more and more often. She assumed it was because of the pregnancy. There was no sign of Cole. He must have been detained in Houston. She would drive into town and meet Stan for dinner. A steak sounded good. And a piece of coconut pie. Maybe Frieda had that on the menu, as well.

When Cole arrived at the old cabin, Tallie was nowhere to be found. Only after checking the river and the dig areas did he realize her Ford wagon was missing. Apparently she'd had enough of the heat, the bugs and the rodents. How long would she be away? Cole felt a sinking feeling. Where had she gone?

It would have been nice if she had told him or someone on the ranch that she was leaving. The idea of her disappearing didn't sit well. He'd become used to her being here every day. He'd driven here with the intention of asking her to come to the house for the night.

On his way back to the estate his cell phone began to ring.

"Hey, little brother." Wade's voice came over the phone.

"Hey, man. Haven't talked with you in almost a month. How was the trip? Or are you still in London?" Wade had been negotiating the acquisition of a boutique hotel chain to expand Masters Corporation's presence in Europe.

"Nope. Got home last night," Wade explained. "There have been some changes. Thought you might like to have an update and I need your signature on a couple of documents."

"How about steaks and a couple of cold ones at Frieda's?"

"Done. Give me an hour and I'll be there."

When Cole got to town an hour later, the small eatery was packed. Not surprising for Frieda's on a Saturday night. Cole spotted Wade at a table along the wall and headed in that direction. The diner was a laid-back kind of place but served the best food in three counties. After each of them gave their order Wade asked, "So, how's it going with your archeologist? Have you been able to reclaim the land where Tallie is digging and move forward with construction?"

Cole shook his head. "No. Tallie is going to be here for a while. I've done all I dare do to *entice* her to leave. I'm just going to let it play out. She had Tom Mitchell call me."

"I was there the day he called, remember?" The grin on Wade's face said he was not above teasing Cole about the entire ordeal, somewhere Cole didn't want to go. Circumstances had changed but he didn't intend to enlighten Wade tonight.

"I don't think it's that damn funny."

"Do you honestly think she doesn't know who was behind all the shenanigans?"

"She does. But she is as good at giving back as she is at taking."

"Really?" Wade tilted his head for a harder look at his brother. "I've always wanted to meet the girl who brought Cole Masters to his knees." He chuckled again. "She must be one hell of a woman minus the mud pack."

Before Cole could answer, the small bell above the door tinkled, indicating a new customer had entered the diner.

"You're about to get your chance to find out."

Cole watched his brother turn and gaze at the sexy woman who'd just come in, her long black hair swinging against her shoulders and down past her waist. She responded to the wave from a man at a table not far away. A man several years her senior.

"Brother—" Wade leaned toward Cole "—I'd have

to say you have a bigger problem than putting up with an archeology dig. Damn. She is hot. I'll trade places with you anytime. Just say the word."

"I don't think there is a word," Cole responded, suddenly overwhelmed with a protective instinct. He wasn't sure what brought it on or what triggered it but his love-'em-and-leave-'em brother could stay the hell away from Tallie. And another quick glance at Tallie with the older man clearly showed they had a close rapport. Dr. Tallie Finley might be taken, anyway. And didn't that set well? Small wonder she didn't want to stay at Cole's house.

Tallie immediately spotted Stan as he waved to her from a table. When she drew closer she was surprised to see David Sloan sitting with him. They were all employees of the museum and all great friends. After hugs all around, they sat and barely stopped talking long enough to look at a menu. After ordering, the two men wanted to know the focus of her dig—why she was here.

"Sterling is tight-lipped," Stan said. "We didn't think he was even going to tell us where you were. So, what's the deal?"

"There isn't one," Tallie replied. Seeing the skepticism on their faces she added, "There really isn't. When my grandmother died she left me a map, supposedly marking the spot of the original village of our ancestors, and asked me to see if I could find it." She shrugged. "So that's what I'm doing. I had some leave time before the Brazil trip so Sterling said if I wanted to do this…do it."

"And here I was imagining the find of the decade and getting jealous as hell," Stan admitted and everyone laughed.

"Dr. Sterling did say something about your host, the

guy who owns the land. Is he really that bad or is Sterling making mountains out of molehills again?"

"He really is that bad," came a deep voice from behind Tallie. "I can guarantee it. Wouldn't you agree, Dr. Finley?"

Tallie tensed as she realized Cole Masters was standing directly behind her. Her dinner partners' eyes were focused above her head; their mouths hung open. She turned partially around in her seat so she could answer him.

"Absolutely. Without any doubt whatsoever he is, by far, the worst landowner I've ever had the bad luck to work with." She forced a broad smile.

"See, I told you," he addressed the group.

"Cole, these are my friends and coworkers, Doctors Stan Bridger and David Sloan."

"And, like Dr. Finley, both of you dig up bones for a living?"

His eyes sparkled. He was so handsome, so charming. He would undoubtedly have her associates eating out of his hand in no time.

"We confess." Stan laughed. "Would you care to join us?"

Had Stan just invited him to sit at their table? She didn't want Cole sitting with them. He wouldn't understand half of their dialogue and she, at least, wouldn't understand his. They were so different. He dealt with blueprints and erecting skyscrapers; she with old maps and digging up the past. She felt the warmth of his large hands on her shoulders as though he was ensuring his claim was known by all. She might be carrying his child but that didn't mean she had become his property.

"Thank you, but I'm here with my brother. We have some business to discuss. Maybe another time?"

Tallie looked to her left toward the table where Wade was sitting. Their gazes met and he smiled and nodded.

Wade stood and made his way over to their table. Cole seemed surprised but made the introductions. Wade seemed keen on holding Tallie's hand far longer than the norm. She couldn't miss the sparkle of interest in his eyes.

"I hope all of you have a nice dinner," Cole said, stepping between Tallie and his brother. "I can vouch for Frieda. Everything on the menu is delicious. It was good to meet you all."

"You, as well," Stan and David chimed in.

Cole and Wade returned to their seats just as a waitress set their plates on the table.

"Don't say it," Cole warned his brother.

"Say what?" Wade asked, total innocence on his face.

"I know you're about to say something crude having to do with my relationship with Dr. Finley. She is just an archeologist doing some work on land I happen to own."

Wade finished chewing and wiped his mouth. "I was merely going to suggest you put it in a higher gear before someone beats you to it. The way you looked at her? The way she looked at you? I know how much you were hurt by Gina. But that was over three years ago. If you let this one get away, you're an idiot."

"Well, thanks for sharing your thoughts."

"Hey, any time, brother."

Eleven

Cole continued to watch Wade with a knowing eye. Often Wade's glance would trail back to Tallie, but he never said another word about her, which was the norm for Wade. He would speak his mind once then drop the subject. The problem was that Cole saw the same thing. He felt what Wade described. The one thing he was dead wrong about was assuming three years was long enough to get over what had happened with Gina and the baby she'd carried.

The emotions that ran through Cole were strong, deep and confusing. His wife had been pregnant with another man's child yet had vowed that she loved Cole. She'd sworn her love to him while all the time she'd pledged that same love to someone else. That was if the woman could love at all. If there was even such a thing as love. If Cole had it to do over, knowing what he knew now, he'd just give her whatever she wanted. Then, perhaps, he wouldn't have ordered her from the house and she wouldn't have driven so recklessly that she went over the cliff, killing her and her baby. But she had played him. And he'd sworn he would never be caught with his pants down again. He wouldn't be the idiot twice.

He'd assumed what he felt for Gina in the beginning was love. But the bitterness that rose within him at her treachery trumped any other feeling. He didn't know, would never know, what love was or if there really was such a thing. The entire concept was dubious, at best, and eventually he'd grown weary of trying to make sense of it. If he needed a woman, he'd find a willing one and that would be the end of it. Never again would he be made such a fool.

He looked toward Tallie. She was talking and laughing with her friends. It hit him hard: this was the first time he had really seen her laugh and show true happiness. A sickening knot grew in his throat as he remembered all the mean pranks he'd thrown her way. Any one of them could have caused her to be hurt in some way. From now on he would do anything necessary to ensure her safety. And that included getting her to move into the house and out of that shack.

"So, what's your schedule like?" Cole asked his brother. Anything to distract himself from thinking Tallie might be a crook in archeologist's clothing.

"I have a full day tomorrow, meetings back-to-back, then a return to Paris for the meeting with Yves Bordeaux." Wade laid his napkin next to his empty plate. "I'm afraid I'm gonna have to cut out on you early."

"I understand. Before you leave...has there been any news on Dad's will?"

"Not a word. Apparently it's more involved than we thought." Wade shrugged. "Valuing a company whose holdings continue to change and grow daily will be a challenge. I don't envy the team of attorneys and CPAs whose task it is to figure it all out."

"I agree. I only mentioned it because I don't like something hanging over my head. Dad acted so different the last few years of his life. There are several deals hinging on what's in that will. It's been months. People are starting to call. I'd just like to get it off my plate."

"I'm with you, bro. That thought has run through my head more than once."

"I'll call the attorneys tomorrow. Whatever Dad decided in the will, all we can do is agree with it or contest it, but it's past time we got to it."

They finished up the business and Wade got Cole's signature on some legal papers. Then, with a handshake-turned-man-hug and a quick slap on the back, Wade made his way to a waiting car that would return him to the county helipad where he would fly back to Dallas.

Cole took one last look at Tallie before he followed his brother out the door into the warm night air. In the parking lot he sat in his car, his finger poised over the start button. About then Tallie and her friends walked around the corner of the building. The younger man hugged her goodbye and got in his small car and drove off. Tallie slipped inside her old Ford wagon and the older man got into his vehicle. He turned his car toward the exit. Tallie followed. Both turned right.

Where were they going? The route to the ranch was in the opposite direction. His hands on the steering wheel and foot on the gas seemed to take over as he pulled his car out behind them. Regardless of telling himself no, that he had no right to do this, he kept going.

Within three blocks the first car turned into the parking lot of a small motel and she drove in behind him. Cole had his answer. He drove past in time to see Tallie walk toward one of the rooms. His hands clenched the steering wheel while his jaw muscles worked overtime.

At the next light, he made a U-turn and headed back to the ranch.

When he got home, he closed the door and tossed his keys on the kitchen counter then made his way to the bar and poured two fingers of Crown Royal before flopping down onto the overstuffed leather sofa. The window gave him a distant view of the acres he'd purchased adjacent to the family ranch for the purpose of building the lodge and cabins for the corporate retreat project. Usually somewhere out in the darkness he could see a small glow from Tallie's barrage of candles she'd begun to leave lit while she'd slept. There were no lights on tonight.

Cole finished the drink and headed to the bar for another. Enough of these and he wouldn't give Tallie another thought. *Maybe. Nah.* With no conscious decision he opened the French door and stepped out into the evening shadows. Still no sign of any light from the shack. Was she still at the motel? He huffed out a sigh. *Let it go.* She'd most likely be there all night. Feeling anxious, he decided to make a quick drive over just to make sure everything was as it should be.

He pulled out his cell phone, called her number and listened to the ringing on the line.

"Hello?"

It was the deeper voice of a man.

"Sorry," Cole said. "I must have the wrong number."

"Are you calling for Tallie?"

"Yes."

"You've got the right number. She's stepped away

for a few minutes but she'll be right back. Would you like to hold or leave a message?"

The man's voice sounded tired, sluggish. Cole had to wonder what the guy had been doing to make him sound so fatigued. *Not your business.*

"No," Cole replied. "This is Cole Masters. I had a question for her but it will wait until tomorrow."

"I'll let her know you called."

Cole terminated the call. So, the good doctor had a man in her life. Good for her. He had to admit he was surprised, but why should he be? She was an incredibly beautiful woman. She probably had men lining up around the block.

Cole felt a sinking sensation in the pit of his stomach. This time he knew exactly why. He wanted her. In his mind he saw her lying back in his bed, those green eyes welcoming, calling him to come to her. He knew how she tasted and he wanted more. He wanted to again run his hands over her silken skin; he wanted to feel the heat from her body. Feel her quiver in anticipation. Anything she wanted of him, he would give her.

Damn. He had to stop this. She was obviously involved with someone. Even if she wasn't, their time together hadn't exactly been a whirlwind of friendship and, in a matter of weeks, she would be gone. But the governor was right. Cole needed to take care of her: see that she slept in safe, cool surroundings and had appropriate food and water. He could also try harder to find someone to help her. First thing in the morning he would put the idea into motion.

Whether she liked it or not.

He heard the ringtone on his phone. It was Tallie.

"Hey."

"Stan said you called. Is everything all right?"

"I just wanted to make sure you were planning on sleeping at the house tonight."

"Oh." She sounded hesitant. If she was coming from another man's bed, how could he expect her to sound any other way? He swallowed back the bile that rose in his throat at the thought of another man touching her, making love to her.

"Tallie, I won't allow you to live in that shack one more minute. It isn't good for you."

"We can talk about that when I get back. Now, if there isn't anything else…?"

"No. Nothing else."

She ended the call and his anger surged. Maybe he had been a bit overbearing but she had to see it was out of concern. He glanced at the lighted dial of his watch. Ten o'clock. Why not just wait for her at the old cabin? He was sure she wouldn't come back to the house. And he knew that if he stayed there and waited for her, he'd have a restless night.

Two hours later there was still no sign of Tallie. Was she really going to spend the night with that man? A red glaze of anger obscured Cole's vision and, with no further thought, he got into his pickup and headed to town. He drove straight to the little motel, walked up to the room he'd seen her enter and beat on the door.

Finally, after another round of knocking, the man opened the door. He'd obviously been asleep.

"Where is Tallie?" Cole almost barked.

The man looked confused. "She went home. Rather, she went back to her dig."

"I just came from there. Her vehicle isn't there and neither is she. When did she leave here?"

"Right after she talked with you. She was upset."

"She isn't the only one." Cole glanced at the bed.

There was no indication that two people were sharing it. The unused pillow was still draped in the cheap bedcover.

"Look, man," Stan said. "She was just here going over some pics on my laptop of my latest dig. If you feel this way about her, you really should be up front. Tell her. She was hurt once. The guy went as far as to ask her to marry him then disappeared when some woman he thought was better came along. Not even a note. Nothing. Personally, I don't think you can find a better woman and, if my wife wouldn't get all bent out of shape, I might pursue Tallie myself. Now, is there anything else?"

Cole muttered an apology for disturbing the man and returned to his truck. When he arrived home, he entered through the back door and trudged up the stairs to his room, shedding his knit shirt as he went. Out of curiosity, he opened the door to the bedroom he'd given Tallie the night she'd been sick. Sure enough a small glow from the lights outside showed a sleeping form. He flipped on the overhead light.

"Oh! Turn off that light," she whispered and pulled a pillow over her eyes. "Where have you been?"

"Out looking for you."

At that she pushed the pillow away and rolled toward him. "Why? Did I misunderstand your *demand*?"

"No, you didn't. You're in exactly the right place."

"Then turn off the light and leave me alone."

Cole ran his hand over his face. The entire time he'd waited for her by the shack, she had been in his house asleep. He didn't know whether to laugh or cry. He flipped off the light and moved toward her bed, sitting on the edge.

"Tallie."

"Hmm?"

"Are you and your friend in a serious relationship?"

The minutes passed until he thought she wasn't going to answer. She sat up and twisted around until she could see his face. "You mean Stan?"

"Yeah." Cole nodded.

"I told you, Stan is an old friend." She glared at him. "He is also married with three kids. You must not think very much of me at all to ask me that. It's discomforting you think most of what I say is a lie."

"Most people lie."

"Well, I'm not one of them," she snapped.

Cole didn't know what to say. Once again he'd put his foot squarely in his mouth.

Tallie threw aside the covers. "I'm going back to the cabin. I should not have come here in the first place."

"Tallie."

"First you strong-arm me into coming here, which I only did because you were right about getting out of the heat. But I am not about to stay with a man who thinks of me that way. You are an arrogant snob. So disappointing." She slid out of the bed and went to the bedroom closet to pull out a pair of jeans and a shirt. "And don't you dare try and boss me around again."

In a heartbeat Cole sprang from the bed and beat her to the closet door. Tallie looked up into his eyes and he saw the glimmer of passion in her emerald depths. Without waiting for permission, he scooped her into his arms and carried her to his bed.

"What are you doing?" she asked. "Put me down."

He set her on her feet but rather than turn away, he slowly began to unbutton the tiny buttons of her nightshirt. When it fell to the floor he removed her panties and she was standing naked in front of him, the memory of a beautiful vision coming true. Her curves were more luscious than ever; roughing it in the trapper's cabin had had no impact whatsoever on her incredible figure.

His erection was straining almost painfully against his jeans. Before he could release himself, Tallie was there, her hands unsnapping then lowering the zipper. Without saying a word she pushed his pants over his hips, freeing his erection.

Cole kicked off his jeans, picked her up and placed her on the bed.

Pushing her back on the bed Cole was once again enthralled as the taste and the scent of her surrounded him. His mouth came down over hers as his larger body molded to her. She was his. He wanted to brand her so that no other man would ever touch her this way.

Tallie writhed beneath him. He remembered how she moved, how she whimpered with need, and how those light, feminine sounds made him fight to keep his control. How she sent him whirling like no other woman he'd ever bedded. He kissed her neck, nibbling on her ear before going farther down her body. Her breasts were ripe and when his mouth closed on a swollen rosy tip, her hands grabbed his hair and held him to her. She arched her back, her breasts swelling beneath his touch.

He rose and with one hand positioned himself at her core She was hot and moist. He pushed in gently, savoring the feel of her. Her breathing intensified. Then as his body began to move, he had no clear thoughts of anything or anyone but Tallie.

The passion between them grew until he felt his body quiver with the need for release. He knew she was close by the way she responded. He pulled out and kissed her belly then farther down. Tallie grew still then cried out as she climaxed. Cole held her until she calmed.

He reentered her and as he pushed in deep he knew he couldn't hold out much longer. He brought her to the peak once again and felt the tingling sensation in his lower back telling him there was no turning back. This time when Tallie climaxed, Cole was right there with her. Then he kissed her gently, pulled the covers over them and held her close.

Tallie loved making love with Cole. She loved being with him even though at times he was overbearing and demanding, always wanting his way. So far, his intentions had been good, but the reality was that she would soon be several months along and someone like Cole Masters didn't appear in public with a pregnant woman at his side. It would ruin his playboy image and the tabloids would go crazy. And, honestly, it was more than she wanted to put herself through.

Cole was devoted to his business, as she was to her job. Both required them to be gone for months at a time. He lived in a world of money and privilege. Hers was a quiet life of digging in the dirt. She couldn't think of one single thing they had in common other than the baby he didn't know about. According to the internet articles she'd read about him, he was a man who hadn't changed his lifestyle in all of his adult life. But having a baby with Tallie would be a big change. For him and for her.

He would have to deal with a stubborn woman who would not listen or follow his demands. She did not do demands. He would have to realize when she'd had enough and know when to back off. She was independent while Cole was overprotective. It was a hopeless situation. Her mind kept silently screaming for him to just leave her alone. Her heart said to take what he was offering and just love him. But how much would he love her when he found out about the baby?

Tallie felt like a rug had just been pulled out from under her. Hopefully she could find proof of her family's beginnings and leave before Cole was ever the wiser.

Twelve

When he'd made love to her last night, it was like their shared night in the Big Easy on steroids. The passion was just as hot as it had been the first time only without the fear involved in opening herself to a complete stranger. He was so strong and, she had to admit, there were times when she didn't mind his demands so much.

Why couldn't he have been a normal guy? One who drank beer instead of imported hundred-year-old whiskey? A guy who liked to watch sports on TV with his buddies instead of from a box on the fifty-yard line? A man who drove his car to work every day, not one who got in one of three helicopters and flew away. He was a billionaire. And Tallie didn't know how to relate to such a person. Or even if she wanted to.

If she could view him as normal, there were a hundred-plus things to love about him. But the hard fact was that he was not a regular guy and never would be. The ego, the arrogance, the expectations, the demands. Life was too short to put up with that. She'd lived through eight long months with John, who'd had the same qualities, and she'd ended up being dumped, her heart and her pride shattered. No way would she put herself in that situation again, especially with Cole. She knew if she ever let her barriers down, the love she had for Cole would be so much deeper, more profound. And if he walked away she might never recover.

Tallie dressed and went downstairs. There was no sign of Cole. She followed her nose to the kitchen where the tea was brewing.

"If you need Mr. Cole," said Martha, the kind maid who worked with Chef Andre in the kitchen, "he said he was going to the main barn."

"Thank you."

Tallie could swing by there on her way to the dig. Grabbing a hot cup of tea, she stepped outside. She passed through the back gate of the estate grounds and followed the natural-stone footpath to the large, sprawling building.

She heard neighing from inside the barn and her pace quickened. She loved horses. She'd had one in her younger years but had had to sell her when she'd left for college. Now, being here on the ranch, she missed that mare more than ever.

Midway down the main aisle Cole stood talking with another man holding a baby. She didn't want to interrupt so she slipped past them and continued down the wide stable aisle, looking at the horses in their stalls. Magnificent was the word that came to mind. Their sleek, shiny coats gleamed under the barn lights. Ears alert, they nickered to her as she passed.

"Tallie," Cole called to her. "Come back. There's someone I want you to meet."

He reached out for her when she got close and pulled her against him, his arm going around her shoulders.

"Tallie, this is my brother, Chance. Chance, meet Dr. Finley."

"Very nice to meet you." He extended his hand.

"You, as well."

"And this young lady in my arms is Emma. She's my wife's niece but we're raising her as our own daughter."

The child was adorable. "Hi, Emma."

"Momie gonna wide hawsee. Daddy say no but Momie not yisen."

"Where did the two of you meet?" Chance asked, switching Emma to his other arm.

"New Orleans," Cole answered. "A little over five months ago."

"That long, huh?" Chance grinned. "That's encouraging."

"When you find what you've been searching for, why waste time?"

Tallie stood there in complete shock. Cole was lying to his brother. Yes, they had met in New Orleans, but everything after that was a trumped-up story. Cole Masters could have any woman he wanted. He certainly hadn't been searching for *her*. In that moment she wished things between them could be different: that Cole was really in love with her and wanted to marry her just because she was who she was. But Cinderella dreams were not in abundance this year.

"Cole!" called a young woman leading a large, dapple-gray thoroughbred toward them. She was beautiful, with angelic features and long, silver-blond hair.

Without pausing she stepped into Cole's arms. "Even when you stay here on the ranch I never get to see you."

"I guess today is your lucky day."

"In your dreams."

"Holly, this is Dr. Tallie Finley," Cole said. "She's an archeologist doing some excavating on that land I purchased a few years ago."

Holly turned toward her, a wide grin on her face. "Very nice to meet you."

"Tallie, this is Dr. Holly Masters, Chance's wife."

"Who's going to put that horse right back inside his stall," Chance stated firmly, which caused Holly to roll her eyes.

"I don't know how long you'll be here," Holly said to Tallie, "but one thing you'll soon learn about the Masters brothers is they are all bossy control freaks. Always have been, now that I think about it."

She turned to her husband. "I'm just going for a short ride, *dear*."

Chance pulled his wife to him and kissed her. "We just found out Holly is pregnant. The doctor said no horses until after the baby is born. Some hardheaded mothers-to-be just refuse to listen to common sense."

"Congratulations," Tallie said. "To both of you. That's wonderful."

"We gonna has baby," Emma chimed in.

"We just moved into our new house on the ranch. If you can spare the time, come over and visit for a while."

"I would like that. Thank you." Tallie was moved by the kind invitation.

Cole took her hand, said his goodbyes and walked with Tallie out of the barn toward the house.

"It was nice meeting your brothers. You have a great family."

"You sound surprised."

"No, not at all."

"It was good to see Chance. The three of us rarely get together anymore. As Holly said, they just finished building their home about five miles away from the original house, the one Dad built for Mom, which is where I've been staying. Chance was in the SEALs but while he was home on leave after an injury he started seeing Holly and he never signed up for another tour. Instead he took over running the Circle M. When the profits began to soar, no one was surprised."

"What about Wade? Does he live here, as well?"

"Wade lives in the family mansion in Dallas. It's close to the airport and built for entertaining and meetings. Since Wade does most of the traveling and entertaining, it works out well."

"And what about you?"

He shrugged. "I live here and there, wherever I'm needed at the time."

"So you were telling the truth that night in New Orleans."

He laughed. "Yeah. For the most part. But I can honestly say I've never spent a night under a bridge."

"You did look like a bum."

"That wasn't exactly the plan, but it had a good outcome, don't you think?"

"I have to go this way," she said, turning away and purposely not answering his question.

"Tallie, why don't you let someone else look for the artifacts?"

She shook her head. "I could use the help. I won't deny that. But it's my dig, Cole. I promised my grandmother I would find the proof that an ancient tribe lived in this area. It's my responsibility. I intend to shorten my work days and not be out in the heat so long. I'll be careful, but I must try and find…what I'm searching for." Whatever that turned out to be.

She could tell Cole wanted to argue with her; she felt his body tighten. But he said nothing and for that she was grateful.

"Then I'll see you later."

"Absolutely."

A week later Tallie had barely finished her morning tea, which she still took outside the trapper's cabin even though she was now living under Cole's roof, when a strange car rolled up to the site. The doors opened and four young women got out of the vehicle; the driver remained at the wheel. They all walked toward Tallie, excitement on their faces. Before Tallie could ask who they were and why there were there, Cole's pickup pulled up next to the car. He got out, grinning from ear to ear. Yep. Whatever this was, Cole Masters was behind it.

Their eyes met and his sparkled with mischief.

"Good morning, Dr. Finley," he said as he nodded to the four women. "Have you met them yet?"

Tallie shook her head. "No."

"Carolyn Hicks, Amy Knell, April Hastings and Kathy Brown. These exceptional students all have a perfect grade-point average and are majoring in anthropology or archeology at area universities."

Cole had a smile that reminded her of the fat cat that ate the canary.

"They all applied for internships at various museums for the summer. All were turned down because of budget restraints. I managed to correct that small issue and here they are. Ready to go to work. They are actually excited to help you dig in the dirt. Go figure."

He turned to the four students. "This is Dr. Finley. She is the one you will be helping."

Tallie was speechless. "Do…do any of you have any experience?"

All but one raised their hands. The one who apparently didn't have experience looked anxious.

"Well, if you have an idea of what this is about and can dig carefully, I can teach you the rest. Welcome. And thank you all. I really do need your help.

"Look in the back of my old wagon and you will find a box with extra hand tools and brushes. Get a small hand shovel, a four-inch rake and two brushes—one small, one large. The site is that way. If you grab your supplies and head over toward that sifter, I'll be with you in just a few minutes. Did everyone bring water bottles?"

They all nodded; two of the women held theirs up.

"Good. Hop to it."

"I can't believe you did this." Tallie turned to Cole.

"What? You don't want them?"

"No. Yes! They'll be great. I was about the same age when I was selected for my first dig. It will give them valuable experience and help me, as well. Thank you, Cole." And without thinking she bounded into his arms and hugged him tight. "Thank you so much."

She felt his arms go around her back and squeeze her gently to him. Then his arms dropped and she stepped back.

"You're welcome." She couldn't miss the twinkle in those hazel eyes. He handed her a manila envelope. "Inside is the basic information on each student and their signed wavers. I'll provide a place for them to stay and all the meals."

For the first time in what felt like forever, Tallie was speechless.

"Tallie?"

"Why are you doing this?"

"Let's just say I want my field back."

"But all of this trouble…it must be costing a fortune."

"It's really not that much. I want to do it, Tallie. I look at it as a donation. Find your artifacts. I want to see your face when you show me the first one." He must have seen her look of astonishment because he made no attempt to hide his grin. "I'll catch you tonight."

Tallie stood in the shade of the giant oak tree and watched until he drove out of sight. If she was dreaming, she never wanted to wake up.

The girls proved every bit as knowledgeable and eager as she'd first surmised. She gathered them in a small circle and explained what they were looking for. She couldn't tell them they were looking for a new civilization, but did confirm they were searching for artifacts from a tribe that dated back several thousand years.

"Beads, pieces of jewelry, pots in part or whole," she told them. "Keep an eye open for anything that looks like it could be made by man. Also, you might happen on petrified seeds, plants or bulbs. There are two grids. Two of you take one, the other two take the second. If you find anything you can't identify, set it to one side for me to look at. Do you have any questions?"

Once all the questions were asked and answered, Tallie left them and walked closer to the cliff. Through her binoculars, she again searched for any sign of caves or openings between the massive rocks and boulders. The same dark, shadowy area she'd spotted last week still called to her. It might be worth the effort to climb up and check it out from a closer viewpoint. But in her condition, she didn't know how a climb like that would be possible.

With stakes and string she outlined a third grid and got to work. The hours flew by. It was almost two o'clock when she heard a strange honk and looked in the direction from which it came. It was a bus. No. An RV. Followed by a car. The massive recreational vehicle came to a stop just to the other side of the old trapper's cabin. The sight brought Tallie to her feet. Cole had said he was going to provide lodging for the students. And here it was.

"Hey, guys," she called to the college students, "I've gotta return to the cabin for just a few minutes. I'll be back as soon as I can. Take a break and make sure you stay hydrated!"

Dropping her tools, she jogged in the direction of the RV. The driver, a robust man in his fifties, was just stepping out when she reached the door.

"Good afternoon," he said. "Are you Dr. Finley?"

"Yes."

"I'm Clay with Big D RVs out of Dallas. If you wouldn't mind, I need you to check the RV inside and out. If you find everything is okay, I'll ask you to sign that you received the vehicle and all is in order. First let me get it set up. Is the location okay or do you want it moved?"

"It's perfect where it is."

"Good. There is some leveling we need to do and it has four extensions, plus the main compartment will about double in size. Let me get the TV and all the extras set up then I'll need you to give it a look."

When he was done preparing the RV, Tallie stepped into the amazing vehicle.

Clay adjusted his cap, scratched his chin and gazed longingly at the river. "Any fish in that stream?"

"I think there might be, yes. You're welcome to see for yourself."

"Good. While you do the inspection, I think I might have a look."

The RV was enormous. She had no idea a recreational vehicle could be so luxurious. There was a master bedroom plus two smaller ones, a whirlpool tub, even two, big, flat-screen TVs with satellite, one in the master bedroom and a larger one in the living area. The entire vehicle was actually larger than her apartment. The air-conditioning was pure heaven. It contained state-of-the-art appliances, granite countertops, even a small chandelier in the main living area. And the kitchen was fully stocked.

As she stepped outside another car drove up and a man got out holding several large boxes of pizza and a case of sodas. "Dr. Finley?"

"That would be me."

"I've got your lunch. Where would you like me to put it?"

Tallie knew Cole was behind all this. He had said he would provide a place for the students to stay and all meals were on him. "Put them over on the porch of the old cabin for now."

"Yes, ma'am," he said and walked in that direction.

Jogging down the hill, she gathered the students and told them about the pizzas and soft drinks. That seemed to lighten their mood even more.

They all gathered on the rickety porch and didn't hesitate to open the boxes and grab ice-cold cans of soda.

"When you've finished eating, you are welcome to go inside the RV and check out your new home." They all looked long and hard at it. First one then all headed in that direction, forgetting about the food.

Cole Masters was a take-charge kind of guy. If she accepted this, what was next? Her heart missed a beat at the thought.

After signing the inspection papers, Tallie drove to the mansion. Finding the door unlocked, she stepped inside and closed it behind her. She stood in front of his office door, waiting for him to finish his phone call, ignoring his gestures to come farther into the room. Finally he ended the call and stood, an unmistakable mischievous light shining in his soft brown eyes.

"The RV was just delivered," she said, wrapping her arms around her chest, suddenly a bit uncomfortable. "Thank you."

"You're welcome. The girls can move in there for the duration of the dig.

"I intend to donate it to your museum after you leave. They can use it or sell it. I don't care. But I do care about your safety."

"But—"

"No buts. The RV is for the students. A guard will be on duty at all times during the evening hours. We don't have any crime to speak of around here but I will feel better if someone is out there making sure it stays that way. You can continue to stay here. You need rest, which it's doubtful you'll get if you try living with those college kids. They'll probably keep you up until four every morning."

There was a moment when neither Tallie nor Cole moved. Tallie was held by the strength of his gaze; she was close enough to see the different colors of gold and brown in his eyes. There was even a touch of green.

Almost in slow motion he dipped his head and kissed her.

She heard him draw in a deep breath as his hand cupped the back of her head, his fingers threading through her hair. Feeling her response, he quickly took the kiss up to the level of a sensual demand. She was lost. The scent of his cologne surrounded her, his strong arms held her firmly against him. But she wasn't going anywhere. His hungry mouth feasted on hers, his tongue seeking hidden places. Absently her hands clutched his shirt, pulling him nearer even though there was only one way they could get any closer. That thought propelled her out of his arms, breaking their amazing kiss.

To become involved with Cole would be to commit emotional suicide. Her heart would become involved and it was almost guaranteed he would then tire of her and disappear.

"I can't do this," she whispered against his lips. "I need to get back to the dig."

She turned and headed for the door.

"Tallie, wait," Cole called to her.

But Tallie didn't stop or slow down. As tempting as he was, she couldn't let herself be swayed into a brief affair regardless of how badly her body wanted him. The effect of his kiss was still raging through her body, the need for him pooling deep in her belly. But she would not be a fool again.

By the time she'd returned to the dig she was in more control. Her mind had cleared enough that she had regained her focus. She had to do more, work harder and faster, so she could leave. Before she had to tell him about the baby and bear his wrath.

By four o'clock she called a halt to the day. The temperature was in the nineties. Everyone needed a break, including her. She had twice stepped on tree stubs, leaving the bottom of her left foot bruised. It hurt like the dickens.

Tallie gathered her backpack from the cabin and headed for the main house on the hill. In a few minutes she had her soiled clothes washing, found a box of crackers and a jar of peanut butter in the kitchen and fixed a glass of iced tea. As bad as she wanted a shower, she made it no further than the large bedroom upstairs. Setting her glass, the crackers and peanut butter on the nightstand, she pulled back the covers and fell into bed. Sleep wasted no time in claiming her.

Thirteen

Tallie woke sometime in the night. A night-light provided just enough glow that she could see and recognize the furniture and doorway leading into the huge en suite bathroom. Throwing back the covers, she walked toward the bathroom. She wanted to get into that huge tub and let the jets massage her from every direction. It would feel amazing.

She turned on the water and heard a soft knock on the bedroom door. She went and opened it. It was Cole.

"I saw the light under the door. Are you all right? Is there anything you need?"

"Nope." She turned toward the bathroom. "I'm good. Just woke up and wanted a bath." She began to remove her T-shirt…and stopped. Cole was still standing in the room. When she stopped, it took him a second to realize he needed to leave.

"Could I borrow another T-shirt? I need to do laundry."

"Sure."

She wouldn't admit it out loud but she preferred staying here versus staying in the RV with four excited, talkative college students. While she was plenty thankful for their assistance, she preferred some peace and quiet.

When she got in the tub, she quickly applied body wash and felt the silken suds roll down her body. She began to wash her hair in the same wonderful herbal solution as the body wash.

When she was done, she grabbed a towel and quickly dried herself off. It was then she again heard a soft knock on the bedroom door. Encircling her body with the towel, she answered the knock. Cole stood there with a couple of navy blue T-shirts.

"Oh, thank you." She reached out to take them. As soon as she did, the towel slipped. Grabbing for it did no good. She looked up at Cole.

He reminded her of a golden warrior with his tanned skin and sun-bleached hair. His shirt hung open, partially revealing a muscled chest and ripped abs. Slowly she lowered her hands, no longer caring that she was naked or that Cole was standing two feet in front of her. She felt his hot gaze roam over her breasts and her nipples hardened under his gaze.

Cole stood in front of her, letting her see the smoldering desire in his eyes. His erection signified that she wasn't alone in her need. He was a handsome man, a brilliant man. Forget about the money. That night in the French Quarter had been a turning point for Tallie. Cole had showed her how glorious sex with the right man could be.

She went to step back but before she did Cole came forward. Not one word was spoken as he gently cupped the back of her neck and slowly pulled her to him. With a deep groan, he plunged his tongue inside her mouth. Cole enticed her to open her mouth wider as though he was willing to fill it with all she needed.

With an almost savage moan, he cupped her face in his hands and he went deeper, searching the hidden depths of her mouth, taking his time as though this was a moment that had to last a lifetime. He tasted of wine and mint. But it was the scorching heat that told her exactly what he wanted. He changed his stance, moving still closer, and his big hands cupped her hips, pulling her hard against his obvious desire. He was grinding against her, making the fire pool in her lower regions.

Suddenly he spun her around and pushed her up against a wall, his body holding her in place. He moaned as he kissed her even more deeply. His hard, muscular body pushed against her, hips moving, letting her feel his erection before taking it away. Tallie couldn't suppress the frustrated groan. She grabbed hold of his shirt and tried to pull him to her. He huffed a laugh and tore the shirt off. Tallie began to unbuckle his belt.

Cole hadn't meant to hover in the doorway while bringing the T-shirt to Tallie. He'd been so overwhelmed by her beauty he couldn't have turned and left had his life depended on it. Again, he couldn't help noticing how voluptuous she looked. It was like watching nature in its purest, most beautiful form. On her face was surprise. In her mesmerizing green eyes, honest desire. He had grabbed on to that need and refused to let go unless she said one word: no.

There were at least a hundred reasons why he should have walked away and only one why he didn't: he'd never wanted a woman so badly in his life.

Her body was hot from the warmth of the water, her skin smooth as the finest silk. She tasted like the wild berries that grew deep in the vistas near the towering pine and oak trees. When he drew back to look at her lovely face, he swallowed hard. Unbridled passion surged through him, his erection straining against his jeans until it was painful. Her eyes were closed, her head was tilted back, her mouth open, lips pink and swollen from his kiss. She grasped his shoulders as he traced a line of heat down her throat to the junction of her shoulder with his tongue. He nipped at the velvety skin and thought he would die of pleasure.

Her hands had stilled on his belt, the passion of their embrace apparently taking her mind down a different path. He quickly unbuckled the buckle and unzipped his jeans, pushing them down just enough. His hands roamed over her back and down past the waist to her hips. He didn't pause before he lifted her and settled her body against him, entering her slowly, watching for any signs of discomfort. She moaned and lifted her legs to go around his hips; her head fell back against the wall and she moaned in ecstasy.

"I can't go slow," he said as he felt his control slipping.

"Then don't," she whispered.

He entered her body fully, completely, with one hard thrust. Tallie whimpered and, gripping his shoulders, pulled his head to hers for another kiss. Cole did not disappoint. The feel of her holding him was unlike anything he'd ever experienced. So tight.

His body began to move, pulling out, entering again. Over and over; again and again. Suddenly she threw her head back, her climax fully overtaking her. It almost took him with her, but he held on, wanting to give her more pleasure. He wasn't nearly finished with this incredible woman who had come into his life so unexpectedly.

With her legs still wrapped around his waist, he carried her to the bed, laying her down on the silken coverlet, never breaking the link between them.

"Tallie," he whispered softly.

She was breathing hard, her body limp and fulfilled, but she managed to open her brilliant green eyes and smile. He threaded her fingers with his and brought them to his lips.

"I want more of you."

She smiled her understanding and nodded with no thought of denying him. Lifting her head off the bed she found his mouth and kissed him, this time letting her tongue explore the depths of him. Her touch set off a ticking bomb in his chest, his gut and his mind. He broke away from her lips, letting his tongue discover her ear, neck and shoulder before coming to her breasts. His hand kneaded one while he suckled the other almost frantically. The dark, rosy-pink tips were swollen and rigid and he suckled first one then the other. Tallie moaned and arched her back, offering herself to him.

When she raised her legs and arched her hips toward his, Cole knew he wasn't going to hold out much longer. With his fingers threaded through her silky black hair and his lips on hers, he began to move.

He pushed in farther, time after time. Her incredible silkiness was so amazing. He inhaled the rich scent of her body; she smelled like lavender, with a hint of wild Texas sage. She altered her position and he knew. He knew what she needed, what she wanted. He felt her still then cry out as the whirlwind carried them both to the heavens and kept them there.

Finally, breathing hard, he fell to one side of her, pulling the edge of the comforter around her. She moved enough to place her head on his shoulder and, with his arms holding her close, he fell into the sweet oblivion he hadn't known in forever, going to a place it seemed only Tallie could take him.

The next morning, Cole slowly came awake with the memories of the night before vivid in his mind. Tallie was still asleep, her head still nestled on his shoulder. Her long hair fanned her shoulders and spread over his chest. She was as beautiful and incredible as ever. She had such passion. Such a wildness that carried him into the realms of the untamed. Their actions were driven by something stronger than passion. It was fierce and uncontrollable, sex in its rawest form. He felt his body getting hard at the thought. He would stay in this bed with her all day and into the night if he could talk her into it. He had never once thought of staying with a woman so long, needing her to stay with no end in sight as they made love over and over again.

Regretfully, business awaited, both hers and his. He pushed the covers back and got out of bed. With one last look at the woman still asleep on the bed, he turned and walked to his room.

Tallie woke in an empty bed. She knew Cole had held her through the night. It was the best sleep she'd had in a long time. Maybe since New Orleans. She smiled at the thought. The sun was just cresting over the horizon when she made her way into the bathroom. She hadn't expected last night to happen but she wasn't sorry. In fact, she felt just the opposite. Cole was an incredible lover. Smiling, she padded to the shower. The water was warm, streaming over her head and down her back as she grabbed for the exotic-smelling soap.

She had just stepped out of the shower and finished dressing when the nausea hit. She couldn't do much more of this, she thought to herself. It had to stop soon. Trembling, she reached out for a towel and wiped her mouth. Standing, she turned toward the sink for the toothbrush and ran straight into Cole.

He was frowning, a look of concern covering his features.

"Do I need to call the doctor?" he asked.

She shook her head. "No, it's just…"

"Tallie, don't tell me it's just a bug. No one gets a virus that lasts this long. Whatever it is, you can tell me."

She had to tell him. To continue to withhold the news was deceitful and just wrong. And if she kept the secret too long, he might think she was trying to set him up. If he hated her for it, so be it. She turned to face him.

"Cole, I was afraid to tell you, but I can't go on living a lie. What I have is morning sickness. I'm pregnant."

The silence in the room was deafening. Cole stared at her as if trying to find some sign she was joking. She saw his Adam's apple bob in his throat as he swallowed hard.

His eyes narrowed while his jaw worked overtime. "You're saying you're pregnant and I'm the father?"

"Yes. It…it happened in New Orleans."

She watched as he swallowed, his features turning dark. He turned away, as though he couldn't look at her anymore.

"That's impossible."

"I assure you it isn't."

Silence cut through the room like a knife. He rested his hands on his hips.

"That was almost five months ago. And you are just telling me now?"

"Until two months ago, I didn't know who you were. Then I didn't know how to tell you."

"What do you want, Tallie?"

Her quick intake of breath filled the silence. "I don't want anything."

Her heart beat wildly in her chest while alarms rang in her ears. This was it. What would he do?

"When were you going to tell me?"

"I don't know."

"What does that mean exactly?" The pure anger in his voice made her jump.

"It means that as soon as I told you, I knew you would accuse me of…all sorts of terrible things. Getting pregnant on purpose at the very least. Of being a gold digger. A tramp." She looked away. "I couldn't deal with that."

"Did you, Tallie? Did you become pregnant on purpose?"

She could only look at him as her eyes filled with tears. "No." It was a whisper, but the best she could do as one tear slid down her face. That Cole had even asked the question was almost more than she could take. "No. I'd just earned my Ph.D. and was about to start on a career that had been a lifelong dream. The last thing I ever expected was to get pregnant."

He looked down at the floor as though the answer was there. "It won't work, you know. Regardless of the planning, the backing, whatever determination you have, it will not work. You're not the first and you probably won't be the last to try this."

Tallie couldn't pretend she didn't know what he was saying. He thought she was using her pregnancy to scam money out of him. She didn't know what to do now. She'd played this scene out in her mind a hundred times but it always stopped with him calling her on it. She'd never ventured to imagine what would happen next.

"What did you hope to achieve by coming here?" He turned and looked at her again and she fought not to cringe at the rage in his eyes. "Does this…dig, this search for a lost civilization, have any basis in fact?"

"What does it matter? You won't believe anything I say."

She reached out to open the door and saw that her hands were shaking. Not surprising. In less than fifteen minutes Cole had gone from the sexy man she was falling in love with to the deadly, dangerous man she'd encountered when she first showed up on his land. A man that any sane person would stay well away from.

"If it's proven to be my child, I will take care of it, certainly. And likewise the mother of the child."

"I'm not asking for anything from you." She opened the door as the first tear fell from her eyes. "I don't want anything. I can take care of myself. I just wanted you to know that you're going to be a father."

With that said, she marched down the hall, her heart broken into small pieces. Her mind was a jumble of twisted thoughts. She had to get her clothes…had to pack up her things… Cole hated her for something she hadn't intentionally done…she had to talk to the girls…

"I'm flying out this afternoon on business." His voice carried down the hall. "Pick out a dress and some wedding rings if you wish. When I return in five days, we will be married."

That brought her to an immediate stop. Slowly she turned to face him, to face his anger.

"I'm not marrying anyone."

"You will be here when I return and we will be married. In fact, there's no time like the present to get the license."

"No." She spun on her heel and continued toward the back door.

Heavy hands gripped her shoulders and she was turned around. "Do not push me, Tallie."

"Why? What will you do? Threaten to destroy the dig? Sue the museum? You know, I feel sorry for you. The very first time I saw you it saddened me that you were so alone. But now, I realize that's the way you want it. You are going to end up a lonely old man who will look back on your life with regrets. But I won't be there to see it."

"I wish I could believe you because I almost bought the whole package. Wife, children, family, a permanent home. You, of all people, didn't have to do a goddamned thing. I was falling for you. I thought..."

"What? What did you think, Cole?" The tears she'd fought so hard to hide rolled down her face. Her heart felt as though it was breaking in two.

"I thought you were the first honest person I'd ever met."

She couldn't stop the small cry that left her throat. Her heart shattered. Into millions of tiny pieces. She had never felt such pain. She lost the battle to control herself as the tears ran in waves down her cheeks. She wanted to scream at him, *I'm not lying to you!*

"I'm a realist, Cole. You are not the average person. I imagine that you and your advisors have to contend with schemers trying to get some of your money every day. I'm not one of them. But I have no way to prove it. I didn't tell you because I didn't want to see that look of betrayal in your eyes."

"There is no look of betrayal. We will marry as soon as I can arrange it."

"No, we won't. I refuse to marry a man who doesn't love me. And you just made it clear that you don't believe me or want anything more to do with me. That isn't love."

"I'm just curious, Tallie. Was the entire New Orleans thing staged?"

"*What?*"

"Was it all part of some plan?"

"There was no plan." Her voice was dull, as though the soul inside her body had given up.

He let out a sigh. "I would think by now you would be willing to come clean. But, no matter—we *are* getting married. No way is my son or daughter going to be born without my name whether the baby was conceived under false pretenses or not. It isn't how I roll. It isn't how this family operates."

"I'm not marrying anyone. I've been through a painful breakup once. I'm not about to go through that again by entering into a marriage I know won't last." She looked at Cole. "Based on what you just said, you must have doubts that you're the father."

He thought about that question. "Should I?"

"No. I'll do the test. That's only fair. But I don't want to marry you, Cole."

"That, my dear, is too damn bad."

Tallie tried to work but her heart wasn't in it. The girls seemed to know something was wrong but didn't approach her and she was grateful. Cole had left after he'd taken her to the doctor's office for blood work then to city hall to apply for a marriage license.

He had looked at her then, his usually golden eyes a flat brown, his mouth pulled into a straight line, his dark brows drawn into a frown. "I expect you to be here when I return."

His words were daggers straight to her heart. He had dropped her off at the mansion, picked up his briefcase and, without another word, walked out the door. She'd fallen onto the leather sofa and hadn't stopped crying for hours. Or was it days? And she had not heard from him since that moment.

She stayed for only one reason: she loved him. She could put herself in his place and doing so helped her understand the pain she'd brought to his doorstep. She felt duty-bound to try to do as he asked when all she really wanted was to run away and hide.

At 4:00 p.m. she called a halt to the day. Rain clouds were hovering and the temperature dropped into the low eighties. She stepped back and looked around her. The only place to go was up. Into the cliffs. There might be caves she hadn't spotted yet. Five months into her pregnancy, she debated if she could climb a ladder. Probably not the smartest thing to do.

After herding the girls to the RV and saying good evening to the two cowboys who arrived for their evening watch, she ambled to her old car and headed for the ranch. She could think of a thousand places she'd rather be.

And the next five days went pretty much the same way. She went to the dig site, worked with the girls until four in the afternoon, then returned to the mansion for another lonely night. She still hadn't heard from Cole since their argument. He hadn't called. It should have made her happy but instead she felt dead inside. This situation was not going to work out well.

But tonight, on entering the house, she immediately

heard his voice. He must be in his office talking on the phone.

"Chances are meant to be taken, Matt," she heard Cole say. "In business. Not on a personal basis."

There was a silence while Cole listened to the person on the other end of the line.

"No, I really didn't give it a second thought, which was stupid on my part. She was hot and willing and I saw no reason to abstain. She had good references, the family liked her… A few months later she tells me she's pregnant. I used protection. In this day and time I'd be a fool not to. It was then I began to question her and everything about her. I hope like hell you did the same in your situation."

There was another silence. Was Cole talking about their time in New Orleans? She had always prided herself that she wasn't an eavesdropper but it would take a bomb to pry her away from that door.

"What are you going to do?"

Silence.

"Think about this, Matt. She's probably after money. It never fails. And usually there is another man touted as just a friend that's the real father of the baby. He is also the banker. And unless you catch him, he will clean you out. Right now she could take you for everything you're worth. Beat her to the punch and offer her a payoff up front. Let her know your suspicions. If she even considers it, you will have your answer."

Another silence.

"Then all I can tell you is to have your attorneys draw up an ironclad prenup. I'm afraid you're gonna need it. I hope I'm wrong but I haven't seen a woman yet that didn't have those twenty-four-carat stars in her eyes. They will even track you down to get some of it."

Long silence.

"Well, good luck. Keep me posted."

Tallie tried to swallow but her throat had gone dry. Quickly she hurried away from the door, down the hall and out to her car. She felt shocked but her mind told her she shouldn't have been surprised. What else had she expected?

Tallie wanted to ask him how much longer this would go on. How much punishment did he intend to dish out for something that was equally his fault? But she didn't. The overheard phone call had pretty much said it all. She needed to leave. Immediately. Before he tried to force her into a marriage that was wrong on so many levels.

Everything bad she'd imagined happening if Cole found out about the pregnancy was coming true. His words had penetrated her shield of self-protection like a laser cutting through butter. What he'd said hurt deeply. He'd spoken of her like some vicious, impersonal stranger. He considered her someone who expected money for a romp in the bedroom. Now he felt compelled to marry her and give their baby a name. He had described their relationship in such a cold, unfeeling way.

She had never had sex without caring for the person she was with, but realistically that's exactly what she'd done. Knowing how he felt about her brought back the tears. And she couldn't blame Cole. She couldn't blame anyone but herself.

She didn't have to be told twice that she wasn't wanted. She would leave with all possible speed. Returning to the dig wouldn't accomplish anything. He would find her there—if he even bothered to look. She would leave her things and arrange for someone to pick them up later.

She climbed inside her old Ford and started the engine. It was past time to go home.

Cole emerged from his office sometime later, tired but stimulated by the conversation he'd just had with the CEO of a company they'd been trying to do a deal with for about four years. The man had finally looked at the figures and was suddenly interested in a merger and the potential money he would make.

Cole smelled food cooking in the kitchen and headed in that direction. Andre was busy making supper.

"I will have this ready for you in about ten minutes, Mr. Cole."

"That will be fine, Andre. Have you seen Dr. Finley?"

The chef looked at him with a confused expression. "Dr. Finley left. She called Carson and said she would send for her things."

Left? Tallie was gone? "What time did she leave?"

"I'm not sure. A couple of hours ago at least. Carson would know."

"Did she say where she was going?"

"No, sir. She did seem quite distressed but all she said to me was goodbye."

Cole thanked Andre and walked into the den. Tallie had actually left. That was a first. Usually it took a herculean effort to get a woman to leave once she showed her hand. Did Tallie expect him to follow her? To track her down and demand she come back? She was in for a surprise if she did.

He hated being played. He was tired of it happening over and over again. Women saw the name Masters and that's all they needed to know. He had actually thought Tallie would still be here now that she had Cole where she wanted him. In fact, that she'd left was a bit unexpected.

Curious, he sped up the stairs and entered the room she'd been using. Her clothes, everything, was there, including the set of wedding rings in the small black case on the dresser. He opened the box. The rings were there, sparkling against the black velvet. So she hadn't taken the rings. It didn't appear she'd taken much of anything. That surprised him.

Returning to the ground level he called out to Martha, "I have to make a quick run to the bank. Hold supper if you can."

When he stepped outside the sky was already turning black. Storm clouds hung low. He saw lightning in the distance; he heard the rumble of thunder. He jumped into the truck and headed toward downtown Calico Springs. It wouldn't take long to sign the papers he needed to sign down at the bank then he could return home and have a nice quiet evening. As he backed out of the parking area, raindrops began to beat against his windshield.

When he rounded the sharp turn just before the town came into view below, he saw the red, blue and yellow lights up ahead. Police had the area roped off, the road closed to one lane while the firemen pulled ropes and ladders from the truck. It was almost the same place where Gina had plunged off the cliff. Without conscious thought, his gaze honed in on the ambulance. By the time he reached the area, his hands were wet, his mouth dry and his heart was beating out of his chest. He slowed and came to a stop. One of the policemen approached the car.

"Sir, you need to keep moving… Oh. Mr. Masters. I didn't realize it was you."

"I had a friend traveling in this area. She would have passed through here. Could you just tell me if that's a Ford wagon at the bottom of the ravine?"

"No, sir. It's an old Chevrolet. Driver is a man, covered in tattoos. It appears he had one too many, was driving too fast and couldn't make the curve. Looks like he will live, though."

Cole let out the breath he'd been holding. "That's very good to know. I appreciate it, officer." When he saw the officer nod his head, Cole continued on. He drove a short distance down the road and pulled over. He drew a deep, shaky breath, striving for calm.

When he had first seen those flashing lights and realized another accident had happened at that turn in the road, he'd almost lost it. Fate couldn't be that cruel. It easily could have been Tallie at the bottom of the cliff. *Oh, God.* Realization came down on his head and shoulders. What had he done?

Tallie was not like Gina and if she had gone over the edge it would be his fault entirely. Torn between relief and worry, he was glad Tallie had not followed the same path as Gina but he was still concerned. Where was she? He once again turned the truck around and headed home. His business at the bank could wait.

Now that the news of the pending birth had soaked in, he was excited about their child.

Tallie was pregnant. She'd said that he was the father and he should have believed her. It was the same scene as had played out with Gina, only that child had not been his. But Cole knew in his gut that Tallie wouldn't lie to him. He'd screwed up big time.

He'd handled the knowledge she was pregnant badly.

He'd done exactly what she'd thought he would do: accuse her of trying to pull a fast one. Of getting pregnant on purpose. He still felt his heart sink to his knees every time he thought about what he'd said. He may have lost Tallie and his son or daughter permanently after his cruel allegations.

She had tied one on at a bar in New Orleans and taken a chance on giving herself to a stranger. It must have taken everything she'd had even with the help of alcohol, to give herself to him. But she'd picked the wrong man. He had been so intent on seeing every woman as a lying, conniving cheat that he hadn't considered staying with her long enough to talk the next morning. He'd walked out on her. What a fool he'd been.

Damn. This was all his fault. He'd screwed up royally. First he'd gotten her pregnant then blamed her that it happened. He had to find her. He had to apologize, to explain. Hell, he had to ask for her forgiveness. He'd never done that before, but he imagined groveling would be involved. A tinge of pure fear ran through his body that even if he found her, she would reject him. It's what he deserved. But he loved her and that was a first for Cole. He would be proud of their child. Proud to call Tallie his wife. He was willing to do whatever it took.

He tried calling her repeatedly but there was no answer. He didn't have her boss's home number. He would have to wait until tomorrow to contact Dr. Sterling. Then he would make her listen. How could he have insinuated she had lied about the baby and accuse her of getting pregnant on purpose? He knew better. Tallie was not Gina. And he had pushed Tallie too far. He just hoped to God she would listen to him. When he found her. *If* he found her.

The morning came. Then another and another. No

Tallie. Her boss at the museum refused to give him her address, citing the laws he would be breaking if he did. He'd dismissed the college students helping her on the site with instructions to call him if they had news of Tallie, but he hadn't heard anything from them. And Tallie was still not answering the only number he had for her.

Tallie was gone. She was smart enough that if she didn't want to be found, he wouldn't find her. He felt as though part of him had been ripped out and thrown away.

He ran a hand over his face. He had to find her. *But why?* asked a little voice in his head. *Isn't this what you wanted?*

Cole sat on the large sofa in the den, the last moments they'd had together running through his mind. Tallie was so amazing, so different than Gina, they could be two separate species. Tallie's intelligence was off the charts. Her sense of humor had him laughing when at times he wanted to break down and have a fit of frustration. Her natural beauty was unsurpassed.

He needed to find her. He needed to sit down and listen this time to what she had to say and to keep his temper under control. He grabbed his cell and called the little motel in Calico Springs. She wasn't a registered guest.

If Tallie had intentionally disappeared, neither he nor his security staff would find her. Her family would stick together and protect one of their own. And what in the hell was he going to do?

Fourteen

Three months later

Cole had come home to pick up some papers and was on his way back out when the phone rang. "Yeah?" he answered coldly.

"Is this Mr. Masters?" a woman asked.

"Yes, it is. Who is this?"

"You probably won't remember me. My name is Kathy Brown and I was one of the four students who worked for Dr. Finley. You gave all of us your cell number in case of any emergency."

"I remember you, Kathy. Have you heard from Dr. Finley? Is she okay?"

"My mother is a nurse at Medical Central Hospital in Dallas. She knew I was working for Dr. Finley and mentioned that she was admitted as a patient."

"She's in the hospital?" His heart sank to his knees. Had something happened to her? All the worst scenarios raced across his mind. Cole was holding back a scream, a demand to know where she was, but he didn't want to frighten the young student.

"Yes, sir," she replied. "She's been there for a week. It's something about her pregnancy. Something has gone wrong." She paused as if putting thought to what else to say. "I just didn't know if you knew. Dr. Finley is such a nice lady and I know you were friends."

Assuring Kathy that Tallie would be all right, as though he actually knew something she didn't—he thanked her for calling and hung up.

Cole's heart began to slam against the wall of his chest. He immediately called for a driver. No time for a shower. Since Tallie had left, Cole had spent his days in the main barn, mucking stalls, grooming, exercising colts in training, his work forgotten until he could find Tallie. Now, he wanted to be there with her as fast as possible.

The helicopter ride to Dallas was excruciatingly long. And when they got there and switched to a limo to drive into the city, every red light seemed to take an hour to pass. Finally the tall, fourteen-story hospital loomed ahead. His driver pulled up under the pergola and Cole bailed. By the time he stood in front of the double doors leading to the ICU he felt as though he'd just run a marathon. With every step he worried. *Does she want me here? Will she see me?* The shoulda's and coulda's followed him the whole way.

He went to the nurses' station in the ICU and asked where Tallie's room was. The attendant looked something up on the computer and said, "Ms. Finley has been taken to surgery. Up two floors. There is a waiting room."

Cole ran for the elevator. When he got off, he quickly

followed the signs to the surgical unit. Eventually a nurse answered the doorbell leading to the surgical ward.

"I'm looking for Tallie Finley."

"And you are?"

"Her husband, Cole Finley." He hardly gave the lie a second thought.

"She has just been taken to recovery. I'll let them know you're here. Have a seat in the waiting room across the hall. We'll notify you when you can see her."

Recovery. That was good—wasn't it? It had been twelve weeks since Tallie had left the ranch. A quick calculation put her at about eight and a half months pregnant.

The minutes slowly ticked by. Every time he looked at his watch, only three or four minutes had passed. He stood and walked to the window. People were coming and going, some smiling, some weeping. He gripped his hands into tight fists. Tallie had to be okay. She just had to be.

Finally a nurse came into the room calling out for Mr. Finley. Cole followed her into Recovery. Tallie was asleep; her face looked ashen. He couldn't not touch her. He went to the bed and picked up one small, soft hand. She stirred and blinked her eyes as though she couldn't believe he was there, standing next to her. Whether that was good or bad remained to be seen.

"You're here," she whispered as if it was a struggle to speak. Her eyes fell away and closed as she concentrated on something going on with her body. She suddenly gripped his hand. Hard. "Are they all right? The babies?"

The babies? Was she delusional? "Sure, honey," he said to comfort her. "They are going to be fine."

Cole wanted to ask why she hadn't called him. He wanted to ask why she hadn't wanted him to know she was here. And why had she referred to his son or daughter as the *babies*? A thousand questions swirled in his mind but, at the moment, none of them mattered. And he had to ask her forgiveness.

A nurse bustled in and proceeded to check Tallie's vitals. She looked at Cole. "Are you the proud father?"

"Yes," he said firmly, his gaze going to Tallie. "I am indeed."

Tears filled Tallie's eyes. A silent message passed between her and Cole. One of pride and acceptance.

"You guys have two beautiful baby boys. We think they are both gonna be just fine. May have to stay in the incubator a couple of weeks, but they are breathing on their own and screaming for that bottle. Give it a while for the drugs to wear off and we can get you into a private room. Then you can feed them if you wish, Mrs. Finley."

"Oh, yes," Tallie answered.

"Your vitals look good. Give it about an hour and someone will come and get you," the nurse concluded and bustled out the door.

Cole could only stare. Twins. He needed to sit down.

"Cole, are you all right?"

He silently shook his head. "Hon, we are having twins. Twins."

He heard her chuckle. "We *have* twins, you nut cake. Why are you here?"

"I love you, Tallie." He kissed the palm of her hand.

"But you don't believe there is such a thing as love."

"I was wrong. I was stupid. I can't call what I feel anything else. I've honestly never felt this way before about anyone. When I thought you had died… Tallie, can you forgive me for reacting the way I did? Forgive me for doubting? And marry me, Tallie. My life won't be complete without you in it. I know we can make it work."

"You're not ready to settle down with a wife and children. You have your work. I'm not going to be the one to negatively impact your life."

"You are the first and only woman I've ever been this drawn to. And you will be the last. I don't want anyone but you." He wanted to scream it to the whole world but gritted his teeth to maintain control. "Marry me, Tallie. Marry me because you love me and because you believe I love you. Marry me with no regrets."

"I love you, Cole. And if you're sure, yes."

"Yes? You will marry me?"

"I'm an easy sell when it comes to you." She smiled and the twinkle was back in those emerald green eyes.

He bent over the bed and touched his lips to hers. It felt so right. He placed a hand on her head and followed with more kisses, loving this woman with everything he had inside. "You are so beautiful," he told her and knew she could see the honesty in his face.

A little while later, a team of nurses came into the recovery room, and rolled Tallie's bed down the hall to a private room.

"Mr.….Finley?" one of the nurses said to him. "While we get her settled in, if you would like to feed the babies with your wife, stop by the nursing station. They will provide a mask and gown."

Feeling excited and numb at the same time, Cole did as the woman suggested. When Tallie was settled in her new room, two nurses placed one newborn infant wrapped in a little blue blanket in his arms and gave one to Tallie.

Cole could only stare at the tiny new life he held. He was perfect. His cry sounded more like a kitten's than a baby's but it was the most beautiful sound Cole had ever heard. He caught Tallie's attention and mouthed "I love you." She smiled and said it right back. There was no expressing the love that grew in his chest at seeing his soon-to-be wife feed one newborn son then the other. Two sons. She had given him two incredible miracles.

The babies fed and back in the nursery, Cole left Tallie alone to rest. He'd kissed her goodbye with a promise that he would be back.

Had she agreed to marry Cole Masters? Still full of emotion, she felt tears of happiness welling up in her eyes. For the first time in her life, she was loved, truly loved, by an incredible man. She never thought she would trust another, yet there was no doubt in her mind that Cole loved her. With that in mind, she closed her eyes.

An hour later she awoke to a soft knock. "Come in."

It was Cole. He was grinning ear to ear while he held the largest bouquet of red roses she'd ever seen. Setting them on a table, he moved to Tallie and gave her a deep, meaningful kiss. "How are you feeling?"

"Pretty good, considering." She pushed herself up against the pillows. It was time to ask him a difficult question that had been bothering her.

"Cole, the day I left the ranch I overheard you on the phone talking to someone named Matt. You spelled it out pretty clearly that I had gotten pregnant on purpose and only wanted your money." Tears filled her eyes and she snatched a tissue from the bedside table. "If you feel that way, why did you come here? Why would you want to marry me?"

Cole sat on the edge of the bed and took the tissue from her, gently wiping her eyes. "I wasn't talking about you, sweetheart. I was talking about Gina, my ex-wife. She and her boyfriend set up this elaborate plan to get me to marry her so she could extract money, tens of millions of dollars, from a few of my bank accounts. The night I kicked her out, she drove too fast around a curve on the edge of a cliff and lost control of the car. She died immediately. So did the baby she was carrying. I never found out if it was mine or the other guy's."

"Oh, Cole, I'm so sorry."

"It made me bitter and hard and unforgiving. When I lashed out at you it was really Gina in my mind's eye. I will regret that until the day I die."

Tallie raised their joined hands to her face and kissed his palm. "I'm sorry you had to go through that."

"God, I love you, Tallie. I actually thought I was in love with her. You showed me what real love is."

Suddenly there was a knock on the door and an entourage of people walked into the room. She recognized Wade Masters, Cole's older brother. And next to Cole were Chance and his wife Holly. Before she could say hello to anyone, another man stepped forward.

"Hello, Dr. Finley," he said. "Congratulations. You and Cole have two beautiful sons."

"Thank you." What was Reverend Blackhawk from her hometown doing here? And what was the formal-looking paper he held in his hand?

"You said you would marry me," Cole told her softly. "I intend to hold you to your word."

"Are you sure?" she asked him. "Now? Here?"

Cole leaned over her and whispered in her ear. "Yes. And when you heal, I intend to show you exactly how sure I am."

Tallie signed her name and handed the form to the reverend, who passed it on to Wade, Holly and Chance to sign as official witnesses. Some twenty minutes later, after Holly did her hair and added some lipstick and a hint of blush, they said their vows and Tallie became Mrs. Cole Masters. His lips had never felt better on hers. When the clapping began, Cole lifted his head and winked at her.

It was, indeed, a beautiful day.

Epilogue

All the people at the museum were gathered around, wanting to have the opportunity to get closer to Tallie's babies.

Tallie left the dual stroller just outside her office as her friends oohed and aahed. Stepping into her office she proceeded to power up her computer. She needed to check the dates of certain meetings and what digs were scheduled for the next month. She glanced at her watch and wondered where Cole was. He'd said he would meet her here.

Outside, she heard the small crowd of people greeting Cole, who had apparently just arrived. Pulling up her email software, she began to scan the nearly three months of messages. It was going to take a lot longer to catch up than she'd thought.

"Hi, sweetheart." Cole walked around her desk and planted a deep kiss on her lips. "Happy six-week anniversary." He grinned that adorable grin. Tallie saw the sparks in his eyes and knew today marked the end of the safe period. Romantic evenings and spontaneous sex were back on. They had come close a number of times but Cole had held firm, a trait she'd told him she didn't especially hold in high regard.

"I have a wedding present for you."

She laughed. "Husbands don't give wedding presents. But what do you have?"

A huge smile covered his face as he held up an item about the size of a football. It was wrapped in a blanket and she watched as Cole began to carefully remove it. Gasps from all the people who were crowded in the doorway made her realize they were not alone.

"Presenting one certified pot—well, most of a pot, from your dig. Dr. Sterling has put his stamp of approval on it. It's what you were looking for, Tallie."

"But how…?"

Cole held it out for her to take. "You had been edging ever closer to the cliffs. I took a couple of men and we climbed up the face of the cliff and found the cave you suspected was there. Inside, it's full of pottery, spear-type weapons, jewelry…a whole bunch of things. We didn't enter the cave more than a couple of feet. I wasn't about to incur your wrath by stepping on something priceless. So, the rest is there for you to discover. Now you have proof positive of the origins of your family's people, Tallie. Your grandmother was right."

Woots and laughter filled the air until Dr. Sterling shooed everyone out saying they were going to frighten the babies. Her colleagues took the piece of pottery with them, continuing to gush as it was carefully passed around.

"Cole, if that is, in fact, proof of my people's origins, it might cause problems with building your retreat."

"So, what are you saying? Find another place for my

project—which I am willing to do. Or cover the cave back up and forget what's there?" he asked, sitting on the edge of her desk. "That's not happening. I spoke with Dr. Sterling about the possibility of incorporating your discovery in what I'm building. What better way to showcase our American beginnings than including a museum presenting remnants and information from the earliest people who ever lived on the land?"

"You would do that, Cole?"

"You were right, sweetheart. This is so much more important than my project."

Tallie was out of her chair and hugging her husband with the speed of a lightning flash. "Thank you. Thank you, Cole."

"I'll tell you what. You finish up here and let's get you and our two spoiled brats home. I think I know of a way you can thank me."

"Well, what do you know? It just so happens I'm finished." Tallie reached over and closed the lid of her laptop. "What are we waiting for?"

"Not a single thing."

Cole grabbed the handle of the stroller and escorted Tallie to the big doors of the museum, waving good-bye to all of Tallie's associates. Then he draped his arm around her shoulders and pushed his sons' stroller with the other hand as they headed to the car.

Tallie thought of her grandmother, who had set this all in motion. As her *ipokini* had told her, all things happen for a reason. Tallie believed her. One small map had changed her path forever. Had changed her life and brought her the man of her dreams.

Life just didn't get any better than this.

* * * * *

Pick up these other sexy Western romances from Golden Heart Award-winning author Lauren Canan!

TERMS OF A TEXAS MARRIAGE
LONE STAR BABY BOMBSHELL
REDEEMING THE BILLIONAIRE SEAL

Available now from Mills & Boon Desire!

* * *

If you're on Twitter, tell us what you think of Mills & Boon Desire

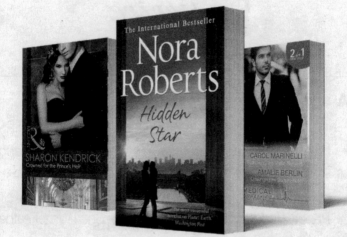